QUINTET

Doctor Banner's Garden

Family Agendas

Ambition

The Ultimate Success

A Son's Father, a Father's Son

BY HUGH AARON

PublishAmerica

Please visit our website at
StonesPointBooks.com
for more books by this author.

ISBN: 1-4137-8487-9
PUBLISHED BY PUBLISHAMERICA, LLLP
www.publishamerica.com
Baltimore

Printed in the United States of America

This book is dedicated to
my daughters Suzanne and Betsy
and
my son Andy
for the joy they have given me.

10/10

For Carol & Win,

My Talented friends.

Enjoy!

Hugh Aaron

TABLE OF CONTENTS

DR. BANNER'S GARDEN

Shortly after I rang the doorbell, a small, bedraggled, bent woman in her mid-sixties came to the door. I could hear a dog barking inside. "I'm here to answer your ad for a part-time gardener," I said, showing her the newspaper clipping.

"Come in, young man," said the woman. Her short hair was bone straight, and she had a strong southern accent

I stood in the doorway, surprised. Her speech was hardly what I expected to hear in Chicago, where the purest American English is spoken.

"Are you a student at the university?" she asked.

"Yes, ma'am. First year."

"Well, young man, you must negotiate with Doctor Banner, mistress of our garden—which is, I must say, in much need of repair. Come in, come in."

She led me to a large all-purpose room, evidently once the dining room, which contained an immense threadbare Oriental carpet. In the middle of it stood a large oak dining table that had seen better days. A pool-table-style light hung from the ceiling over the center of the table, which was strewn with books—Hemingway, Forster, Myrdal, Einstein, Dostoyevsky, Chekhov, Rolland—on a bewildering variety of subjects. It seemed that nothing had ever been put away. The entire room looked chaotic except for a prim, elegant corner in which stood, to my amazement due to its inconsistency with the rest of the furniture, a massive mahogany cabinet that housed a state-of-the-art Capehart phonograph and amplifier. It was veiled in dust. I could see another room through the almost-closed sliding paneled doors along one wall. At one end of the room where we stood were two overstuffed chairs and a couch. An afghan partially covered a figure lying on the couch.

"Clarissa, this is the young man who answered our advertisement for a gardener," explained the woman who had answered the door. "Come over here, young man, so Clarissa can see you."

The figure under the afghan was a woman well into her eighties. She had evidently been dozing. Her small, web-lined face was framed in a scant wreath of stark white hair. Through an open doorway that led to the kitchen, I glimpsed a large, white-haired, sad-eyed dog sizing me up.

I stood looking down at the reclining woman, her head framed by a white pillow. Her eyes remained closed, but her voice was commanding when she finally spoke.

"Before I would consider employing you, I must have your assurance that you respect plants. Do you meet that qualification, young man?" She sighed.

"Well, I used to work in a nursery, ma'am," I responded.

"That hardly answers my question," she said with authority, her eyes still shut. "Can you distinguish the weeds from the cultivars? That's what I must know, young man. And what is your name?"

"Pete...Pete Albert," I said weakly.

She opened her eyes and turned her head to gaze at me. "Two good first names. Do you have a surname?"

"No, ma'am. Only first names."

"Well, at least you have a sense of humor. Now I shall see whether you have common sense. One dollar and a half an hour—is that satisfactory?"

"Yes, ma'am."

"I think twelve hours a week will be sufficient."

"That's okay with me, ma'am."

"When can you start?"

"Tomorrow afternoon, ma'am."

"I'm not a ma'am, Mr. Albert. I'm Doctor Banner," she said, visibly annoyed.

"Yes, ma'am—Doctor Banner."

"Show him the garden, Justine. But before you do, help me to my bedroom. My nap has been interrupted and I wish to rest some more."

Justine, who had been standing by the doorway to the kitchen tentatively smoking a cigarette, as if anticipating an early termination of my interview, hurried over to the couch to help Dr. Banner to her feet. Obviously the old lady was too weak to get up by herself.

"May I help?" I volunteered. At Justine's nod of acceptance, I moved in to support Dr. Banner under her legs and arms.

"I do declare, what superhuman strength you have, young man," said Justine as I lifted Dr. Banner.

"You needn't do this," Dr. Banner commanded. "I got here on my own, and I can leave on my own. Put me down, young man."

"You got here with my help," Justine reminded her, "and I haven't recovered from it yet." She turned to me. "So for my sake do not put her down. Here, this is the way to Clarissa's room."

I didn't know what to do until my burden made the decision for me.

"I'm quite capable of directing him myself," Dr. Banner said to Justine.

"Why, of course you are," replied Justine. "I wouldn't think of coming between you and your rescuer." Justine made a sweeping motion with her arms. "Go, young man. Your guide is an expert."

"Straight ahead, Mr. Albert," said Dr. Banner, apparently not only reconciled to the situation but enjoying it, "to where peace and harmony prevail."

I entered the bedroom and gently placed her on the bed.

"You may leave now, young man," the doctor said, waving me off. "Thank you."

I returned to the common room, where Justine was seated at the table snuffing out a spent cigarette in an overflowing ashtray and lighting another. The dog ambled creakily into the room and sniffed my shoes.

"My name is Justine Faray," the woman said, shaking my hand, "and that's White Princess," she said, pointing to the old dog. "Hello, sweet princess. Yes, Clarissa will see you again soon, dear." She stroked its fur, then turned to me. "Now, before we proceed, I must make one thing clear. The cellar is off limits, most definitely. Nothing must be disturbed there. Is that understood?" I nodded my head.

"Then please sit down and rest your weary feet. Now, let me take you through Clarissa's neglected paradise. I trust that after you've seen it, the magnitude of your task will not discourage you before you begin. Look upon the garden's restoration as a challenge, a noble endeavor, with consequences far beyond the space itself."

I must have looked confused. "I don't expect you to understand my absurd ramblings," Justine volunteered, "but I hope you will understand someday—if not now, then in years to come." She looked down at the dog. "You stay, White Princess. Now, I'm going to take Mr. Albert on a tour of paradise lost—soon to be regained. Right, Mr. Albert? A paradise soon to be regained. What a glorious thing to contemplate. Come, Mr. Albert. To the garden, sir, and let us dream of a new world."

Justine led me out the rear entrance of the old house onto a tiny wooden porch. She pointed out where White Princess resided for part of the day—a small corral surrounded by a rusty wire fence. We stepped off the porch onto a soft, damp dirt path that led into the garden. It was a large, triangular plot of tangled growth bordered on one side by a parking lot that belonged to the university hospital. On another side a thick, high privet hedge shielded the jungle from the street, which was walled with an endless string of low apartment buildings. On the third side stood the doctor's house itself, a two-story, twenty-foot-wide Victorian affair with an ornate sandstone face. Many such houses once filled Chicago's Southside grid, but only a few specimens remained by the fifties, looking unappreciated.

"As you can see, you have your work cut out for you," said Justine.

"It'll be a challenge, that's for sure," I said, surveying the unruly garden.

"Ah, but what opportunity this disaster offers. What can be more satisfying than transforming the ugly into the beautiful? Now, if you've seen enough, let's go back to the house."

We walked along the path in silence viewing the plants and enjoying the surroundings. Bending down to feel the soil in my hands, I found myself eagerly looking forward to being in touch with the earth on a regular basis.

As we entered the common room, Justine lit another cigarette, then beckoned me to sit down at the worn oak table. "I presume, Mr. Albert, you are a man of your word and you will show up when you say you will. Please understand, sir, next to White Princess—yes, even before myself, good, ol', dependable Justine—the garden is the most important thing in Clarissa's life. Its curative power surpasses any of the medicines those quacks have prescribed. Clarissa and I maintained it with loving hands until finally it got beyond us." She laughed. "It would appear that old ladies don't revive each spring the way the plants do."

Justine went on to explain that the university allowed Dr. Banner, a professor emeritus, and her assistant to use the house rent-free for as long as the doctor lived. Although she was in her mid-eighties and hadn't taught at the university for more than ten years, she still conducted biological research in the cellar of the old house. Scores of cages full of peeping mice were stacked there

I had no inkling then how crucial those two old ladies would be to my future. I knew that my college years were one of the most influential times in my life. I was at an age when I sought to absorb all the learning I could, not because I had to, as in high school, but because I wanted to. And I was at an age when I was sophisticated enough to ponder life's meaning but not yet too preoccupied to ask. The two women were about to instruct me on why we live and why we die.

It became my custom several afternoons a week to study amid the formal echoes of the high-vaulted university library. I was drawn by the serenity of its simulated antiquity, a refreshing contrast to the raw atmosphere of commercial Chicago only a few blocks away.

I was not alone on these afternoons. A slight young man with an appealing smile that seemed to say life was a lark often sat across the table facing me. Because I thought that life was quite the opposite, I made no effort to introduce myself. Besides, he looked too fast for me.

One afternoon when I raised my eyes from a book to contemplate Aristotle's statement on the soul, our gazes met.

"I'm not sure he's worth it," the young man said.

"You mean—"

"Who you're reading. Aristotle."

"But it's required," I said, intrigued by his audacity. "Anyway, I don't agree. Take his definition of the soul: it's the source of movement, the end, the essence of the whole living body. Not bad stuff, I'd say."

He laughed. "Hell, that stuff held back science a thousand years. No offense. I'm sure you'll get an A. Well, at least a B." He reached over the table and shook my hand. "Lenny Gladfeld at your service. Of course, you and I know that Freud discovered the soul, not your buddy there."

"Of course," I said, impressed. "Name's Pete Albert."

"Where are you from?" It was a reasonable question, seeing as the student body, several times larger than normal due to returning veterans such as myself, was from everywhere.

"The East," I said, expecting that he wouldn't recognize the name of my hometown.

"Well, that's pretty specific. I'm a native Chicagoan. How'd you like a home-cooked meal once in a while?"

I was dumbfounded. Such generosity toward a total stranger. "Sure. Why not? This cafeteria food does get a bit boring."

"My mother loves to cook. Let me have your phone number and I'll be in touch."

"I'm renting a room in a private home. I'll give you that number," I said.

The family I lived with offered to let me use their phone, within reason. As long as I didn't fall in love with one of the coeds, there was little danger that I'd abuse the privilege. I wrote down the number on a piece of paper and handed it to him.

"Are you one of those seasoned guys on the GI Bill, or an inexperienced, child like me?"

The distance between us seasoned veterans and students entering the freshman class from high school was palpable. Although not so far apart in age, we were years apart in our view of life. We were serious, hardened, and wise. The protected eighteen year olds still wanted to play.

"I was in the war," I said.

"Is that so? You look young. I'd take you for still being wet behind the ears."

"I was drafted right out of high school four years ago."

"Where were you?"

"Southwest Pacific."

"Really?" said Lenny, looking interested.

"My, you're a wordy guy. I see you can't wait to talk about it. Well, I was right here in Chicago keeping all the women at bay."

"Must have been tough," I cracked.

He looked at his watch and rose from his chair. "I gotta go. You'll hear from me. This is the beginning of an enormous friendship. I can tell."

As I watched him walk away, I realized that I liked him. His exuberance, his sophistication, and his obvious brilliance compensated for what seemed like naiveté and insouciance.

Being compulsively dependable, I did, of course, show up for work on time. The garden—a riot of excess growth, weeds well ensconced in the perennial beds, lily of the valley running rampant, massive thickets of roses—was to me no less exciting than a lump of clay to a sculptor. I found it especially appealing that by restoring the garden to its former splendor, I might also help restore the doctor's flagging health.

Through the month of September, I worked three afternoons a week bringing order to the morass. My relationship with the old women remained on a professionally distant plane. Justine greeted me at the door each time, a cigarette drooping from her pale lips.

October came, and the garden, covered with blowing leaves, was turning brown. After knocking at the front door, I waited bundled up against a strong wind coming off the western prairie.

Admitting me, Justine whispered, "Hush, walk tippy-toe. Clarissa had a most difficult night and is resting."

As I entered the common room, the sliding doors were uncharacteristically fully open, revealing a parlor beyond. The room was dominated by a massive concert grand piano and a large, old Victorian settee.

"What's wrong with Clarissa?" I inquired, concerned.

"Wrong? Nothing's wrong, unless you wish to call the natural process of wearing out wrong," said Justine as we both took seats at the table.

"Then she's not ill?"

Justine lit a cigarette and placed her lighter next to an open book that she had evidently been reading. "Why, Clarissa has never been ill a day in her life, at least not in the fifty years I've known her."

"But she seems so fragile," I said, confused, for Justine's statement didn't square with my observations.

"Don't be fooled. You see only her physical self. Her mind is as alert

13

as the day we met when I became her student at the university. She was doing remarkable original medical search, which later won her the Nobel—"

"Doctor Banner won a Nobel Prize?" I exclaimed loudly.

"Shh, she might hear. If she knew I informed you of her award—one among many, I might add—she would boycott me for...let's see, the last time I mentioned it to someone, she ignored me for a month afterward. So don't you dare reveal that you know. Do I have your word?"

"Of course. But I can't imagine why she's so secretive about it," I said.

"Because people glorify Nobels, put them on a pedestal. Clarissa wants to be accepted for the person she is, not for what she's done."

I hadn't considered it in that light.

"I suppose from now on you'll quake in her presence," said Justine with a twinkle in her eye.

"I'm trembling already. Is she still doing research?"

"Oh, yes, although not the way it used to be. I have to push her these days. As I say, Clarissa's mind is one hundred percent functional. It's her will that's failed." Suddenly becoming sad, fingering her cigarette lighter, Justine stared off.

"I see."

"I'm afraid you can't, my boy. Clarissa's eighty-five; she's been at the center of the world's attention for most of her life, and now she finds herself without a future, cast off to the side by a new generation. Oh, we have this house that the university allows us to use until she dies. As a professor emeritus, she has no financial worries. So I do my best to keep her will alive. It's difficult. She and I know that we don't have the time left to do anything worthwhile. I might have a few more years than she does, but by myself I'm worthless, absolutely worthless. We're a powerhouse together; alone I'm a cipher. And when Clarissa goes, I refuse to be alone."

Her frankness, a confession certainly, went to my heart.

"You count in your own right, Justine. I can tell that you are something, really something."

"How kind of you. You surely know how to make an old hag from the swamps of Louisiana feel good, I must say. But I'm afraid that my sense of reality, my knowledge of life's limitations, is too overwhelming for me to be swayed by the sweet words of a handsome young man. Still, you may repeat them anytime the urge strikes you."

"The urge is coming on again—"

"Go on, you," she said, reaching over the table and gently caressing my face. Then she quickly straightened in her chair. "How about some tea?" she said. She retreated to the kitchen and returned with cups, tea bags, and a steaming pot of water.

We looked out the window at the formerly weed-choked chrysanthemum bed, which I had cleaned out two days earlier. It was now in abundant flower. "I declare," she said. "After only a month, the garden is becoming a marvelous sight to behold."

"Yeah, it's shaping up, isn't it?" I said, joining her gaze.

"You have been most diligent, sir, and on behalf of myself, I do wish to reward you with something extra." With this she handed me a book. "Are you familiar with E. M. Forster?" I shook my head. "No? Well, you certainly should be. Please take this marvelous gem, *A Room with a View*, as a token of my regard."

"I don't know what to say."

"Say nothing. Just enjoy the book, and think of me as you enter its world. Please look at the title page."

I read aloud, "'To Pete, the ultimate gardener, for providing my room with a most gracious view. J. Faray.' Oh, Justine. Thank you." I walked over to her side of the table and hugged her.

"I'm too old for such a shameful expression of affection, sir. Desist, I say. On the other hand, would you be so kind as to do it again?"

By the end of October I had completed preparing the garden for the harsh Chicago winter, tying up the shrubs to protect them against fracturing under the weight of the heavy snow that was sure to come, and mulching the flowers with fallen leaves that I hauled from beneath the trees on the street.

The garden needed less attention in November. On my last afternoon, an unusually mild one for so late in the season, Dr. Banner appeared on the garden path. Her rippling, silky white hair was now neatly contained, and her pale but leathery complexion was disguised with rouge. She wore a heavy wool scarf about her neck. Justine supported her by one arm. I was kneeling, tying up the last shrub.

"Stay, White Princess," said Dr. Banner to the dog, who was standing at the door of the house. "Clarissa will return shortly."

I stood to greet the women. "Here, take my other arm, Mr. Albert; let's walk through our little paradise. It pleases me to look out my bedroom window again. You have brought order to chaos—the very noblest of human endeavors. Do you think that lily bed would look better over there?" She gestured across the garden. "I think so," she said. "Let's do that in the spring. May we expect you in the spring?" I nodded. "Yes, it will be something to look forward to, won't it? It will make the winter more endurable."

Clarissa, don't overdo it, now," warned Justine. "Don't you think you've had enough?"

"Perhaps you can return in early March, Mr. Albert," said Clarissa, deliberately ignoring Justine's cautious advice.

"Let's go back to the house, Clarissa," Justine suggested.

"Shut up," Dr. Banner snapped. "I don't need you to tell me what I should or should not do. Now, if you wish to leave the garden, then go. Mr. Albert and I are having a conference."

Justine, her eyes brimming with tears of hurt, released Dr. Banner's arm and headed back to the house.

"Let's continue, Mr. Albert. Show me everything you've done. Everything. I want to miss nothing."

We toured the remainder of the garden and, as the doctor wished, we discussed its every detail, missing nothing.

"Those shrubs are very overgrown. I suggest they be cut back to the ground," I said.

"Yes, of course. Let's do it," agreed the doctor. "By all means, let's do it. And those shrubs over there as well. They're as ancient as I am, I daresay. Indeed, they were there when I arrived. I understand that you're from New England."

"Maine, Doctor Banner."

"Then you descend from hardy stock. Solid, independent, climate-hardened individuals. My progenitors were also New Englanders, rebels from Rhode Island."

Of course, the doctor was descended, as were many mid-westerners, of New Englanders who had migrated to the Midwest for the rich, alluvial soil of the plains, which was far less backbreaking to till than that of my rocky New England. But if they expected a less harsh climate, they were mistaken.

"I'm afraid I can't lay claim to such genes," I said. "My parents came from Germany in the thirties."

"Ah, I see. But they had the foresight to see that Europe would be engulfed in flames. Obviously, good stock. One must always keep in mind where one comes from to better understand where one is going. Now, let us go indoors. Chicago outdoors in mid- November is no place for a woman in my cellular condition, don't you agree?"

"I'm curious," I said as we approached the house. "I notice you have a Capehart phonograph."

"Yes," the doctor said apprehensively.

"It's the very best made. State of the art," I commented.

"Maybe so, but a ridiculous machine. It's far too complicated to operate."

"Is that why it's gathering dust?"

"A most perceptive conclusion," she said with a smile.

"If you have records, I think I could show you how to use it," I offered.

"I have some records, yes, but I have little patience for deciphering the ways of mechanical devices."

"Could I play some of my own records?" I ventured.

"And what sort of records might they be?" she asked cautiously.

"Classical: Beethoven, Mozart, Brahms, a little Bartok."

She seemed delighted. "Yes, that would be excellent. We must have a concert. When could that be, Mr. Albert?"

"Can I bring a friend?"

"What sort of friend?" she said.

"My girlfriend."

"I think not," she said immediately.

"She's a pianist," I pursued, not realizing the nature of the woman I was dealing with. "I know you would like her."

"I'm afraid, young man, you did not hear me. I repeat, when would you like to play your records?"

"Saturday afternoon," I said, somewhat crestfallen, "after I'm done working in the garden."

"Saturday then. I'm sure it will be a gala afternoon. It has been at least a year since I've listened to any of our friends."

"Our friends?" We had reached the steps to the rear porch.

"Brahms, Beethoven, Mozart, and Schubert. They are among my best friends. But Bartok and I definitely do not get along."

17

"If you have time, I could play one of your records for you now," I proposed.

"Now? Such an impulsive lad. But yes, I suppose I could take a ration of Schubert. Lately my mind has been imagining the andante of Schubert's Opus 99 piano trio. Yes, it would be nice to hear the real thing. Do you know it?"

"I'm afraid not," I said. My knowledge of classical music was severely stunted from living in the jungles of New Guinea, and listening to it was an ongoing revelation.

"Well, young man, you're in for a treat. Let's hurry," she said, almost tripping as I helped her up the stairs."

Upon entering the common room, I immediately went to the Capehart and, after wiping off the layer of dust with my sleeve, lifted the lid while the doctor looked for a record among a pile of papers stacked on a chair.

"You'll find the andante on the second band," she said, handing me the Schubert.

We sat at the table listening to the melody pour out. Hearing the music, Justine emerged from her bedroom and joined us, saying nothing. She had probably been stewing ever since the doctor had sent her from the garden.

My friendship with Lenny Gladfeld was a happy one. I found him to be a devoted and complicated friend. Good looking, blond, and pixyish, Lenny dreamed of someday vanquishing the mysterious unhappiness within himself, which he hid under a happy-go-lucky manner. Out of necessity, but unhappily, he lived at home with his affluent parents. As I got to know them, they frequently invited me to dinner at their sumptuous apartment. Afterward Lenny and I would spend hours in his room listening to his enormous classical record collection, which consisted of orchestral and operatic works that were new to me.

Lenny's father, a power in the Chicago scrap metal business, was a small man like his son. Both men projected an overweening self-confidence. The father lacked the son's wit and refinement, and the son lacked the father's intensity and sense of clear purpose. When they discussed matters in my presence, which was rare, Lenny was always curt; his father would react with pained silence.

As we sat around the dining room table the first time I was invited to dinner, Lenny's father advised him that the Cadillac wouldn't be available for his use on a particular Saturday night. "Hell, why tell me?" Lenny retorted bitingly. "It's yours. Are you asking my permission?"

"I figured you'd like to know so you could make other plans," the father explained.

"Oh, sure," Lenny went on, his tone unaltered. "You always have my interest at heart, don't you?"

His father shrugged as he lifted a spoonful of soup to his lips. "There's no pleasing this kid."

"Please, both of you, don't, don't," Lenny's mother pleaded, fixing an apologetic gaze on me. "Out of respect for our guest. Please forgive them, Pete."

Lenny's mother assumed the role of protector and constant arbitrator, although Lenny told me that she wasn't well, and the task appeared to exhaust her.

"You have a beautiful place here," I said, following Mrs. Gladfeld's lead. "I'm afraid I'm not used to such elegant surroundings."

"What does your father do?" Mr. Gladfeld asked.

"He's a struggling small businessman. A neighborhood grocery store. He makes a living, and we're happy."

"My father here makes much more than a living, and we're unhappy," said Lenny bitterly.

"Stop it, Lenny. Please stop it," said his mother, closing her eyes as if to block out the animosity in the air.

"Listen to your mother. It's not good for her," said Lenny's father. "If you don't give a damn about me, at least think of her." Addressing me he explained, "Any aggravation causes her angina to act up."

"Yes, and recently they discovered I have diabetes. Lenny, will you help your father clear the table before dessert?"

As Lenny and his father disappeared into the kitchen with the finished plates, Mrs. Gladfeld, the loving center in a hostile circle, attempted to draw me in with her.

"I'm so happy that Lenny has found you as a friend," she confided. "You are such a good influence. Like an older brother. I wish I understood what he's got against his father. It hurts me to see him so bitter."

I too failed to comprehend Lenny's hostility toward his father. "I think Lenny should get some help," I suggested.

"Help? What kind of help?"

"Psychological help, Mrs. Gladfeld."

"He's not crazy, Peter. Are you saying he's got something wrong with his—"

"No, no. I'm only saying he should talk to a professional who can help him discover what's at the bottom of his unhappiness. Then he can deal with it."

She sighed. "I think Lenny needs someone, a role model, to show him how to be happy. A good friend like you. Or maybe a nice girl."

I nodded, realizing that she hadn't understood. She expected more of me than I could deliver.

The men returned and Mrs. Gladfeld got up to get dessert.

"I see you and my mother have become close friends.," Lenny observed, pleased.

"Of course. We have you in common," I said as Mrs. Gladfeld returned with a homemade layer cake.

"You shouldn't, you know," Mr. Gladfeld warned. "The doctor said—"

"I know, I know. But just this once. All right? I'll make an exception in Pete's honor," said Mrs.Gladfeld as she placed the cake before Lenny.

"Yeah, let's all make the big sacrifice," said Lenny, slicing into the cake and serving us.

"Hmmm. I haven't had anything this good since I was home. Thank you, Mrs. Gladfeld, for a marvelous home-cooked dinner," I said gratefully. Without my mother's extraordinary cooking, I felt deprived from the moment I had arrived in Chicago.

"You must come again, Peter, and come often. This is now your home away from home," said Mrs. Gladfeld warmly.

"Yes, you're always welcome here, Pete," Mr. Gladfeld chimed in. "Maybe some of your civility will rub off on my son."

I passed the first winter in Chicago concentrating on my undergraduate studies, dating Vicki, and falling in love with her. She had wide, gentle, dark eyes and a beguiling fragility and dreamed of someday becoming a concert pianist.

It was a winter of deep snow and long weeks of subzero cold, more severe than any I had known in my native New England. In January I stopped in to see Dr. Banner and Justine to find out how the doctor was feeling and to reassure them that I hadn't forgotten the garden.

"Why Pete, how nice of you to think of us and drop by," Justine said as she greeted me at the door with her usual exuberance, reeking of cigarette smoke as she hugged me. "How long has it been? I estimate not since our record concert almost three months ago. What a sweet boy you are. Shall we have some tea? Come in, come in. Please sit down, my boy."

"How have you been, Justine?"

"Well, you know. Justine just goes on and on. Justine the dependable."

"And Doctor Banner? How is she?"

"She has her good and bad days. At eighty-five, that's how it is." Justine squashed a cigarette into the butt-filled ashtray, then nervously lit another. "Clarissa," she shouted. "You must see who has come to visit."

"You know I'm busy," Dr. Banner called back from the cellar. "I have no time for nonsense."

"I hope you'll excuse her, Pete. Clarissa is in the midst of some very important work, perhaps as momentous as the work that won her the Nobel. She's down there, the first time in months, surrounded by an array of cages filled with our lovely mice."

"What is she working on?" I inquired.

"Cancer, dear boy. She has discovered that the propensity for cancer is carried in our genes, that there's a hereditary factor. Indeed, we traced the disease through thousands of generations of my lovely mice. But just as important, Clarissa is convinced that the environment is a contributing cause."

"Possibly, possibly," said Dr. Banner as she shuffled slowly into the room out of breath from climbing the cellar stairs. "Come, White Princess, dear."

White Princess straggled feebly across the room, then plopped down at the doctor's feet as soon as she sat. Clarissa bent over and stroked the dog empathetically. The old woman and the aged dog had reached a similar stage in their biological lives.

"The genes and environment combined," continued the doctor. "The early results are pointing in that direction. We're just beginning."

"Clarissa, do you know whether anyone has ever received a second Nobel?" asked Justine.

Dr. Banner laughed. It was a wild cackle, unrestrained and primordial. "Dear lady," she said, "you know as well as I do, I shall be gone long before my work is completed. And so will you, with your stubborn addiction to cigarettes."

"But aren't I a statistic in the great national experiment?" said Justine. "My raison d'etre, really? I'm a mouse, a most mousy mouse. See, see my beady eyes?" Justine pulled her eyelids into slits with her fingers.

"No, you are more stupid than the mice. You are at least aware of the consequences," said the doctor bitterly. "An experiment on a grand scale is currently in progress, Mr. Albert. Because of our changing social mores, smoking is increasingly prevalent among women. In twenty years, as the incidence of lung cancer in women increases, we shall have statistical proof that smoking is a major cause of cancer."

"Peep, peep," said Justine. "Don't I sound like a mouse? If only I were as pretty."

As Dr. Banner stared contemptuously at her, Justine popped a cigarette between her lips, then struck a match with an exaggerated flourish and lit the Lucky Strike. "Clarissa, dear, how could I dare outlive you?" Abruptly she turned to me. "Well, Pete, have you read the Forster?"

I nodded. "Yes, I finished it last night."

"And how did you like it?"

"What Forster?" the doctor inquired.

"Let's talk about it," Justine said, as if the doctor were invisible.

"What Forster?" the doctor said again.

"The author. Not in your field. This is between my friend and me, if you don't mind."

Dr. Banner departed in a huff. I realized that the war between them hadn't abated.

"Now, let's you and I, a mere statistic, have a profound discussion over tea, my boy. As I was saying, or maybe I hadn't said it yet, Forster was all for casting aside rigid convention and being a free spirit. Did you find that in his book?"

As planned, I resumed working in the garden in early spring. It provided me the extra money, beyond my government stipend, to take Vicki to concerts and movies and to keep up with my rich friend, Lenny. On many Saturday nights he picked me up in his father's brand-new, long green 1948 Cadillac, and we glided dreamily along the eight or so miles of the Outer Drive bordering the lake to the Near North side. There we dined in splendor at the renowned Imperial House. Having come from a lower-middle-class family and a poor, small, industrial town in Maine, I was dazzled by all the unfamiliar luxury. At the beginning, Lenny paid the entire tab, but soon I insisted on paying my own way, difficult though it was. Inevitably Lenny would drink too much and lapse into a tirade against his wealthy and too-generous father.

"Gardens are for old ladies and D. H. Lawrence," said Lenny as we drove along the Outer Drive on our way to the restaurant. "I wouldn't be caught dead working in a garden."

"I can use the money, Lenny. I don't have a rich father like you. Anyway, I love gardening, feeling the cool soil in my hands. And I love the physical labor after poring over books all week."

"The world has all types. So what's with the old ladies?"

"Well, Doctor Banner is a professor emeritus and a biological research scientist, and Justine was her student and now is her assistant. The university has let them live in this old Victorian house until they die."

"What I mean is, exactly what is their relationship?" said Lenny, as if pursuing some predetermined assumption.

"I just told you," I said, annoyed at the suspicious way he asked the question. "What do you mean by 'relationship'? Justine came up from New Orleans, and they've been doing this research together for more than forty years."

"Probably lesbians," said Lenny, concentrating on the road as we turned off the highway.

"I...I don't know," I said, surprised at the idea. "I've never thought about it. Anyway, what does it matter? If they are, it would seem perfectly understandable."

"Someday I'd like to meet them," said Lenny.

"I doubt if that would be possible," I replied, vexed that he expected an introduction to be a routine thing. Anyway, I feared that the doctor, a rigid, house-bound, irascible woman, might be offended by Lenny's outrageous, rebellious nature.

"Just because I said they're lesbians? C'mon, Pete."

"Of course not. It's just that they lead a kind of self-enclosed existence. They seem to shield themselves from the world. Nothing personal, but I don't think they'd welcome you. You'd be intruding."

"Why not ask? Tell them I'm a good friend who'd like to see their garden," Lenny urged.

"Because you love gardens?" I said, trying to be clever.

"How did you know?" said Lenny, responding in kind.

I pondered the possibility. "There *is* a chance that you and Justine might hit it off."

"Really? Why so?"

"Because you're both renegades," I said.

Furthermore, a common theme pervaded their personalities: Each had a tragic, self-destructive nature. Lenny's motive was suspect, but he did propose an intriguing possibility that aroused my curiosity. What were the women really to each other?

We parked the Cadillac in a garage and walked, whooping and hollering and generally enjoying ourselves, to the Imperial House restaurant. Greeting Lenny as Mr. Gladfeld, the maitre d' ushered us to a choice table.

"I'm paying for myself this time, Lenny," I told him as the waiter approached.

"Bring me a Rob Roy, will you, waiter? Make it two," said Lenny, ignoring my words.

"I don't want one," I protested.

"They're both for me, waiter. You see, my friend here refuses to become an alcoholic."

He turned to me after the waiter took off. "You're not paying because I'm not paying either. My father is. It's going on his tab. He has an account here."

"I don't like this," I said, uncomfortable.

"Too fucking bad. You can't afford it anyway. Not on your measly government stipend."

"I'm not so hard up. I've got the gardening job, remember?"

"Oh, I forgot. You're loaded."

"Y'know, Lenny," I said, deciding to come clean with how I felt,

24

"I don't admire you for what you're doing, taking advantage of your father the way you do."

"I hate the bastard."

"But why? He gives you everything."

The waiter delivered the drinks, which Lenny quaffed one after the other.

"That's exactly why I hate him. He makes sure I owe him."

"You're mixed up, Lenny. He loves you. I've seen how he looks at you."

Lenny signaled the waiter and ordered another two drinks, which promptly appeared as if they had already been poured. Apparently this waiter knew his customer.

"Too bad for him. I still hate the bastard," Lenny said, his tongue thickening. "See, they knew I'd want these." He raised the first glass to his lips and swigged it down.

"Why are you slowly destroying yourself? Why are you doing this?" I said, feeling helpless and worried. "Godammit, Lenny."

"Is that what I'm doing? Hey, I have an excellent idea. Let's go to the crazy hospital. I'll walk into emergency and say, 'Here I am, you lucky people. My friend says I'm addicted to alcohol. Cure me. I dare you.'"

"Okay. Let's go. I'll drive you there," I said, flinging down the menu that I held in my hand.

"Well, I will someday," he said. "I really will. But not today." We ordered, but Lenny was blubbering drunk by the time the meal was over, so I had to drive us home.

My girl, lovely Vicki, the daughter of equally affluent parents, saw me regularly in spite of her parents' objections on religious grounds. She was Greek Orthodox and I was Jewish. On Sunday afternoons we took the Illinois Central, the IC, commuter line downtown to Orchestra Hall, where in the uppermost balcony we sat enthralled with both the music and each other. We meet weekdays in the library to study together, and afternoons we relaxed in the student lounge, where Vicki practiced on the grand piano. Playing Mozart and Beethoven, she always attracted a crowd of admiring listeners. Our conversations were mostly about ourselves, our future together, and our mutual problem: her parents. I told Vicki of the garden, Dr. Banner, and Justine. She had not yet met Lenny.

Through that spring of 1948, I worked not only the prescribed twelve hours a week in the garden but often, at Dr. Banner's request, an additional eight hours on Saturdays. She supervised me closely, showing me how to distinguish the weeds from the flowers and instructing me to move certain plants from one spot to another. She was like an inspired artist obsessed with her creation.

"No, leave that, Peter. That's a flower. But that"—she pointed with her cane—"is a weed. Of course, a weed is only by definition. To a romantic, a weed may be a flower; to a realist, a flower may be a weed." She pointed to something that we had discussed last fall. "By all means, this shrub should be moved."

I dug up the plant, then lifted the heavy root ball to transplant it to a new location that she recommended.

"Oh, how wonderful to be young and strong," she exclaimed in admiration. "Make the most of your energy, Peter. The law of conservation of energy does not apply to us humans. Use it while you can, because, I assure you, it doesn't last. But I must say, I have recovered some of mine—a scintilla perhaps, but that's something."

Actually the doctor *had* regained a great deal of her waning physical strength. Justine no longer had to offer her arm, and although Dr. Banner still carried a cane, she used it more to call attention to things. "I don't need this anymore for support, but it makes an excellent pointer," she said.

"I see I've used up my ration of energy for the day," the doctor announced a short time later. "I shall repair to the house and lie down for a brief rest, after which I'll be ready for a wild night listening to Bach."

"I'm about ready to knock off, too, Doctor Banner."

"Yes, let's knock off. Such expressions you young people have. Did you know, Peter, it's not our tools or our scientific discoveries that most set us apart from other animals? It's our invention of language."

Upon entering the common room, we found Justine sitting at the table, reading a book, as usual. White Princess was lying at her feet.

"Peter's all yours," the doctor told Justine as she departed for her bedroom. "Come with me, White Princess. Time for a nap."

"Your restoration of the garden has done wonders for her," Justine told me after we heard the bedroom door close. "She hasn't had to stay in bed for weeks."

"Could it really be the garden?" I wondered out loud.

"My boy, don't you know that a garden is the best restorative in the world? That's the purpose of natural beauty, to nourish body as well as soul. Sit, Pete. My, how hard you work. Would you like some tea?"

I nodded and sat down opposite her. Often cynical and self-deprecating, Justine seemed pleased with herself lately. Our friendship had warmed so that I began confiding in her, telling her of my friends and my conflict with Vicki's parents. Justine listened, always sympathetically, commenting without pressing advice on me. When I had a complaint against some injustice, whether real or imagined, she always took my side like a doting parent. She also asked to hear in detail about the concerts, movies, art exhibits, and plays that I attended.

"I enjoy working in the soil," I said. "It's a welcome change from the classroom and studying. I consider it a stroke of luck that I found this job. Especially while living in the city."

"Well, Clarissa and I are lucky to have found you, my boy," she said as she handed me a steaming cup of tea.

"I hope the garden brings you pleasure, too."

"It does, it surely does," she said, gazing out the window at a rainbow of spring colors.

"Someday I'd like to show it to Vicki."

"She's..."

"My girlfriend. A terrific pianist, and a terrific person," I said with unbridled enthusiasm.

"Of course, a fine boy like you would have none other. And an accomplished pianist, too, my, my," she said with wonder.

"Trouble is, because of our different religions, her parents object to our relationship. They won't let me set foot in their home."

"How stupid of them." She sipped some tea, then asked all of a sudden, "Do you love her?"

"Yes, I think I do."

"Do I hear some reservation in your words?" she said, studying my face.

"No, no. It's only I'm afraid to—"

"To commit."

"Right."

"Yes, I can appreciate that. It's a big step," she said, taking another sip of tea.

"Then you know how hard it is from experience?" I said.

She burst out laughing. "Lord no, my boy. No man ever wanted me, and I confess I never found a man I wanted. My commitment has been to science, and to Clarissa, with no regrets. But Clarissa has not been as fortunate as I. She had fallen in love with a certain gentleman, a man famous for his achievement in music, but he wished to live in Europe, where, at the time, he had more opportunity to advance his career. Now, don't you ever mention to her what I'm telling you. Clarissa was unwilling to abandon her research here and the generous grants that made it possible. Anyway, being the patriot, she refused to leave America. How she agonized over having to tell him that she wouldn't join him. I watched it, the pain she suffered. Yes, commitment can be hard, if there are conflicting needs."

"I can't explain my hesitation," I confessed. "What am I afraid of?"

"Another person is a responsibility," said Justine seriously. "It's the basis of all love and friendship. Someday you will find the courage. And I hope not too late."

"My friend Lenny has a similar problem," I said.

"And who might Lenny be?"

"He's a classmate. His parents are rich. He has everything. They keep nagging him to go out with girls and get married. But he has no desire to."

"It's unfortunate that parents don't realize that their children are as different from themselves as any stranger on the other side of the earth. I won't go into the scientific basis for that difference right now. Just take my word for it. And what career does your friend Lenny plan to follow?"

"As far as I can tell, drinking a lot, and doing nothing while waiting for his father, whom he hates, to die."

"That's most sad, most sad," she said, clicking her tongue.

"It is. Because he's positively brilliant. We have good times together; we go to movies and concerts, art exhibits and plays. He's read everything. He can discuss any subject intelligently. He's much smarter than I am."

"You are in no position to judge," Justine said. "Each of us has a special talent. It's only a matter of finding it. Pity is, most of us don't have the opportunity to use it. Haven't you noticed how living gets in the way of being who you are? No, you are still too young to make that discovery. Tell me about some of your escapades. What about the last art exhibit you went to. Where was it?"

"At the Art Institute. Look, since you're so interested, why don't you go?"

"Me? Don't be silly, my boy," she said, dismissing the idea with a wave of her hand.

"I'll take you."

"And have you seen with an ugly, beady-eyed old hag? Why, Pete, you'd be the laughingstock of your friends. No, this house is enough for me. This house and my mice and literature and Clarissa are all I need."

Seeing that Justine was most definite, I pressed my offer no further.

Dr. Banner awakened from her brief nap and came into the room, with White Princess tagging along behind her. "Well, that was a refreshing rest, I must say."

"Did you know that our friend is a frequent concert goer?" said Justine, pleased that I appreciated such things.

"I wouldn't say frequent, Justine," I said, dismayed at her inclination to exaggerate. "I can't afford to go very often. Maybe once a month."

"Yes, I have observed that we have music in common as well as the garden," said Dr. Banner. "But they are all that is necessary. Fine music is western civilization's greatest gift to mankind. And loving it gives us hope despite our penchant for inhumanity toward one another. Well, young man, how would you like to escort me to Orchestra Hall as my guest this Thursday evening? I have two of the very best box seats in the house."

"I don't have a car, Doctor," I said, bewildered by the invitation.

"We'll use a taxi, Mr. Albert. I always do."

"Your offer is pretty hard to refuse," I said.

"Then you'll be my date."

"It's about time," said Justine, turning to look out the window. "You haven't used your seats in years. Dear garden, what magic you have spun."

When I called at the house on the evening of the concert, the taxi was already waiting. As Justine opened the door, I stood there smiling, barely resembling the gardener she knew. Wearing a sport jacket and tie, hair neatly combed, face close shaven and as shiny as my polished shoes, I used everything I had at hand to make myself a proper escort.

"How handsome you are, Pete. Why, if I were a couple of years younger I'd go for you."

Dr. Banner soon joined us at the door. She looked glamorous— old-fashioned, ornate, overdone glamorous. Her makeup was thick and garish, her brassy dress fitted too loosely, and she was bedecked with sparkling necklaces and bracelets and oversized pendant earrings.

"And look at you, Clarissa," said Justine. "What a beautiful couple you two make." Justine seemed as excited as a mother seeing off her children to their first prom.

"Such nonsense. I'm old enough to be his great-great-grandmother."

"Oh-ho, your friends at the concert will talk, Clarissa. Won't that be fun?" said Justine. "Oh, you are both so lovely. It brings tears, tears." Her eyes moist, she embraced the doctor and kissed us both on the cheek.

"Stop it, stop all this silly emotion," Dr. Banner protested, but the tone of her voice belied her delight. She hugged White Princess, who barked and licked the rouge on her face.

As the taxi took off, I heard Justine holler, "Good-bye, my queen and my prince. Enjoy yourselves."

The concert seats were indeed the best, a box to the left of and overlooking the string section, located so we could see the conductor's profile and watch his expressions during the performance. But why two seats? I soon learned that my seat had been occupied by many colleagues from around the world who came to visit the doctor during her active years at the university.

As made our way to the box, I sensed that the entire audience was watching us as if royalty were arriving. Many reached for the doctor's hand or waved. Smiling and nodding, the doctor acknowledged their greetings. She was back in the throbbing world again.

"Boy, what seats!" I exclaimed as we sat down.

"They've been mine for fifty years. The very best in the house, wouldn't you say?"

"Absolutely," I said with fervor.

Several people from the audience approached Clarissa. "How nice to see you again, Doctor. We've missed you."

"Yes, it is nice to see you too," said the doctor, grinning.

"Good to have you back, Clarissa. How are you? You do look wonderful. I hope we'll see you again. And the research...?"

"Why, thank you. Oh, I'm just fine. Yes, fine. Thank you. Yes, it has been a while; yes, the research has been very demanding. When will you see me again? Soon, very soon, of course."

A steady stream of greeters kept coming.

"Yes, yes, thank you, dear. It's nice to see you. Very nice. My companion? This is Peter, my protégé. No, no, not in my field, dear. In life."

Between such visits, we managed to converse briefly.

"Some of the most famous scientists and politicians and artists in the world have sat where you're sitting," she pointed out.

"As your guests?"

"Of course. But most of them are now gone. I'm one of the last to leave."

Gazing up toward the lofty balcony, I was surprised at how far away it was. "That's where Vicki and I sit," I said to Dr. Banner. "I can't wait to tell her."

The doctor joined my gaze. "Ah, seventy years ago I used to sit there with my parents. It's all they could afford. Although the stage appears no larger than a postage stamp—yes, I remember—the music is the same there as it is here. And nothing else matters."

Not exactly. From Dr. Banner's spot, the music was all-enveloping. I was immersed in sound as I had never been before. We watched the conductor instruct the orchestra to begin as the soloist sat and adjusted himself at the piano. Concentrating her gaze on the orchestra, closing her eyes from time to time as if in a reverie, Dr. Banner said nothing throughout the entire performance. Knowing how deeply she loved music, I wondered why there was so little of it in her home. Why was the piano always closed off behind doors in the parlor?

After playing Beethoven's Fifth piano concerto, the soloist bowed to enthusiastic applause. Then it was intermission.

"What a pianist. He's incredible," I said.

"Yes, perhaps the world's best. Would you like to meet him?" the doctor proposed.

"You're kidding. Arthur Rubinstein?"

"Peter, I don't—as you say—'kid.' Let's go backstage."

We wended our way through the crowd and entered a door that led to an area where the musicians were gathered in small groups drinking coffee. A woman was assisting the pianist, who was putting on his coat. Spying the doctor, he came forward to meet her, leaving his assistant behind holding the garment in midair.

"Clarissa, my dear," said Rubinstein, giving her a long embrace. "Where have you been? How are you?"

"Your playing has made me feel young again, Artur. As always, it was brilliant."

"You are my most adoring fan, save none."

"I'd like you to meet my gardener, Peter Albert. I would say that, after me, he is your most adoring fan."

Reaching for my hand, he looked at me squarely. "Very nice to meet you, Mr. Albert."

"Same here, Mr. Rubinstein. It's my honor, sir."

"I must congratulate you on your choice of a date. Clarissa is the most exciting woman I've ever known."

"Pish-posh, Ruby. You say that about all the women you know."

"Yes, but only in your case do I mean it. Unlike myself, who must travel the world, you are famous without ever having to leave Chicago. Well, I must be off. Will you come to see me while I'm in town? We could have lunch and reminisce about old times."

"Perhaps, Ruby, perhaps," said the doctor tentatively. "If I'm up to it. You know I have some good days and some bad ones. I'm not in circulation all the time."

"But you look marvelous. What about tomorrow? I must leave the next day."

"That wouldn't be good," said the doctor immediately. "I'll not be recovered from tonight."

Was she closing down again, I wondered. What was there about the world that she had withdrawn so and was now cautious about reentering?

"Then when I return in a year for my next booking. What about then?" said Rubinstein, pressing for a commitment.

"Certainly. If I'm still able."

"I'll call you then. Remember, we have a date."

Rubinstein kissed her on the cheek. "Good-bye, sweet lady." And to me, "Good-bye, young man."

We stood quietly, watching him leave. "I can't believe I shook his hand," I said.

"They are hands of gold, Peter. His touch is magical. Of course, he is quite a ladies' man, you know. Couldn't you tell? Now, we had better return to our seats before we miss the rest of the concert."

After our taxi drove up to the house, the doctor paid the driver. As we emerged, we saw Justine waiting in the open doorway to welcome us back.

"Well, well, well, look here, the music lovers return," she said and preceded us to the common room. "Shall I put on a kettle?"

"By all means," said Dr. Banner. "Will you stay for some tea, Peter?" White Princess scampered up to her, tail wagging like a metronome. "Hello, White Princess, dear. Have you missed me? Let me kiss you." Hugging and kissing the dog, she repeated, "Good girl. Good, good girl."

"Sure," I replied. "I'm still under the spell of the music. You must go, Justine. What seats! Right over the orchestra. You can watch the conductor in profile. And the music just swells up toward you from the stage. I've always had seats way up in the high balcony where the stage looks miniature. I've never had such an experience before."

"I had great company right here," said Justine. "You have your music, I have my literature. What did you think of the concert, Clarissa?" Without waiting for an answer, she flew into the kitchen and returned with a steaming kettle and three mugs with teabags. Apparently she had the water already heated in anticipation of our arrival.

"The new conductor was most impressive" was all that the doctor had to say.

"He's not new, Doctor Banner," I pointed out. "He's been with the orchestra for a couple of years."

"My, has it been that long since I've attended a concert?" said the doctor. "What splendid direction. How expressive, how imaginative his interpretation, not like the stiff, old German they used to have."

"What German was that?" I said.

"Never mind. It was before your time," she said curtly.

Justine began pouring the hot water. "You loved—"

"Please, that's enough," said the doctor, cutting her off.

"I was merely going to say that you loved his conducting at the time."

I wondered what Dr. Banner had refused to explain. What was there about the German conductor that she avoided talking about?

Seeing the doctor scowl, I thought it best to go on to another subject. "I wish Vicki could have been with us," I said. "Rubinstein is one of her favorite pianists."

"Ruby performed?" said Justine, surprised. "What did he play? Did you visit him after the concert?"

"An excellent rendition of the Beethoven Fifth concerto, as usual," said the doctor.

"Of course, you saw him after the concert. I imagine he was thrilled to see you, one of his former students."

"You were his student?" I exclaimed in astonishment.

"Clarissa studied under him for...how many years was it, Clarissa?"

"It was long ago, a time long forgotten. He was very young, younger than I, and before he became famous."

"And you visited him, of course," said Justine.

"Certainly, I saw him," said Dr. Banner, as if stating the obvious. "He is as flattering and as charming as ever. One can't believe a word he says. I strongly suggest that instead of asking meaningless questions, Justine, you stick to pouring tea. Now, Peter, this girl of yours, Vicki, how good is she at the piano?"

"You should hear her play. Her teacher says she's good enough to be a concert artist someday."

"Maybe so. But does she have the dedication?"

"She practices constantly, hours every day," I said.

"Good. A good sign."

"Would you like to meet her?"

"I'll think about it."

Dr. Banner's reply puzzled me. What could possibly be the harm in meeting Vicki, in talking to her or listening to her play? But I knew that the doctor was not one to be pressed. I switched the subject to Lenny.

"I'd also like you to meet my friend Lenny. He's absolutely brilliant, and he has the world's largest record collection. Maybe someday, with your permission of course, I'll bring him to visit."

"Perhaps someday."

"We could listen to some of his wonderful records on the Capehart. I'm sure you'd love them."

"That may be. We'll see. It has been a most enjoyable evening, Peter. Thank you kindly. You have been a perfect escort. Now I must retire."

"It's I who should thank you, Doctor Banner."

She came to me, at first shaking my hand, then kissing me on the forehead. "Good night, sweet boy. We'll do it again. Next Thursday, perhaps?" Then she left for her bedroom with White Princess straggling behind, as usual.

Unaccustomed to such luxurious entertainment, which was, of course, far beyond my means, I was only too eager to accept Dr. Banner's offer. Through the rest of the season I escorted her, and on each occasion she was no less enthusiastic than on our first outing. Indeed, I began to suspect that the concert was the highlight of her week.

Dr. Banner's transformation from the irritable, distant, demanding, bedridden old woman who had interviewed me nine months earlier to the currently involved, expansive, more giving spirit was miraculous. She had dropped her formal ways with me. I was now "Pete" instead of "Peter" or "Mr. Albert," and she inquired in subtle ways about my personal life. Justine attributed the change mostly to my zealous restoration of the garden. She said it had taken her out of a boring rut. But I was puzzled about Dr. Banner not wanting to meet my friends.

"It's not them, my boy," Justine said. "You must understand that for some years now she has removed herself from the center of things. It's the disillusionment that comes when the world passes one by."

"But she's had all those honors."

"Precisely. They're in the past. What's left? She has the will and determination for more, but society - the world - has abandoned her, given her—us—this house and the garden instead of the wherewithal to continue her research. You have most of your life ahead of you to accomplish wonderful things. She has all of it behind her; deprived of long-term challenge. Our work with the mice in the cellar is limited. I have no illusion that it will produce anything of value. But it keeps Clarissa alive. She's as capable as ever, no less than when she and I were young. Clarissa needs challenge as much as food in order to live. Can you understand, my boy?"

"Y'know, at the concert she just glowed," I said, reliving the experience in my mind. "As we moved down the aisles to our seats, people everywhere greeted her, said how pleased they were to see her again, and after we were seated they came to ask her how she was. She was radiant."

"Yes, that was good. She was back in the world again. Keep taking her to concerts. Will you?

By the middle of May, the taming of the garden was complete, and only routine maintenance was necessary, requiring no more than one or two afternoons a week. Having become accustomed to my presence, however, Justine pointed out that I needn't wait for my garden chores to have an excuse to visit.

But as my familiarity with Dr. Banner increased, I noticed that the reverse was happening in my relationship with Justine. It was as if she purposely drew away in order not to dilute the other developing closeness. At times she exhibited a new brusqueness. Had I said or done something that hurt her?

I conceived an ingenious proposal. "Could I bring Lenny over?" I asked Justine one afternoon. I told her that he was well read. And were he to play his records on the Capehart, it would be like bringing a concert hall into the room. He also drank too much, I said apolo-getically, but wasn't Justine naturally drawn to anyone who indulged in excess?

"We would have Doctor Banner's permission of course," I reassured her.

"Clarissa's permission be damned," said Justine. "This place is as much mine as hers. Hah, it belongs to neither of us. It belongs to the university. I'd be pleased to meet your friend. Perhaps we could get drunk together."

Inhaling deeply on her cigarette, Justine lapsed into a coughing fit.

"I wish to hell you'd listen to Doctor Banner and quit," I said sharply.

"I appreciate your concern, my boy, but I've gone beyond the point of redemption. Here we are, three old hags with nothing but ourselves to live for. You've brought us beauty and young strength and yourself. Now we have somebody more than ourselves to worry about. It's about time."

Although it was only two in the afternoon on the day that Lenny and I visited, a large bottle of white wine stood on the oak table, which was tidier than usual. The books, instead of being strewn about and open, were closed and stacked along the far edge. Justine's short, straight hair had been neatly combed; uncharacteristically, she wore lipstick.

A lit cigarette between her fingers, she greeted us at the door.

"Justine, I'd like you to meet—"

"Oh-ho. A fellow smoker, and a drinker, too," she said. "You poor boy. Pete has told me all about you. A brother in arms." She embraced him as if their meeting were a loving reunion, then she patted his back

Lenny grinned, joyous at finding another renegade. "You suicidal too?"

"Of course, my boy, but more important, I'm statistical. Hah, my death will have meaning. Tell me, what is your unhappiness about? Come, come into our labyrinth." Obviously Justine and Lenny were symbiotic. She took his hand and led him into the common room. "Let's begin with some wine, a cigarette, and some Forster. Pete has informed me of your appreciation of my favorite author."

"If you'll excuse me," I said, "I have some work to do in the garden."

"Go, do your labor while Lenny and I bask in unforgivable overindulgence and sloth," said Justine with a wave of her hand.

As I left the room to take up my chores, I overheard Lenny say, "I've been waiting all my life to meet you."

"Likewise, my boy. Pete tells me you're quite intelligent."

"Actually, I'm brilliant. An IQ of one-ninety."

"Well, I see that modesty is not one of your strong points."

"I wish I could just be average. Being smart's a damn curse."

"How so? I'm a greater admirer of a superior intellect. It's such a rare commodity," said Justine as she poured two glasses of wine.

"That's the trouble. My classmates hate me for it. Getting a perfect grade on every test and knowing the right answer in every discussion hardly contributes to my popularity."

"Ah, I see. Yes, we live in a society that wallows in mediocrity. Stand up to it. Be courageous. Don't let it bring you down to its level, and you'll do great things."

"Me, do great things?" Lenny snorted. "Not a chance. I'm cut out to fail."

"Nonsense. Are you aware that down through history it has taken only one person to make a difference? One person can change the world. So can you." She reached across the table and patted his hand.

"Now, let's imbibe, get pie-eyed if you're so inclined."

Raising his glass, Lenny toasted, "To freedom."

"To freedom? But why, young man?"

"Because...because I'm not free."

"Ah, how sad, a novice in life and already a prisoner," commiserated Justine. "And who, my dear boy, is your keeper?"

"Myself. Just myself," said Lenny in disgust.

"My heavens. The worst kind. But are you sure? I used to blame myself for being sinful. Then one day I discovered who I was, that sin is only in the eye of the perpetrator, and I've been free ever since."

"Teach me how, Justine," begged Lenny. "I'm dying to learn."

"All in good time, my boy. Reading Forster is a good beginning."

"Forster reaches me like no one else," said Lenny brightly. "I suppose it's because he and I have something in common—personally, I mean."

"And what, may I ask, is that—personally?"

"Well, we're both men."

"What powers of observation. A good start. What else?"

"We're both rebels, in our own way."

"And your way is...?"

"It's my father," said Lenny, his voice steely. "He expects me to be like him, to come into his business—the junk iron business. It's the last thing I want to do. He doesn't understand that I'm not like him."

"An unfortunate and not uncommon error, my boy: a parent who thinks he has literally reproduced himself. I'd suggest a few lessons in genetics."

"Wouldn't do any good. He has all the answers," said Lenny, pouring a second glass of wine for Justine and himself.

"What does your mother say?"

"She loves us both. What can she say? So she stays out of it."

"A loving mother. That is fortunate."

"Yes. Since I'm an only child, she gives me everything. More than I need, or want."

"Ah, a singleton. But you love them both?"

"My mother, yes. My father? I hate him." He refilled his glass and immediately quaffed it down. "But I suppose I love him too."

"Such ambivalence, my boy," said Justine sadly. "The torment of childhood. Is that also your prison?"

"Why…why, I hadn't thought of it that way but…Well, I suppose it is, partly."

"I'm sure someday you'll become reconciled in your mind and forgive him. Every parent makes mistakes—some innocent and, too often I fear, some intentional. Those of us who don't forgive our parents for their errors suffer all our lives, but I think you're too smart to let that happen. You say your father is only partly the cause of your unhappiness. I'm not satisfied, my boy, with your flippant answer— if I may say so—concerning what you have in common with Forster."

"Well," said Lenny, his tongue thickening from the wine, "we're both homosexuals."

"Really. Now that is a revelation," said Justine without a sign of surprise. "You do come to the point."

"No one knows. Pete doesn't know. My parents don't know. Only I know. And now you." Lenny finished his third glass as if it were water, and refilled a fourth.

"What a terrible burden you carry, my boy. Now I clearly know who your keeper is."

"I doubt whether in my lifetime society will ever accept my sexual preference. What about yourself?"

"I am a woman, my boy. What do you expect?"

By now Lenny's tongue had become thick and his thoughts hard to control. "Well, you live with the doctor."

Justine laughed until tears filled her eyes. "I see. The wine is fortifying you, eh? For your information, my boy, I like men. I like you, and I like Pete, and I suppose if Rhett Butler had asked me to go to bed with him, I'd have given it a try, but since he never did I buried my urges in work. Now all is calm, and my hormones have settled down. Today I just like living. I'm content with what I've got, with my books, my mice, Clarissa, and having new friends like you."

Dr. Banner, dressed in a white laboratory coat, came into the room from the cellar, with White Princess in tow. "Who, may I ask, is this young man?"

"Why, this is Pete's good friend Lenny, and my newest fan. Lenny, this is Clarissa, my extraordinary companion."

Standing, wobbly, quite under the influence, Lenny reached to shake the doctor's hand.

"Pleased to meetcha, Clarissa. I understand you're a Bach lover."

"You understand correctly, Mr...."

"Just Lenny. I answer to no other name. May I put on some Bach?"

Clarissa smiled at Lenny's outrageous, irresistible informality. "I would have no objection."

"Would you like a glass of wine, Clarissa?" said Justine.

"No, no thank you."

"Wine and Bach. They're made for each other. You must have some wine," urged Lenny.

"Well, all right, a little," said the doctor, who then addressed the dog. "Clarissa's going to have just a little wine, White Princess. You stay. That's a good girl."

Justine went to the kitchen, then returned with a large glass and filled it to the brim from the decanter.

"Attagirl," said Lenny approvingly. He put Bach's Toccata and Fugue in D Minor on the Capehart.

"What do you say we have a record concert some evening, say next Saturday?" he asked after they'd listened for a while. "I have some Rubinsteins that'll send you to the next galaxy."

"How did you know, young man?" said Justine, winking at Lenny, having guessed that Pete had informed him of the concert at Orchestra Hall. "Rubinstein's my favorite pianist. And an old buddy of Clarissa's. By all means, let's have a concert. Say yes, Clarissa. I'd love it."

"Well, for your sake," said Clarissa reluctantly.

"Thank you," said Justine with a bow.

I returned from my gardening labors for the traditional teatime to find Lenny and Justine still at it, a bit boisterous from the wine, and by then declaring themselves old friends in spirit. The room was foggy with cigarette smoke. But most surprising, Dr. Banner was thickly engaged in the repartee, and "feeling good" herself.

"What's going on?" I said.

"Clarissa here has consented to have a concert on the Capehart next Saturday evening," said an excited Lenny.

"It's 'Doctor Banner,' not 'Clarissa,'" I whispered into Lenny's ear.

"I'll put on some tea," said Justine, rising to go to the kitchen.

"I must say, Pete," admitted Dr. Banner, "I like your friend, and I confess to letting myself be cajoled. How can one deny the pleasure of listening on the Capehart with such a lover of fine music? I trust you'll join us," said an unshackled Dr. Banner.

"I think the Bach did it," said Lenny. "Right, Clarissa?"

Did I hear him call her Clarissa again? Audacity was part of Lenny's charm.

"Well, of course, one can never hate a lover of Bach," said Dr. Banner.

"Could I bring a friend?" I asked. "Well, I mean Vicki."

"Certainly, my boy," Justine piped up, returning with teacups and a steaming teapot. "It's about time we met her."

"Is that okay with you, Doctor?" I pursued cautiously.

"I suppose so," she said indifferently.

"In fact, we could have a live concert too. I'm sure we could get Vicki to play for us," I added.

"Say, what a wonderful idea," Justine exclaimed. "But of course we wouldn't want to impose. Clarissa, we must have the piano tuned. It has been such a long time since you've played, dear."

"Because they no longer obey, my sweet," said the doctor, spreading her gnarled, swollen, arthritic fingers before her on the table.

"But aren't we lucky? Suddenly we are surrounded by new, fresh lives," said Justine ecstatically. "It's far from over, Clarissa."

"Why, yes, I agree."

"Then you'll try again? As we used to?"

"Oh, I'll see."

"Try what, may I ask?" I queried.

"To shake the world, my boy," said Justine.

"Terrific! Shake it, Clarissa. Shake it to its molten core," shouted Lenny.

For some time, Vicki had wanted to meet the "old ladies." When she and I were together, which was three or four times a week, I rarely failed to refer to something Justine had said, or to Dr. Banner's opinion on a musical performance, or to the new blossoms in the garden. Although I believed I did this in all innocence, it was unthinking of me. My allusions only whetted Vicki's desire to meet the ladies all the more, but I had to stall and make phony excuses because of Dr. Banner's curious aversion to meeting my girl.

Now at last, Vicki would meet them. We were going to a party at their house on Saturday night. Vicki said she could hardly wait. It would also be her first chance to meet Lenny, whom I often mentioned admiringly. I broke the good news about the party to her while we sat on a bench in Jackson Park.

"Wait till you meet Justine," I said. "She just loves everybody. And Clarissa, Dr. Banner, studied under Rubinstein. Can you believe it? While we were watching him perform, she never said a word about it."

"It's hard to believe that after all these months I'm really going to meet her," said Vicki, overjoyed at the prospect.

"Now I know why she has that concert grand in the living room."

"A real concert grand," said Vicki in wonder. "What I'd give to play on a concert grand."

"Well, you can. I told them you'd play something."

"What? How could you, Pete?" she said vehemently. "I couldn't possibly."

"I don't understand your objection. You play in the student lounge all the time where anyone can listen."

"That's not the same as giving a performance."

"You wouldn't be performing, Vicki."

"Of course I would."

"Christ, I told them you'd be willing—"

"Without consulting me," she interrupted, anger flashing.

"Doctor Banner should hear you play, Vicki. She'd appreciate you more than anyone I know."

"Well, I'm sorry," Vicki said, calming down. "But I don't want to be judged."

"Okay, okay, if that's the way you feel."

"It is, Pete. Please try to understand."

I kissed her. "I love you, Vicki. I wouldn't want you to do anything you didn't want to do."

That cool May Saturday evening, Lenny fetched me in his father's Cadillac, then we drove to Vicki's home. Lenny called at the door so I wouldn't have to deal with her parents and risk a scene.

On the way over to the doctor's house, Lenny, outgoing and always appealing, informed Vicki of the program he had planned on the Capehart. They were her favorites too, she said. Beyond their common love of music, their personalities seemed to mesh.

"At first you'll probably take Clarissa for a sourpuss, but don't be fooled," Lenny said, proud of his insight. "She's got a real funny bone. Right, Pete? And Justine's the opposite; she acts like she doesn't give a damn about anything, but she cares about everything."

Justine greeted us at the door. "Oh, you're here! Our stars are here, Clarissa," she shouted, as if amazed that we showed up. She drew Lenny to her, pulling him through the doorway. "Come in, come in, you lovely boy. And this is Vicki, is it? Come in, sweet girl. Immensely delighted to meet you."

As she hugged me, she said softly in my ear, "I must say, your taste is impeccable."

Clarissa entered with White Princess following. "This is Vicki, Clarissa," said Justine, and to Vicki she said, "And this is White Princess."

As Lenny warned, Clarissa greeted Vicki with a cool, "How do you do."

"I'm happy to meet you, Doctor Banner," Vicki replied.

We walked into the dining room, as neat and immaculate as during Lenny's first visit. Glancing at the Capehart, I noted that it was now polished, its mahogany grain shimmering under the floor lamp beside it. Turning to the parlor, I observed that the piano too was now shiny, the keyboard exposed, the cover raised.

We sat around the oak table as Justine asked Vicki about herself, about her music and her ambitions. Dr. Banner merely listened without comment, without displaying any interest. But I was sure she was taking in every word.

"We've just played a game on Vicki's parents," I said.

"Instead of Pete, I picked her up in my father's Cadillac," Lenny informed them.

"So they think I'm going out with Lenny," said Vicki, giggling. "And were they impressed with the car."

"Yeah, they wanted to know which model it was, and how I liked it. I played right along. Was that okay?" asked Lenny.

"Perfect," replied Vicki.

Lenny lapsed into hysterical laughter. "I told them it was the best Caddy I'd had in years."

"If they knew you were Jewish, they'd have had a fit," said Vicki.

"What a pity. My, my, prejudiced parents. And what is their faith?" asked Justine.

"Greek Orthodox. They want me to marry a Greek boy."

"Ah, yes, Pete told me. No doubt that marrying one's own kind makes for peace, but it's not the best, genetically speaking, wouldn't you say, Clarissa?"

"Hmph."

"You're quite a beauty, my girl," said Justine. "I would highly recommend intermarriage. Your children would be both handsome and smart."

"It is none of your business," Clarissa declared.

"For God's sake, Justine," I said, embarrassed for Vicki.

"I was merely speaking genetically," explained Justine. She turned to Vicki. "So, like someone else in this room, you too have parent problems?"

"They liked me, Vicki," said Lenny. "Maybe we should swap parents."

"I love them. I don't want different parents," said Vicki firmly.

"And, of course, they love you," said Justine.

"Yes, except my father doesn't show his feelings."

"But you know he loves you," Justine said, pouring tea for all of us.

"I think he does. He bought me a grand piano for my sixteenth birthday."

"A significant gesture, I'd say," said Justine, handing Vicki a steaming cup.

"Hell, he could easily afford it," I cracked.

"If only we could talk, if only he'd let me in. I'd give anything," said Vicki.

"Tell us about your dreams, dear girl. I understand you can make a piano sing like a human voice," Justine said, smiling tenderly. "Would you kindly play something for us?"

"What have you been telling these people, Pete? I thought—I mean, didn't Pete explain? I'm sorry, really sorry, but—"

"Just play something and show them that I'm not exaggerating," I said.

"I thought we agreed that I wouldn't perform," she protested.

I could see the daggers in her look. "She plays in the student lounge all the time," I said.

"And I told you that's not the same as giving a performance."

"This wouldn't be a performance," I persisted.

"Of course it is. How could you do this?"

"Doctor Banner should hear you play," I said stubbornly. "I told you she'd appreciate you, and Lenny hasn't heard you."

"I'm sorry," said Vicki, more calmly now. Then she said to me in a clear, firm tone, "And I told you I don't want to be judged."

"Pete explained your reluctance—your understandable reluctance," said Justine sweetly. "But my dear, you needn't worry. It's all in fun, and as Pete said, you're among friends."

"I quite know how you feel," said Clarissa, suddenly breaking her long silence. "When I was young, I hated it whenever my parents asked me to play for their guests. After all, they weren't *my* guests. I wished to play only for my own pleasure and for others of my own choosing. Yes, I quite know how you feel."

"Thank you for being so understanding, Doctor Banner," said Vicki, looking toward the parlor to scrutinize the piano, an old Steinway, older than any she had ever seen. "Do you still play?"

"Sadly, my playing days are over."

"Your piano is beautiful. I've never seen such an old Steinway."

"Yes, fifty years ago it stood on the stage of Orchestra Hall."

"It was a gift from the conductor," said Justine.

"Shush, Justine," said Dr. Banner firmly.

"Hah, your German boyfriend the conductor," said Justine in defiance, referring to a secret romantic liaison of Clarissa's youth.

"I shall not dignify your foolish words with a comment," the doctor declared angrily.

"I don't mean to be intrusive—you need not answer—but why did you stop playing?" asked Vicki.

Dr. Banner rose, walked to the piano, and sat on the bench. She placed her hands on the keyboard and played a chord. "See, my fingers are like the twigs of a petrified tree, not like yours. Let me see your hands." Vicki walked over to the piano. "Here, sit beside me," said Dr. Banner. As Vicki did her bidding, she took Vicki's hand in hers. "What glorious fingers; how slender and supple they are. I would give years of my life to have such hands now."

Ever so lightly, Dr. Banner positioned her twisted fingers on the keys, pressed them down slowly, then moved them over to a new position. We heard an exquisite melody issue forth, the first chords of Mozart's Piano Sonata in A Major, the eleventh. Then her fingers stumbled and stopped.

She closed her eyes as if imagining that her fingers had resumed their tripping course across the keys, as if the melody were still magically filling the room. But it was not a fantasy, after all; the music was impossibly real, marvelously lovely. The sonata was alive. Vicki had taken up where Dr. Banner, who gently removed herself from the bench, had left off.

For the next fifteen minutes or so, Vicki played the piece flawlessly to its triumphant end, pouring herself into it with relentless intensity. Her world was entirely circumscribed by the keyboard. That somehow frightened me. It crossed my mind, as she became lost in a distant, glowing trance, that I was witnessing an overwhelming adversary.

When she was done, we clapped until our hands ached. We shouted bravo, and I kissed her and said, "Thank you, thank you. I love you, Vicki." Lenny kissed her and Justine embraced her and Dr. Banner held her hand. "Well done, young lady, very well done, I must say. Isn't she superb, White Princess? Yes, we'll be listening to more music, but nothing as beautiful as what this lovely young woman has played. Vicki, my dear, how would you like to visit with me some afternoon?"

"Oh, Doctor Banner, I would like that. Whenever you'd like," said Vicki, enthralled.

"How would tomorrow afternoon do? Anytime after I awake from my nap at three."

Meeting my approving eyes, Vicki replied, "I'll be here promptly at three."

"Not too promptly, my dear," said the doctor, amused. "I'll need a few moments to return to reality."

"I'll bring Clarissa back to reality. Come at three, Vicki," said Justine.

"Make it three fifteen, my dear. I look forward to it," said the doctor, throwing Justine a disapproving glance.

Lenny loaded some records in the Capehart. "I hope you're putting on my friend Ruby Rubinstein," said Justine. Then to us, "It's time to celebrate, my dear friends. Let's all have some wine. Perhaps we'll get drunk."

When the music began, Vicki and I withdrew to the Victorian couch in the now-darkened parlor while the others remained seated around the oak table in the dining room. Invisible in the gloom, Vicki and I held each other and kissed, urged on by the tremendous tension of Sibelius's Second Symphony. Later, after the ladies had retired to their rooms, and Lenny was lying spread-eagle across the table with a pillow under his head, we played El Amour Brujo—Love the Magician—and, inspired by its raw, erotic power, we made love.

"Oh, my god, Pete. It's morning," Vicki said, leaping from my arms. The rosy glow of the dawn had penetrated the parlor. "My parents must be going crazy with worry."

"They'll blame Lenny," I said gleefully. "Maybe now they'll appreciate me."

"Where is he?" she said. "Lenny, Lenny," she called.

"Here I am, I think," he responded groggily as he tried to sit up on the dining room table.

Vicki began combing her hair and organizing herself. "Please take me home," she said to Lenny just as Justine entered the room in her robe.

"I haven't had such a bacchanalian night in ages," she said. "Did I hear amorous sounds after I went to bed, or do I have a keen imagination?"

"We were listening to El Amour Brujo," I confessed.

"Really?" said Justine with a raised eyebrow. "A very erotic piece, indeed. But whatever you say, my boy. Whatever you say."

"Thank you for a fantastic time," said Vicki, smoothing the wrinkles in her dress.

"It's been marvelous having you, young lady. You must come again for another concert."

"Say good-bye to the doctor for us," I said.

"I will," said Justine. "I haven't seen her so spirited and free in years. It was like old times again. You gave her a marvelous gift."

"What gift do you mean?" I asked.

"Yourselves, my boy. Just your young, happy selves."

Admitting Vicki at the front door the following afternoon at three, Justine bowed, and with a sweep of her arm said, "Come in, young lady, do come in. Your fellow musician awaits." Vicki followed her into the common room. "Clarissa will be with you presently. I'll retire to the garden to commune with the wildlife. If you'll excuse me, dear," she said, picking up a book from the dining room table.

The dining room was back to normal; the Capehart lid was closed, and the sliding doors to the parlor were closed. Seated, waiting in silence, Vicki watched Justine through the window as she entered the garden, sat on a cast-iron bench amid the tall shrubs, and opened her book. Soon Clarissa appeared, her eyes still showing the effects of having just awakened from a nap. Vicki stood to meet her.

"Good to see you, my dear Vicki," she said, looking at her wristwatch and shaking Vicki's hand. "Three fifteen exactly. Excellent. No need to stand. Please sit down." Directing Vicki to sit at the table, she moved a chair beside her for herself.

"Thank you for having me, Doctor Banner. I'm very honored."

"Yes, yes. I'm sure you are, but you needn't be. You and I are the same, both members of the human race. However, I am the one to be honored that you would take the time to listen to what an old busybody has to say. You see, I must rest on my laurels, and frankly they are a most uncomfortable bed to lie in." She reached across the table and picked up a sheet of music. "Now, I have this music, a piece that an old friend composed many years ago. I would like you to learn it and, when you are ready, play it for me. Would you do that?"

Vicki took the music. "It looks extremely difficult," she said after studying it briefly.

"Yes, it is. But I think you can master it. Indeed, I know you can. You see, it was composed for me, but I can no longer play it, and even when I could I played it poorly."

Vicki shook her head. "Oh, Doctor Banner, then I doubt whether I could."

"We shall see, won't we? But I must warn you, I'm rarely wrong, especially in such matters. You have a rare talent, my dear. Rare indeed. Your touch is magical. You can do with musical notes what few can do: you imbue them with feeling."

"You're making me blush," said Vicki, truly turning pink.

"Of course. But for all your modesty, don't you believe that eventually you will have the ability to master any work?"

"Yes, I do. How did you know?"

"Because I too felt the same way when I was your age. Not only about music, which soon enough brought me to my knees, but about science. I pursued a goal unswervingly until I succeeded. And I see the same sense of purpose in you. Only you are far better, even at this early stage of your development as a talent, than I ever was."

"It's true that I want to perform on the concert stage," said Vicki, astonished at the doctor's insight into her being. "But I've not told a soul for fear they'd laugh at me. Most of all my parents."

"Of course, you realize the competition is merciless," said the doctor, looking into Vicki's eyes for a sign of hesitation.

"I don't care."

"To be talented is not sufficient. You need that extra, indefinable quality that separates genius from ordinary brilliance."

"What do *you* think, Doctor Banner?" said Vicki, knowing that she would receive an honest answer from one whose validation had suddenly become all-important.

"If I were a betting woman—which I confess I am," said the doctor, who then whispered into Vicki's ear, "but please don't tell a soul—I'd bet my life on you."

Vicki's eyes danced with delight. "Thank you, thank you," she gushed.

"Have you informed Peter of your ambition?"

"I've mentioned it, but he doesn't take it seriously. I think he considers it an idle dream."

"Forgive me if I'm intruding," the doctor said cautiously. "I take it you love him."

"With all my heart."

"You may be faced with a choice. Have you considered that possibility?"

"A choice? What choice?" said Vicki anxiously.

"Between your career and love," said the doctor, watching Vicki's eyes react to her every word.

"I don't understand."

"A long time ago, when I was your age, or perhaps a few years older, a young man and I fell in love. We were both at the cusp of our careers, his in music, mine in science. In order for us to marry, one of us would have to sacrifice our calling. He was offered the conductorship of a prestigious orchestra in Europe. At that precise moment I had been given a major grant with which to pursue my research at the university. And here you see me today."

"I don't see the comparison, Doctor Banner."

"Well, young lady, please think about it. Everything good in life exacts a price. But aren't you already dealing with a decision that is costing you?" She paused, waiting to see whether Vicki would anticipate her next words. "I'm referring to your parents' disapproval of Pete, their anti-semitism."

"True," said Vicki, fingering the music sheet nervously. "It's not only because I love Pete, but because they are so terribly wrong. They won't even let themselves know him."

"So you see, if you believe in what you think is right, if you believe in your feelings, if you remain true to yourself, you will be compelled to sacrifice others who are dear to you. Do you see my point?"

"What can I do? I will never give up Pete," said Vicki, feeling at a loss.

"Of course not, my dear. But it may not be your choice. Oh, dear child, I don't want to make you unhappy over this. I simply want you to see that life consists of choices, and we can make only one at a time. Whether we have made the right one is never easy to determine, quite simply because there is no way of knowing how the alternative would have worked out. It all comes down to making the most heartfelt of the choices available."

"I understand what you're saying. And I thank you for your concern," said Vicki respectfully.

Clarissa stared out the window. "Look, Justine is coming in from the garden. What do you say we have a spot of tea?"

"I'd love it, and how about a Beethoven sonata on the Capehart."

Justine came in from the garden holding a small bouquet of flowers, which she proceeded to put in a vase. "I heard you say 'sonata,'" she commented. "Let it resound, dear girl, let it resound until the teacups rattle. I presume you know how to operate the contraption."

"Put the pot on the stove, will you, and leave the poor girl alone," said Clarissa as she and Vicki laughed.

Whenever Justine greeted Lenny or me at the front door, she did so with enormous enthusiasm, making us feel not only welcome but also special, as if we were a surprise gift. So it was that soft spring evening when Lenny and I appeared at the door to take Clarissa to a chamber music concert, the last of the season, at Mandel Hall, only a few blocks away. We were shaven and powdered and dressed in suits and ties.

"Come in, you adorable, handsome men. They're here, Clarissa. Your two gorgeous escorts," said Justine in her customary fashion.

"You're embarrassing me," I said as we stepped into the entrance hall.

"Not me," said Lenny, grinning from earlobe to earlobe. "Keep telling me how gorgeous I am."

"So it's chamber music tonight, eh?" said Justine. "At Mandel Hall, is it?"

"All Schubert," I said. "Yes. We're walking over."

"Oh, oh, heavenly, heavenly," said Justine, popping a cigarette into the corner of her mouth.

Clarissa appeared in her usual garish going-out regalia. "Good evening, boys," she said, tossing a shawl over her shoulders.

"Evening, Doctor," I said.

"Same here, Clarissa," said Lenny.

Each of us took Clarissa by the arm. After Justine rushed to open the door with flair, we conducted the doctor out onto the sidewalk.

"Good evening, sweet princes and princess," said Justine, blowing a kiss.

"Foolish woman. You're just envious," said the doctor, after which Justine slammed the door shut behind them.

On our walk the couple of blocks to the hall, the conversation was nonstop.

"We invited Justine, but she wouldn't come," I said.

"I didn't know. It was cruel of me to say what I did. I wish she'd join us, but I knew she wouldn't," said the doctor. It was the first time I had ever heard her express any regret for her harshness toward her loyal companion.

"Why won't she?" asked Lenny.

"In all the many years we've been together, she has never come to a concert with me. Quite simply she fears crowds."

"It's as if she lives another life in her literature," I commented.

"Yes, that's her escape, just as music is mine," said the doctor.

I wanted to change the subject. "We would like to pay for the concert tonight," I informed her.

"Actually, it's on my father," Lenny explained. "I got my allowance today." "Really? At your age you still have an allowance? My, how unfortunate," said the doctor sardonically.

"We're splitting it between us," I told the doctor. "You're paying for the other half indirectly."

"Ah, from your wages in the garden," she said. "Well earned, Peter. Well earned."

Lenny and I were pleased. Her allowing us to pay struck us as an act of generosity on her part.

As we entered Mandel Hall and worked our way down the aisle to our seats, Clarissa was greeted with the same smiles and welcoming nods and handshakes that she encountered at Orchestra Hall. People came up to her to chat even after we were seated.

"Are you aware that you're causing a stir among my former colleagues?" said the doctor devilishly. "The young women wonder what magic potion I've given you. I told them I've mesmerized you into thinking I'm the most beautiful woman here."

"But you are, Doctor," I said, laying myself open to a put-down.

"Of course you are," Lenny chimed in, foolishly seconding me.

"Words wasted. Such ridiculous words," said the doctor, not at all unhappy but, to my amazement, actually giggling. "Oh, the musicians are now seated. Now, for wonderful music, my soul food. So be quiet."

That summer I remained in Chicago running the night shift at a gas station on 51st Street. At least once a week I spent a few hours working in Dr. Banner's garden. Vicki went off to music camp in Vermont, much to her parents' relief—anything to keep us apart— and Lenny hung aimlessly around the city, bored and gradually destroying himself with alcohol. He must have spent a good deal of time visiting Justine, for whenever I showed up to work in the garden, I usually found him sitting at the oak table in lively conversation with her. Justine, a natural if not a passive listener, thrived on being needed. She, better than anyone I knew, could relieve Lenny's torment, at least for a while.

On occasion I was baffled by Lenny's apparent disinterest in women, except as asexual friends, but I shrugged it off as a meaningless and temporary aberration. Often I worried aloud to Justine about Lenny, both before and after she became his confidante.

One afternoon in August, Justine invited me in to chat. By this time I was working only a day a week in the garden, for it needed only minimum maintenance this late in the summer.

"Would you like some tea before you start work?" she said after closing the door behind me.

"No, thanks," I said. "Have you seen Lenny?"

"It depends. How far into the past must I go? From time to time he comes by, and we settle matters of the world together. Why do you ask?"

"I think he's avoiding me. Have you seen him *lately?*"

"Such ambiguities, dear boy. What do you mean by 'lately'?" said Justine, seeming to evade my question by complication.

"I mean this week," I said, pinning it down.

"No, not yet this week."

"I'm worried. The last time I saw him he seemed depressed, and he was drinking a lot."

"Yes, the poor boy has been deeply troubled," said Justine, exhaling a plume of cigarette smoke.

"Maybe if he found the right girl, he'd find himself," I suggested.

Justine squinted at me to ascertain whether I was serious. "I see you have a very limited understanding of your friend's problem," she said with a certain sting.

"It's his parents," I said unequivocally.

"No, my boy, it's our society, but I have said all I intend to say, and I wish to discuss the matter no further."

"What is Doctor Banner up to?" I said in view of Justine's refusal to dwell on Lenny. "I haven't seen her for some time." In fact I hadn't seen her for weeks. According to Justine she was hardly ever home.

"She's been busy out there in society doing her patriotic duty."

I interpreted that to mean that the doctor was actively espousing her anti-cancer crusade against cigarette smoking. But I soon discovered I was mistaken.

"But right now she's in the garden working like a zealot," said Justine. "I wish you would tell her not to overdo it. She won't listen to me."

Seeing that Justine was a bit contentious, taken with a foul mood no doubt, I immediately went to the garden, where I found the doctor on her knees on the damp ground weeding a flower bed, with White Princess lying near her.

I knelt down beside her and we worked side by side for a couple of hours, sometimes talking, sometimes lapsing into an easy silence. It was obvious that the doctor's metamorphosis from a discouraged, incapacitated shadow to a vital, enthusiastic person was complete. Throughout the concert season when I was her escort, she still had her bad days and often had to cancel our plans, but to hear her talk now, she was routinely up and about, rarely needing a cane, taking in the fragrance of the flowers and their parade of colors as if she had discovered sensation for the first time.

"Ah, Pete. This fall I think I shall have you plant some flowering shrubs and shorten the flower beds. It will reduce the maintenance."

"Okay, if that's what you want. But I'm having no trouble keeping up with it now," I said.

"I see. Then you plan to stay with me forever?"

"Well, I'm only in my second year."

"Of course. Then I shall have you a while longer."

"Absolutely."

When Dr. Banner tried to get up by herself, I gave her my arm. She ignored it at first, but, having no success from being on her knees so long, she finally grasped it for leverage, which allowed her to rise to a standing position.

"Thank you, Peter." She laughed. "Were it not for you, I'd probably have to spend the night on my knees."

"Praying for help, I presume," I said, joking.

She grunted in appreciation. "Have you decided on a career? I gather you're still in the general undergraduate program."

"Doctor, I haven't the faintest idea what I want to do."

"I presume you may have gathered that I aspired to being a concert artist, and look what happened," she said, chuckling. "Few of us become what we dream of in our immaturity. All my life I've been frustrated over how little I've accomplished. And now there is no time left."

"But the Nobel—"

"An accolade representative merely of world opinion. It was never a prize, *the* prize. What I wish for myself - simply to pursue my research - is far more important. Still, I suppose I'm pleased with the quality of what I've achieved. And what about you, Peter? Have you ever considered politics?"

"No, never have."

"You war veterans bring much maturity to our scene. Your experience provides a world view. Our nation is in such dire need of exemplary leaders. Men like the two Roosevelts. I hope you'll favor my friend Henry in November."

"Henry Wallace is definitely not my choice, Doctor," I said frankly.

"Henry knows what ails our country and what medicine to apply. He knows that more than anyone else, I assure you."

"But he's surrounded by fellow travelers. Aren't the Communists behind him?"

"Nonsense. That's the ultimate absurdity, propaganda spread by his enemies. There will be a giant rally at Soldiers Field next week. I shall be introducing him. You must come and listen. Will you?"

"Okay, to please you."

"Well, thank you," she said. "In the end, I believe you'll be pleasing yourself."

"I'm amazed at all the things you're doing these days—the music, the research, the garden, now politics. You've changed so, Doctor."

"You had a hand in it. You made the world beautiful again. I had forgotten that my life isn't over, that despite the wasting of my body, my inner being is still as vital as ever."

One hundred thousand souls thronged the rally. Clarissa stood on the rostrum, paused momentarily before the microphone awaiting silence, then in her aged, cracking, imperative voice spoke.

"It is now almost three years since our victory in the Great War," Clarissa began. "In generosity, and not without self-interest, we have forgiven our enemies and are set on a mission to rebuild the world and be its model. But to do this, we must also rebuild ourselves: eradicate our slums, give our minorities equal opportunities, and use our science to create plenty, cure disease, and take us to the stars rather than destroy cities and cause human suffering. We must educate our masses and provide security and health care regardless of ability to pay; establish a cultural renaissance of great art, great music, and great literature; and keep ourselves a unified people regardless of origin, arm in arm together, each for all, all for each.

"There's only one man who can lead us successfully up this rainbow of the future. Only one man: your candidate and mine, Henry Wallace. Ladies and gentlemen, my good friend and our next president, Henry Wallace."

One hundred thousand adulatory souls roared their approval. Henry raised Dr. Banner's tiny arm with his. "Henry and Clarissa, Henry and Clarissa," the crowd roared. I could hardly believe my eyes; I could hardly believe my ears.

September was now upon us. A year had passed since I answered the ad for a gardener. More than plants had flourished in Dr. Banner's pleasing and peaceful oasis plunked in the middle of the South Side brick and asphalt desert. Our lives, too, intermingled and grew together, flowering no less dazzlingly than the cultivars that Dr. Banner coaxed and treasured. But nothing endures, neither the ugly nor the beautiful.

The morning after the rally I dropped by to tell the doctor that I had attended it and was inspired by her message. She opened the front door, a book in her hand, appearing groggy, apparently having fallen asleep on the couch.

"Is that you, Peter?" she said.

"Yes, Doctor."

"Come in, come in. No need to stand there," she said, sweeping me inside by using her book like a wand.

"I'm sorry if I'm disturbing you," I said.

"Not at all. I was just awakening from a much needed nap after a long night."

"And what a night, I'd say. My god, Doctor, you had one hundred thousand people in the palm of your hand. They went wild. A gigantic chorus: Henry and Clarissa, Henry and Clarissa. Your speech…inspiring."

"So you've changed your mind, and you'll vote for Henry?"

"No, Doctor. But I'd vote for you," I said eagerly.

"Such flattery is wasted on me, young man. Well, if you won't vote for my man, then you must at least take me to this Thursday's concert. Dame Myra Hess will be soloist."

"Yes, I heard. But I promised Vicki I'd take her," I said innocently. "She's her idol. Why don't you ask Lenny?"

"Are you telling me whom I should ask?"

"It was only a suggestion," I said, flinching, realizing too late that I was compounding my mistake.

"Your audacity is boundless, young man," she said, and in a fit of anger threw her book across the room. "I believe I made my preference clear."

"I can't take you to this concert, Doctor," I said standing firm. "There will be other concerts."

My statement had a familiar ring. Hadn't my mother spoken to me in the same manner when I was a child?

The doctor put her face so close to mine that I felt her spittle as she spoke. "She is not good for you, Peter. I warn you, she will break your heart." Her tone was sardonic.

"Vicki?" I said. Clarissa remained silent. "I think you resent her," I ventured.

"That is absurd. Certainly not. I fear for you. She is good, very good at her art. I perceive that her music is all-consuming. Someday, and very soon, she will have no room for anything else."

"We love each other."

"Of course you do. But do you want a life languishing in her shadow, taking a back seat to her music? As certain as I know the results of my mice experiments, I predict that she will someday appear on the stage at Orchestra Hall. She will have all the world's adulation. You have much to offer, my son. Make a mark in your own right. She can never help you become somebody."

Refusing to see that she had my interest at heart, I felt that Dr. Banner was mad with resentment, mouthing total nonsense. Hadn't she herself said that being somebody wasn't important? "You don't understand," I said.

"If you could only see, Peter. I speak from experience. You are very young."

"And you are very old," I said heatedly. "You've forgotten what it was like."

"I've forgotten nothing. It's only puppy love. Take my word for it, and it will pass," she declared.

"You don't know real love," I shouted, losing control. "How can you? You're a dried-up old woman. You missed your chance a long time ago. Don't take it out on me."

"How dare you, how dare you?" she thundered, and struck me forcefully on the shoulder with her cane.

"You're wrong, wrong, wrong, goddamn you."

"You insufferable, arrogant child. Leave my sight."

Taut with rage, I stomped from the house, passing Justine returning from the market with a bag of groceries in her arms.

"What's the matter, my boy?" she said, alarmed.

"She's a jealous, domineering old witch," I shouted and ran on.

"What have you said to him?" Justine demanded as she entered the house. "What have you said?"

"He's blind with a foolish infatuation," said Clarissa, breathing heavily. "I tried to make him focus on his own life."

"No, Clarissa. You're only denying your own mistake when you didn't follow your paramour to Europe," said Justine fiercely.

"Nonsense."

"Nonsense? It's time you admitted that the Nobel has been a meager substitute for him, for the conductor, for love. I hope you haven't turned away our Peter for good. I hope you haven't. Because I love that boy, and I need him, even if you don't."

"After he apologizes, I would gladly accept him, and only then," said Clarissa as she walked out of the room.

Because of her parents, my life with Vicki was no picnic. I could not call on her at home, so we met on campus or in the evening at street corners. On the night of the Dame Myra Hess concert, we arranged to meet at a certain hour in the third car of the Illinois Central commuter line heading for the Loop. I found her on schedule seated by herself, and kissed her lightly.

"I wish I could take you out in finer style, Vicki. I wish I had a car, or a rich father with a car," I said.

"This is fine," she replied. "I don't mind. I'd be willing to walk the whole ten miles downtown to hear Myra Hess play." She stopped and listened to the train wheels clicking and clacking down the tracks like castanets as we hurtled north. "Anyway, this is fun. I never travel the IC. I love looking at the people. And I love the feeling of rushing through space.

We sat side by side jostled by the sway of the car. Streaks of light flashed across the window by our seat. Her eyes darted with excitement. She read every advertisement within view. For her the ride was clearly an event in itself.

"To me it's just a way of getting downtown, that's all," I said.

"I love to feel the experience. Just feel it, Pete," she said. "You feel it, don't you? See what I mean? Isn't it wonderful? It's like music."

"You're like music. My music," I said, interested only in my girl.

She smiled as we debarked. We walked up Michigan Avenue to Orchestra Hall, entered through the big doors, and climbed the narrow flights of stairs to the uppermost tier of seats. From such a height, the great expanse of the stage appeared miniature.

"Oh, I'm so excited," she said.

"That's where Doctor Banner and I sat," I said, pointing to the seats that Clarissa and I had occupied. "The very best seats in the house, I'd say."

"They are. They are," she said, impressed. "Oh, how I'd love to sit there so I could see Myra Hess close up."

"I'm afraid that will never happen. Not those seats," I said mournfully.

"Why not? I mean, you sound so...so definite. Maybe someday when Doctor Banner is unable to come, she'll let us use her tickets."

"I'm afraid not. We had a big fight."

"Why?" she said, surprised. "I thought she liked you very much."

"That's the trouble," I said. "She likes me too much...like a mother. She wants to possess me."

"I don't understand."

"You won't believe this," I said, wanting her to take my side. "She thinks I should give you up."

"Where do I come into it? You were arguing about me?"

"She thinks your love for the piano comes before your love for me," I said, seeking a negative confirmation.

"One doesn't preclude the other," said Vicki sensibly. "I love you and I love the piano. Why can't I love both?"

"I agree. She's absurd."

"Pete, you're not threatened by my desire for a concert career, are you?"

I hesitated.

"Are you, Pete?"

"Of course not," I finally replied. "But I see how much the playing means to you. When you were playing the Mozart at Doctor Banner's, I could see that you were completely lost in the music, as if in a trance, and it frightened me."

"That's...that's ridiculous, Pete," she said, dumbfounded.

"It was as if the music were suddenly an adversary. That's the only way I can explain it," I said.

"Oh, Pete. Don't think such things," she said passionately.

The musicians drifted onto to the stage until every musician's seat was occupied. A cacophony commenced as they tested their instruments, drowning out the buzz of the audience, then they became silent. Myra Hess appeared threading her way through the violin section, followed by the conductor who bounded to the podium. The audience burst into thunderous applause at the sight of the pianist who bowed then sat at the piano, watching the conductor as he raised his baton, and with a flick activated the soft strains of a Mozart concerto soon joined by Myra Hess's full, pure notes.

But rather than watch her, I watched Vicki, who was completely enchanted. Dame Myra Hess's command of the keyboard was stunning. After a half-hour the piece was over and the pianist acknowledged the audience's approval, with several curtain calls. Vicki went wild with excitement, standing and applauding with gusto until her hands must have ached.

"If only I could play like that," Vicki declared over the shouts of "Bravo." "Oh, if only I could, I'd give anything, anything."

As we made our way to the train after the performance, I was lost in thought. But Vicki was still under the spell of the concert. I dared to intrude on her excitement. "Tell me, Vicki. What would you give to play like Dame Myra Hess?"

"Certainly not my life," she replied, "because then I'd defeat myself, wouldn't I?"

"Like William Kappel, who died young, at the peak of his piano career?" I suggested.

"Yes, that's too tragic. Such waste. But I'd give up part of my life."

"Would you give up love?" I asked cautiously, after we boarded the train and seated ourselves.

"What are you getting at, Pete?"

"Doctor Banner believes that you're incredibly talented. She says that you're completely dedicated to the piano and she has no doubt that you're headed for a successful concert career."

"Really. She said that? I...I hope she's right."

"She also said that there'll be no room for anything else."

"She shouldn't...How can she...? The piano won't be everything, Pete. I know there's more to life than—"

"According to her," I pressed on, "not if you're serious about becoming another Dame Myra Hess. The piano will consume you completely. Nothing else will be as important to you. Be honest, Vicki."

"I...I don't know what she's talking about. I don't have to choose; I can have both you and my piano. You know, she makes me very angry."

"I think I want to become a journalist," I said, having finally decided on a career, partly as a result of the doctor's probing. "That means I'll be traveling. Will you come with me wherever I go?"

"That's not fair, Pete."

"I know it isn't. And if you become a concert pianist, you'll be traveling all over the world. I won't be with you. I'll have my own career. Do you understand?"

We got off the train a few blocks from Vicki's house, a distance that normally she would walk by herself. But tonight she wanted to prolong our being together. Had she some premonition that the future would hold few such occasions? There was more serious business between us to talk about.

"My parents will be asleep," she said. "I think it will be all right if you walk me to the house."

The moon was full and bright. A fresh breeze from the western prairie rustled the dry brown leaves on the trees that bordered the sidewalk. We strolled through the lamp-lit streets in silence to Vicki's elegant home and stopped at the end of the driveway.

"My love, I don't want to lose you," she said, her eyes welling with tears as she embraced me and we kissed.

Suddenly we were enveloped in a brilliant spotlight. I heard an angry voice coming from the house.

"Stay away from my daughter, you son of a bitch," said the voice whose source I could not see due to the glare.

Startled, Vicki and I froze. Two men wearing bathrobes appeared at the edge of the light. A young man, Vicki's cousin, stood beside Vicki's father with his fists raised. Her father was pointing a gun at me.

"I'll kill you if you ever come here again, you goddamned kike," her father said.

Vicki lunged at her father, swinging her handbag and beating him on the head with it. "Run, Pete," she screamed. "Run! Please run."

"How can you do this, Victoria?" cried the older man. How can you strike your father?"

Terrified, and unable to decide whether to help Vicki or take her advice, I remained stationary, refusing to move. The younger man drew closer to me, ready to beat me up.

"Call him off, Daddy, or I'll leave your house forever," Vicki screamed. The threat prompted her father to signal the younger man to quit.

"Please go, Pete. I'll see you tomorrow," Vicki pleaded, then she dashed for the open front door of the house, where her mother, wringing her hands, was watching.

Vicki cried herself to sleep that night as her father stood outside her door begging for forgiveness.

Time would prove that he had created a chasm between him and his daughter that would never be bridged. Indeed, instead of keeping Vicki and me apart, he only drove us closer together, at least for the time being.

October passed, then November. Henry Wallace lost. The garden went untended. Without preparation for the coming winter, some of the plants were bound to succumb. I hadn't shown up once; I never called. I was so involved with myself that I didn't realize the implications of my actions, that my inattention was painfully cruel and unforgiving, my reaction unpardonable.

Lenny had continued to drop in to see Justine from time to time. He told me that she was hurt by my behavior and decided that I added up to less than what I had seemed.

One warmish November afternoon, Lenny and Justine were talking on a bench in the garden.

"I'm so glad you came to visit today," said Justine. "I was just thinking not more than ten—well, maybe twenty—minutes ago, wouldn't it be wonderful if my friend in arms, a fellow smoker, fellow hedonist, and fellow Forster fan, were to pay me a visit? And wishing it was all I needed to make it come true. Wouldn't you say that's a rare talent?"

"I answered your call, Justine. I received the vibes. It's mental telepathy pure and simple."

"So to what may I really attribute the honor of your visit?"

"I needed an ear," said Lenny bluntly.

"You have them both. And if I had more, they'd be yours," said Justine in a rare mood.

"Thankyou, Justine. You are the only one I can talk to."

"As one rebel to another," said Justine with a wide grin. "What is your trouble, my boy?"

"I want to leave home and become independent, but I have no money."

"Have you ever heard of that noble calling: work?" said Justine, fixing her eyes on his.

"I'm not like Pete. I'm cerebral. I have no skills," said Lenny, spouting his usual excuse.

"Oh, my. Such a handicap. There is a thing called unskilled work, but unfortunately it doesn't involve the application of brain cells. You move objects from one place to another, or affix one thing to another, or—"

"You're making fun of me," said Lenny.

"Yes, I am, dear boy. Why don't you go to work for your father? You tell me he wishes you to participate in his enterprise."

"Never. That wouldn't be independence."

"Of course. Such ideas are the ravings of a desperate mind. But I have just the solution. While I was walking along Fifty-third Street the other day—"

"That's a distance from here," interrupted Lenny. "What were you doing there?"

"Occasionally I become adventurous and perambulate along our crime-ridden streets. You can imagine how prepared I am to foil any attack."

"They'd have no idea what they were getting into," said Lenny, pressing himself against Justine's side in jest.

"Most perceptive, my boy. Well, as I was saying, I noticed a sign in the window of a filling station. 'Help Wanted,' it read."

"Pump gas?" Lenny winced.

"Why, yes, and you would also make your contribution to the pollution of the air. What do you think of that?"

"Hey, as my father would say, if there's money in it, go for it."

"Good. A philosophy that drives our civilization. It will make you free," said Justine, pressing her body against Lenny's side in return.

"I know that once I'm on my own, free, I'll feel a lot better about myself. It won't fix everything but—"

"As long as we live, our lives are never completely 'fixed,' as you call it," announced Justine.

"I have one reservation."

"Go on, dear boy."

"I don't want to fall into the trap of being slave to a job."

"Yes, I see what you mean. Actually, a slave to yourself. But there are jobs and there are jobs."

"I don't get your drift."

"Most of us live lives of compromise," said Justine, measuring her words. "In order to survive—that is, have a roof over our heads and food on the table and support a wife or husband and who knows how many squealing kids—we hold jobs that bear little relation to our desires, and even our talents. 'Quiet desperation,' Thoreau called it."

"Precisely what I'm saying," said Lenny, nodding.

"Ah, but my boy, to find what one wishes most to do, for which one has a talent—and all of us have a special talent of one sort or another—regardless of monetary reward, that's nirvana."

"Well, for me it's not pumping gas, that's for sure."

"But it can be one step on the road to happiness, no? You need only keep your goal in mind, to do the work that makes you most happy."

"And how many in this society have found happiness in what they're doing?" asked Lenny.

"A minute minority, I fear," Justine replied, sweeping her breeze-driven hair from in front of her eyes. "As I say, most people compromise. It takes courage to be oneself and say to hell with the practical—and superfluous—demands of society."

"What about you? Have you found your nirvana?"

"Oh, yes, oh yes," said Justine. "I'm fascinated by what Clarissa and I are doing. I can hardly wait each morning to check on my little mice to see how they're reacting to our experiments. We're on an exciting search, even though we may end with nothing. And I have time to indulge myself in Forster and his like. This and—in recent months—you and Pete and Vicki complete my happiness."

"You give me hope."

"Yes, hope. By all means, hope must be maintained. Hope is the cousin of surprise, of not knowing what will happen next, the very essence of the excitement of living. Can you imagine how dull life would be if we knew the future?"

"If only I could be like Pete, then my happiness could be complete," said Lenny, looking off into the distance.

"You are referring to his heterosexuality, I take it."

"That's right."

"I see. Yes, he is considered normal and not you. But that's a judgment made by others. I think you're smart enough to realize that each of us is an individual, the same and also different in many ways from every other individual. To paraphrase one of my favorite authors, Shakespeare, Have you not eyes, hands, feet, and so on? Have you not a brain, and a soul? But those are obvious similarities. You, dear boy, are not radically different, and perhaps far less than you know.

"Be assured you are not alone," she continued. "And if you depart from the norm in one way or another, why is that bad? You see, it isn't. Society is intolerant of differences and seeks to level us all. It fears the offbeat. Thank god we die. If it weren't for the new generations, we would grow more and more alike. That would be an extreme tragedy." She sighed and stretched herself. "Shall we have a drink to variety? Let's wend our way back to the house and imbibe."

"Justine, what would I do without you?" said Lenny as they rose from the bench. Justine took Lenny's arm, and the pair began strolling down the garden path.

"The feeling's mutual, my dear friend," said Justine. "Most mutual. Rather, what would I do without you?"

December. Lenny did not take the gas station job. Instead, his drinking increased, and he began seeing the ladies less and less often. Soon he hardly saw them at all. He was thinking of committing himself to the mental hospital, as he had once suggested, to dry out. He was drunk the evening he called to tell me that Dr. Banner was not well. White Princess had died.

I was at the door the following afternoon after class. Justine answered my knock.

"Go away. We don't want any," she said through the door.

"It's me, Pete."

"And what do you want?" she said coldly.

"Can I see you and Doctor Banner?"

There was a long wait before she opened the door. "Pete? You're here at last." Apparently having forgiven me for my long absence, she hugged me. "After all these months. It's a sight to see your handsome face, your beautiful blue eyes, your muscular frame, and yes, your very own self. Welcome. Come in, come in, my boy."

I followed her into the dining room, and we sat as we used to at the oak table. The room looked chaotic as never before: newspapers, books, dirty dishes on the table, on chairs, on the Capehart, which was dust-laden again. Through the window the garden appeared brown, dead, wild pockets of leaves covering the flower beds, scraps of paper, having blown in from the street, strewn here and there. Even an occasional tin can and soda bottle were visible.

"Lenny told me about White Princess," I said.

"Yes, her time had come, as it must to us all."

"Poor Doctor Banner," I remarked. "First, Wallace loses, then this. It must have been painful. I know how much the dog meant to her. Is she home?"

"She's in her bedroom, where she must remain."

"Isn't she well? May I see her?"

"I don't think she'd be pleased to see you. She doesn't forgive easily."

"I'm willing to apologize."

"I fear it's too late for that," said Justine, downcast. "Furthermore, it is she who owes you an apology. Oh, Pete, dear boy, it's too late."

"Too late? I don't understand."

"She's dying. I'm afraid she's lost her will to go on. She won't cooperate with the doctor. Nothing I do pleases her. White Princess is the only creature that has ever truly made her happy." Justine's eyes filled with tears and she shook her head emphatically. "Not me. Never me."

"Sure you have, Justine."

"No, never. It was never enough."

"No one could have been a more dedicated companion than you," I said.

"You pleased her, my boy. You made her happy again. She became the spirited person she used to be. It was truly remarkable. All because of you."

"If I could see her, maybe that would help."

"Perhaps. But she's too ill today. Your absence saddened her more than you realize." Justine was speaking for herself as well.

"The garden's a mess," I commented, looking out the window. "I'll clean it up, tie up the shrubs, make it ready for next spring. That's sure to lift her spirits, just like before."

"Next spring?" said Justine. "That's awfully far into the future. Awfully far."

"I'll come by tomorrow, okay?" I said, trying to reassure her.

She rose to accompany me to the door. "If tomorrow comes, if it comes." She hugged me again. "How nice to have you back, my boy. After Clarissa, you are the only family I have left."

That evening Clarissa, frail and needing Justine's support, walked to the common room to lie on the couch, where Justine served her hot broth. Later Justine would change the bed-sheets before Clarissa returned to her room.

"I'm so helpless," said Clarissa. "I'm sorry to impose."

"It's all right, dear. That's what I'm here for."

"No, you're my assistant, not my caregiver," said Clarissa, mustering up a firm voice.

"Now, you know if I were ill, you would take care of me, wouldn't you?"

"No, my sweet." Clarissa smiled slightly. "I'd hire someone to do it."

"Well, it amounts to the same thing."

"Do you think so? I surely don't. I lack your kindness, your solicitude. You have a soul, and I have only a calculating, logical mind. Take me to the window, good friend. Let's gaze upon the garden."

With Justine's help, Clarissa slowly worked her way to the window, and the two stared out together.

"How brown and sere and lifeless it is now. It's what I have become," said Clarissa.

"What foolish talk. The garden is only sleeping, and in a few months it will come to life, just as you will," said Justine, contradicting her own true belief.

"No, my sweet. I have no illusions. I shall not see our garden wake up again. Oh, look, some scraps of paper have blown in; I see a soda bottle, and over there a tin can. How dare they? You must call Pete in the spring."

"Are you sure? I thought he was persona non grata."

"By then he will not have to deal with me. Help me to the couch again. My legs are becoming buttery."

Back at the couch with Justine's support, she reclined as Justine tucked her in under an afghan.

"I'm sure he's forgiven you," said Justine.

"As I said, whether he has or not will be a moot point, dear," said Clarissa weakly.

"And have you forgiven him?" asked Justine.

"I have forgiven life, everybody, the world. It has been a magnificent trip. I have no complaints. Now, let's talk about what will happen when I'm gone. You must bring the research to a conclusion."

"Clarissa, dear."

"The results must be published. The world must know. Too many are suffering needlessly."

"*Clarissa.*" Justine spoke her name firmly.

"Will you stop Clarissa-ing me?"

"Clarissa, I'm going with you," said Justine resolutely.

"Please, dear woman, I'm serious."

"Hah, and you think I'm not? What is my life without you? You are all I have. With you gone I'd be desolate, of no use to myself, to anyone, not even the mice."

"But you have years to go," Clarissa protested, "and there's the research."

"We can arrange for the university to take it over. And as for how much longer I would live, I don't want to be one of our statistics. My poor lungs are already like concrete; they barely keep me alive. I don't have that much longer. Furthermore, the rebel in me revels at the prospect. I, Justine Faray, will choose the when and how of my own demise. It's the ultimate control. I have never felt so powerful. I'll go at the pinnacle, Clarissa, don't you see? I think it would make a good ending for a heroine in a novel. I must write a letter to Forster."

"I do not approve. I most definitely do not approve."

"What can you do about it after you're gone?"

"Oh, Justine. My good Justine. It is so humiliating," said Clarissa.

"What is?"

"Being a burden. The end of life."

"Then you see it my way," said Justine, brightening.

After a silence, Clarissa said meekly, "Yes."

"Now, let's make ready for the day. Do you want to dictate a going-away letter?"

"I'm still quite capable of moving a pen."

"Of course. Perhaps a joint message," suggested Justine.

"I can imagine nothing better," said Clarissa happily.

"When should we start?"

"Now, my dear. Now is the time, before it's too late. But I'm tired, so you write while I dictate."

"Whatever you wish, dear," said Justine, her pen poised.

After I contacted Lenny, he and I went directly to the ladies' house after class the following afternoon and knocked on the front door.

"Why don't they answer?" I said, worried.

"Maybe they're asleep," said Lenny, trying to ease my concern.

"At three in the afternoon? Let's try the back door."

We ran to the rear of the house and banged on that door, but again there was no response. Lenny helped me drag the old iron garden bench to the dining room window, and I stood on it and peered inside

"Clarissa's lying on the couch. I can just make her out. A shadow of herself," I said. We moved the bench to another window. "I can see Justine. She's slumped on the table. Something's terribly wrong."

Lenny broke the windowpane with a stone that he had picked up from the ground. He unlocked the window and lifted the sash; I followed him in. Justine was seated at the table, her face lying sideways on her arms. Clarissa was stretched out face up on the couch under the afghan, a wraith of a person.

"They're asleep," said Lenny. "Must have had a wild night."

I walked over to Justine and shook her. "Wake up, Justine, wake up," I said, panicky. "Something's definitely wrong." I placed my finger on her neck seeking a pulse. "This is terrible. Justine's gone." I rushed to Dr. Banner and felt her neck. "Doctor Banner too. This is terrible."

Lenny picked up a bottle from the table and examined the label. "These did the job. My god."

Slumping in a chair, I buried my face in my hands and began to sob. "Why did you, Justine. Why?" I cried.

Lenny placed his arm over my heaving shoulders. "I loved her too," he moaned. He began to sob himself as he bent over me and hugged me to him.

"I was too late. I could have prevented this," I said.

"You shouldn't blame yourself. Did you ever see them do anything they didn't want to do?" said Lenny, blowing his nose.

"That's true. There was no stopping them," I agreed.

"And they knew their own minds. They never had doubts," said Lenny.

"I'll miss them as long as I live," I said.

"Me too. As long as I live."

"I dread having to tell Vicki," I said. "She and the doctor had something special between them. What was it?"

"For god's sake, Pete, it was music."

"No, it was more than just music," I insisted. "Maybe Vicki brought the doctor back to her own youth. They're so much alike, really. Both determined to make it big."

"I hadn't thought of it that way. It makes sense," said Lenny as he picked up a sheaf of papers neatly stacked amid several books on the table. "Here's their research paper." He began reading aloud, "'The Genetics of a Propensity for Malignancy Abetted by the Inhalation of Tobacco Smoke.' And here's a note: 'For the university. Please continue what we have begun. C. Banner, J. Faray. P.S. The mice are in the cellar and have enough food and water for several days. Please be kind to them. J. Faray.' Oh, that woman."

I rifled through the papers and picked up another one. "It's all here in this letter," I said, "in their own handwriting. It says that Doctor Banner leaves the Capehart to you, and the piano to Vicki. Justine leaves her books to me, except the Forster collection, which she gives to you."

On opening one of the books and seeing that it was inscribed to Lenny, I handed it to him with the letter. He read the inscription for me to hear. "'May these volumes help you declare your freedom and shake the world to its molten core. In boundless affection, Justine.' My god. The letter is dated only yesterday. Look at this. 'With gratitude for bringing us a beautiful last beginning. Your loyal admirers, with love, Justine Faray, Clarissa Banner.'"

He handed the letter back to me. "They signed their own names," I said. "It's clear that Justine had no intention of surviving Clarissa. I can imagine the arguing that went on between them about that. Justine never doubted who she was, and nobody, Clarissa included, could ever persuade her otherwise."

I read the letter further. "Doctor Banner gives the furniture to the Salvation Army. She donates all she has, two thousand dollars, to the university for biological research. Seems Justine had no money."

"Well, we know that Clarissa had a bundle after getting the Nobel," said Lenny.

"I guess they spent every cent on their research project," I said. "The university stopped supporting it years ago. Look, here's a letter addressed to E. M. Forster."

"Aren't you going to read it?"

"Can't. It's in a sealed envelope."

"Y'know, yesterday Justine said that Doctor Banner was dying, but I wonder..."

"About how she died?"

"Yeah. Oh, Justine wouldn't exaggerate," I said emphatically. "But I didn't think it would happen so soon. She expected me today. Don't you get the feeling that it's too neat? Everything's so orderly, so planned."

"You think Clarissa took pills too?"

"Well, she liked to run her own show."

"An autopsy could be performed, I suppose," Lenny suggested.

"Why bother? They're gone. Everyone will assume the doctor died a natural death. Let it end there."

"But it's not really the end, is it, Pete? These women will be with us the rest of our lives," said Lenny, becoming teary again.

"Very true. Let's not disturb anything. We should call the police."

Apparently Clarissa and Justine had arranged to be buried near each other. A week later Lenny and I stood by their graves and speculated on their pasts.

"They had fame," Lenny said. "Did you see Clarissa's obituary in the *New York Times*?"

"No," I admitted.

He withdrew from his pocket the obituary that he had cut out of the newspaper. "It's on the very first page," he said. "'Famed Cancer

71

Researcher and Celebrity Dies. Doctor Clarissa Banner, winner of the Nobel Prize in 1936, is noted not only for her discoveries in cancer research but also for her dedication to the advancement of democratic principles and justice in a free society.'" Lenny gazed at her grave, not yet marked with a permanent gravestone. "A heavyweight, that woman."

"But not a word about Justine," I said, disgusted. "It's as if she never existed. Her contribution was enormous and no one will know."

"I don't think Justine would give a damn," said Lenny. "Her life revolved around Clarissa. She basked in her reflected glory. That was enough for her."

As I considered Lenny's statement, I was beset with regret. "I deserted them. They depended on me for much more than just the garden."

"Don't punish yourself," counseled Lenny. "You couldn't have known."

"But I should have; I should have been more aware. I missed seeing so much."

"We're all blind to one another. It's the way things are. I think Justine's suicide was absolutely wonderful. What courage. What a woman." Lenny sat on a nearby gravestone and started sobbing. Eventually composing himself, he went on: "We'll be their survivors. We'll keep their memory alive and tell everyone about them. Now that you've decided to become a journalist, you could write about them."

"That's what I'll do," I said, suddenly inspired. "The world must be told what marvelous women it has just lost: Justine and Clarissa. Do you think Doctor Banner would mind if I called her Clarissa?"

"Hell, no. Anyway, she's in no position to complain," said Lenny with a chuckle.

"I wouldn't put it past her."

"Amen, my friend," he said as we strode away.

FAMILY AGENDAS

June 3, 1950

Dear Steven:

I want you to know how sorry I am that I cannot attend your college graduation. I'm still not fully recovered from my heart attack and the doctor advises me not to travel. I hope you'll understand. What do you plan to do after graduation? I have a proposition for you. Because of my health situation I'd like to take it easy, retire. How would you like to come home and take over the business? You would be the boss. Maybe you'd want to consult with me from time to time, seek my advice, but the business would be yours. I know you would do well. After all, you were brought up in it, ever since you were ten years old when you used to sweep the shop floor. All I would ask of you is enough income from the business, which wouldn't be much, so that your mother and I could live out our lives comfortably. If you agree, you'd be taking a big load off my mind and have a great future for yourself. I know we haven't always agreed in seeing things the same way in the past, but please give this serious thought. I promise to stay out of your hair. It would be all your show, guaranteed. It's an opportunity that few sons can have.

Love, Dad

Late in the evening a few days after writing this letter, Morris was sitting in his armchair reading the local paper. His wife, Pearl, was lying on the sofa reading a women's magazine. It was her favorite pastime. This is how Morris and Pearl spent most evenings. But this evening was full of anticipation. They knew that Steven couldn't resist Morris's offer. At about ten o'clock the doorbell rang.

"It's Steven," said Pearl, jumping up to answer the door.

"Nonsense," said Morris, a short, bald, portly man. "I mailed the letter only a few days ago."

"No, it's Steven. I can feel it. Mothers know such things," said Pearl, almost tripping on the hall rug on her way to the door.

"Ridiculous," said Morris, who was inclined to only tolerate Pearl's excitable nature.

She opened the door and shouted so Morris could hear, "Oh, Steven. Son. Give your mother a big hug." As they embraced she shouted even louder. "It's Steven, Morris. Didn't I tell you?"

Pearl quickly ushered Steven into the living room.

"Why are you yelling?" said Morris, getting up from his chair and taking Steven's free right hand while Pearl continued clinging. "Good to see you, son. Got here real fast, I see."

"Hello, Dad," said Steven, grinning. "Drove straight through. Thirty hours."

"Without stopping?" said Morris. "Don't you think that was foolhardy?"

Steven flinched. "Oh, I pulled off on the side of the road and slept in the back seat for a few hours. That's all I needed."

"That was smart," said Morris, nodding approval.

"Steven's very sensible, Morris. You know that." It was just like Morris to find some kind of fault, she thought to herself.

"I thought maybe I'd get a letter from you," said Morris, "but coming here straightaway, this is quite a surprise. I gather my proposition appealed to you."

"Come, let's all sit down," said Pearl, leading Steven by the hand to the sofa as Morris returned to his chair.

"Dad, you know I've always wanted my own business."

"Well, I was never sure," said Morris. "I remember that by the time you were seventeen you refused to work in the shop and instead went to work at that lab. I really could have used you."

In fact, father and son had had quite a row at the time, one that neither of them would forget.

"I couldn't work for you, Dad. You were impossible to please, and you didn't pay me enough. I made more money at the lab."

"Well, I was supporting you. What did you expect?"

God forbid they should reenact that argument, thought Pearl. She'd put in her two cents' worth. "He expected to be paid as much as the other workers," she said to Morris. "I didn't blame him. I've heard all this before, so let's stop it."

"You look good, Mom. You've trimmed down," Steven said, welcoming his mother's interference.

"Take a good look," said Pearl, who was still on the plump side. She swirled around holding her arms out to reveal her figure. "Willpower did it, sheer willpower. Come over here. Give your mother another hug." Steven, tall and lanky, engulfed his mother in his arms. "It's so good to have you back," she said. "First the war, then college. We've hardly seen you in the past seven years."

"I've been home for Christmas for the past four years, Mom," said Steven, gazing up at the ceiling in resignation.

"So we've seen you for just a few days in four years," said Pearl, sitting again. "You'd come and then you were gone. Poof, you were like a phantom. It was as if you didn't want to be with us anymore."

"Of course I wanted to be with you," said Steven, throwing up his hands. A frequent refrain every time he came home, his mother's complaint was a good reason to stay away. "Would I have come at all if I didn't want to?"

"He's got another life," said Morris for the nth time since Steven left home to go into the service, then college. "Lay off him."

"I know he has another life," Pearl insisted. "They all grow up and have other lives, but it's important that they remember who loves them the most, who they can always depend on: their mothers. Me. And now you're here to stay, son. Really to stay."

"That's right, Mom."

"Your room is all ready," said Pearl.

Morris laughed. "She's had it ready for years. Look, Steven and I have some business to talk over. Would you mind shutting up?

Pearl opened her mouth to protest, then changed her mind. "It's late anyway. I'm going to bed." She embraced Steven yet again. "You must be exhausted. Good night, dear. Don't keep him up too late, Morris."

Morris waited until Pearl left the room. "That woman. She thinks you're still a kid."

"I suppose it's typical," said Steven, admitting to himself that on occasion he enjoyed basking in his mother's attention, even if it risked being smothered. "How are you feeling, Dad?"

"Feeling?" said Morris, somewhat puzzled. "I'm okay."

"I mean since the heart attack. Are you sure you're okay?"

"The heart attack? Oh, well, these days you're up and around right away, y'know. As I said, I'm okay." Morris preferred to avoid the subject.

"But you've still got to take it easy?" inquired Steven.

"Sure, sure. I've got to take it easy. Doctor's orders."

"That's why you're turning the business over to me. Right?" said Steven skeptically.

"Isn't that what I said in the letter?"

"Sure, Dad, I didn't mean…if your proposition is what you say it is."

"Of course it's what I said." Morris sounded impatient. "You'll be the boss. The business is yours."

"To run any way I see fit?"

"Look, I meant what I said. I won't interfere."

"Will you put that in writing?" Steven asked cautiously.

Morris was indignant. "He wants it engraved in rock yet. I already put it in writing. You've got the letter. What more do you want?"

"A formal agreement."

"What's wrong with you?" said Morris, about to explode. "You want a formal agreement with your own father? My word isn't enough? C'mon son, you've got my solemn word. You'll learn that any agreement is worth no more than the word of both parties. Putting it in writing doesn't mean a damn thing. If either party wants out, whether it's in writing or not will make no difference."

But Steven was insistent, even at the price of becoming a victim to his father's infamous wrath. "Yeah, I understand what you're saying, Dad. But I don't want it in writing just to bind us, because if it doesn't work out for either of us, I think we ought to call it quits. I see the agreement serving as a reference point—you know, spelling out the details so there's no misunderstanding."

"Well, okay, if that's what you want," said Morris, mollified by Steven's sensible explanation. "Write one up."

"Do you know a good lawyer?"

"What? You want a lawyer to do it?" Morris exploded again, then said more calmly after a momentary silence, "That isn't necessary."

"To do it right it is," said Steven, giving his father no quarter.

"Tell me, is that what they taught you at that college of yours?" said Morris, reluctantly paving the way for giving in. "Trust no one, not even your father? Well, if that's what you want, then you find a lawyer. I don't know any lawyers. I don't use them, don't trust them. They make federal cases out of everything just to build up their fees."

One down, another to go, thought Steven. Now he'd drop the bomb. "Dad, I want Robert to come in with me."

"Robert?" yelled Morris. "Your brother's got a good job. And he's a married man. Some day he'll be a father and need a big income. How do you expect the business to feed three families?"

"Three families?"

"There's also your mother and me, remember?" said Morris.

"I'm not a family, Dad. I can get along on very little."

"I don't think it's a good idea, bringing Robert in," said Morris, getting down to the nub of his objection.

"He's a natural salesman, just what I'll need. I want him in. If you won't agree to it, we don't have a deal."

Morris was outraged. "We haven't even started and you're making ultimatums. Who do you think you are?"

"Your son," said Steven, smiling.

Morris chuckled. "Well, that you are. Chip off the old block, eh? If you run the business the way you drive a bargain, you'll do all right, that's for sure. How do you know he'll go for it?"

"We had a long talk. He agreed."

"Way ahead of me, aren't you?" Morris said, shaking his head. "Okay. But he's your responsibility. Just remember you'll have to contend with Deborah if things don't go right."

After changing into her nightgown, Pearl came down to the kitchen to finish cleaning up after dinner. "Did I hear you say Robert will be in the business?" she asked as she walked into the living room.

"That's right, Mom. He'll be a real asset."

"That's very generous of you, Steven. Ever since he was born you've looked out for your younger brother. Haven't you noticed, Morris?"

Pearl felt blessed that her sons were close and that Steven was downright protective of his brother. Her sons weren't like her sister's two sons, who despised each other.

"Yeah, but don't let it get in the way of business, son," Morris warned. "Robert has to perform, or else. That's the way it is in business if you want to survive."

"Okay, okay, I understand," said Steven, nodding vigorously, grateful that he was getting his way.

"He doesn't have your stuff, y'know," said Morris almost under his breath, hoping that Pearl wouldn't pick up his remark.

"Dad says he's feeling pretty good," said Steven. "He's not just saying that, is he, Mom?"

"He's got to watch it, don't you, Morris? You've got to take it easy."

"Hey, I'm as good as can be expected for an old guy," said Morris with a chuckle.

"You're not old, Morris. We're just middle aged. Wouldn't you call us middle aged, Steven?"

"Of course you're middle aged. You don't look old and you don't act old." Steven took his mother's hand and twirled her around.

"I guess I've still got some vinegar left," said Morris.

"I can testify to that," Pearl began. "Why just last night—"

Morris gave her a hard look and deliberately changed the subject. "How long do you expect to stay here?" he asked Steven.

"For as long as he wants," Pearl interjected. "What are you asking?"

"I'm asking if it's temporary, that's all. My desk is in his old room."

"So what? You'll just have to move it back to where it was," said Pearl in a huff.

"Not that you're not welcome, son," said Morris. "I just thought maybe you'd like to be more on your own. I mean, you know, girls—that sort of thing." Morris shot his son a knowing look.

"You're giving him ideas, Morris. Steven's a good boy."

"What do mothers know, eh, son?" said Morris with a wink.

"Yeah, I think I'd like to stay here, at least for a while," said Steven. "It'll save money, for one thing. But I can sleep on the couch, Dad. You can keep my old room as your office."

"No, no, I wouldn't think of it. A man needs his privacy," said Morris, regretting that he brought up the subject.

"When do you want me to start?" Steven said as he withdrew a cigarette from his shirt pocket and lit it.

"Smoking, eh?" said Morris approvingly. "So now you're a real man."

"He's a good boy. Why do you insist on leading him astray by telling him that smoking makes him a man?" said Pearl.

"All those years he wouldn't drink coffee or beer, wouldn't touch cigarettes. That's a hell of a thing for a grown-up man. Tell me, how did you get away with it while you were in the army? The other boys must have made fun of you. Tell the truth."

"Not at all. In fact they loved me," said Steven, happy to dispose of his father's theory.

"I don't believe it."

"Because I gave them my weekly issue of beer and cigarettes," Steven explained triumphantly.

"Can you beat that? Bought them off. Smart kid. Tell me, when do you want to start? It's up to you. Maybe you'd like some time to settle down, get together with some of your old buddies, that sort of thing."

"Most of them are gone."

"I suppose that's the way it is. They go to college and don't come back," said Morris sadly. "Nobody stays in their hometown anymore."

"Except for our son," said Pearl as she gazed at Steven adoringly. "We're very fortunate."

"Most of my friends found opportunities in the big cities."

"Thanks for not being like them," said Pearl, embracing Steven. "Here is all the opportunity you could ever wish for. Well, I can't keep my eyes open. I must say good night. Your bed's all made, Steven."

"Night, Mom," said Steven. Then he turned to his father. "I'll start tomorrow morning, Dad. The sooner the better as far as I'm concerned."

"We'll drive to the shop together."

"No," said Steven. "I'd rather go by myself in my car in case you want to knock off early."

"Oh, I expect to put in a full day," said Morris.

"I thought you still have to take it easy."

"Well, I do," said Morris, feeling caught. "But putting in a full day isn't a strain. Especially with you there taking over. And what'll I do at home? Just sit and twiddle my thumbs?"

"I thought the idea was that you'd step aside and—"

"Well, it is. I am stepping aside," said Morris, his impatience mounting. "I'll just be there, that's all. You know, making sure everything's running smoothly. In case you have any questions. There has to be a transition period, Steven. You just can't show up and take over without some guidance. Christ, you're impatient. Slow down, will you? Just slow down."

"I didn't mean—"

"So we'll go in separate cars," said Morris. "I don't get it, but if that's the way you want it, that's what we'll do."

"No, I'm sorry. We'll go together," Steven said, feeling guilty.

"Now you're making sense. Relax, son. I'm handing you a great future. Now, I don't know about you, but I'm going to bed." Morris rose from his chair. "It's good to have you back, son," he said as he walked out of the room.

To celebrate Steven's arrival, Pearl invited Robert and his wife, Deborah, for a family get-together the following evening. Answering the doorbell promptly at six, Pearl greeted her second son and daughter-in-law with warm hugs.

"Robert, Debbie. Good to see you. Dinner will be ready soon. Why don't you sit here?" she said as they walked into the living room. "We have to wait for Morris."

"Don't you want help, Mom?" asked Deborah.

"No, no. Thanks anyway," said Pearl with a wave of her hand. "I think Steven wants to talk with both of you. You'd better stay."

"Yes, I'd like you to hear what he has to say, Deb," said Robert.

"I know what he has to say," said Deborah, annoyed. "I told you I'm against the idea."

"Well, at least you could listen. Hear it from the horse's mouth."

"So I'm a horse, am I?" said Steven, striding into the room.

Robert stood and embraced his older brother. "Hi, Steve."

"Hi, Rob." Steve patted his brother on the back, then turned to his sister-in-law. "How about a little welcome, Debbie?"

"Sure, Steven," said Deborah, rising and hugging him with little enthusiasm.

Steven sat in his father's chair. "I hope we can settle things before Dad gets here," he said quietly. "Have you thought over what I proposed on the phone this morning?"

"Sure, I'd love to come into the business," said Robert." But..." Robert looked to his wife.

Deborah explained. "We'd like to start a family, which means I'll have to give up my job to stay home with the baby, so we'll need Rob's income."

"He'll have income from the business, Deb. A secure income," Steven pointed out.

"How can you be sure?" said Robert. "Until now the business has supported only one family. It'll never support three families."

"Why not, if we make the business grow?" Steven countered. "With your sales skills and my management savvy, it's bound to grow. And it only has to support two families. I won't be drawing a salary until I see that the business can afford it."

"How will you live?" asked Robert, genuinely concerned.

"I've saved enough to live on for a year, and I'll be living here."

"How long do you think that will last?" said Deborah. "The last time you stayed here, there was a big argument and you left for years."

"Dad and I have an understanding now. We'll get along," said Steven with confidence.

"Sure. Good luck," said Deborah skeptically. "So, if Rob joins you, what will his salary be?"

"As much as you're earning now," Steven said, addressing Rob. "You won't have to sacrifice a thing. And you'll be part owner, which is something you'll never be with your present employer."

"That's true. Sounds pretty good to me, Deb. What have I got to lose? I've always wanted to be with Dad."

"But he never wanted you. It was always Steven," said Deborah bluntly.

"How can you say that?" said Robert, looking hurt.

"That's right. How can you say that?" said Morris as he walked into the room. "Give me an incident. Just once. I've never played favorites with my sons, Deb."

"Well, if you recall you told Rob that he's not entrepreneurial enough to have his own business," said Deborah, feeling awkward at being overheard.

"Well, he isn't entrepreneurial, and he doesn't have to be. Not with Steven as his partner," said Morris.

"Here's your chair, Dad," said Steven, getting up. "I'm glad to hear you say that. You agree then that Rob and I will make a good team?"

"Absolutely," said Morris, taking his chair. "The three of us will."

"Just a minute, Dad," objected Steven. "You said—"

"Until you've got your feet wet, I'm sticking around," said Morris. "I don't want either of you making any avoidable blunders, see? After all, I've spent most of my lifetime building this business. It's my child, understand? So although I'm handing it over to you, I want to make sure you take care of it the way I did."

"I thought our two sons were your children, too," said Pearl, coming into the room from the kitchen.

"Well, of course," said Morris, flustered. His words touched an old argument between them. "I didn't mean—"

"Sure, you did," said Pearl, cutting him off. "You have the business. My sons have always been mine, haven't they, Morris?"

"Yes, you've made that clear more than once," Morris said bitterly. "All you ever did was spoil them."

"You never took to them when they were babies," Pearl reminded him. "There was never time for them while they were growing up. It was always the business."

"You wanted food on the table, didn't you? You wanted them to grow up healthy, didn't you? It was a depression. I was breaking my butt keeping the business alive, working day and night. I had no time for kids. Haven't I explained this to you a thousand times?" Morris said, hot under the collar.

"I'm in no mood to argue," said Pearl. "It's almost time to eat. I'll call you in a few minutes," she said, turning to go back to the kitchen.

"I'll wash up," said Morris, following her.

"You've always been her favorite, Steve," said Robert when their parents had left the room.

"You're crazy. I'm the one she always beat."

"That's what I mean. She never beat me," said Robert, slapping his brother on the back.

"Only because I was the older one, the bigger one," said Steven, touching Robert gently on the face.

"It's pretty obvious to me who she loves most," said Deborah without rancor. "Mothers are known to have a close attachment to their first born. You can't deny that, Steven. You were always the most brilliant, the one most slated for success."

"Well, he is, isn't he, Deb?" said Robert. "They just sent me to a state college. But Steve was top student in high school, summa cum laude at a top university, and now...look at him."

"Just a minute, Rob," said Steven, feeling embarrassed. "The GI Bill paid for every cent of the tuition. And I pumped gas for spending money. Dad didn't contribute a cent."

"Yeah, maybe so. But who did Dad call to take over the business?"

"There you go putting yourself down whenever you talk about your brother," said Deborah angrily. "You're wrong. You're brilliant, too, but in a different way."

"Yes, Deb's right," said Steven. "For instance, I can't sell the way you can. You've got it all over me in that regard. I need you, Rob. Without you, I wouldn't be doing this."

"Do you mean that?" said Robert, feeling flattered.

"Certainly, every word of it. The future of the business depends mostly on you."

"Hear that, Deb?" Robert said, nudging Deborah with his shoulder.

"I see you've made up your mind," said Deborah resignedly. "Okay, I won't stand in your way. I only hope that nothing will interfere with our plans to have a family."

"I'll do everything in my power to make you and Rob secure, Deb," Steven assured her. "I love him. Just remember that."

"I don't doubt that, Steve," Deborah responded. "Only I don't know how much power Dad will let you have."

"All of it. You'll see. I have his word, and soon it will be in writing. The lawyer is drawing it up now."

It was a tradition ever since she and Morris first got married that Pearl had the entire family over for Sunday breakfast. At first the event included her parents and Morris's parents. For Pearl it was the highlight of the week. After the boys were born, there were eight attendees, but over the years, as each of the parents died, eventually only four came, then three when Steven left. When Robert married Deborah, they were back to four. But now they were five again and hopefully growing.

The following Sunday while waiting for Deborah and Robert to arrive, Steven made a phone call. It was prearranged that he would phone Caroline, his girlfriend in Chicago, before she went to church.

"Everything's fine, Caroline. Just fine. So you've got to come. You'll love it here. It's not crowded like Chicago; the air is clean, and the people—I can't wait to introduce you to everyone. I've told you all that already."

"I'm not sure it will work," Caroline said at the other end.

"You want us to get married, don't you? So what's holding you back?" said Steven.

"My parents are putting up a big fuss."

"Your parents again? You said they didn't matter. For god's sake, we've been through this. You said their prejudice wouldn't stop you, right?"

"That's true. I can't let them dictate who I love."

"I won't insist on a rabbi if you won't insist on a priest."

"We'll have to elope, Steven. That's the only way it can happen."

"Fine. It'll be a justice of the peace, as we agreed. So you'll come?"

"When, Steven?"

"Well, as soon as you can get away. Think about it."

"What about your parents? They won't be thrilled."

"My parents? I can handle them. They won't interfere." Steven wasn't aware that his mother had entered the room.

"Do they know about me?"

"Sure they know about you. I wrote them."

"Well, have they asked?"

"No, they haven't asked."

"I love you and miss you so much."

"Good-bye, my love. Talk to you soon. Just come, okay? I miss you."

Pearl withdrew to the kitchen and put a percolator of coffee on the stove. "Would you like a cup?" she asked Steven as he ambled in.

"Sure, Mom."

"Here, help me set the table. Robert and Deb will be here soon. They come over for breakfast every Sunday morning, the way they used to when we were a family. And now we're together, a complete family again." Pearl hugged Steven from behind. "It's good to have you back again, son," she said into his ear.

"It's good to be back, Mom."

"I suppose we won't be a really complete family until you're married. Then I'll have two daughters." Pearl poured two cups of coffee and handed one to Steven. "That's the wonderful thing about having sons. You end up having daughters, too. I hope you pick a girl that deserves you, a girl we can all be comfortable with, one of our own kind."

"I don't need one of our own kind, Mom. I just need someone I can love and who loves me."

"There's more to marriage than love, son. There's mutual understanding and common interests, which come from having a common background. Find a nice Jewish girl who can make you a nice home and give you fine Jewish children. It'll be much easier that way, and everyone will be happy."

Pearl had been relieved when Robert chose Deborah for his wife. But Robert was never daring. Perhaps because he was the less favored son, he tried harder to please by conforming. In most families, the oldest sibling is the most conservative and adopts the parent's ways. Not so with Steven. Having a rebellious streak, Steven was less predictable than Robert. Pearl made a mission of bringing him back into line.

"Mom, I'd like you to get one thing straight. I'm not living my life just to make others happy. You should be happy if I'm happy. If you aren't, I can't help it. A good human being is good no matter what his or her background. That's what I go by."

"Well, I hope you're not serious about that Catholic girl you've been going with at school," Pearl said, knowing full well he was. "Is that who you were talking to?"

"Oh, you heard me? Then, yes, and it's none of your business," said Steven sharply.

"Oh yes it is. Your happiness is my business," said Pearl, accidentally pouring too much coffee into a cup.

"Let's drop it, Mom."

"Drop what?" inquired Morris as he came into the kitchen in his pajamas and robe. "What's all the talk about?" Not waiting for an answer, he sat down at the kitchen table, picked up the morning paper, and began reading.

"Your son and that shiksa from school," said Pearl.

"That, eh? Don't worry. He'll be too busy to think of girls for a while. Anyway, how could he be serious? He isn't even supporting himself, so how can he afford a girl?"

Pearl resented that Steven's personal affairs hardly concerned her husband. All he cared about was the business.

"Look, you two, you have no say in this, so butt out. Get it?" said Steven angrily.

"Look at this," said Morris, referring to the paper. "It says that we're headed for years of prosperity because of the demand for goods created by the war."

"That's what I've been saying, Dad," said Steven. "The business can't lose."

"Yeah, but they talked like that back in the twenties, and look what happened. No siree, I don't believe this for a minute. Our economy will always have its ups and downs. When times are good, just remember it's only temporary. Hell, we'd still have a depression if it weren't for the war. Even Roosevelt couldn't get us out of it."

"It's a different world, now, Dad," said Steven.

Morris turned a page of the newspaper and continued his speech as if he hadn't heard Steven's words. "All I see is rising prices. People going into debt buying fancy cars and homes with big mortgages."

"Don't you think that's better than falling prices and nobody able to buy anything?" said Steven, referring to the Great Depression, in which he was brought up.

"Listen to this kid," said Morris, turning to Pearl, who only shrugged. "It's the twenties all over again. You weren't there, I was. We'll have a depression as sure as the sun will rise. Sooner or later. You don't know what it was like to have to survive because you always had food in your stomach and good clothes to wear. I saw to that."

"I was proud of your father. He worked days in the business and nights managing a telegraph office—from eight in the morning to midnight for years so that we could make ends meet. We were among the lucky ones. He was employed. Most of our friends were on welfare."

It was a story that Steven had heard over and over.

"It will happen again as sure as the sun rises," Morris said. "And there'll be no second Roosevelt to tackle the problem."

"Boy, that coffee smells great," said Robert as he and Deborah walked through the back door and into the kitchen.

"Sit over here," motioned Pearl, pouring three more cups. She gazed at the couple and sighed. "You can't imagine how happy it makes me to see us all together again."

"One happy family," said Robert. "I'm happy for you, Mom. It's the way Sunday mornings used to be. Bagels and lox, home-ground coffee, and fried eggs."

"Remember once a week early in the morning when the bread delivery man, the egg man, and the milkman would congregate around our kitchen table to drink Mom's home-ground coffee?" said Steven, waxing nostalgic. "They'd discuss politics for a good half hour. The egg man, with his checkered coveralls, was a dyed-in-the-wool Republican and hated Roosevelt, eh, Dad? And you and he would end up shouting at each other every time. Still you remained friends."

"I felt sorry for him," said Morris. "He was a good man, hard working, struggling like the rest of us to make a living. His only trouble was, being a Republican, he didn't know what was best for the country. I tried to set him straight. And you know, I think after a few years he was beginning to waver. After we got into the war, he stood behind Roosevelt like the rest of us."

They all laughed, especially the boys, who saw that their father hadn't stopped arguing his point.

"This is the first time I've heard this," said Deborah, feeling left out of an apparent private joke. "I was too young."

"It was a terrible time and a wonderful time, Deb," said Morris, becoming misty eyed.

"Everyone looked out for one another. We were so grateful for every little thing. A fine, generous spirit spread among us. Because things were so bad for so long, we had only ourselves. When the war came, suddenly we had a cause and everyone was ready to pitch in. We were undaunted. You know what I mean, Steven. You were over there."

"Yeah, and I really wanted to go. Our outfit believed in itself. We never doubted why we were fighting," said Steven, seconding his father's picture.

"I wanted to go, too, but—"

"Still too wet behind the ears, eh, Rob?" said Morris, giving his son a shove.

"Thank God," Pearl interjected. "I couldn't have endured the possibility of losing both my sons."

"A man felt guilty if he stayed behind," said Morris.

"Now we're all together again," Pearl said, surveying her brood. "And Steven got a good education out of it."

"God bless the GI Bill," said Steven, grinning.

"We sure as hell couldn't have sent you to college. Tell me, what did they teach you at the University of Chicago?" Morris said, implying that it couldn't have amounted to much.

"Everything," said Steven, playing along.

"Everything?"

"I became educated. I learned how to think about things."

"That's pretty general," said Morris, extending his empty cup to Pearl for a refill. "I mean, in my day most of us just finished grammar school, then off we went to work. But we learned to be practical early, you know. Work hard, save your money, make every penny count. Still, I know there's more to the world than just surviving. There's science and engineering. You learn all that in college, eh?"

"And literature and music," said Steven, knowing this would elicit a rise.

"I don't see what good they can do for you," said Morris, who indulged in neither.

"They make life richer," said Steven.

"We have everything, Steven, as long as we have each other," announced Pearl in her wisdom.

"Sure, Mom. I know," said Steven in total agreement.

"I'm sorry we couldn't go to your graduation. I just wasn't up to it," Morris apologized.

"Did that girl graduate, too?" asked Pearl.

"What girl?" inquired Robert.

"I wrote you about her," Steven told his brother.

"Oh, that girl," said Robert, placing his hand on Steven's shoulder. "Yeah, that girl."

"You didn't tell me about her," Deborah said to Rob.

"A guy goes out with a girl. What's there to tell? You're not serious, are you, Steve?" asked Robert.

"I love her, that's how serious I am."

"Oy, it's a calamity. A calamity," intoned Pearl, pressing her hands to both sides of her face.

"Why do you say that, Mom?" said Deborah.

"She's Catholic," Robert explained.

"Look, this is nobody's business but mine," said Steven. "So let's change the subject. Dad, while we're all here, let's get the contract signed." Steven stood and started for the door.

"What contract?" said Morris. "Do you know what he's talking about? Where are you going?"

Steve returned immediately with some papers. "You know, the one we discussed."

"I don't remember any contract," Morris said, claiming innocence.

"It stipulates that you'll step aside and turn over the business to Rob and me," said Steven, trying to hand the papers to his unwilling father. "Remember we talked about it? I suggested we make it formal, and you agreed."

"What's wrong with taking me at my word?" demanded Morris.

Steven threw up his hands in disgust. "Do we have to go over all this again?"

"I'll take his word for it, Steve," Robert put in.

"That's not enough," insisted Steven. "It has to be in writing."

"How dare you?" said Morris in righteous indignation. "What do you mean it isn't enough? It's my bond. I'm your goddamn father. Without me you wouldn't be here. It took me ten years to pay the hospital and doctor for your mastoid operation. I saved your life. And you want it in writing yet."

"I'm shocked at you," said Pearl, holding a plate of hot bagels in midair. "If you can't trust your father, who can you trust?"

"Damnit, Steve," said Robert. "It's no big deal. We'll just hold him to his word."

"He's already broken it," said Steven, discouraged. "He agreed to let me have a lawyer draw this up. He's already going back on his word."

"Gimme the goddamned contract," said Morris, tearing the papers and pen from Steven's hands. He dropped the papers on the kitchen table and signed. "Feel better now? It not worth the paper it's written on. So if I don't live up to it, you gonna sue me? Is that what you'll do?"

"No, of course not."

"So what in hell is this all about? What in hell did they teach you at that college? Don't trust anybody, don't trust your father? First lesson I learned is either you trust someone or you don't. When it comes to trusting, no piece of paper, nothing in this world except a person's integrity, can make a difference."

"Business is business, Dad," said Steven, removing the papers from in front of Morris and passing them to Robert.

"Sure it is," said Morris. "The whole world of business, every transaction, is based on trust. Did you know that? When we fill an order, how do we know we'll be paid? We trust, that's how."

"I guess we've taken this as far as we can," said Steven, seeing there would be no reprieve.

"Come over here, you two," said Morris as he stood up. Steven and Robert stood on either side of him. "Pearl, get the camera. Take a picture of the three of us partners in crime, eh?"

Pearl rushed from the kitchen and immediately came back with the camera.

"No, Dad, just two of us are partners," Steven said, reminding his father of the facts.

"Sure, sure. That's what I meant. My sons with their dad."

"Get in with them, Pearl. I'll take the picture," said Deborah as Pearl, overjoyed, moved a chair in front of Morris and sat down.

"We're all together at last. This is the best day of my life," said Pearl, her faced wreathed in happiness.

"Say cheese," said Deborah as she snapped the picture.

After two months Steven was still living with his parents. He was putting in long hours partly because the business needed his attention, partly because he needed to keep busy to assuage his loneliness. Caroline had not yet joined him as planned. He was drawing a barely livable salary and depended on his parents for meals. In view of his mother's opposition to Caroline, he couldn't very well have her stay with them. Although he had some savings, he had to be frugal and couldn't afford to put her up elsewhere.

One particular evening he arrived home at seven, his usual hour.

"Just get back from the delivery out of town?" Morris asked from his armchair, where he was reading the evening paper. Steven nodded; he looked tired. "I've got a few things on my mind I want to talk to you about," said Morris, putting down the paper. "But go clean up first."

Pearl walked in from the kitchen after Steven had left the room. "When are you going to tell him?" she asked Morris.

"Now is as good a time as ever," Morris said with a grunt.

"Well, I don't want to be here when you do."

"He'll come around. What choice does he have?"

"I don't want to lose him now, Morris. Be gentle. If he objects, don't lose your temper, the way you're apt to."

"Me lose my temper? Never," said Morris.

Pearl bent over and kissed him on the cheek. "Of course not, dear," she said, then walked back into the kitchen.

Steven reappeared—his jacket and tie removed, a glass of wine in his hand—and sat on the sofa opposite his father. "Okay, what's up?" he said.

"As you can probably tell, I've been feeling pretty good," said Morris.

"You've never talked about your heart attack," commented Steven.

"My heart attack?"

"Well, yes, your heart attack," said Steven, confused. "That's why you asked me to come. Remember?"

"Oh, sure. I've been feeling so good that I don't think about it."

"That's wonderful, Dad. But take it easy, stop worrying about the business so much. I want you here for a long time," said Steven warmly.

"I appreciate what you're saying. That's what I want to talk to you about."

"Taking it easy? You can pull out of the business entirely right now, Dad. Rob and I have things pretty well in hand."

Morris cleared his throat. "I need to stay in the business, son. What would I do sitting here at home? I'd die. Do you know that a big percentage of men who retire die within two years of quitting work?"

"But didn't you know how you'd feel when you asked me to come home and take over the business?" said Steven, suspecting what his father was leading up to.

"Well, I didn't expect to get back to my old self. I didn't think I could handle things the way I used to, but, as you can see, I'm just as good as before."

"I do see," said Steven with a laugh. "Sonofabitch, I wanted to talk to you about this, too."

"You mean about my staying with the business?"

"No, about your leaving. We can get along on our own. Rob and I have things under control."

"I wouldn't say that," said Morris, holding up a finger. "In the past two months we lost money. I never had a loss month, never. Do you call that having things under control?"

"But we've got more expenses now, like our advertising program and Rob's salary," explained Steven.

"I never had to advertise before," said Morris.

"Look at it as an investment in the future, Dad."

"I think it's necessary that I stick around, even if only to keep a lid on things," said Morris.

"Goddamnit, Dad. You promised."

"Well, I meant it at the time."

"I'm not so sure," Steven said, swigging down the last of his wine.

"Why would I ask you to come home if I didn't? Look, son, you'll make the major decisions. I just have to keep my hand in the business. It's my life. Don't you understand?"

"So what will your function be?" asked Steven.

"That's what you call it, a function?" Morris shook his head. "Well, I'll run the shop."

"With Rob in charge of sales and you running the shop, what am I supposed to do?"

"You're chief honcho, Steven. You'll find things to do."

"Rob and I own two-thirds. We can force you out," Steven said warily.

"Force me out?" Morris yelled. "You'd do that after all I've done for you? You'd do that to your father? I don't believe what I'm hearing."

"I didn't really mean it."

"But you're thinking it. Look son, after I die the business will be all yours and Rob's, free and clear. But I see you have a lot more to learn about business, and I want to make sure you don't make any more mistakes."

"What mistakes?" Steven asked.

"Advertising, for one. We don't need it. It's a waste of money. It hasn't helped our sales one sliver. Hell, they've gone down. And, so far, Rob hasn't done a thing."

"Advertising takes time to be effective," said Steven, trying to contain himself. "It may take a year or more before we see results.

Rob's effort will kick in, just give him time. Hell, it's been only a little over two months."

"Then there's the fortune you've spent renovating the showroom. Goddamnit, Steven, what was wrong with the old showroom? And Rob tells me you're thinking of buying a building. That's stupid. Why tie up money in real estate, money we can use in the business?"

"The old showroom was obsolete. It needed updating. It's our face, Dad. We have to make a good impression. As for buying a building, the current owner keeps raising the rent, and he won't give us a long-term lease. In the right location, real estate is a good investment. We'd be diversifying."

"I can't allow it," said Morris, as if he were issuing an edict.

"I'm not planning to do it right away," said Steven. "It's a long-range thing."

"Just forget it and cut out the advertising, now," said Morris, brooking no argument.

"You're making it impossible for me to make us grow," said Steven.

"Listen to me. I want to keep the business solvent for you and Rob. Don't you understand? We can't spend money as if we had unlimited capital. There's no substitute for cash. It's the only sure thing. We have to be ready for the next depression."

So this is what's behind his thinking, mused Steven. "What next depression? Are you crazy? Dad, the future is as bright as the sun," he said, flinging his arms toward the ceiling.

"That's what everyone thought in the twenties. The good times would go on indefinitely," said Morris, frustrated that he wasn't being heard.

"This is not the twenties. And the thirties are gone forever."

"Your generation doesn't know. History repeats itself," warned Morris. "Didn't we have a second world war after the war to end all wars? I don't want to live my old age in poverty. If the business goes down, your mother and I go down with it. Remember, you and Rob are still young enough to start over again. But not your mother and me. No, we must conserve all we've got. Don't you see?"

"Sure, Dad, I do see," said Steven, acknowledging the futility of their conversation.

"Rob and Deb are late," said Pearl as she walked in from the kitchen. "Are you sure you told Rob seven?"

"Of course I did," said Morris, "and I told him there'd be hell to pay if he didn't come on time. He knows his mother."

"The food won't taste the same if I serve it a minute late," said Pearl, annoyed. "I work in the kitchen all afternoon. The least he...the both of them...can do is be on time. I should think Deb would see to that. She should be more assertive."

"She's got plenty of that, Mom," said Steven.

"You think so?" said Pearl. "Maybe it's not enough."

Out of breath with Deborah in tow, Robert rushed into the room from the front entrance. "Sorry we're late."

"I was downtown shopping, and the traffic was impossible," explained Deborah.

"I'm going to wash up," said Morris.

"When you're done in the bathroom, so will I. I didn't get a chance before coming here," said Deborah.

"She knows the consequences of arriving late for dinner in this house," said Robert, nodding vigorously.

"Being on time for a meal is a way of showing respect for the cook," said Pearl defensively. "Help me set the table, Deb." Pearl led her into the kitchen.

"You're pretty quiet," said Robert, sitting down. "Something wrong?"

"Plenty," said Steven. "I feel Dad has betrayed me...us."

"I don't understand."

"Dad isn't quitting."

"I'm not surprised," said Robert, resting his head on the back of his chair.

"You're not? You never said that," said Steven.

"I figured you knew he wouldn't."

"Why should I? I took him at his word. He signed an agreement. Now he says he's fit, feels fine, and he wouldn't know what to do if he wasn't in the business."

"I can appreciate that, Steve. He has no hobbies. He'd be bored," said Robert matter-of-factly.

"But that's not what he wrote me. That's not why I agreed to come home. If it weren't for his heart attack—"

"What heart attack?

"His heart attack, his heart attack," Steven repeated. "The one he had a few months ago."

"First I've heard of it," said Robert, shrugging. "Dad didn't have a heart attack. The doctor found his blood pressure slightly elevated, that's all. So they told him to relax more, be under less pressure."

"Wasn't he laid up in the hospital for a few weeks?"

"Of course not," snorted Robert.

"Son of a bitch," Steven hissed, standing and slamming his hands against the wall. "Son of a bitch."

"It's time for supper, boys," called Pearl, poking her head into the living room. "Now, no more talk about business. Let's eat. After dinner, "I Love Lucy" is on TV. Who wants to watch it with me?"

"I don't feel like eating," said Steven, turning away.

"You've got to eat. Look at you. You're too thin already," said Pearl, repeating her litany.

"Mom, goddamnit."

"What's wrong with you?" demanded Pearl. "Why are you so touchy all of a sudden?"

"C'mon, Steve. Thing's will work out," said Robert, trying to make light of Steven's discovery.

"What things?" asked Pearl, looking from Robert to Steven. Neither answered. "What things? Tell your mother."

"Dad isn't keeping his word," Steven finally replied. "He lied to me. I can't trust him."

"Oh, that," said Pearl dismissively. "Don't give it a thought. He changes his mind a dozen times a day. Talk to him. Now, let's be a happy family and sit down together."

Pearl took both boys by the arm and directed them to the kitchen, where they joined Morris and Deborah around the supper table.

"So what have you two boys been cooking up?" said Morris, in high spirits. "Don't look so glum, Steve. Look at what your mother made. Now, is she a good cook or isn't she a good cook? Except for my mother's hamburg, your mother's can't be beat."

"What's wrong with my hamburg?" demanded Pearl, ready for war.

"Nothing, except my mother's was better," said Morris, raising his arm as if to defend himself.

"There's no satisfaction from this man. Your mother's hamburg was garbage," said Pearl.

"That's enough," said Morris, suddenly angered. "Shut up, Pearl."

"Lay off her," said Steven. "She does everything for you, Dad. So just lay off. This is great, Mom. I can't imagine any better."

"How could you know?" said Morris. "You weren't around when your grandmother was alive."

"It's true," said Pearl, "we didn't see much of you then."

"I was off fighting a war, then getting an education, remember?"

"I know, son," said Pearl wistfully. "But it seems as if you were born only yesterday and gone the next day."

"I should have stayed away," said Steven under his breath.

"How can you say such a thing?" said Pearl. "At last, we're together, one happy family."

"No, Mom. We're not a happy family," said Steven. "I'm one unhappy guy."

Pearl suspected that Morris was the source of his unhappiness. "I'm sure you and your father can work things out," she said.

"He's unhappy because I put a lid on his spending," said Morris. "The war, is that where you learned that everything's expendable?"

"Sure, we just dumped our equipment into the ocean when we were finished with it," said Steven sarcastically. "You're being absurd. I know we have limited funds."

"No you don't the way I see you throw my money around," Morris shot back.

"You can keep your goddamned money," said Steven. He turned to Robert and Deborah. "What do you say you and I put up some of our own money for working capital? I've got a small nest egg. Hell, to raise cash I'll even sell my car and use public transportation."

"We're not loaded, Steve," said Robert. "But I could probably contribute a small amount."

"No, Rob, not a cent," said Deborah. "We need it for the baby."

"What baby?" said Pearl, suddenly perking up. "You're not expecting, are you?"

"Yes, Mom, I'm pregnant," said Deborah shyly.

"Oh, Deborah," said Pearl, rising and rushing over to embrace her.

"Our baby will be born in seven months," announced Deborah.

"Oh, how wonderful, how marvelous," said Pearl, hugging Deborah again. "Morris, isn't this something? Finally, a grandchild with our blood. You say you're two months along, Debbie? And you're sure everything's all right?"

Deborah nodded, delighted at Pearl's excitement.

"Well, yes, it certainly is something," said Morris. "I guess now we can't cut Rob's salary as we planned, eh, Steve?"

"It's Dad's idea," said Steven, apologizing. "I never intended to."

"Cut his salary?" said Deborah, alarmed. "How could you think of doing such a thing? You promised—"

"Don't worry. I won't let him," assured Steven.

"I'd really like to pitch in," said Robert.

"No, Rob. You heard me," said Deborah adamantly. She turned to Steven. "You have only yourself to worry about. You can't expect Rob to put up his own money when he has two dependents. I think it's too risky, anyway."

"Then I'll do it alone, Deb. And I'm happy for both of you."

"If you want to put up your own money, that's okay with me," said Morris. "But when it's gone, don't look to me for more, understand?"

"I don't want anything from you, Dad. You lied to me. I don't trust you."

"That's a terrible thing to say to your father," said Morris, wounded.

"Steven, he's your father," said Pearl. "He deserves your respect."

"Oh, yeah? What about his heart attack? It never happened. You deliberately deceived me," said Steven, speaking to both of them.

"Would you have come home if I hadn't had one?" Morris said. "What else would have brought you back? We wanted you to come home."

"Why? You aren't retiring. Far from it. What do you need me for? It's obvious you didn't ever want to quit the business. What in hell am I doing here?" Steven said, asking himself as well as the others.

"It was for your sake, Steven, for your sake," said Pearl.

"What are you talking about? Before I graduated I was offered a good job in Chicago. I had things all lined up. I didn't need Dad's business. I didn't need to come home and have to deal with this…this lying and deception and—"

"It was the girl," said Morris.

"That shiksa," said Pearl contemptuously. "She wasn't good for you."

"You tricked me into coming here to get me away from Caroline? That's all it was, a lousy trick? Damn you," Steven shouted.

"Please, Steven. Try to understand," begged Pearl. "It wouldn't have worked. Catholics and Jews don't mix. When you're young and impressionable, the blood runs hot, and you don't have any judgment. We want you to be happy for the rest of your life. She wouldn't have been good for you."

Steven trembled in outrage at his parent's deception. They used his wish to have his own business as a ploy to get him back, which, of course, explained his father's refusal to step aside. And their prejudice repelled him. Suddenly it all became clear.

"How do you know she wouldn't be good for me?" he demanded. "You haven't even met her. You judge her without knowing a thing about her."

"She's Catholic. Isn't that enough?" said Pearl.

"Goddamn you both," said Steven, standing. "This is it. I'm leaving. I've got to get away from you."

"Where are you going?" said Pearl, in panic.

"I don't know yet. Maybe back to Chicago. For sure, I'm not staying here."

"Don't be hasty, Steve," said Robert. "Without you, the business has no future. I have no future. Don't desert us. Think of the big picture."

"Of course the business has a future," Morris objected. "How do you think it got a past? But Rob is right. I want you to stay, Steven. We'll work it out. You have my word."

"Your word? That's a joke."

"I swear," said Morris in earnest. "Everyone has heard me. You all heard me, right?"

All nodded, but Steven wasn't satisfied. His distrust was too great. "I'm not staying. I'm leaving this house. It's no use."

"Just this house, is that right, son?" said Pearl.

"You can't run my life, Mom. I survived a war and got through college, no thanks to anyone but myself. I make my own choices, for better or worse. I can't stay here."

"I did what I thought was best for you," Pearl said, embracing him, tears in her eyes. "Please, try to understand. No one loves you more than your mother, the one who carried you in her womb. Remember that."

"Steve, if you quit, I'll quit," Robert warned.

"What's wrong with you, Robert?" said Morris. "I'm still here. We're a team. You have nothing to worry about."

"Without Steve I don't see a future, Dad. You'd like to coast, but I—we—want more than that."

"Before long we'll be needing a larger place, Morris," Deborah added. "Actually, we'd like to buy a house, and we can't afford one on what Rob is earning."

Seeing the consequences of his leaving, Steven backed down. "Look," he said to Robert and Deborah, "I'll stick with it for a while longer, for your sakes. See how it goes, but—"

"Good man. You won't regret it," said Morris.

"Oh, son, you're making me happy," said Pearl, relieved.

"But—" said Steven, struggling to get a word in.

"Thanks, Steve," said Robert. "Together I know we can make this thing grow."

"But I want to take some time off, say a couple of weeks, maybe a month," Steven said finally.

"Sure, go ahead," said Morris. "Rob and I can handle things just fine."

"A month. That's a long time. Why a month?" said Pearl, fearing that his being away could lead to his never returning.

"I don't know. Maybe it'll be less, maybe only two weeks. I'll see," said Steven, intentionally noncommittal. "It depends on how things work out where I am."

"Where are you going?" asked Pearl suspiciously, suspecting the worst.

"Away, just away."

"You're going to Chicago," Pearl said accusingly. "You're going to that girl."

"Maybe. So what?" said Steven, irritated. "It's none of your business, Mom."

"Leave him alone, Pearl," said Morris. "He's coming back. That's all that matters."

"Not if he's with her," said Pearly sharply.

"I said I'd be back," said Steven. "At least I keep my word. Do you want it in writing?"

"Hah, you're the one who wants things in writing," said Morris, stamping his foot on the floor.

"Shut up, Morris," said Pearl.

"Lay off Steve, Mom," said Robert. "Have a good time, fella. Rest, and come back all fired up."

The two brothers embraced. Their love for each other was the salve that healed Steven's outrage.

"Good boys," said Morris, pleased. "The three of us will make an unbeatable team. Right, Steve?"

Keeping his location a secret, Steven disappeared for almost three weeks. Of course, everyone speculated that he had gone to Chicago, and Pearl was certain he was with "that girl." The Saturday night he arrived back in town, he called Robert. The following morning, when the family usually gathered for one of Pearl's Sunday breakfasts, Robert revealed that Steven had returned.

"Did he tell you where he was staying?" Pearl inquired as they sat around the kitchen table sipping freshly brewed coffee.

"Some motel in town," answered Robert. "I didn't ask him which one."

"Why didn't he call?" Pearl complained. "He's been gone more than three weeks and he never called."

"It's not quite three weeks, Mom," Robert reminded her.

"He's still angry with us," said Morris, feeling guilty.

"Do you think so?" asked Pearl. "But he said he'd join us for Sunday breakfast, didn't he, Robert?" Pearl said, seeking reinforcement.

"Yes, he did," confirmed Robert, trying to put his mother at ease. "I don't think he's angry any longer," he said, without any basis in fact.

"I hope not. No one loves him more than his parents," said Pearl. She cocked her head when the doorbell rang. "That must be him. Let him in, Robert."

Robert walked to the front door and opened it. "Hi, Steve. God, it's good to see you."

Pearl and Morris lit up when they heard Robert greet his brother. "Steven couldn't be angry or he wouldn't be here, right?" said Morris.

"Is it you, Steven? Is it you, son?" Pearl shouted as she burst into the living room and embraced Steven tightly, tears flowing. "Give your mother a good, long hug. Morris, it's Steven. He's here."

Deborah and Morris followed, all smiles.

"Hi, Mom. Why are you crying?"

"I wasn't sure you'd come back."

"Let me have my turn," Morris cut in, gently pulling her away. He hugged Steven to him. "Good to see you, son. I never doubted you. I want you to know that."

Steven broke from his father's embrace to look at Deborah. "How's the mother-to-be?"

"Everything is normal," said Deborah, beaming.

"Good," said Steven. He searched everyone's face to make sure he had their attention. "I want all of you to meet someone. I'll be right back."

He went to the front door and opened it. In walked a tall, young, auburn-haired, neatly dressed woman.

"And who might this be?" asked Pearl warily.

"This is Caroline, Mom. Caroline, meet my mom and dad, Pearl and Morris."

Caroline extended her hand to Pearl. "I'm delighted to meet you both. Steven has told me so much about you, how supportive you've been."

Morris took the hand that was intended for Pearl. "I'm happy to meet you, Caroline. Won't you sit down?" As Caroline sat on the sofa, Morris muttered to Pearl under his breath, "Is she the one?"

From the moment Deborah laid eyes on Caroline, she wanted to be her ally. "I'm happy to meet you, Caroline. I'm Deborah, Steve's sister-in-law." There was something about Caroline's manner, her smiling eyes, her relaxed voice that led Deborah to believe they could be friends.

"I know precisely who you are, Deborah. Steve has told me about you and your pregnancy. It must be so satisfying. Congratulations."

"Why, thank-you," said Deborah warmly.

"And this is my brother, Rob," said Steven.

"It's my pleasure," said Robert.

"No more than mine, Rob. I understand you are one super salesman."

"Just an ordinary salesman, that's all," said Rob, blushing.

Steven eyed his mother, who had been obviously silent. "Aren't you going to welcome Caroline, Mom?"

"You haven't answered your father's question."

"What question?" asked Steven, baffled.

"Is she the one?"

"The one, the one," repeated Steven. "You mean, is she the gentile? Is that what you mean? Yes, she's the one."

"I've so been looking forward to meeting you," said Caroline, extending her hand to Pearl again.

"How could you, Steven?" said Pearl, ignoring Caroline's outstretched hand. "Bringing her into our home, yet."

"You needn't concern yourself. We're not staying here," said Steven sourly.

"Why not?" said Morris. "You can't afford to stay in a motel, not with what you're taking from the business."

"If Caroline isn't welcome here, neither am I," said Steven, his voice brittle.

"They're staying here, Pearl," said Morris with authority. "Have you had breakfast, Caroline?"

"Yes, thank-you. We ate at the motel."

"How do you feel about staying here, Caroline?" asked Steven.

"I don't want to offend Pearl."

"This is my place, too," said Morris before Pearl could reply. "You're not offending me."

As distasteful as Caroline's presence was to her, Pearl feared alienating Steven. And no doubt, soon Caroline would be leaving. Reluctantly she conceded. "If she's staying here, though, it means one of them will have to sleep on the living room couch."

"I don't care where they sleep, as long as they stay here," proclaimed Morris.

"We'll stay until we find an apartment," agreed Steven. "We'll sleep in my room, Mom."

"I don't approve of that," said Pearl, her lips tight. "In my time we didn't do such things."

"Well, in my generation we do," said Steven, "and we've been doing it for some time even though it's been a secret."

"And look what it's done to our morals. No one has morals anymore," said Pearl, as if that were her concern as well.

"The only difference between Steve's generation and ours is we did it in the backseat of cars," growled Morris.

"How can you say that?" Pearl objected. "We were married."

"You have a short memory, eh, Pearl?" said Morris, pinching Pearl's buttock.

"You've been a mystery person until now," said Deborah, taking Caroline's hand. "Steven has kept you a secret...I mean the kind of person you are. But I see he shouldn't have. I'm sure we can be good friends."

"I want us to be," said Caroline from her heart.

"How long will she be staying?" Pearl asked.

"As long as I stay," said Steven evenly.

"You mean you're not staying—" said Morris alarmed.

"Indefinitely?" Robert finished the sentence for his father.

"It depends on how things go. If I stay, Caroline stays with me. It's that simple. Any more questions?"

"Things will go fine, you'll see," said Morris.

"We'll do just great, Steve. I can feel it," Robert said, echoing his father's sentiment.

"You're a good man, Rob. I'm not worried about you," said Steven, expecting his father to respond.

"Then what are you worried about? Me?" said Morris calmly. "Y'know, son, I always dreamed that someday my boys would take over the business. I didn't build the business strictly for myself. You didn't know that, did you? I always thought it would be there for both of you, maybe go on for generations, at least through yours. It's sort of my legacy."

"While you were gone, Steve, there were a few foul-ups," said Robert, interrupting his father's monologue.

"Minor problems, that's all," said Morris, directing his next words to Robert. "If you had written the order up correctly, we wouldn't have had problems."

"You didn't read it right," Robert protested.

"A typical salesman," said Morris. "That's why we need you, Steven. A company needs a man with entrepreneurial smarts. A Yiddisher kop, know what I mean?"

"Hey, thanks for the compliment," said Robert, feeling put down.

"I love you," Deborah said to her husband, "but I don't think you're the entrepreneurial type. Maybe that's why I love you." After kissing him on the lips, she turned to Caroline. "Would you consider moving to our town, Caroline?"

Steven answered for her. "Caroline comes from a big city where most people are strangers to one another—"

"I'm fascinated that everyone seems to know everyone else here," Caroline interrupted him. "Or so it seems from what Steve tells me."

Steven tried to assuage his mother's anticipated disapproval. "You won't have to put up with us for very long, Mom."

"Good," said Pearl. Then she turned to Caroline. "I'm sorry, dear. You may be a fine person, but I don't approve of mixing religions. You should find a Catholic boy, and Steven should find a Jewish girl. That's how I feel."

Robert stared at the floor and Deborah turned away, embarrassed.

"I understand, completely," Caroline replied without a moment's hesitation. "My parents won't let Steve set foot in their house. They think he has horns. He would meet me a block away until I moved into my own apartment. You see, they really drove us together—not that we wouldn't be together otherwise. I love Steve and I'd love him no matter what he was."

Deborah raised her eyes and looked at Caroline admiringly. "I feel the same way about Rob, Caroline. The fact that I'm Jewish too had nothing to do with our falling in love. My parents didn't approve of Rob because they felt he had no future."

"I never knew that," said Pearl, astonished.

"They sure as hell never let on at the wedding," said Morris.

"They wanted me to marry a professional man, a doctor or lawyer," Deborah explained. "Certainly not a salesman. Your generation doesn't judge a person by who he or she is, do they?"

"My generation tries to maintain our differences," replied Morris. "It keeps everything familiar and safe. Know what I mean?"

"But it doesn't keep things safe, Morris," Deborah said. "It creates more insecurity."

"Deb, I know we're going to be fast friends," said Caroline.

"So, Miss," said Pearl, "my question is, how long will you stay?"

"That's the wrong word, Mom," said Steven firmly.

"What's the wrong word?" said Pearl, bewildered.

"Miss."

"Well, what then?" said Pearl innocently. "Isn't that how you address a single girl nowadays?"

"She's not a Miss. She's a Mrs.," said Steven, fastening his eyes onto his mother's.

"Oy, gevalt. Do I understand that—"

"Caroline is my wife, Mom. Here's your ring, Caroline. Let me put it on you."

Steven gently slipped the ring on Caroline's outstretched finger, then kissed her.

"Well, whaddya know?" said Morris, all smiles. "Congratulations, son, and you too, Caroline."

"I must sit down. Let me sit down," Pearl exclaimed, dizzily falling into a chair.

Robert embraced Steven, then slapped him on the back. "Hey, Steve. You did it. God, this is great." Robert raised a cup of coffee into the air. "Here's wishing you the best," he declared.

Deborah grasped Caroline's hands in both of hers. "Welcome, sister-in-law. Being an only child, I always wanted a sister. This makes me so happy."

"Me, too, Deborah. I'm a singleton also."

"Congratulations, Caroline," said Robert, taking Caroline's hands away from Deborah. "But what's a singleton?"

"Deb and I are singletons—only children. But no longer."

"I don't know what to do," said Pearl.

"What to do?" said Steven impatiently. "There's nothing for you to do. Caroline and I are married. We'll set up housekeeping and get on with our lives."

"You'd better start right now," said Pearl, suddenly resolute. "I don't want her in this house."

"Don't do this, Mom. Please don't. Caroline's my wife now. Accept her."

"That's the way I feel," said Pearl, refusing to face Steven's gaze. "Your whatever-she-is is not welcome in this house."

"Dad, bring her to her senses," Steven pleaded.

"I'll try, but don't expect miracles," said Morris meekly.

"You've all heard me," said Pearl, leaving the room.

"Your mother is a stubborn woman," said Morris, shaking his head. "It'll take a while. Give it time, son." He turned to Caroline. "I'm sorry. Please try to understand."

"But I do. I understand completely," said Caroline sincerely.

"The family problem is one thing, the business is another. Nothing's changed. That right, son?"

"Sure, Dad. I'll see you at the shop in the morning."

During the following month, Pearl refused to acknowledge Caroline's existence. Although this strained her relationship with Steven so severely that he rarely came around, she hung on to her animosity as if her life depended on it.

Fed up with the estrangement, Morris confronted her one evening in the living room. "Tell me, Pearl. How much longer are you going to boycott Caroline?"

"Forever."

"Stop being ridiculous. You're making everyone miserable—not only Steven, but Deborah and Robert. I have enough to do to keep up a peaceful business relationship with our sons. Your attitude only complicates the situation."

"She's not one of us, Morris. Wait until kids come and she brings them up Catholic. What will you say then?"

"I don't care what she brings them up. That's not our business." Morris picked up his newspaper and read a few lines, then, without lowering it, muttered, "Anyway, she's pregnant."

"I knew it, I knew it," said Pearl, bolting from the sofa where she had been reclining.

"Won't you be thrilled to have another grandchild?" said Morris.

"Why thrilled? We'll have gentile children. Is that what you want for the next generation?"

"Pearl, I need us to have peace. Y'know, I haven't been feeling so hot lately, and it would help if—"

"What's wrong, Morris? You haven't said anything about this before."

Ever since Morris was found to have high blood pressure, Pearl was concerned about his health. She observed his waning vigor and wondered whether something besides simply aging was responsible. He was only in his early sixties.

"I suppose it's age," said Morris. "I just don't have the get-up-and-go anymore."

"You can't expect to stay the same," said Pearl, trying to put his mind at ease.

"I know that. It's…well, some strange things have been happening."

"Tell me. Tell me," said Pearl, anxious.

But the answer never came. There was a knock at the door and Robert strode into the room. "Hi, folks. No TV tonight?"

"Your mother and I have been shooting the gab," said Morris. "What are you doing here?"

"I've got to talk to you about the situation."

"What situation?" said Morris, tossing aside his newspaper.

"Well, everything—Mom, Steven, the business." Robert sat stiffly in one of the recliners.

"Things in the business are going smoothly," said Morris.

"No, they're not," Robert said.

"Steven seems happy. What else is there?" said Morris, genuinely curious.

"Not with Mom, he isn't happy. Mom's a problem."

"How can you say that?" said Pearl defensively. "I'm not the problem. His wife is. As for happy, you and Deb—you're happy."

"Sure, I'm happy with Deb, but not with everything else. If things keep on as they are, Steven's going to—"

"What's he going to do?" said Morris, sitting upright from his slouch. "He hasn't complained to me."

"Because he knows it won't do any good," said Robert.

"Well, what's his complaint this time?" said Morris resignedly.

"You're his complaint. You won't let go."

"Sure I've 'let go,' as you call it. I do what I have to do and I leave him alone."

"He's not running the show the way you promised. The business isn't going anywhere," said Robert, leading up to the nub of his complaint.

"So what does he want? Does he want me to stay home and twiddle my thumbs?"

"I'm not here to speak for him, Dad. I'm here for myself, for Deb and me. We don't feel secure about the business; if there's ill feeling, the business won't get better. You've got to let go."

"Let go? Let go? How can I let go?" ask Morris, waving his arms while words poured out. "The business is all I have. I struggled through a depression and through the war when materials were impossible to get. Now the business is where I always wanted it. Maybe it's not growing by leaps and bounds, but it's holding its own. What do you boys want of me? You want my soul, too?"

"Calm down, Morris," said Pearl. "Getting upset isn't good for you."

"Calm down?" Morris screamed. "They want me out. How can I be calm?"

"No, Dad, we don't want you out," Robert said. "All we ask is that you do one thing and stick with it instead of trying to do everything."

"That's what I've been doing—one thing."

"Hell, you have," Robert shouted uncharacteristically.

"Well, maybe it's better that both of you leave," said Morris with finality. "Maybe that's the way it has to be."

"Do you mean that? Is that what you want?" said Robert, incredulous.

"We'll lose our boys, Morris," moaned Pearl. "I don't want to lose our boys."

"Goddamn them. They don't know a good deal when they see it," said Morris.

"This whole thing has been a trick," Robert said, echoing Steven's earlier accusation. "Both of you just wanted to keep us around."

"Your mother wants you around. As far as I'm concerned, you can go to Timbuktoo."

"What a cruel thing to say," said Pearl. "You love them as much as I do."

"Of course I love them," said Morris, regretting his ire, "but I can't let them run my life. I agreed to bring them into the business for your sake, Pearl. For your sake. I don't need them. I can handle things just fine. But you wanted the boys near. You wanted to get Steven away from Caroline."

"You always said you were building the business for them," Pearl shouted. "Someday it would be theirs. You always said that."

"Sure, after I'm gone, but not while I'm still going strong."

"We're getting old, Morris. The doctor told you to ease off. If we wait too long, the boys will be settled doing something else."

"We're not trying to run your life," Robert interjected. "But you're trying to run ours."

"You can do whatever you want," Morris said, shifting in his chair, "but not in my business."

"I thought it was our business," said Robert.

"It is, it is," replied Morris, caught short. "What did I say?"

"If something happens to you—" interrupted Pearl.

"Like what?" Morris demanded. "What's going to happen to me?"

"You were just saying you're not feeling so good," answered Pearl.

"What's wrong, Dad?" said Robert, apprehensive.

"It's age, just age," said Morris.

"That's what I said, you're growing old," Pearl agreed. "Wouldn't it be smart to have the boys take over in our declining years?"

"I'm not ready," declared Morris. "Don't you understand?"

"When will you be?" asked Pearl. "When you can't walk up a flight of stairs? I won't forgive you if the boys quit. Where's the money going to come from in our old age? We need them. Don't you see that?"

Ignoring Pearl, Morris turned to Robert. "Did Steven send you?"

"Of course not. Steven is quite capable of speaking for himself. And I think he'll be doing it soon—tonight maybe."

"So you came here on his behalf?"

"I came here to prepare you, to explain what you're doing to him."

"Well, I'm prepared," Morris sneered. "Satisfied?"

As if prompted, Steven walked into the room. "Hi, folks."

"Hello, son," said Pearl, standing but keeping her distance. But Steven walked up to her and took her in his arms. He kissed her on the forehead, bringing tears to her eyes. She was hungry for any expression of affection from her favorite son.

"I'm surprised to see you here, Rob," said Steven.

"I just dropped by to—"

"Rob tells me you're unhappy," said Morris, ready to do battle.

"Damnit, Dad," said Robert.

"Well, let's not beat around the bush," Morris said, challenge in his voice. "Let's get it out in the open. What's your gripe?"

"You know what it is," said Steven quietly. "You aren't keeping your promise."

"And what promise is that?"

"You're stringing me along," said Steven.

"No, I'm not. Go ahead, tell me what promise."

"To not interfere. You won't let me do my job," asserted Steven.

"And what do you think your job is?" asked Morris.

"This is a game," said Steven, growing impatient. "Running the company. I'm supposed to be in charge, damnit."

"You are. Doesn't your business card say you're president?"

"C'mon, Dad. Christ, you know what I'm talking about."

"I was just telling Robert that maybe you ought to quit. There's no pleasing you," said Morris, throwing up his hands.

"Don't listen to him, Steven," said Pearl. "Morris, you hear me. If the boys leave, so will I."

"You can't mean that," said Morris, shocked.

"I do. I mean every word."

"Dad's right," Steven said to Pearl. "I ought to leave. He's impossible."

"Don't you dare leave," said Pearl.

"There's nothing to keep me here. I may as well be working for someone else. You refuse to accept Caroline. Both of you are making our lives miserable."

"I understand she's having your child," said Pearl with sarcasm.

"She was gang-raped," said Steven bitterly. "I can't be sure who the father is."

"Stop it," said Pearl angrily. "Stop fooling with me."

"She's having your grandchild, Mom."

"Really, then it's true," said Pearl, suddenly mollified now that the prospect had become a reality. "My, now we'll have two grandchildren. And of course you'll bring her - or him - up Jewish. I hope at least one of them is a girl. Morris could only make boys."

"Sure, blame me," said Morris with a sneer.

"Well, I hear the male determines the sex of a child," said Pearl. "You've done good, Steven."

"It was nothing," said Steven, grinning, delighted at his mother's approval.

"But why did it have to be with a shiksa?" Pearl sighed.

"Look, I'll keep out of your way," said Morris, caught up in the happier atmosphere. "For your mother's sake. You're in charge."

"I'm sorry, Dad. That's not enough. It won't work," said Steven.

"What's not enough? I said I'll stay out of your hair."

"I want you to retire. Travel, take it easy, stay out of the business."

"You mean quit? With my boots still on?" said Morris.

"That's right. I'll spell it out for you. Q-U-I-T."

"You must be dreaming," said Morris with a nervous laugh.

"Listen to your son, Morris," said Pearl. "We can travel, see the world, like the sailors do."

"Dad, you'll finally have time to enjoy life," Robert added. "Do all the things you've always wanted to do."

"What things are you talking about? I've done what I always wanted to do. Steven's asking me to drop dead."

"No, Dad. I'm asking you to start living," Steven said emphatically.

"What do you think I've been doing all my life? I built a business. Hell, I even made you. What do you think of that? Maybe I should regret it."

"Morris," shouted Pearl.

"I said maybe."

"This is it, Dad. You step aside or else I go," said Steven, his ultimatum final.

"Me too, Dad. I'm sorry," said Robert.

Morris glared at one son, then the other. "You'd do this to your father?"

"Laying on the guilt won't work," said Steven, refusing to budge. "I've heard it before."

Perhaps there was room for some bargaining, thought Morris. "Tell you what, I'll do just the buying. How's that? Nothing else."

"No, Dad. It's either you're out or I'm out. That's the way it has to be," said Steven, holding firm.

"You heard him, Morris. You and I will be able to spend time together," said Pearl.

"Doing what?"

"Well, to start we could visit the relatives in California."

"I never had any use for them. They aren't my type," Morris growled. He turned to Steven. "It looks like you'll have to go. I'm sorry."

"Dad, do you know what you're saying?" Robert asked.

"You've had your chance, Morris," said Pearl. "I'm moving in with Rob and Debbie." She paused as if a startling thought had occurred to her. "Steven, can't you and Rob outvote your father?"

"Yes, we could," said Steven, as if a light bulb had gone on in his brain."Together we own two-thirds of the voting shares."

"Well then," said Pearl with a leer.

"You mean you want us to force Dad out?" asked Robert in disbelief.

"For his sake as well as mine," stated Pearl.

"It's a goddamned conspiracy," said Morris, outraged. "You would do this to me?"

"What do you think, Rob?" said Steven, ignoring his father. "If you want me to stay then Dad has to go."

"You're conniving right in front of me," Morris howled. "You sons of bitches."

"As Mom says...," stated Robert, playing along at pretending that his father had disappeared.

Steven took pity on his father. "We'll let you come in part-time, Dad. Check the books, chin with the customers, that sort of thing."

"Well, isn't that damned decent of you. You think you can get away with this? My own sons, my flesh and blood would send their father out to pasture. Now you listen to me, I'm going to fight you. You haven't heard the end of this. I'll show you how much vinegar I've got. I'm taking you to court."

"I thought you hated lawyers," Steven reminded his father. "Besides, you signed some papers, Dad."

"I wasn't in my right mind. And I'll prove it."

"Morris, stop being silly," said Pearl. "Let's go to that place you wanted the boys to go to."

"What are you talking about?" said Morris, still steaming.

"Timbuktoo. What's it like there?"

Steven thought that his father's threat to fight him in court was hollow, but Robert, sensing his father's desperation, believed otherwise. So did Deborah. She had never seen Robert so upset. All the couple's plans to establish a home and raise a family were in jeopardy. But worse, such a battle would tear the family apart forever. She realized that Robert, although no longer living with his parents, had never left home. She knew that family harmony was fundamental to his sense of well-being.

The next morning Deborah visited Pearl. She wanted to hear her view of the conflict in order to better decide what she and Robert should do. But she had another motive, too.

"Robert is beside himself over Dad," said Deborah as they sat at the kitchen table sipping their cups of Pearl's freshly ground coffee. Deborah seemed more concerned over Robert than their suddenly uncertain future.

"You mean the court business?" said Pearl.

"That, too, but mainly the effect it will have on Dad's health and what it will do to our family," said Deborah.

"I know," said Pearl, cooling her coffee by blowing across the surface of the steaming cup. "I'm working on him, trying to make him see things rationally."

"He must be angry at you for siding with the boys."

"Oh, yes, he's angry all right," said Pearl, not looking worried. "He won't talk to me except when he wants to eat, and then it's silence at the supper table. But he'll get over it. Morris can't stay angry for long about anything."

"What if he goes through with it?" said Deborah anxiously.

"Let's wait and see, Deb," Pearl said, patting Deborah's hand.

"Rob is having second thoughts about staying. If Dad brings this thing to court, I think he'll quit," said Deborah.

"Has he talked to Steven?"

"Steven is determined to take over no matter what Dad does," said Deborah, spilling her coffee onto the tablecloth as the cup was halfway to her lips.

Pearl rushed to get a sponge, not missing a beat of the conversation. "Good for him," she said as she sopped up the coffee. "Robert should help Steven. I want my boys together. You know how much Robert worships Steven, and as children how Steven always looked out for Robert. That's the way they've always been, natural partners."

"But they're so different from each other," said Deborah, censoring her true opinion that they are downright incompatible.

"Yes. Isn't that wonderful?"

"You don't seem worried by Morris's threats," Deborah said, surprised by Pearl's equanimity.

"I am, of course," said Pearl, "but I have a weapon that will change his mind. If he brings this to court, I've threatened to leave him. And he can't survive by himself. He needs me to take care of him. Pick his ties, little things like that—but important just the same. What will he do for meals? Maybe he thinks his mother made better hamburg than me, but he knows I'm the world's best cook. Do you think he'd ever give that up? No, Deb, not a chance. You tell that husband of yours not to worry. Morris will come around. Our family will stay together."

"I feel better already," said Deborah, draining her cup. "But we're not really together, Pearl. Will you ever accept Caroline?"

"When the moon turns to cheese," said Pearl coldly.

"She's a good person, Mom."

"Maybe, but that doesn't matter. She's not our kind."

"She's no different from us, Pearl. We've become friends. I like her." Deborah silently studied Pearl's face for any sign of a concession, but Pearl was impassive. The time had come for Deborah to come clean. "I've asked her to come by."

"You what?" Pearl exploded. "I don't want her in this house."

"Please, Mom. Give her a chance. Hear what she has to say."

"About what?" said Pearl, as the cup she was balancing rattled nervously in its saucer.

"About everything, anything, so you can see what she's like," said Deborah. She grasped Pearl's hand tightly. "Are you afraid to like her?" she asked.

"What do you mean?" said Pearl indignantly. "Certainly not."

"Well?" said Deborah.

As if on cue, the doorbell rang. "That must be her." As Deborah headed for the door, Pearl was left at the table feeling trapped.

Deborah led Caroline into the kitchen. "Hello, Pearl," Caroline said, extending her hand. As usual, Pearl ignored it. "I hope I'm not intruding."

"Humph. This isn't my doing," muttered Pearl, refusing to look at Caroline squarely.

"Why don't you sit, Caroline?" said Deborah. She accepted the invitation by sitting beside Pearl.

"Steven is sick over Morris," said Caroline. "He's not sleeping. He has no appetite." Caroline expected that Pearl would care enough to respond.

"Are you giving him good food?" asked Pearl.

"I love to cook for him," said Caroline, which made Pearl turn her way. "I'm not as good as you, Pearl, but he tells me I'm second best."

"Well, isn't that something? said Pearl, giggling. "So you cook, too."

"Nobody cooks like Pearl, Caroline. Don't even try to measure up. The boys are spoiled," said Deborah. "Would you like some coffee?"

"Why, yes, that would be nice," said Caroline. "I was flattered when Steven said I was second best."

"And well you should be," said Pearl, looking into Caroline's eyes for the first time. "How is your pregnancy coming?"

"I feel good. My weight is under control."

"You look beautiful," said Deborah as she placed a cup of steaming coffee before Caroline.

"I glowed when I was pregnant with each of my boys," said Pearl. "But I never went back to my old trim self after I had Robert. I hope it won't happen to you, dear."

"You look fine to me," said Caroline.

"Really? You think so?" said Pearl. "I've been watching my diet, you know."

"I'm worried about Steven," said Caroline, fingering a spoon. "He's become so impatient. Sometimes he snaps at me for the littlest thing. The other day he became angry over nothing: I forgot to put tomatoes in his salad. I know it's this battle with Morris. It's eating him up inside."

"Pearl and I were just talking about it," said Deborah. "Robert is troubled, too."

"Steven shouldn't worry," said Pearl. "As I told Deborah, keeping our family together is the most important thing in the world to me. And I'll make sure that nothing interferes. I have ways to change your father-in-law's mind. To be honest, you're my biggest obstacle."

"Pearl, I hope not. I don't want to be."

"You are what you are, and that's the problem," said Pearl.

"My being Catholic shouldn't prevent us from being friends," said Caroline gently. "I want to like you, and I want you to like me."

"It's the child," said Pearl, looking very serious.

"You mean—"

"There's no place for a Catholic child in our family."

"But I'm not insisting that our child be brought up Catholic. She can be Jewish if she wants."

"You mean that?" said Pearl, astonished.

"Certainly."

"But I thought your people made sure their children were brought up in their own faith," said Pearl. It was a practice that she approved of. After all, didn't Jews insist that children of a mixed marriage be brought up as Jews? Indeed, a rabbi required that an alien spouse convert before he would conduct a marriage ceremony.

"I'm not that kind of Catholic, Pearl."

"Then your people don't think much of you," said Pearl.

"There are many more who think like me," explained Caroline.

"Jews are no different, Pearl," said Deborah, pointing out what Pearl well knew.

"Aren't you a practicing Catholic?" asked Pearl, challenging her own supposition.

"I don't go to church every Sunday, if that's what you're asking, but I was brought up a Catholic. I'm comfortable being one, and I want to be nothing else. I'm sorry if that doesn't please you."

"Well said, Caroline. I'm that kind of Jew, too," stated Deborah.

Pearl couldn't help but admire Caroline's explanation. "It is well said. You do stand by your convictions."

"I think our different beliefs needn't separate us," Caroline suggested. "Rather I think we should respect each other's. Don't we want the same thing: to keep our men happy and together?"

"It's really our common bond," said Deborah, thrilled over Caroline's irresistible appeal.

"That and being women—their women," added Caroline.

"I'll have to think about this," said Pearl, finding her assumptions being threatened. "I was brought up a certain way, too—to protect our people from the rest of the world, to keep us from disappearing from the earth."

"I have no personal objection to the Jewish people surviving and multiplying," said Caroline, tossing Pearl's agenda right back at her. "And none of my Catholic friends has any objection. Don't you feel the same way about my people?"

"Yes, I do," said Pearl. "Only you don't practice birth control, so your people will always outnumber us."

"Mom, no one is telling us Jews to practice birth control," said Deborah with a laugh. "We don't have to do that if we don't want to."

"I'll bet that some Catholics do practice birth control even if the Pope says not to," said Pearl.

"You're right," said Caroline. "Some of my friends do." She shifted in her chair uncomfortably. "May I use your bathroom?"

"You know where it is," said Pearl.

After Caroline excused herself, Pearl commented, "When I was pregnant I had to go often, too."

"You see what she's like, Pearl," said Deborah. "How can you not like her?"

"I admit she's very nice. Steven would only choose someone like her, so why not someone Jewish?"

"Because that's not important to him," Deborah explained. "Don't you realize if you don't accept her, you'll alienate Steven.? You could lose him for good."

Pearl remained silent for a few moments, staring into her cup, then said, "I thought I had lost him when he left for Chicago, then when he came back ---"

"You'll risk losing him again, Pearl."

"Do you really think so? Would he turn against his own mother?"

"He loves her. When you were young would you have forsaken your love for Morris for that of your parents? You're making him choose. Why can't he have both her and you?"

Pearl sighed. "It's so hard, so hard. I want him to be happy."

"He will be, if you'll let him."

"Hmm. I see, I see."

Caroline returned to the kitchen and sat at the table as Pearl swirled the coffee in her cup a few times while she pondered her new view of this captivating woman sitting beside her. "Well, maybe you and I should start getting to know each other a little better."

"I'd like nothing more," said Caroline, reaching over and putting her arm around Pearl's shoulders. The older woman slowly put her arm around her new daughter-in-law.

"So what are we going to do about our men?" said Deborah, wanting to get down to the business of bringing harmony into the family once again.

"I told you, Deb. Leave it all to me," said Pearl.

"Hello, girls. Why Caroline, what a nice surprise," said Morris, strolling into the kitchen to replenish his coffee. "Leave what to you?"

"Leave you to me," said Pearl, refilling his cup.

"Concerning what?" said Morris.

"I want you to call off the lawyer," declared Pearl.

"Not on your life," Morris said resolutely. "You stay out of it, Pearl."

"The girls here are telling me that the boys are miserable."

"Good," said Morris. "They deserve to be, after doing this terrible thing to their own father. What do they expect to feel—proud?"

"Would you at least talk to them?" asked Deborah.

"Sure, I'll talk to them, if they're willing to be reasonable."

"They love you, Morris," said Pearl, expressing what she felt should be the overriding reason for making peace.

"And I love them," said Morris. "They're good boys, the apple of my two eyes. Why are they doing this to me? And you—why are you taking their side?"

"Because I want you to take it easy from now on. With the time we have left, I want us to have a new life together—the life we didn't have before."

"Oh, Pearl, my Pearl," said Morris sweetly. "You can't teach an old dog—"

"Let's try, try to learn how to live," Pearl interrupted, kissing him. "Let me teach you."

"You can't," said Morris, looking into her loving face with gentle eyes. "I don't know any other way." He turned from Pearl. "It's good to see you here, Caroline. So you and Pearl, are talking?"

"Let's make a deal," Pearl cut in. "You want me to accept Caroline, I want you to let the boys have their way." Pearl looked struck by the brilliance of her own proposal.

"What kind of a deal is that?" said Morris. "You're wrong and I'm right."

"Of course, Morris. Isn't that how it's always been?"

The courts moved slowly. Weeks passed and Morris's suit hadn't yet come up. Forced to step aside in the business, Morris fumed and threatened. Ignoring him, the boys deprived him of all responsibilities. Steven felt sure that his father's case had no merit. Robert, although troubled about his father's lot, hitched his future to Steven. Thanks to Steven's management ability and progressive ideas, the business thrived.

The Sunday morning family breakfasts continued without Morris, who, stewing in disappointment, took breakfast at a nearby cafeteria. But Pearl, although she felt bereft by Morris's absence, insisted that the rest of the family keep the tradition without him. Now she had four children with two grandchildren on the way.

"It's wonderful having my children all together again," she said as they sat around the table.

"Thank you for including me, Pearl," said Caroline, who felt genuinely welcome.

"When you told me you weren't planning to bring up your child in the Catholic faith —"

"That's not what she said," said Steven, cutting her off. "She told me she said that our son or daughter will be free to make a choice when she's old enough. She may well choose Catholicism, or Buddhism, or whatever. We don't care."

"I'll see to it that she chooses correctly," said Pearl.

"No you won't. It's not your decision. If I catch you —"

"If our daughter wants to adopt Judaism, I won't object," said Caroline, annoyed at her husband's aggressiveness. "But she must be free to choose."

"She needs to belong, Caroline," said Pearl. "And that has to start early. A person needs the comfort of knowing that they're not alone in their beliefs."

"She'll feel she belongs to us, Pearl. She won't need anything more until she can think for herself."

"We're not religious," said Deborah, "but our son will know he's Jewish. The rest will be up to him." Deborah looked to Robert for agreement.

"We're a dying breed," moaned Pearl. "The next generation won't be true. All this intermarriage is making everyone the same."

"We're Americans, Mom," said Steven. "That's enough for me."

"What about God?" said Pearl.

"What did He do for my buddies who I watched die beside me?" Steven said resentfully.

"What did they do to deserve what happened to them? They were no worse than I am. Either He failed or He doesn't exist."

"I've never heard you talk like that," said Caroline, staring at her husband.

"I told you I'm a heathen. I mean it," said Steven.

"You always said it jokingly," stated Caroline. "Then you don't believe in God?"

"We didn't bring you up to be a heathen, but you are, aren't you?" said Pearl as if her son had become a stranger. "We made sure you went to Temple, at least for the high holidays. What happened?"

"Yeah, and at Temple I was bored every minute. I went only to please you."

"How did you get this way?" asked Pearl, suddenly seeing how little control parents have over their children. "Denouncing God is a terrible thing."

"I don't need Him," said Steven. "From what I see, much of life's a crapshoot."

"But we can move things in the right direction for ourselves, don't you agree, Steve?" said Robert, espousing his own approach to life.

"Sure, and that's the challenge of living: making decisions that turn out best for yourself."

"Sometimes you have no control. Look what's happening with your father," said Pearl, wiping away a tear. "That's when we need God."

"We have damn little control," said Steven, digging his fork into the heap of home fries on his plate. "Things are bound to go wrong no matter how much we plan."

"Damn little control." It was Morris's voice. He had just walked in the back door and into the kitchen.

"I'm sorry things have happened this way, Dad," said Steven contritely. "I didn't want to take over on these terms."

Morris waved his hand. "Damn little control," he repeated.

"The business is going great guns," said Robert, hoping the news would please his father. "Compared to last year, sales have doubled. I think things are pretty much under control."

"And the business should keep doubling with the sales promotion program we have in place," said Steven. "The future has begun, Rob."

"I hope not," said Caroline.

"You can't mean that," said Steven, startled. "I don't get you. Except for Dad, it's going our way at last."

"I never see you now," complained Caroline. "When will I see you if you get busier?"

"If he's like his father," said Pearl, "you'd better reconcile yourself to being a businessman's widow."

"I want you home every night and weekend, you hear?" said Deborah to Robert.

"You've got me," Robert replied, getting up and moving another chair to the table. "Dad, why don't you join us?"

"I always wanted my own business," said Steven. "Now that I have one, I'm going to make the most of it. I plan for us to go statewide, then eventually nationwide. Someday, even international. The potential is there. We'll go public. I'm going to build the business beyond your wildest dreams, Dad."

Accepting Robert's invitation, Morris sat down, intrigued with what was being said. Could his business ever have national, even international, possibilities? Or was Steven an unrealistic dreamer?

"Whoa, Steve," said Robert. "I never heard you talk like this."

"You can come with me part of the way or all the way. It's up to you," said Steven.

"Pearl, he's a chip off the old block," said Morris suddenly. "Look at him. He's me all over again."

"Didn't you know, Dad? We're the same," said Steven proudly.

"Except he doesn't have principles," said Morris, addressing his wife. "That's where he and I are different. He's ruthless. A man with principles wouldn't do this to his father."

Robert cleared his throat. "I'm sorry, Steve, but I don't approve of what you're doing. You're going too fast."

"How's that? You want to make a lot of money, don't you?"

"How much money do we need?" said Robert, seeking his wife's input.

"I like money as much as the next person," said Deborah, "but I want Rob and me and our child to be a family."

"And you want a nice house, don't you?" said Steven.

"Rob's making enough already for us to buy a house," said Deborah.

"And he'll make a lot more. You'll be able to buy a bigger house," said Steven confidently.

"We won't need a bigger house," stated Deborah firmly.

"I can't keep putting in the hours the way you do, Steve," complained Robert. "You heard Deb. She wants me home for supper every night."

"I don't understand you, Deb," said Steven. "First you were worried that the income wouldn't be enough. Now it's too much."

"I don't want to see what happened to your parents happen to us, too," said Deborah. She touched Pearl's arm. "Forgive me, Mom."

"Oh, you're absolutely right," agreed Pearl. "For Morris the business was always more important than the family, and we suffered for it, especially you boys."

"Just a minute," objected Morris. "It was a depression; there were no jobs. I was one of the lucky ones. I was night manager of the local telegraph office, which paid me peanuts—eighteen dollars a week. We couldn't live on it."

"We've heard all this before, Dad," said Steven, exasperated.

"Well, you're hearing it again," said Morris loudly. "So I started the business and ran it during the day. Just try building a business when nobody has any money. There I was, working sixteen hours a day to put food on our table and clothes on our backs. I did it for ten years. We were the fortunate ones, Pearl. We managed—because I worked my ass off. For us. Would you rather we'd gone hungry?"

"I know how hard you worked, dear," said Pearl, feeling her comments had been unfair. She knew that they had not been easy times, and Morris always provided.

"Then what do you want of me, Pearl?" Morris demanded.

"Only that you let our sons be. Nothing else."

"They've sucked my life dry," Morris snarled.

"It's their turn now, Morris," said Pearl.

"No, it's still my turn."

"It's not the same now as it was then, is it, Steven?" said Caroline. "You don't have to work that hard today, do you?"

"Since the war the whole world has opened up," said Steven.

"Everything's there to be had for anyone who's willing to work for it. And I am."

"But we don't need everything," protested Caroline.

"Exactly, Caroline," said Deborah as their eyes met.

"I don't understand any of you," said Steven, baffled. "I can make us all rich someday, and you don't want it. What's wrong with you?"

"Maybe we're all asking what's wrong with you," said Caroline, who welcomed having the issue out at last. She had not seen Steven's obsessive drive before they were married, and now it worried her.

"Nothing's wrong with him," said Morris, seeing himself in Steven, seeing that the father is visited on the son involuntarily. "I know how he thinks. I've always said he's the entrepreneurial type. Such people have drive; they make things happen. Steven's one of them. Without his type, the world would come to a stop. Trouble is, there's not enough room for two of us in the same company. I know now that I made a big mistake."

"No you didn't, Dad," Steven said. "Call off the lawyers. I'm going to make you rich."

"Do you think money matters to me anymore?" Morris said with contempt.

"It matters to me," chimed in Pearl.

"I can't help what I am, Caroline," said Steven. "But without you, I'm not worth much. I need you at my side."

"Don't worry, Steven, I'm with you," Caroline said sincerely.

"Our vow includes for richer, too, you know," said Steven, squeezing Caroline around her waist.

"I won't forget it," said Caroline, laughing.

"You just have more money to pay the price, isn't that right, Steven?" said Pearl sarcastically.

"But you stayed with Morris just the same," Caroline said.

"I put up with him, yes. I love the lummox," said Pearl, wrapping an arm across Morris's shoulders.

"I feel the same way about Steven," said Caroline to Pearl.

"True, a good woman sticks by her man," stated Pearl.

"What do you mean? You threatened to leave me," said Morris, removing Pearl's arm from his shoulders and kissing her hand.

"It hurts me to see you suffering, but you don't know what's good for you."

"What's good for me is to keep working," said Morris, slicing the air for emphasis.

"I have much to tell you about husbands and business, Caroline," said Pearl. "Come over for lunch tomorrow."

"I'd be glad to. What time, Mom?"

"Come early, about eleven."

"Steve, Deb and I have been talking. I don't think I want to stick it out," said Robert guardedly, anticipating a row.

"Don't say that. You can ease off. I'll let you ease off."

"That's not it," said Robert. "I can't stand by and see what's happening to Dad. This court thing…I want it to stop. It'll destroy all of us."

"Good boy, Rob. Good boy," Morris interjected.

"He doesn't have a leg to stand on," said Steven, missing Robert's point. "He can't win. I'll see to it that they'll have enough income. They'll be all right."

"If he loses, so do we," said Robert, gazing at his smiling father. "We've lost him as our father."

"You and I, Rob, we'll throw the bastard out, eh?" said Morris, feeling vindicated. "Whaddya say to that, Steven, my boy?"

"Damnit, the business is going great guns and you—"

"I'm sorry, Steve," said Robert. "You and I can do anything. He can't. We're stripping him of part of his life."

"Listen to me, both of you," said Morris. "Give me a few more years. That's all I ask. Then it will all be yours."

"No, Dad. I don't want it," Robert said. "I've had a job offer. You've been driving me pretty hard, Steve, and I can't keep up."

"I just said you can ease off," said Steven, feeling desperate. "We'll hire another salesman and you'll be sales manager."

"It's more than that," said Robert. "The pace is too fast for me. I'm thinking of quitting sales."

"Why?" said Steven. "You're such a natural. You'll be wasting your talent."

"Maybe so, but I think I can do something else just as well."

"So what's that?" said Steven.

Deborah looked at her husband in admiration.

"Teaching," Robert replied. "I'd like to teach."

"I see. I had no idea," said Steven. "Well, now that I think of it, you are an empathetic soul. You probably would make a good teacher."

"Teaching?" exclaimed Morris. "How much will you make teaching?"

"Enough for us to live comfortably," said Deborah, offended by Morris's implication.

"Everything I do has to be your way," said Robert, voicing his other complaint to Steve. "You're just like Dad."

"I suppose I am," admitted Steven. "I catch myself seeing in me what not long ago I thought was bad about him."

"Has my way been so bad?" Morris said to Robert. "I'd say you like it."

"I didn't say being like Dad was bad," said Robert, addressing his brother. "It's just not my way."

"Today I don't think your way is either bad or good," Steven said to Morris. "I understand how it is, that's all."

"Your father's a good man," said Pearl. "And don't you forget it."

"Maybe my working days are over," confessed Morris, "but I'm not complaining."

"You must be kidding," said Pearl. "All I hear from you are complaints."

Ignoring Pearl's comment, Morris continued, "I want you to be happy, all of you, nothing more. And Caroline, I can see why Steven loves you. You're a fine woman, especially for a gentile." Everyone laughed, and laughed again when he gazed at his wife and said, "Isn't she, Pearl?"

"So, I've been wrong," said Pearl, shrugging. "Not like you, who's never been wrong."

"Oh, I've been wrong," said Morris, winking at Caroline. "And I know when I've been wrong. I just wouldn't admit it."

"That's a confession I never thought I'd hear this side of the pearly gates," said Pearl.

"What are you going to do, Steve?" Caroline asked.

"What do you want me to do? I'll do whatever makes you happy."

Caroline fastened her eyes on Steven's. "Even give the business back to your father?"

"I can't do that. I've gone too far. I can taste the future. Don't ask me to give it up. Please."

"Your happiness is my happiness," said Caroline. "All right, stay with the business. But take your father back."

"He's impossible. You're impossible, Dad. You refuse to see how things are today. It's nothing like the way it was. You're still back in the Depression."

Morris remained silent for a while before he answered. "That may be, and maybe not," he said, measuring his words. "It's not up to you to tell me where I am. I know where I am. The issue here is: are you going to steal my business from me, the business I spent a lifetime building, or are you going to give it back?"

"He's right, Steve," said Robert. "It's his business, not mine or yours. Don't do this to him."

"If I were to give it back, it wouldn't be the same business anymore," said Steven. "You know that, Rob. Dad, listen to me, it's grown, it's expanding, it's an organization now. Today it's more than you can handle or want to handle."

"Morris, let's spend the rest of our years enjoying life together," said Pearl again. How she yearned to break free of their long years of routine. "You've earned it, and so have I. Listen to Steven."

"Pearl, I want to, I really do," said Morris, softening. "But you've got to understand, it's not in me to sit around the house doing nothing. I have to work, or...or...or..."

"Or what, Morris? Or what?" Pearl demanded.

"I'll die," said Morris in a strong, clear voice.

"Die?" said Pearl, laughing nervously. "You don't mean that."

"I do, Pearl. I do. I know myself. It's work or...or death."

"Dad, I don't want you to die," said Steven, finally perceiving his father's profound stake in the business.

"Neither do I, Dad," said Robert. "You've got plenty of years left in you. Listen, Steve, can't you compromise?"

"What about you, Dad?" said Steven. "Can you compromise? If you will, so will I."

Morris raised his eyes to Steven's. "I promise you...I know you've heard my promises before—"

"Getting me to come back home the way you did was pretty low, you know," said Steven, implying that Morris's promise had better be genuine.

"That was your mother's scheme, not mine," said Morris.

"How can you say that? You went along with it, didn't you?" said Pearl, defending herself

"This time I'm not doing it for your mother, I'm doing it for myself. I promise to let you run the show. Now you all heard me."

"You'll put that in writing?" said Steven.

"In writing yet?" Morris said, grinning. "That's the way this generation likes things, always in writing. Sure I'll put it in writing. We'll get the chief justice of the Supreme Court to draw up the papers."

"There you go," Steven said. "You're feeling bitter about this already."

"No, I'm not, Steven. Believe me I'm not. I'm just joking a little. Look, I only want to keep my finger in the business, know what I mean? You're doing big things, bigger than anything I could handle. I know that. I'd be satisfied being a small part of it. That's all. You tell me what my job is and I'll do it. I know it will give me satisfaction and joy seeing you doing well. That'll be enough for me."

"You're making sense, Morris," intoned Pearl. "Listen to him, Steven. I'll see to it that he keeps his word. We're all witnesses, aren't we?" Everyone nodded vigorously. "I ask only one thing: you'll make him take vacations. I want him to take me on a safari in Africa."

"What?" said Morris, incredulous. "Are you dreaming? Where does that come from?"

"Well, maybe not a safari and maybe not Africa, but you get the idea, don't you?" said Pearl, smothering him with kisses.

"You're on, Dad," said Steven, embracing his father as tears welled up in his eyes. "I love you."

"Did I call you a bastard?" asked Morris.

"Yes, you did," Steven said with a grin as he damped his tears with a handkerchief.

"How could you be if I'm your father?" said Morris. "Your mother would know. Isn't that right, Pearl?"

"Now Morris, don't be funny. Let's take a picture. Everyone go into the living room," said Pearl, dashing out the door and immediately returning with a camera.

"I love you, and you make me proud," said Caroline, kissing Steven on the lips.

Pearl placed the camera on an end table, pointed it toward the sofa, then set the timer. The men sat on the sofa and their wives sat on their laps. Pearl rushed to sit on Morris's lap just before the camera clicked.

"This'll be the shot of the century," said Morris. "Get up, Pearl. My old thighs can't take it anymore."

"Neither can my buttocks," said Pearl, rubbing her cheeks.

"Y'know," confessed Morris, "if we had gone to court, I think it would have killed me. Thank God I'm still here. I want to stick around to see all of you grow. We're six now, and soon we'll be eight."

"No, Dad. Nine," said Deborah.

"Where do you get nine?" said Morris, confused.

"We're having twins," said Deborah and Robert in unison, and everyone laughed and began dancing around the living room.

AMBITION

Jack and Helen White lived in a comfortable house built to their specifications and filled with expensive furnishings. The kitchen had the latest imported appliances, all in stainless steel. A mahogany table, rimmed with pearl inlay, commanded the dining room. Jack and Helen's guests, Dan and Anna Black, had just risen from the hand-carved mahogany chairs to retire to the living room.

"Make yourself comfortable," said Jack, gesturing to the sumptuously upholstered sofa and chairs around an enormous rose-tinted glass cocktail table. "How about an after dinner drink, Dan? Anna?"

"No thanks, Jack," said Anna. She sat upright, refusing to submit to the welcoming soft upholstery. This was her first visit to her husband's boss's home, and a white home at that.

"Sure thing," said Dan, sinking into one of the chairs. Relaxed, Dan basked in the Whites' acceptance. Although Dan reported to Jack in the company, he felt free to be himself in their relationship. The two couples had become close friends.

"How about you, Helen?" asked Jack.

"Of course not. You know how I hate that stuff," Helen replied sharply. She detested that Jack included her in his ritual. And she resented more that he carried on an act of pretense: They were not a happy couple, yet she went along.

"Just thought I'd try. You know, help celebrate Dan's joining my department," said Jack, hoping to make her feel guilty for not participating.

"I'll celebrate with water," Helen said, forcing her tight, thin face into a smile for her guests. She adjusted her neatly coiffured hair.

"Now folks, I don't need to celebrate," said Dan, trying to ease the visible tension between his hosts. "It's enough to know that Jack has given me an opportunity to show what I can do."

Jack poured drinks and handed one to Dan. "I asked for you because I know you can handle it," Jack said. "I've been watching you out on the road, watching how you've managed to expand your territory despite, well, your visible handicap. You're always on top of things. You're dependable, and everything you do is in an orderly fashion—all features of a successful executive."

Jack dropped onto the couch, drink in hand, and gazed approvingly at Dan.

"That's my husband. I'm proud of you, too, dear," said Anna, gazing at Dan adoringly. How handsome he is, she thought, lean and tall, such strong Negroid features, quite different from hers, which were aquiline. She was lighter skinned and could almost pass for white.

"Thanks, Anna, but I wish you two would stop laying it on. If I were white, you'd see me blushing. But I want to thank you, Jack. It's a courageous thing you're doing. You must know you're taking a chance bringing me in."

To make sure that Jack would stick by him under any circumstances, Dan aired his reservations right off. He had been betrayed more than once in previous jobs.

"How so?" asked Jack. "My decision is based strictly on your performance and qualifications," Jack said in his best executive mode.

"C'mon, Jack. You know what I'm saying."

"Your color is not a factor," Jack said categorically.

"Sure it is." Dan laughed. "It has to be."

These white liberals live in denial, thought Dan. He knew that with them his color was an advantage. And what's wrong with that?

"In business, as far as I'm concerned, all that matters is a person's competence. You rise or fall on that basis," Jack said.

Dan prided himself on his realistic assessment of what life was like in 1970s American society. Accepting his blackness as a handicap, knowing the constraints it imposed, he devoted his energies to cleverly working around it. "You and I know that not everyone sees it that way," he said. "There's going to be resentment, I can tell you from experience. I can just imagine how my white colleagues feel, the ones you passed over. And do you realize that even my own people resent my success, the fact that I wear a business suit and drive a high-priced car?"

"It's true that the neighbors and friends we had when we were struggling no longer talk to us," added Anna. "I don't understand it. We're still the same, but you'd think we've become royalty or something. It's very sad."

In fact Anna had tried to persuade her husband to move to a white neighborhood to get away from the bad feelings. But Dan feared that would be worse.

"Yes, it's a rotten shame," Helen said. "I can sympathize, Anna. When we were first married, Jack and I were victims too, not of our own people but of the rest of society."

"That's hard to believe. I mean you seem so...so accepted. Why were you victims of —"

"We're Jewish," said Helen.

"Oh, I didn't know."

In all the time they had known each other—the Christmas parties they attended sitting at the same table, the gatherings at the CEO's house—wasn't it remarkable that this fact hadn't been recognized? Of course, Jack had never brought it up, and Helen certainly hadn't. Just as Dan wanted white acceptance, so Helen wanted WASP acceptance.

"How could you have known? We have a good, neutral, Anglo-Saxon name. It used to be Whitman. And we don't look Jewish—that is, after I had my nose operation."

"I look Jewish, though, wouldn't you say?" Jack said, turning his face so that all could see his profile. Although he catered to Helen's ambition to fit in, it was not his issue.

"Exactly what is the Jewish look?" asked Dan.

"See this nose? It's a Jewish nose," Jack said sarcastically. He stood up and turned completely around so that his nose was visible from all angles. "More like a Roman's or an Arab's or an Englishman's or maybe a Hottentot's," he said, indicating how ridiculous nose labeling was. "In any case, until I changed my name to White, it was a Jewish nose. As you say, Anna, we're accepted—now."

Sinking back again into the depths of the couch and sipping his drink, Jack felt good about his liberal leanings, his sympathy for the underdog. He went on.

"My grandparents who came over from Lithuania still kept to the ways of the old country. That's what they called it, the 'old country.' And my father, who fought in World War II, became the first generation of assimilated Americans. But they were still excluded. It took two generations for us to become generally accepted on an equal footing with the establishment. Of course, there are exceptions out there, but you rarely know who they are. So you and Dan are where my parents were, and where Helen and I were when we started out."

Yes, Jack understood their plight; he had made it despite his handicap, and he was proud. America had come a long way since his parents' day. Although Helen had to work at fitting in, Jack felt as though he had arrived.

"Well, that's not quite the way it is," Dan objected. "Sure we're assimilated. We've had eight or nine generations, maybe more, to do it in. Not all in my generation are sure that they want acceptance, that they want to join your society. It may be that gaining acceptance is insurmountable. Unlike you, we wear our Jewish noses all over our skin."

"I see. Then I should ask, where do you stand?" asked Jack, curious and surprised at Dan's resistance.

"I'm testing. When you pass me over the white guys, there's got to be resentment. It may be too much to take. I may be doomed; only time will tell. I may have been better off where I was, working the road alone."

Dan gulped down his drink. He realized he was close to turning down his advancement. His very ambition could well be the cause of his ultimate defeat; he could lose what he had. Yet he had to be honest and make Jack realize that he would accept the job only with Jack's total support against any future obstacles.

"You were happy there, Dan," said Anna, as if reading her husband's mind. "I don't want to see you get frustrated and angry, the way you used to be. Remember how you got nowhere in every job you had even though you were better than most of the others? All I want is peace. I'll love you even if you have to sweep the streets."

Anna moved to sit on the arm of her husband's chair and held his hand.

"Anna, you shouldn't give in," Helen proclaimed, gazing at Jack. "Behind every successful man is a woman. I've encouraged my husband every step of the way in his climb to near the top. And I expect some day he'll become president of the company. I just know it. You must change your attitude for Dan's sake."

"Look, Dan, I know how you feel," said Jack, standing to refill his glass. "I've been there. I remember what it was like when the other kids in school called me 'Kike' and 'dirty Jew' and 'Christ killer.' And I remember when the members of the country club in our town blackballed my father. So all the Jews got together and formed their own club. You realize it's people's ignorance and learn to ignore it. Bear in mind, I'll be there behind you."

Jack had good reason to feel triumphant about himself. He understood Dan's plight, and wanted to make sure Dan knew it.

"You mean protect me?" said Dan, suppressing a rising anger. "Thanks, but I don't want anyone's protection. I want to make it on my own."

But Dan knew that his argument was somewhat specious. The truth was he didn't trust anyone, least of all an upper-class white liberal.

"No one makes it on his own," said Jack unequivocally. "Where did you get such an idea? Everyone who's made it had someone who took an interest in him—a sponsor, so to speak—someone who recognized his talents and gave him a boost, a chance. When and if I move up, you'll move up with me. That's the way it works, see?"

"You'd make a great CEO, Jack," Dan said in all sincerity. Jack was convincing. Maybe he was secure under Jack's wing. "Doesn't Bossman plan to retire one of these days?"

"I admit I'd like the job, but I wouldn't be surprised if he died in the saddle. Anyway, he's not that old. The company is his sole interest, it's his life."

It was Jack's, too, although he hadn't recognized it. He had never worked anywhere else. Having a fragile marriage, he found his greatest satisfaction on the job.

"Just a minute. What about the conversation I had with him at his birthday party?" said Helen.

"He just talks. I told you not to take him seriously," said Jack, intentionally putting her down. She was always driving him. Her ambition to see him top man drove him to distraction.

"He told me he's grooming Jack to replace him when he retires," Helen said, addressing Dan and Anna.

"The key phrase is 'when he retires,'" said Jack sourly.

"He's sixty-eight. Why do you doubt him?" said Helen, raising her voice, reviving a constant argument between them. "Why are you so cynical about this?" She couldn't understand why Jack took such a negative view of things, why he fought her concerning what he wanted most. "He owes you," she continued. "After all you put up with over the years, all the shit, the groveling—"

"Shut up, Helen," Jack said harshly. "You don't know the man. I do."

"There's a rumor around the company that you'll be our next CEO, Jack," said Dan, hoping again to ease the atmosphere. "And it will be soon."

"Yeah? Well, if it happens, you'll step right into my vice-president's slot. So if you want to dream a little—"

"Let's drink a toast to that," Helen said, grateful for Dan's remark. "Here's to the company's next president and vice president. Pour me a little something now, Jack. What about you, Anna?"

"I don't drink, Helen," she said.

"Well, it's time you started. If you're going to be a vice-president's wife, you must drink something—wine at least. Pour her some wine, Jack." After everyone had a glass, Helen made a toast. "To Jack and Dan, the company's next president and vice president."

"What's his mood this morning?" Jack asked Sally Love, who was seated at her desk just outside Bossman's office. She was slender and petite and full of efficiency.

"Shh, not so loud," Sally said, looking at her watch. "Better get in there. You know how he is about not being late."

"See you tonight?" asked Jack.

"You're free? On a Friday night?"

"I can manage it."

"I can hardly wait," she whispered. "I've missed you so. Now, go."

After knocking on the office door, Jack entered to find Christopher Bossman seated at his desk reading a file of letters. A full head of wavy silver hair capped his wrinkled face, which had gone flabby from having recently lost weight. After several minutes

Bossman raised his head. "Have a seat, Jack," he said, then returned to what he was reading. Finally after several more minutes he faced his visitor. "Do you have any idea why I asked to see you this morning?"

"Either to raise my pay or fire me," Jack responded, sitting with one leg over another as they both laughed.

"You're half right."

"You mean I'm fired?" said Jack confidently.

"Yes, you're fired."

Jack was momentarily caught off guard. "I see. Well, I was only kidding," he said. "My god."

"I'm not kidding. You're fired from your present job, Jack. I'm moving you up. How long have you been with us? Twenty years?"

"Twenty-five, Chris."

"That long? You started with us selling on the road. Fresh from B School, as I recall."

"That's right," Jack said. Hadn't he spent his entire career with the company? Hadn't he given Bossman the best years of his life? Why couldn't Chris say that to him? Jack scanned the teak-paneled office with its couch and custom-made visitors' chairs as if searching for the courage to speak the words.

"And you've held about every middle-management job in the company," said Bossman, glancing at the papers before him.

"Just about, except janitor." They both laughed. There was a time long ago, before business school, when he would have taken a janitor's job and been thankful. Ambitious though he was, he was willing to start at the bottom then. But as he rose in the ranks, Helen's ambition surpassed his own. To be a janitor—now that would show Helen a thing or two.

"Do you remember what you wrote on your job application when we first hired you?" said Bossman with a grin.

"I hate to think. I was a brash kid then, full of ambition, my future spread out before me. Raring to go. I could have said anything."

"You did," said Bossman admiringly. "One of the questions on the application was—and still is, by the way—'What position in the company do you aspire to?' And you answered, 'President.' See?" He handed Jack a paper from the file he was reading, but his hand trembled and he dropped the paper in Jack's lap.

"God, I had balls."

"No, Jack, you knew what you were capable of. And you've stuck with me. I bet you've had offers through the years. Is that right?" he asked, meeting Jack's eyes.

"Occasionally," said Jack, lying. He had never been pursued, nor did he pursue.

"I'm curious. Why did you stay? Most men of your generation try to better themselves by moving from one company to another."

"I stayed for the good pay and challenging assignments, and because I kept moving up. But I stayed for you most of all. Don't get me wrong: I'm not buttering you up when I say I've always considered you capable and fair."

He stood and returned the paper to Bossman.

"Well, thank you, Bossman said. "I don't always succeed, but I try."

Bossman considered himself a topnotch executive. Although he had inherited the business from his father-in-law, he had made it grow so that it hardly resembled the company it was when he assumed command.

"You must know I've liked you from the beginning," Bossman continued. "I like your style. But that's not why I've kept you around. I'm more practical than that. I knew the day would come when I'd have to step aside and replace myself. And I think now I'm ready to do that."

"Well, to tell the truth I think I'm ready, too, Chris. I've been ready for some time," Jack said, not sure whether his words sounded arrogant, but what did it matter?

"Is that so?" Bossman said with a laugh. "You still have balls, Jack."

"Is that so bad?"

"Oh, I'm not being critical." Bossman tented his hands. "It's what it takes to run this outfit. You know as well as anybody that you have to walk over bodies to reach the top, and you'd better bury them in order to stay there. Running a business from the top is merciless."

"I don't think I've operated that way." Jack said, repelled by Bossman's philosophy. "For me, patience does it. I've left no bodies in my wake." His conscience was clear. His decency was overwhelming.

"No? You'd better look again. Are you forgetting what happened to Gary when you took over his job?" said Bossman gruffly.

"I thought he retired," said Jack. "Couldn't take the pressure, was burned out. That's what he said." Indignant at Bossman's suggestion, Jack returned to the chair and sat stiffly erect.

"Retire at fifty-two? Don't you believe that.? Pressure? He put it on himself. I had to can him. You were there, ready. Now you've held his job for the past five years. What's it done to you?" Bossman slapped the top of his desk in emphasis. "Hell, it's agreed with you. You're better than ever."

"I see Gary once in a while. He still hasn't found a decent job. At his age—"

"Either you make it by then, or you're finished." Bossman closed the folder on his desk and slipped it into a drawer. "The only way left is down. Those who make it by their mid-fifties, like you, are old enough to have good judgment and young enough to have the energy to use it. When you get as old as I am, you still have the judgment but, well, a lot of the energy's gone. You start seeing what you've missed outside the business, things you didn't have time to do but always wanted to, and you decide you'd better go for it before it's too late." Becoming pensive, he fingered his desk calendar. "Maybe for me it is too late."

"Why do you say that?" Jack asked. "You still have plenty of vigor. Hell, I can't keep up with you."

"You haven't tried lately," Bossman said with a tinge of sadness.

"So what are your plans, Chris?"

"I'll move up to chairman, do some traveling with my wife, spread goodwill around the world about our company. Make sure you're doing a good job."

Jack took a deep breath. Reality had suddenly struck. "Okay, Chris. When do I start?"

"When do you think you can be ready?"

"Right away, actually. I've already got the perfect man to fit into the vice-president's slot." This was like a happy dream. Everything was falling into place. All he had ever wanted, all Helen had ever wanted, and, yes, all Dan had ever wanted would now be realized.

"Good, then you can take over on Monday." Chris stood up, signaling the end of the discussion. "I know this may seem rather sudden, but I have reasons for wanting you in this chair right away, reasons I'd rather not discuss now but will become clearer in time."

"Well, I'd like to have a week to acquaint my replacement with what I've been doing."

"And who might that be?"

"Dan Black. He came up from sales and has been my assistant for the past two years. Excellent man. Very bright, ambitious, a quick learner," said Jack, expecting to be praised for his foresight.

"Black, Black. Isn't he our token black employee?"

"I don't see him quite that way. As I said, he's very able," said Jack warily.

"A black man as an officer. Hmm. I don't think so, Jack." Bossman's face appeared troubled.

"What's his color got to do with it?" Jack demanded.

"I'm concerned about our company's image," said Bossman, sitting down. "He won't fit in socially. How can he entertain a customer at the country club? Not only that, there's a pile of prejudice out there, and his presence at such a high level will reflect on us."

"I've been grooming him for my job, and I promised him that someday after I moved up he'd take over," said Jack, standing at the edge of Bossman's desk.

"Pretty cocksure of yourself, aren't you?" Bossman snapped, piercing Jack with his gaze."

"As you say, I've got balls." Jack grinned, hoping to diffuse the issue.

"Listen, you'll be our president. That's all you need concern yourself with," Bossman said, leaning back in his chair.

"Well, I'm concerned about Dan. I gave him my word. I feel I owe him." It was a matter of honor to Jack.

But it wasn't a matter of honor to Bossman. Trustworthiness, yes, but for him honor had no place in business.

"That's no problem. It will be out of your hands. I'll take care of the matter," said Bossman firmly.

"How?"

"As I say, just leave it to me." Bossman rose from his seat and walked over to Jack, placing his arm over his shoulder as he led him to the door. "Now, rest over the weekend. When you come in on Monday, you'll be in charge of the whole works. What do you think of that?"

"Sure, the whole works, but it seems not all the works," said Jack without enthusiasm as he headed to the door.

"Everything has its limits. Life has its constraints. It will be your show, Jack. You have my word."

Bossman opened the door and Jack walked out. As he strode past Sally, she saw his troubled face. She knew why Bossman had wanted to see him. So why the look on Jack's face? She'd find out that evening.

As Sally was setting the dinner table for two, Jack, using his key, entered without knocking. The apartment was tastefully furnished; modern art adorned the walls. A Pullman kitchen adjoined a large room that was divided for dining and comfortable seating. A doorway at one end of the room led to the sole bedroom, where Jack had spent many weekday nights in Sally's arms.

"Oh, Jack, isn't it wonderful? she said, kissing him. "I knew you'd become CEO someday, and now here you are. Congratulations, darling."

"You knew before I did," Jack said, pulling out of her embrace.

"Of course, darling. Why are you surprised? Working for Chris, I know everything that goes on."

Indeed, Sally was Bossman's right hand. She knew every detail of the company's workings. And she was privy to all of Bossman's secrets, including a most crucial one, which she hadn't yet divulged to Jack.

"I suppose it was in the cards. Bossman likes me. I don't doubt that I deserve it. But everything boils down to politics. I think I got the position because I was smart enough to play up to him all those years."

Jack removed his suit jacket, unbuttoned his tie, and sank down on the couch. He was clearly deflated. It was hardly the reaction that Sally expected, and it confused her.

"Come on, Jack," said Sally as she placed two heaping plates of salad on the table. "You know it's more than that. He wouldn't have chosen you if you weren't capable."

"That's true, too. Anyway, whatever the reason, now I've made it. Hell, what do I care how."

"Why the lack of enthusiasm? I don't understand. We should celebrate, go dancing, do something that's fun," said Sally, taking both his hands in hers and pulling him from the sofa.

"I'd rather not, if you don't mind. We'll have dinner, and I'll spend the night. That's all I want. Tomorrow morning I'll go home."

"What's wrong, Jack? You seem, well, depressed."

"I'm not sure I'll really be in charge, that he'll actually turn over all the reins. It's a gut feeling."

Jack began pacing the room like a caged animal.

"Don't worry. Sure he will. After ten years of working for him, I know him better than anyone else. He's tired, Jack. He was always a patient man, but now he loses his temper often. Haven't you noticed how much time he takes off? He wants out. The other day when I walked into his office, he was trembling and couldn't stop. When I spoke, he ignored me, as if I wasn't there. He's not well, Jack."

"He seemed fine today, as sharp as ever."

"Yes, today he was his old self. But I don't think you have to worry about being in charge. You will be. And I can help."

"Well, I'm off to a bad start already," said Jack, sitting down at the table as Sally placed a plate of steaming spaghetti before him.

"How so?"

"He won't let me move Dan Black into my old job, make him a vice president," said Jack testily. A question flashed through his mind, gone as soon as it began: Was his problem with Dan's promotion or his own autonomy?

"I'm not surprised. He doesn't think much of blacks in business. You know that's why we don't have any—except Dan, our token," said Sally matter-of-factly.

"He's concerned about Dan's ineffectiveness because of his color and the prejudice out there."

"Don't you think he has a point?" said Sally, sitting down at the table across from Jack. Although she held nothing against black people herself, she realized that Bossman was not the sort of man who would risk a business advantage for a principle.

"Are you agreeing with him?"

"Absolutely not. I'm merely saying there's a reality that must be faced. He's simply not willing to pay the price."

"Don't you think he should?" asked Jack, holding a fork full of spaghetti in midair.

"Yes, I do."

"Well, that's a relief. These people must be given a chance. But it's more a personal matter. My own integrity is on the line. I promised Dan my old job; I've been grooming him for it for two years."

"Tell Chris how you feel, stand up to him," said Sally. Being courageous herself, she admired any act of courage on the part of others, although she was also practical.

"I did. He's adamant," said Jack, stuffing his mouth with food.

"So what are you going to do?" asked Sally, twirling the pasta around her fork.

"I don't know yet."

"Let it pass, Jack. Don't make a big deal out of this and risk the opportunity."

"How can I let it pass? I've waited more than twenty years for it. But I'm fighting him even before I've got the job. This is not the way to begin, damnit." He slammed his fork onto the table and quaffed some water from a glass.

"I'm sure Dan will understand if you explain the situation to him. He's probably run into this sort of thing a hundred times. They all have. He wouldn't want you to jeopardize your position to keep a promise." Sally daintily placed her fork full of pasta into her mouth.

"It's not that simple," Jack said, becoming increasingly exasperated the more he thought about his interview with Bossman. "If I'm supposed to be in charge, there can't be any exceptions."

"Why can't you bend a little once in a while?" Sally suggested, retrieving a slice of bread from the basket on the table.

"It's how I feel about myself," said Jack, lifting another fork full of spaghetti to his lips. "Can I take the job, knowing I may be overruled, my orders countermanded? I can't live with that. I need Dan to be second in command."

Sally sighed. "I know you'll do what's right."

"And what do you think that is?"

Sally bent across the table and kissed him despite his mouth being full. "Let's finish eating, then go to bed. I'm hungry for you as well as dinner."

"You haven't answered my question," Jack insisted.

"Whatever you decide will be right. I'm with you either way."

"Even if I turn down the job?" said Jack, having worked himself into entertaining the idea.

"Even if you have to become a street bum."

"If I don't take the job, at my age there may not be any other alternatives, you know." Age was Jack's biggest enemy, and his biggest fear. But how big was yet to be learned.

"Don't be dramatic, Jack. Let's eat and make love."

The next morning, Saturday, Jack slipped the key into the door of his own home. There he found Helen, neat and prim as usual, sitting in the living room knitting. She was used to such morning arrivals, although not usually on weekends.

"You didn't call last night. Where were you?" Helen demanded.

"I told the receptionist to call and tell you I had to stay over in the city. Didn't she call?" Jack stood at the entrance to the living room, making no move to come in.

"Of course not. Why do you think I'm asking?" Helen said icily.

"Well, I'm sorry."

"So am I. Don't you think you're staying over a lot lately?"

"It's the job," said Jack, turning to leave.

"The kids never see you," said Helen, raising her voice. "We haven't had dinner together as a family in months. I may as well be a widow."

Jack swung around. "What do you expect? You wanted the house, the cars, the boat, the summer place, the condo in Florida. You don't get all this by screwing off."

"Why can't I have all this *and* you?" Helen said, putting down her knitting to concentrate on her husband. "Why does it have to be either or? It seems the higher up you move, the less we see you." Sensing a full-fledged fight about to begin, Helen felt helpless to find a way to stanch it.

"How many times have I told you it's the price you have to pay when you move up the ladder?" Jack said, his words taking on a recognizable sameness. "My job is a twenty-four-hour affair. That's what it takes to succeed at it. That's business. I don't know any other way."

Although he knew that his excuse was phony, Jack had used it so often that he believed it.

"I don't think Chris works as hard as you do, and he's president," said Helen, repeating her oft-expressed admiration for Bossman. She simply couldn't resist a rebuttal.

"You're wrong. He's had it. He's stepping down," said Jack, relishing being able to give her news that she hadn't yet heard.

"No! Why, he's not that old, is he?"

"He's got twelve years on me."

To Jack, he and Bossman seemed generations apart, perhaps because of Bossman's fatherly quality, or perhaps because of his dominant position.

"That isn't old," said Helen.

"It is for some men, maybe most men. Anyway, he wants me to be CEO."

"CEO? You, CEO! That's marvelous. I just knew it would happen some day. Finally! When do you start?"

She jumped up from her chair and wrapped her arms around Jack. This was Helen's dream, the culmination of her wifely ambition that one day she would be the woman behind the top man.

"Right away. Monday."

"Oh, Jack, it's what you've always wanted. To run the whole show. That's how you are, you know."

No need to mention that it's what she always wanted, of course.

"How am I?"

"Controlling. You're very controlling," Helen said, withdrawing her embrace.

"That's your opinion. I don't see myself that way."

"I'm not surprised. You're not one to look at yourself objectively."

"Is that so? And you do?" said Jack, steaming. "By the way, I may have to stay over even more often now."

"I don't see why. After all, you'll be the big cheese. You can delegate some of your duties to someone else. Isn't that the sign of a good executive?"

Smart lady, thought Jack. Of course she's correct. "That's not the way it works," he said. "More responsibility demands more time, not less. Anyway, I'm not sure I'll take the position."

Jack threw out this last idea more to aggravate Helen than to consider it. It was only a possibility.

"What? Not sure? How can you say that?" said Helen, verging on outrage. "It's what you've been aiming toward all your working life. How many times have I heard you say you have to be top man, chief honcho, before you die? It's been your dream."

"Yes, that's true. But I didn't count on the price I'd have to pay."

"What are you talking about?"

"I'll have to sacrifice Dan Black."

"I don't understand. He called last night."

"What did he want?" said Jack, alarmed. He wondered whether Bossman had already taken action. And if he had, that could well clinch his decision to reject Bossman's offer.

"He didn't say. He seemed agitated. He said he has to talk to you and would call this morning."

"Good, I want to talk to him, too."

"What's going on? Let me in on it, for god's sake," said Helen.

"Chris won't let me move him into my old position, and unless that happens I know Dan will quit. You know I told him he had the job. He's counting on it."

"So he'll find another job. He's a bright, capable young man," said Helen, failing to see her husband's dilemma.

"Exactly. Perfect for the job. So he's being penalized for his color."

"That's not your concern," said Helen, wishing the matter would disappear. "After all, it's Chris's company. You have to do things his way, the way you always have."

"No, if I'm going to be in charge, I have to do things my way. That's the real issue," said Jack.

"I know. As I said, you are a controlling person. And it drives me wild sometimes. So don't let it kill this chance, maybe the only chance you'll ever have, to be the president of a company. Listen to me, Jack. Are you listening?"

"I have to do what I have to do, what I can live with," said Jack emphatically. Helen's argument only stiffened his resolve to do what he wanted regardless of her wishes.

"What does that mean?"

"It means..." He hesitated. "I don't know what I'll do."

The doorbell rang, breaking off the conversation that was surely headed into another storm.

As Helen went to answer the door, Jack sat down and closed his eyes. He was in a quandary. Hearing Dan's voice, he opened his eyes and raised his head, dreading what was bound to follow.

Helen returned to the living room with Dan in tow. "Speaking of the devil, look who's here," she said.

Rising from his chair, Jack extended his hand, which Dan refused. Jack searched his friend's face. "What's wrong, Dan?"

"You know damn well what's wrong," Dan replied.

"Here, sit down. Please sit down. What happened?"

Dan remained standing. "C'mon, Jack, stop pretending you don't know."

"Know what? I swear I don't know what you're talking about," said Jack, aware that he was being honest only in a technical sense.

"Goddamned hypocrite, giving me the line that you've been there and all that shit. You're all the same, you whites, and you Jew whites are the worst hypocrites of all."

Jack rose as if to do battle. "Just a minute, Dan—"

"You're insisting on playing this thing out, aren't you?" Dan said.

"So help me, I have no idea—"

"You want to hear me say it? Okay, I've been fired," Dan shouted into his face.

"Fired? Who fired you?" Jack said, maintaining the fiction of his ignorance.

"You, you sonofabitch."

Jack reeled at Dan's accusation. "Hell, I did."

"At five yesterday a memo appeared on my desk dismissing me. Something about downsizing. My severance pay, and a letter of reference signed by you. I called last night, but Helen said you weren't here. Didn't want to face me, huh, Jack?"

Jack sat down and tried to sort out his confusion. Obviously, Bossman made him a patsy. "Certainly not," he said. "I wasn't here. It couldn't have been my signature, Dan. I had nothing to do with this."

"As for downsizing, it's the first I've heard of it," said Dan. "You never said anything about it. Who else is being let go, Jack?"

"No one that I know of. Not even you, as far as I'm concerned." Jack reached to touch Dan's arm.

"Then what's this?" Dan said as he thrust the memo into Jack's hands.

"That's not my signature," said Jack. "It's a stamp. Christ, this is terrible. I'm sorry, Dan. I'll look into this first thing on Monday."

"You do that, because if I don't have my job back I'm suing the company and you personally for discrimination. Do you understand?" Dan threatened.

"Calm down," Jack implored, trying to find an opening.

"Calm down? How can you expect me to be calm? After the years I've put in, working my ass off, thinking I had a future. You've just been leading me on. What a damn fool I've been."

Dan's words pierced Jack like bullets. "I don't blame you for the way you feel. Look, I'm sure I can fix it. Someone's made a terrible mistake."

"Yeah, and it's you." Dan was relentless.

"It isn't. I swear."

"Well, the proof's in what happens next, eh? If you're not responsible for this, then you can correct it, right?"

"I said I would. I'll do my level best to make it right," said Jack, anticipating a confrontation with Bossman.

"Your level best isn't good enough," said Dan. "Just make it right." He turned to leave.

"I'll show you out," said Helen.

"Never mind. I know the way. Don't I, Jack? The way out," said Dan as he slammed the door behind him.

"Who did this?" asked Helen.

"Bossman. Who else?" Jack said bitterly. "And he had the gall to do it under my name when he knew damn well how I felt."

"Can you get Dan his job back?"

"Not a chance. Once Bossman makes up his mind, the decision is irreversible."

"But Dan will sue you," Helen said, fearful of the publicity as well as the cost.

"I'm not involved in this, and I can prove it. There's nothing to worry about," said Jack confidently.

They sat on the couch next to each other, the closest they had been in weeks.

"What about your new job? As I see it, you must back up Bossman," said Helen, always the pragmatist.

"It's out of the question. He'll keep interfering. I don't want the job," said Jack, spontaneously making up his mind.

"Don't be so hasty. If you turn it down, I'm afraid to think what will happen."

"I'll be finished. It's obvious," said Jack. "I'll have to leave the company."

He envisioned the end of his career. But the alternative, to be Bossman's rubber stamp, was impossible.

"I want you to take the job," Helen said without equivocation. "Where can a man your age find something as good? I read how companies want to hire only young men. If you don't put aside this incident with Dan and accept Chris's offer, you'll be impossible to live with, I know. If you say that none of this is your doing, then what's the problem?"

"The problem is me, Helen. It's the way I am. This thing with Dan is an indicator for how things will be in the future." If you don't see how impossible the whole thing is, I have nothing more to say."

Jack got up and strode toward the door. "I'm going for a walk," he said. "I don't know when I'll be back. Forget about making lunch."

First thing Monday morning, Jack headed for Bossman's office.

"You said you could get away Sunday," Sally said as he approached her desk. "You didn't call."

"I'm sorry," he replied. "You know I've been preoccupied."

"What's wrong? Is she putting pressure on you?"

"Nothing like that. I'll tell you after I see him."

"I'd like to kiss you," Sally said coquettishly.

"No, Sally," said Jack, all business. "I'm in no mood to play."

"I'm not playing," Sally said. Then she realized that there was some kind of trouble afoot. "Never mind," she said. "He's waiting for you."

Bossman was standing, looking out a window, when Jack entered. He turned. "Ah, Jack, what's on your mind?" He directed him to sit on the couch opposite his desk. "You've got some ideas on how to expand our company, I'll bet. Well, that's fine. That's what bringing in young blood is all about. So tell me what you're thinking."

"Dan tells me he's been fired," Jack replied, ready for battle. He sat with his arms spread across the back of the couch.

"Is that what he said? That isn't how I'd put it. He's a casualty of downsizing. I've merely begun a process that I knew you'd introduce as soon as you took the helm. We've grown fat, Jack. If I remained CEO, I'd be doing something about it."

Bossman walked to his desk and slowly, cautiously, lowered himself into his chair.

"Who else is being let go?" Jack demanded.

"At this moment no one, but, as I say, you'll be doing the rest," Bossman said.

"You know I had plans for Dan."

"And you know I didn't agree with your plans."

"But you didn't have to let him go. I might have found a way to make him happy," said Jack, containing his anger.

"And you might not have. Then you'd have had no other option but to do what I did. He was a problem about to happen. I decided, especially where you had a conflict, to rid us and you of the problem before it developed. Good management practice, that's what I'd call it."

Jack had to admire Bossman's rationale. He knew that this man was no pushover, but he couldn't let it go. He'd see it through to wherever the argument brought him, even to his departure.

"You didn't have to do it in my name."

"Who else's? You were his superior; he worked in your department," Bossman countered.

"I think you've done a low-down thing, Chris. You've hurt a qualified man, and you've damaged my credibility," said Jack, getting down to the nub of his complaint.

"Your credibility?" Bossman inquired. "How is that affected? He's gone. Only he knows what happened. No one else knows. I'm sure the other execs are happy to see him gone. You were passing him, a black man, over them. I've been told there was resentment. And if he's the good man you say he is, he'll have no trouble finding another job. Your reference letter can only help him."

"Don't call it my letter," said Jack. He was bursting to blow.

"Well, you would have given him a good reference, wouldn't you? So what's your problem?"

Jack met Bossman's eyes squarely, "You are, Chris."

"Me!" Bossman laughed. "I'm not your problem, Jack. I'm your future."

"I don't think so," Jack said, paving the way for his possible departure or, if his gamble succeeded, the alternative of having it all on his terms.

"What are you saying?" Bossman asked with alarm.

"I'm resigning, Chris."

"Hold on there, Jack."

"I don't want the job; I'm leaving."

"You're being ridiculous," Bossman said, baffled and frightened. "What's changed between Friday and today?"

"I suppose I have," Jack said. "Until now I've always done things your way. It's time I began doing things my way."

"Who's stopping you?" Bossman asked. "I told you you'd have a free hand running the business. It would be strictly your show."

"It's off to a pretty bad start, I'd say."

"Look, Jack, reconsider," said Bossman, trying in vain to conceal his anxiousness. "I didn't know how strongly you felt. This is only one incident, the first and last, I promise you."

"Then I can have Dan back?" said Jack, sensing Bossman's panic.

"That's a fait accompli. You go on from there," said Bossman, reverting to his customary self-confident manner.

"No. That's my condition. I insist that Dan be rehired and made my executive vice president."

"Impossible," said Bossman indignantly.

"Then it's over," said Jack, getting up from the couch and striding toward the door.

"Come back. Be reasonable, Jack. Look, there's more to this."

Bossman's hands began trembling, and the tremors spread to the rest of his body, devolving into involuntary, jerky motions. Jack turned, astonished at the sight of the seizure, watching as Bossman's torso gradually calmed.

"I...I'm not well," said Bossman. "Parkinson's. It's progressive. I can't go on much longer. Please, I need you; the company needs you."

Jack was startled "Parkinson's? How long—"

"The first signs began a couple of years ago. It seems I've got the worst kind."

"I'm sorry to hear that, Chris. But unless you agree to my condition—"

"Goddamnit Jack," said Bossman, regaining his old vigor. "Aren't you listening? I'm going downhill, becoming useless. Soon I'll be little more than an uncontrollable zombie. I have no future. But you have. I'm giving it to you. Are you willing to let it slip through your fingers because of a fucking black man who probably hates your white guts? Wake up, son."

"Are you willing to let me go because I have the need to stand by my commitment to another human being? I don't care what color he is," Jack said defiantly.

"You're a crazy idealist. There's no room for idealists in business, Jack. It's all a matter of survival; it starts with the individual and extends to the organization. If you don't see that, then maybe you've been the wrong man all along."

"Maybe you're right. The wrong man for you." Jack extended his hand across Bossman's desk for a final handshake, which Bossman refused. "Good-bye, Chris. I'm sorry about your illness."

He crossed the room and strode out the door leaving Bossman shouting into the air after him, "Jack, Jack, you're passing up the opportunity of a lifetime. You'll never find one to equal it again. You're a damn fool, Jack. Hear me, Jack. You're a goddamn fool. You're throwing away twenty-five years. I thought you had more sense." There was a pause then he muttered, "Well, you're not the only flower in the garden."

"What's he shouting about?" Sally asked as Jack went to her desk, pulled her up from her chair, and kissed her. "What are you doing, Jack? What's happened?"

"It's over, Sally. I'm through."

"He fired you?"

"I quit," said Jack proudly. "I'm a free man, free as a feather."

"Why? Tell me. What about me? What should I do?" Sally said, fearing that his leaving might well have an adverse effect on their relationship.

"Stay where you are. It's a good job. He needs you now more than ever."

"You'll take me with you wherever you go, won't you?" Sally pleaded.

"Of course," said Jack unconvincingly.

"I'll miss seeing you every day. I'll miss you, darling."

"Same here."

"I'll still have you one or two nights a week, won't I."

"Well, not for a while," said Jack, anticipating her protest. "Until I find a job, I have no excuse to stay over."

"Oh, Jack, I'm losing you. I'm afraid. I want you. Please don't abandon me."

"I'll be in touch. Just give me some time."

"That's my enemy," said Sally, turning away from Jack and staring at the floor.

"Enemy?"

"Time," she said, holding back an urge to cry.

Jack went home to relax and sort out what had transpired, and to begin thinking about what to do next. He found Helen sitting in the living room, knitting and watching TV, as usual.

"You're home at this hour?" she said, looking at her watch. "Something's wrong. What's wrong? Are you ill?"

"Do I look sick?"

"You look strange."

"How so?"

"You look...well...beaten, depressed," said Helen, her eyes exploring every facet of his face.

"I'm not depressed," said Jack with conviction.

"But something's wrong," Helen insisted, able to read her husband's moods from long experience.

"That depends on how you see it."

"See what?" Helen said impatiently. "For god's sake, stop it. Something's wrong. What is it?"

"Nothing's wrong. I just quit the company."

"You what?" said Helen, incredulous.

"You heard me."

"Are you out of your mind?"

"Maybe, maybe I am," said Jack, enjoying the outrageousness of his act.

"But why?" Helen said more calmly. "I can't imagine any possible reason to toss all those years of work and sacrifice into the ash heap."

"Bossman and I simply don't agree on some fundamental matters."

"Such as? What matters can be so fundamental that you'd quit?" Helen pursued.

"You know what it is: He fired Dan over my objection. Don't you get it?"

"I get it," said Helen. "Bossman's preempting your position. It's your pride then. That's all it is."

"Yes, he's preempting my authority, and it's not my pride. It's a matter of right and wrong. It's the principle of the thing," said Jack, turning to leave the room.

"So for the sake of a minor principle, you've given up the position you've been working toward forever. I don't understand you."

"I know you don't, Helen," said Jack, stopping in his tracks and turning to her. "And I don't expect you to."

"What are you going to do now?" said Helen coldly.

"I'll find a job."

"A CEO's job?"

"Possibly, possibly, though unlikely, I admit."

"You'll have to drop down a peg or two," Helen warned.

"Or three, maybe. I'd also consider going into business...if I could raise the capital."

Putting her knitting aside, Helen stood up and went right up to him. "I'm very disappointed in you," she said. "Very disappointed. I thought you were a star, but really you're no more than a...a sad failure."

"I'm sorry, Helen. But that's the way it is," said Jack sincerely.

"When are you going to grow up, learn to compromise?"

"Hell, I've compromised for most of my career. It's time I stopped."

Helen had to agree. She knew well her husband's long history of frustration with Bossman's arbitrary edicts.

The doorbell rang. "I'll get it," he said.

Jack was startled to see Chris's wife as he opened the door. "June Bossman! What a surprise," Jack shouted so that Helen could hear. "Come in, come right in."

"Hello, June. Come, sit next to me," invited Helen.

"Thank you," said June, a tall, handsome, gray-haired lady, athletic and smooth skinned. "I appreciate you're willingness to see me. And you, Jack."

"You knew June was coming?" Jack asked, suspecting a plot.

"Well, yes. June called, asking to come over and talk," Helen said defensively.

"Then you knew what happened right along," said Jack to Helen.

"Of course not."

"Jack, I didn't tell Helen why I wanted to see her. It has to do with you anyway. Now I can tell you both what's on my mind."

"Then you know what's happened between Chris and me?"

"Don't I now?" June said with irony. "Chris is devastated. He was counting on you."

"I'm sorry, June. Really sorry," Jack said.

"I know you are. Chris can be very obstinate."

"He's not the only one, I assure you," said Helen, meeting Jack's eyes.

"I came here to enlist Helen's help in persuading you to change your mind," said June.

"Hah," interjected Helen. "That's a joke, me change Jack's mind."

"Won't you, Jack?" June said. "Change your mind? Chris's days are over in the business. You are the perfect person, the only person who can keep the business prospering. Won't you stay, for my sake if not his; for the business's sake, for the sake of all the employees?"

"It has to be my show, June. Chris says he'll let go, but I don't believe he can, or will," Jack explained.

"Oh, he has to. You can be sure of that. Do you know he had a terrible attack after you left the office? I had to go there and take him home."

"I'm sorry to hear that. I didn't mean to make him—"

"Oh, it wasn't your fault. Anytime he gets upset it comes on," June said, then paused momentarily as she prepared the way to clinch her appeal. "Did you know that forty-nine percent of the stock in the company is in my name?"

"No, I didn't know. I always thought—"

"My father started the company. He took Chris into the business after we were married. When Dad retired, he turned the management over to Chris. In other words, my future, my income, my welfare are tied to the company's continued success. It's important to me that the management be in good hands. Do you understand what I'm saying?"

"Yeah, I do," Jack said, softening

"So you'd be doing it for June," said Helen, making sure that Jack saw it that way.

"That's right You'd be doing it also for me. I'd see to it that you get stock options. If you'll forgive me for being presumptuous, Jack, it's an opportunity that you're not likely to find anywhere else. Chris knows he has to let go, and he will whether he wants to or not."

Although June's winning civility and cleverness were gradually wearing down Jack's resistance, he was not ready to give in. He would play out his advantage for all he could get.

"Are you familiar with the Dan issue?" asked Jack. He saw Helen look toward the ceiling

"No. Who is Dan?"

"An African American, a good man, my former second in command whom I planned to move into my slot. Chris fired him—in my name, yet," said Jack, feeling hot just mentioning the incident.

"Why don't you hire him back?" asked June.

"Chris won't hear of it. He absolutely refuses."

"Well, that's too bad. I'm sorry for the man," said June, not rising to Jack's bait. "But Jack, don't you think with all that's at stake—the future of the company, your career, and my security—your decision shouldn't ride on a single issue of an arbitrarily fired employee? I'm appealing to you for your help, and I guarantee you will be rewarded for it. I know you have good sense, so, I beg you, please—"

"It would be for my sake, too," Helen put in. "It will restore my faith in you."

"If Chris will really step aside…"

"I assure you he will. He has no choice," promised June. "Physically. I want him to continue living his later years as comfortably as possible, without the stress of the business. He can't cope anymore. He was such a powerhouse, and now…how sad it is to watch him deteriorating. He doesn't want anyone to see."

Staring out the living room window toward the street, June became suddenly melancholy.

"So that explains why he's away from the office so much. I thought he was making deals," said Jack.

"Oh no, Jack. He tires so. He can only put in a few hours a week. He's home the rest of the time. I've insisted that we spend our remaining years together, just the two of us. He's promised that we shall, and I intend to hold him to it."

"I'd like to think it over. If I could be sure—"

"You have my word it will be as you wish it. Be our leader, Jack. Be our CEO," said June, every word filled with sincerity.

"You have to do it, Jack," said Helen. "How can you resist such an appeal?"

"Okay, you've convinced me. We've got a deal. I'll let Chris know in the morning," said Jack, feeling suddenly uplifted.

June stood, took Jack's hand, then embraced him. "Thank you, Jack. You won't regret it. But why don't you let him know now?"

"You mean phone him?"

"No, no," said June. "He's outside in the car waiting. I'll signal him to come in. Is that all right?"

"You mean he's been out there all along?" said Jack, astonished.

"He didn't think you'd want to see him."

"Well, of course have him come in," Jack said, feeling awkward.

At this June went to the door and called to Chris. "He'll be greatly relieved to know of your decision," she said as she turned to Jack.

Chris entered and kissed June on the cheek, shook Jack's hand vigorously, and embraced Helen. "From the happy looks on your faces, should I take it you've had second thoughts, Jack? We're in synch again?"

"Your wife is a super saleswoman," Jack responded. "She's very persuasive. I think I'll put her on the staff."

They all laughed. Humpty-dumpty seemed put back together.

"It's good to have you aboard again, Jack. The company's yours to run. You're the boss now," Bossman reiterated.

"The only boss, right?" said Jack, seeking confirmation that his terms were understood.

"Of course. There's only room for one. You and I know that, don't we?"

Bossman put his arm around Jack's shoulder. "You know, I've always thought of you as a son." He looked toward his wife, then added, "The son I never had."

"The son *we* never had," June said. "The son I could never give. I...I'm sorry, Chris. But we let that go a long time ago, didn't we?"

"I suppose so, but it no longer matters. Now we have a son just as good as one of our own flesh and blood," Chris said as he embraced Jack again. "I knew I could count on you. Thank you, my boy."

"It's what I've wanted, Chris. What I've been waiting for. Just let me do it my way, okay?"

"Certainly. Your way, no other. You have my word. Well, we must be off. I'll move the stuff out of my office so you can move in."

"You don't have to do that," said Jack, surprised. "Believe me, I'm fine where I am."

"Wouldn't hear of it," said Bossman. "Everybody knows that my office is the boss's office. It goes with the job. Now, you take the day off. Let's go, June. These kids have a lot to celebrate."

The older couple strode down the walk to their car. As they drove off, they waved back to Jack and Helen standing in the doorway.

"Isn't this wonderful?" said Helen, slipping her arm into Jack's. "I know you're doing the right thing. I can feel it in my bones."

"Some woman, that June," said Jack in genuine admiration.

"Yes, isn't she? But Chris deserves credit. After all, don't you think he put her up to it?"

"Sure, he did. He's an operator. He knows how to get to me."

"I'm proud of you, Jack."

"Why?" he asked, still smarting from their earlier argument. "I'm the same man you condemned a short while ago. What did you call me, 'a sad failure'? I haven't grown up."

"I didn't mean it," said Helen. "I was upset. It was foolish of me."

"Sure, sure," said Jack, unconvinced.

Dan always confided in his wife, Anna. They were truly a team doing battle against a prejudiced society as they struggled to rise within it, all the while dealing with the resentment of their own people for doing so. Anna saw her role as counterbalancing Dan's tendency to distrust people. By moderating his paranoia, she had certainly helped him advance in Bossman's company.

"I'm sure he's coming to offer you your job back," said Anna as they sat in their living room expecting Jack to arrive at any minute.

"Maybe," Dan said, skeptical as usual.

"Why are you so down on him? Isn't Jack a loyal friend?" Anna said.

"He was. I'm not so sure now."

"Come on, Dan. Don't be so cynical. Have you ever seen a sign of prejudice in him?

"No, but in a crisis the truth comes out. I trust whites only so far. The prejudice is there even when it's against their principles. They can't help it. It's ingrained." Dan removed a pen from his pocket and began nervously manipulating it between his fingers.

"I don't believe that," Anna said firmly.

"You haven't been out there, Anna. You don't know."

"He's here," Anna said, getting up to answer the doorbell. "Please come in, Jack. It's good to see you again."

"Likewise," said Jack, embracing Anna.

Jack walked up to Dan and extended his hand, but Dan remained in his chair and refused it. "Well, thanks for seeing me, Dan," said Jack.

"I'm always willing to listen."

"I know you are. That's why I called."

"Please sit down," said Anna, directing Jack to a chair. "Can I get you some coffee, tea?"

"No thanks. I can't stay long. How are you doing, Dan?"

"As well as can be expected." Dan shifted his pen from one hand to the other. "I've got a few feelers out."

"But nothing definite, eh?"

"Get to the point," Dan demanded. "Why are you here?"

Anna glared at Dan. "Don't be so pushy," she said.

"It's okay. I don't blame him," said Jack. "Listen, did you know I turned down the CEO job?"

"You did?" Dan said, looking flabbergasted. He returned the pen to his shirt pocket. "I don't get it. It's what you've been working toward for years. Everyone knows you're the best man; hell, you were groomed for it. Why did you turn it down?"

"Because Bossman fired you, that's why," said Jack, enunciating each word slowly to make his point.

Dan burst into laughter. "I don't believe this. You're the one who fired me."

"That's what I've been trying to tell you. I had nothing to do with it. I told Bossman I'd take the job only under the condition that I can hire you back. But he wouldn't hear of it."

"You actually quit on my account? Incredible!"

"That's right," said Jack, enjoying Dan's amazement. "The issue of your continued employment was pivotal; I saw that he had no intention of giving me a free hand."

"So now we're in the same boat," said Dan, beginning to warm to his adversary.

Jack shifted uncomfortably in his chair. "Well, not exactly."

"You found an opportunity elsewhere, is that it?" Dan said. "Hey, if it doesn't pan out, let me know. I can refer you to a good headhunter."

"Thanks Dan, but...well, it seems I'm going to be CEO after all."

"Congratulations, Jack," said Anna. "I'm happy for you. Then that means Dan—"

"You see, Bossman is seriously ill, Parkinson's, and deteriorating."

"What a shame," said Anna. "I'm sorry to hear that. Aren't you, Dan?"

"Yeah, I wouldn't wish it on anyone. Where does that leave me?"

"Given the situation, that the future of the company is at stake, I felt I had no choice but to accept the position," said Jack, uncomfortable at his weak attempt to justify himself.

"I see that, but—"

"I could do nothing about your situation," said Jack, evading Dan's eyes. "I'm sorry. Bossman was unyielding. Either I reject the job, or I accept it for the sake of the company's future, for the future of all the employees."

"You mean for the white employees, because that's all you have now, except for a few black laborers.

"Certainly not. Color wasn't a consideration," Jack objected.

"It is for me," said Dan, beginning to shout. "What other consideration is there?"

"I'm trying to explain, Dan. It's not what I wanted, but I had no choice. Would you have me let the company ultimately fail because of Bossman's growing incapacity?"

"Of course your ambition had nothing to do with your decision," Dan said sarcastically.

"Sure I'm ambitious. So are you," Jack shot back.

"Except I have limitations. It seems to me that you have terrific leverage. You could have it all your way. Am I right?"

"To a point. But not regarding you. As I said—"

"You're so self-righteous, so good intentioned, so pure," Dan sneered. "What about Sally, your little sideline? You're a pro at betrayal, Jack."

Jack turned red with anger. "You sonofabitch."

"I think it's time you left," said Dan, rising and moving toward the door. "No one swears at me, especially in my own home. I've heard enough."

"Forgive me," said Jack contritely. "I'm a little on edge."

"What have you got to be on edge about? You got what you wanted."

"I'm sorry you're taking it this way."

"There's no other way to take it," said Dan, positioning his face almost against Jack's. "Just leave. I'll see you in court."

Anna opened the door. "You'd better go, Jack. Give my best to Helen."

"Bring some sanity back to him, Anna."

"No, Jack. He is the way he is and I wouldn't dare change it. Good-bye." Closing the door behind Jack, she turned to Dan. "I apologize," she said.

"For what?"

"For being wrong. He could have insisted on taking you back, but he chose not to."

"Then you see the way it is."

"Yes, I see the way it is. He wouldn't stand behind you."

"I'm going to make them pay," said Dan with determination. "It will cost them plenty before I'm through."

"What good will that do? Why can't we just get on with our lives?"

"I want justice, that's all," said Dan.

"No, you want retribution. You don't believe in justice. You keep saying there isn't any." She took him by the arms and shook him.

"Yes, yes, that's true, there isn't. Goddamn their world. Whatever you want to call it, I need to settle this before I can go on."

"I know, darling. I know," said Anna, embracing him and pressing her lips to his.

Jack moved into Bossman's well-furnished office with little fanfare. The entire company accepted his role of CEO as perfectly natural. But for Sally, who was Jack's most dedicated booster, it spelled disaster.

"No, I don't understand why you hired her and didn't use me," she complained as she sat in front of Jack's, formerly Bossman's, desk.

"Because you're Chris's girl Friday," snorted Jack, as if no other explanation were needed.

"Mr. Bossman is hardly ever here. I sit twiddling my thumbs all day. Do you expect me to be happy doing nothing? Furthermore, I know the job. I'm familiar with everything that goes on. It's just common sense that as CEO you'd want me."

"I couldn't take you away from Chris," said Jack.

"For god's sake," said Sally, leaning into the desk, her annoyance mounting. "Didn't he suggest assigning me to you?"

"He didn't mean it. I happen to know that losing you would be a blow to his pride."

"How do you know?" said Sally with contempt.

"Well, I can put myself in his position."

"You're being ridiculous."

"I don't think so," said Jack with finality as he shuffled some papers.

"It's something else, isn't it, Jack?"

"Not at all. Now you're being ridiculous."

"Either you give me back my old job, or I'll have to leave," Sally threatened.

"You still have your old job."

"No, my old job is with the CEO. It's either or. I mean it."

"I don't like ultimatums, Sally," said Jack, his voice hard.

"Neither do I. You've got the job you want. Why can't I?"

The confrontation had gone on long enough for Jack. He was about to dismiss Sally regardless of the consequences when Bossman walked in.

"Hello, Sally," he said. "As soon as you two are done, I have something to discuss with you, Jack."

"Mr. Bossman, regarding your suggestion that I work for Jack—"

"I have no problem with that," said Bossman. "In fact, it's a good idea. Knowing the ropes as you do, Sally, you could be a great help to him. Take her, Jack, with my blessing. As you know, I can call on the rest of the staff to help me with the little I have to do."

"There, could it be any clearer?" Sally said, expecting that this would seal her wish.

"What's the problem?" Bossman asked.

"I'd like to talk to Chris alone, Sally. If you don't mind."

"I see," said Sally, hurt and confused. She rose abruptly from her chair and dashed from the office.

"It's not a good idea for Sally to work directly under me," said Jack.

"Why not? She's extremely efficient, and as I said—"

"I know how competent she is. It's not a matter of...Well, I don't know how to put it. In this job I've got to think straight, not let emotions get involved. You know that better than anyone."

"So what has Sally got to do with not thinking straight?" said Bossman innocently.

"We've...we've been sleeping together."

"You've been...For Christ's sake, Jack, haven't you learned you don't shit where you eat?" said Bossman, outraged.

"I know. That's why I don't want her around me on the job."

"Then you have to end the relationship. Will you do that?" said Bossman.

"I don't know. It all depends—"

"On what?" Bossman pounded his knuckles on his side of the desk.

"I need her," said Jack plaintively.

"Damnit, this is a complication I didn't expect. What about Helen? Does she know?" said Bossman, increasingly tense.

"I don't think so."

"But you don't know for sure?"

"Well, I think she suspects something," said Jack, being honest. "Our marriage isn't perfect."

"Sounds to me like it's damn imperfect. You realize that her role as the CEO's wife is critical to your job."

"I know, I know," said Jack apologetically. "Don't worry, I won't do anything to jeopardize the marriage."

"Then you'd better end it with Sally. What if Helen finds out? Sooner or later that's bound to happen." Bossman remained silent as he let his prediction sink in. "Do you hear me?" he pressed.

"Yes, I hear, but I can handle the situation, Chris. Don't worry."

"No, you don't handle it, you end it. Right away," Bossman ordered, pounding the desk again, but louder.

"Okay, Chris. I'll do what has to be done."

Bossman nodded. He was satisfied. "Now, let's get down to business. Next Monday we're having a visitor I'd like you to meet."

How clearheaded Bossman seemed, mused Jack. You'd never think he was ill. He was his old self again. And dangerous. Could June keep him in check, as she promised?

"Sure thing," Jack replied. "I'll mark it on my calendar. Who is he?"

"He's chairman of the SuperGeneral Corporation."

"The multinational? Don't they own our biggest customer?" asked Jack, warily.

"That's the one. I'll say nothing more until you two meet. I'll be away for a few days—we're going to Bermuda for a long weekend. Remember, do what I asked. And I'll see you next Monday."

Bossman, still disgusted with Jack, turned on his heel and disappeared through the doorway.

Immediately Jack picked up the phone. "Sally, would you come to my office, please? Yes, right now." He organized the papers on his desk, then went to a window that looked out on the company's parking lot. Studying the parked cars, he rehearsed in his mind what he would say. When Sally entered the office, his back was to the door.

She stood at the entrance. "After what Mr. Bossman said, do I have the job?"

"No, Sally. There's more to it," Jack said, whirling around and striding to his desk. "Please sit down."

"There's more to what?" said Sally, still standing. "It's very simple—"

"No, it's not," Jack cut in. He paused, then added, "We're lovers. That's not simple."

"That needn't interfere with my work. I'd never show my feelings while I'm here; I'd never embarrass you," Sally promised.

"The point is that it would interfere with my job, Sally. In my position I can't do anything that would jeopardize my marriage. Having you here next to me every day would be too risky."

"Jeopardize your marriage?" said Sally, her voice rising. "What marriage? You constantly tell me how miserable you are."

"It's true, but it's the price I must pay. I have no choice," said Jack resignedly.

"What about the price I'm paying? I have no future, not with you, not in my job, none."

"I'm sorry," said Jack truthfully. "That's why I'm being open and frank with you. So you can get a future."

"I don't believe this is happening. I've supported your ambition to be CEO. In subtle ways I've led Mr. Bossman to see your abilities, boosted you at every opportunity, and this is what I get? Don't do this to me, Jack. I love you. Don't you love me?"

"Of course I do. It's the way things have panned out," said Jack, spreading his hands out from his sides.

"I'll never forgive you for this," said Sally. "Never." She ran from his office in tears.

Jack jumped from his chair to pursue her, but he was left standing, his hands now extended in futility.

Bossman returned home still upset over Jack's revelation. He was sitting in the living room, a newspaper in his lap, staring off into space when June walked in. "You look tired," she said. "How was your day today, dearest?"

"Look at this," Bossman said, pointing to a headline in the paper. "Our mayor is in trouble because he was found to have a mistress."

"Oh," said June, clearly uninterested.

"Do you think that will affect his mayoring?" said Bossman seeking a rise from June. "He's doing the job. Isn't that all that counts?" He was curious: Would June act as he acted in Jack's case?

"I don't agree," June said, suddenly reacting. "He's also the moral leader of our community. He sets an example for the rest of us. I couldn't trust a man who's disloyal to his wife. I think he ought to resign, or he should be booted out."

"Well, we've got a case closer to home, my sweet," Bossman revealed.

"Really?" said June after a moment's hesitation. "Are you confessing something?"

"Me?" Bossman laughed. "Hell, I'd never confess to something like that. I wouldn't want to hurt you. I'd keep it to myself forever." He gazed at June with adoration.

"Until I learned about it," said June with a sparkle in her eyes.

"How could you? I'd be ever so discreet," said Bossman, enjoying their game.

"A wife suspects," said June. "She knows, maybe not the specifics, but that something isn't right."

Bossman reread the headline, then blurted, "Do you think Helen knows?"

"What are you saying? You mean Jack—"

"He's got an affair going with...guess who?"

"I haven't the faintest notion. Stop keeping me on tenterhooks."

"My gal Sally."

"Sally? Your Sally?" said June, her eyes widening in astonishment. "I thought she'd have more sense. My god, poor Helen."

"Of all the women a good-looking guy like Jack can attract, he picks one from work," said Bossman, shaking his head.

"Don't you think it's a mistake keeping him on? I don't feel I can trust him anymore."

"You're making a moral judgement, June. In business, morality is unimportant. The only consideration is whether he can do the job. No question he's the best person for it. Anyone else would have to undergo a learning curve. And this is a man I know, a man I'm comfortable with."

"Still, I'm not comfortable with him," said June. The subject of morality in business was a frequent source of argument between them. "I have to live with him as much as you. I say get rid of him," said June firmly.

"Please, June," Bossman beseeched, "you're mixing your personal feelings with a business decision. You've got to separate the two."

"I've never understood your thinking. I've seen you tolerate downright crooks, in my opinion lowlifes, among our employees and customers, and yet you keep dealing with them. I simply don't understand why you do that, especially when you're at the top and you can tell them to go to hell."

"Because they serve my company's goals," Bossman said without hesitation. "I know what they're like. I have no illusions about them. My personal feelings about them are unimportant. I'd do business with the devil if it advanced the fortunes of the business."

"I'm asking you, for my sake, Chris, to get rid of Jack. I'm sure you can find someone else. Forgive me for saying this, but I know that some day I...I might have to deal with him alone. I can't do that knowing what I know. I've lost respect for him."

Bossman knew that he was losing the argument. "Well, I told him to end the relationship," he said with a sigh.

"What did he say?"

"I think he will. I made it clear he has to if he wants to keep his job. He's already felt the power of being top dog, and I don't think he'd toss it away for a woman."

"That doesn't change it for me," said June, undeterred. "Now he's being disloyal to another person who presumably loves him. He'd forsake Sally for his own benefit. That's unforgivable."

"You're damning him no matter what he does," said Bossman weakly.

"Get rid of him, Chris. Do it for me. I pity poor Helen, but there's nothing I can do on her behalf. She's strong. I'm sure she can weather this."

"It's too risky if Jack goes," said Chris, feeling caged in. "I'd have to stick around for another year or two to train a new man. June, I'm not up to it. I don't have the energy, the drive anymore. Can't you see? This damn disease is killing me, figuratively as well as literally."

"I know, dearest," said June, stroking him. "I see what's happening to you. I'd rather you'd not have to worry about the business, but isn't there another way? I mean, why do we need the business? Can't you sell it?"

"Sell it?" said Bossman, startled. "I thought you wanted it."

"Certainly not. I always thought you expected me to keep it going for...well, for your sake. We have no one to leave it to. Why not, as you would say, cash in? I'm sure we could live out our lives comfortably on the proceeds. Don't you think so?"

"'Comfortably' is an understatement, my sweet. We'd be downright rich. It's worth millions to the right buyer."

"Then that's the answer. It would be best for both of us. Only, are you sure you can live with that decision?" said June, studying his face.

"My love, you are the one who will have to live with it," Bossman said sadly.

"Oh, Chris, we don't know that."

Bossman's eyes brightened. "It so happens I have a meeting with the chairman of SuperGeneral Corporation on Monday. It's a big sales deal. They're looking to sign a contract with us as a major supplier. I wonder if they would consider an acquisition instead."

At ten o'clock on Monday morning, Bossman entered Jack's office accompanied by the chairman of SuperGeneral Corporation, a distinguished, tanned, dark-suited gentleman.

"Good morning, Jack," said Bossman. "I'd like you to meet George Buyer."

Jack rose from his chair and extended his hand across his desk "Pleased to meet you, Mr. Buyer," he said enthusiastically.

"Same here, Jack. I've heard a lot of good things about you."

"Sit down, George," said Chris after taking one of the chairs facing Jack's desk. "I was telling George how easy the transition went after you took over."

"Well, you're a good teacher, Chris. The best there is, I'd say."

"George is checking us out to see whether we can satisfy his company's needs," said Bossman, glancing toward his guest.

"Really?" said Jack, pretending this was news. "I think you'll find our quality second to none."

"It's not a question of quality," said Buyer. "It's quantity that concerns me. I'll be plain: Our requirement will occupy a third of your company's capacity. That means you'll have to dedicate yourselves to our needs. The question is, are you prepared to do that?"

Jack looked at Bossman for assent. "Certainly we'll have to take that into consideration before—"

"Yes, and so will we," Buyer interrupted, displaying a no-nonsense demeanor. "There are bound to be times when you'll have to sacrifice some of your other customers to meet our schedules. In other words, are you willing to come to bed with us?"

"There is the alternative we discussed, George," said Bossman.

"Of course, and we'll seriously consider it."

"Excuse me," said Jack, puzzled. "You're passing me by. What alternative?"

"We could buy you out," Buyer said succinctly.

Jack looked to Bossman again. "I'd say that's a pretty remote poss—"

"Not necessarily," Bossman interrupted. "George's company has been seeking a company like ours for some time. While our company would provide a guaranteed supply, his would give us a built-in customer, unlimited capital, and management depth."

Jack fumbled for a response. "Well, of course, I can see—"

"Do you think you can get us a complete set of financials, including five-year projections, your customer list, and the annual wages of all your executives, by early next week?" Buyer said to Jack. "We have a board meeting on Friday and we'll need time to study your figures before presenting them to the members."

Jack was struggling to cope with his displeasure at the turn of events. Obviously Bossman and Buyer had already discussed a buyout before they entered his office.

"That's a tall order, but—"

"Do it, Jack," Bossman directed. "Drop everything else if you have to. Just do it."

"Sure thing, Chris. No problem, none at all," said Jack, putting on his most cooperative air.

"If we have a deal, Chris here says he'd stick around for a while to make the transition smooth," said Buyer. "What about you? Could we count on you giving a hand?"

"Of course," said Jack, wide eyed, astonished. "Isn't that a CEO's job? You can depend on it. I've got a professional team here. We'd all pull together to ease the way."

"Good," said Bossman. "I told you Jack would cooperate, George. Now, you have to catch a plane. I'll have someone drive you to the airport."

Buyer and Bossman rose from their seats, and Buyer shook Jack's hand.

"Good to meet you, Jack," said Buyer. "I have a feeling we'll be doing business. Just get me those financials."

They departed, and Jack sat back in his desk chair shocked and totally deflated. Minutes later, having seen Buyer off, Bossman returned and sat in the same chair as previously.

"You've just met one of the giants of the industrial scene in this country, Jack. A no-nonsense guy, wouldn't you say?"

"Why are you doing this?" said Jack, suppressing a wish to explode.

"Doing what?" said Bossman, genuinely baffled.

"You know goddamn well. You pleaded with me to be CEO, and now you're selling out from under me."

"What difference does the ownership make? So you'll be CEO for SuperGeneral, if they go for it."

"Oh, they'll go for it," said Jack sardonically. "This company is a gem."

"So, what's troubling you?"

"I don't know where I'd stand with them. With you I know."

"It seems you really don't," said Bossman, impatient with Jack's chronic dissatisfaction.

"You know I'm capable of running the company like a...a fine-tuned instrument. You and June can retire, travel the world, do anything you want without a worry. Why sell? I don't get it."

"And I don't get you, Jack. You'll be in the big leagues. You'll have a chance to rise in a multinational organization. If you've got the stuff, which you certainly have, your future will be unlimited. With our company, you've gone as far as you can go." He slashed the air to indicate an abrupt terminus.

"I've gone as far as I want to go," said Jack.

"Big fish in a small pond. Is that it?"

"I suppose that's part of it," admitted Jack.

"I'm surprised at you. I thought you were more ambitious than that," said Bossman, eyebrows raised.

"I like running my own show. I don't want to take orders from a paper-pushing executive a thousand miles away in some skyscraper who can't possibly know what makes us tick."

"I've done nothing but praise your abilities," said Bossman. "They don't know our business. We can talk to George. I'm sure they'll give you complete autonomy."

"I'm not so sure. Companies like SuperGeneral want to have their own boys running the show," Jack said, refusing to concede an inch to Bossman's argument.

"Not in our case. They have no one who knows the ins and outs of a company like ours, not the way you do. They'll need you. You know, Jack, I'm amazed to see you react like this. I thought you'd welcome the opportunity to be part of something bigger."

"Bigger, maybe, but not better. Not for me. It's just that I'm not ready for this."

"Well I am, my friend," said Bossman adamantly.

Jack was steaming when he arrived home after work that evening. "Do you know what that bastard is doing?" he said as soon as he entered the kitchen, where Helen was preparing supper.

"What bastard are you talking about?" said Helen derisively.

"Chris."

"Only a few months ago he was your savior, your idol," said Helen, cutting up some vegetables for a salad.

"He's betrayed me," said Jack, sitting at the kitchen table.

"You still have your job?" said Helen, turning to Jack in alarm.

"For now."

"For now?"

"He's selling the company to a giant corporation," said Jack, slamming his fist on the table.

"What does that mean? I don't understand such matters."

"First, it means that I don't know whether the new owner will keep me on. And, second, even if they do, I won't have a free hand to do things the way I want."

"You can't be sure of that though," said Helen.

"I know how these big corporations operate. Some central office always calls the shots."

"I don't see anything bad about that. It seems to me that as long as you do your job, you'll have nothing to worry about."

"What the hell, I didn't expect you to understand anyway," said Jack, getting up to leave.

"I'm simply giving you my opinion," said Helen, hurt by Jack's remark. "I don't pretend to know about these things. If you say there's a problem, I'll take your word for it. I don't see one. That's all I can say. But I have a problem, and I'd like you to clear it up for me. I received a call from Sally this morning. You know, Chris's girl Friday."

"From Sally? What...what did she want?" said Jack, sitting back down.

"It seems you and she have something going," said Helen, stopping what she was doing and sitting across the table from Jack. "At least that's what she says. What do you say?"

"You're my wife and I love you, Helen. That's all that counts." He stood and went over to her.

"No, Jack, that isn't all that counts. You haven't answered my question. Do you have a relationship with this...this girl?"

Jack began pacing. "Not anymore. It's over."

"Then you've been unfaithful, is that right?"

"Helen, I love you, no one else."

"You've been unfaithful, say it," Helen commanded.

"Yes," said Jack plaintively.

"Not just yes. Say it," said Helen, refusing to let go.

"Yes, I've been unfaithful," said Jack contritely.

"So be it. You're a son of a bitch."

Helen stood and beat on Jack's chest with her fists. She burst into tears. "How could you, how could you? I wish I didn't love you. How could you?"

"I don't blame you," said Jack, willingly submitting to her condemnation. "Our marriage isn't ideal. You must know that."

"What marriage is?" said Helen. "No relationship is consistently smooth sailing. Why didn't you come to me if you were unhappy? We could have talked. Somehow we could have worked things out. No, instead you run to the nearest floozy who'll spread her legs."

"I've worked and worked year in and year out for you, Helen. You wanted this fine home, the clothes, the Mercedes, the whole bag, and I've given it to you. It's all been for you."

"Bullshit. You bask in our prosperity as much as I do," said Helen, dabbing at her tears.

"Sure, I admit it. I like the trappings, too. But I wouldn't want them without you. I feel proud of what I've given you, what I've done."

"We were the happiest when you were just starting out and we had nothing," Helen said sadly. "Remember those days?" She sat down again at the kitchen table.

"Yeah, I sure do. We were happy then. But I don't think it was because we had nothing."

"Why do you think it was?"

"It was because…because we believed in each other. We were allies against the world, against anything that might arise. We were—"

"Best friends," said Helen, finishing his statement. "We had complete respect for each other."

"That's right. That's it. Respect."

"And we've lost that. I suppose I as much as you. How did it happen?" she said, dreamily.

"I do love you, Helen. I could never leave you."

"But I could leave you. And I might yet. I don't know if I can ever trust you again."

"I don't blame you. I beg you, don't leave. I need you, and you need—"

"I could take you for everything, do you realize that?" she said coldly.

"We could have what we once had," said Jack, rattled. "I'll make it up to you. I promise. We'll get it back, our old love. You'll see."

"What about Sally?"

"It's over. I swear."

"Then fire her. Do you hear me? Get rid of her now."

"Why penalize her?" Jack said. "It's all my doing. At least let her keep her job."

"No, it took two. You say you want me to be with you. Do you or don't you?"

"Yes, I do."

"Then fire her," Helen shouted.

"It's not fair to her."

"I mean it," said Helen, losing patience. "It's either her or me."

"But...but, Christ, okay, I'll let her go."

"Tomorrow. Not a day later. Is that understood?"

"Yeah."

"I'm not ready to forgive you. I'm goddamned angry." Helen watched her husband hang his head, unable to face her. "Now I'd like you to do something else. I'd like you to call Dan and hire him back."

"I can't do that."

"Why can't you? It's within your power."

"Dan's burned his bridges. He's filed suit against the company and me for discrimination. Soon after he was let go I went to his home and explained to him and Anna what happened, that it wasn't my decision, but he was so angry that he wouldn't listen. He feels that I sacrificed him for the CEO's job, and there's no convincing him otherwise."

"Where is he working now?" Helen asked, ready to intervene if need be.

"I have no idea. A few requests for references have come in; personnel took care of them. I saw to it that he was given the best. I'm sure he's found a job. He's a good man, even capable of running a company."

"I think Chris treated him pretty shabbily. Don't you?" she asked, calm now that the subject had changed.

"Chris saw only what he thought was best for the company. He had nothing personal against Dan. I don't think he's got anything against blacks. He just won't take any risks, and he saw Dan as a risk in a higher position."

Helen pondered Jack's statement. "Do you think that's why he's selling the company, to avoid any risk?"

"By cashing in?" said Jack, considering the suggestion.

"Uh-huh."

"I hadn't thought of that. You might be right. But not for himself. He knows his own days are numbered. He must be doing it for June. You know what a dedicated couple they are."

"Yes, they are beautiful together, aren't they. They have something we don't have," said Helen with envy. "Do you think we could ever find it again?"

"I want to," said Jack, going to her and embracing her.

"So do I," said Helen, pulling away, "like nothing else in the world, but I'm not ready for this, you bastard."

"Oh, it's you," Dan said into the phone when Jack called the house a few months later. "I have nothing to say to you. Yeah, I heard Bossman is selling the company. No, I don't know who the buyer is. Oh, you know but you can't say? Well, I'm sure you'll make out. You always knew how to take care of Jack first. No, I wouldn't be interested in coming aboard again. I've got a job. Who with? Well, I can't say either, but I'm happy where I am. Yeah, I'm sorry too. We used to be a good team. But I didn't quit, you know."

"What did he want?" asked Anna, who had overheard Dan's side of the conversation.

"Now that the company will be sold, he wants me to come back as his executive VP."

"Then he was probably being truthful when he told you it was Bossman who fired you," said Anna, ready to change her original opinion of Jack's motives.

"That wasn't the issue, Anna. I know now that he didn't want to let me go. I know it was Bossman. Sally told me. It's that Jack was willing to sacrifice me to save his own skin. He preached that he was color blind, and he probably is, but he wouldn't stand by his principles. Don't you see that?"

"Maybe you expected too much," said Anna, viewing it from Jack's perspective.

"We were friends, close friends. I expect my friends to be loyal," Dan said.

"Then you won't ever forgive him?"

"Forgive? Sure, I'll forgive him. I'll have to, but I'll never trust him. The way things are turning out is beyond anything I could have dreamed."

He picked Anna up in his arms and kissed her fervently.

"Stop it, Dan," she said, laughing. "I'm serious. Do you think Bossman and Jack have a clue?"

"Not a chance. We're going to spring it on them without warning. God, how sweet retribution is."

"Don't be too harsh, Dan."

"They deserve what they gave."

"You know how much I like Helen," said Anna. "She was…is my friend. You mustn't hurt her."

"No one is going to hurt anybody. It's just that we'll be realigning the power," said Dan, humorously smacking his lips.

"It's remarkable the way things are turning out," said Anna in wonder.

"I've still got to protect myself. No matter how high I go, there are people who will hate me for my color, and I can never be sure who it is. It's a tough call. Once I have power, they'll fawn all over me and down deep probably hate my guts—not for what I do but for who I am. It will be that way as long as we live in the States, Anna. Don't you forget that."

"I know, darling. I realize we can never be completely at ease," Anna said, wanting to share her husband's burden. "And it's a constant strain. But don't you think some of our white friends may not be guilty? They may not see us as different."

"I agree, oh yes," conceded Dan. "I'm sure some of our friends accept us on an equal footing. But how do you know who they are? You can't tell by their everyday actions. Take Jack. Who would have thought he wouldn't back me up?"

"So you don't trust any of the whites reporting to you?" said Anna, seeking to understand precisely where Dan stood.

"I do as far as doing their job is concerned, because I have the power. But on a personal level, no. As for our own kind, I'm not even sure of them."

"My god, Dan, how can you say that?" said Anna, dismayed over the extent of Dan's distrust of others.

"Don't doubt for a minute that there are plenty of our people who resent my success. They're thinking I got where I am by sucking up to Whitey. We have such a low opinion of ourselves that they can't give me credit for succeeding on the basis of sheer competence."

"It's so hard," said Anna sympathetically.

"Sometimes I wish I wasn't so ambitious. But I can't help myself. It's in my blood."

"I know, darling. I admire you because that's the way you are. You keep fighting and refuse to give in. I do admire that in a man…my man." She kissed him on the cheek. "When do you see Jack and Bossman?"

"Tomorrow morning at nine. It's the lawyers' turn now. Between ours and theirs, the deal should be done in a few hours."

The meeting took place on schedule in the company's meeting room, with Jack, Chris and June Bossman, and George Buyer sitting around the long table.

"George wants to review a few details before the lawyers arrive," said Bossman. He looked at his watch. "They'll be here soon, so let's move on. The floor is yours, George."

"Thank you, Chris. Often there's a misunderstanding over roles after an acquisition takes place, even when it's in writing. So I want to clarify what Jack and Chris's relationship with the company will be after we take over. I asked June to be present so she'll know firsthand what's expected of her husband, what was agreed to. Of course, as a shareholder, June, you'll be needed to sign some papers. Now, Chris has agreed to be a paid consultant for five years. I take it you'll be doing some traveling, Chris?"

"Some, I suppose, yes," answered Bossman, meeting June's approving eyes.

"And you'll let us know where you are so we can call on you when necessary?" Bossman nodded. "Actually, your consultant's position is little more than a formality, because, as I understand it, Jack has been running the company without your help for the past six months and he'll be able to handle any problem that comes up."

"Better than I could," Bossman interjected, nodding to Jack. "He's a pro, doing a fine job, as I said."

"Yes, you've said that, and we have no reason to doubt his competence. However, we do like to have depth of management in an organization. To have so much hinging on the leadership of one man is pretty risky, wouldn't you say?"

"Oh, I certainly agree. Between Jack and me, we had depth," said Bossman, missing George's drift.

"But you see—forgive my frankness—we won't have you if you're incapacitated. I understand you're not well."

"Where did you hear that?" Bossman said with indignation.

"We have our sources, Chris. It's our job to leave no stone unturned before committing ourselves."

"Well, it's only a minor thing. Nothing that would prevent me—"

"Please, Chris," George interrupted. "I wouldn't say Parkinson's is minor, so, on considering your possible disability, we've taken steps to deal with it."

"Jesus, I'm not dying tomorrow, George. I'll still be around and kicking five years from now."

"With my love and God's blessing, dear," said June, patting his hand.

"I sure hope so," said Buyer. "However, we must take into account every eventuality. Jack, we're creating a new division consisting of several of your competitors whom we are planning to acquire over the next couple of years. We've appointed a CEO to head the division, and he's the man you'll report to. He'll be your president until the division consists of more than just your company."

"I see. What…what will my position be?"

"You'll be his executive VP, working directly under him."

"Then I won't be in charge?" Jack questioned, confirming his worst fear.

"Not at first. Eventually you will. As I indicated, once your boss moves up to division status, you become president."

"Why are you doing this?" Jack said, disturbed. "Based on the figures, do you have a complaint with the way I've been running the company?"

"Certainly not," assured Buyer. "But you don't know our company. We prefer to have a man at the helm who's familiar with our way of operating."

"Well, that's only half the picture," said Jack, fighting to preserve what he had. "What about knowing my company's culture? Your man will have a long learning curve to contend with."

"Not really. Our man knows your company like a book," Buyer said with satisfaction.

"How could he? Just from seeing our figures? That's impossible," Jack said.

"Not from the figures. From firsthand knowledge and experience," said Buyer, smiling.

"Who are you talking about?" asked Jack, shaken. "There's no such person. You're joking."

George looked at his wristwatch. "I think he's waiting outside." He walked to the door and opened it. "I hope I haven't kept you waiting long. Come in, Dan. Come in."

When Dan entered the office, Bossman's and Jack's jaws dropped in disbelief. "I think you all know Dan Black." The silence was thick. "He'll be our man in charge," said George. "Do you have any questions?"

Jack ignored Dan. "What in hell is this?" he said coldly. Do you expect me to play second fiddle to…to this man?"

"Well, thanks for the compliment, Jack," said Dan.

Jack turned to June. "You pleaded with me to be your CEO. And I delivered. Why are you doing this to me?"

"We're not doing anything to you, Jack," said Bossman. "We've advised George of your capabilities. As the new owner, it was his decision, not ours."

"I'm sorry about how things have turned out," said June. "But are they so bad, really? Your position is secure. Am I correct, George?"

"Absolutely. I think I've explained our reasons adequately, Jack. You have a future with us. Give it time."

"Look, Jack," said Dan. "We were a team once. We can be again. And by the way, Sally Love will be working for us. Great, huh?"

"There's nothing between Sally and me," Jack exploded. "Damn you for bringing her up."

"I didn't mean anything by it," said Dan, regretting his reference to Sally, "except to inform you that she's joining us. Cool off, Jack."

"I'm not taking a backseat, George. I've worked hard to get where I am and I'm doing a good job. There's no reason on Earth to demote me," said Jack.

"Be flexible," Bossman said. "For god's sake, you'll be in a bigger pond where there's an opportunity to grow. Look at Dan—what it's done for him already."

"You goddamned hypocrite," said Jack, forgetting all protocol. "You're the one who stopped Dan cold on his way up and said he'd be a liability."

"Calm down, son. It wasn't a matter of his ability."

"What was it? Say it, Chris. Tell us what it was."

"And what is it with you now? You tell me," said Bossman, nearing the end of his patience.

"Gentlemen, I don't think this is pertinent to our purpose here," Buyer said. "Let's be calm. Jack, do I understand then that you will not accept the position under Dan?"

"You understand right."

"Talk some sense into him," Bossman said to June. "He listens to you."

"Reconsider, Jack," June implored. "Think of Helen. Think of the future you're throwing away. Please, don't be rash. Think it over."

"It's too much, June. I can't. I just can't."

"You're a very proud man, but you've got it wrong," June said, genuine pity in her voice.

"That's not the way I see it."

"Then it's settled," said Buyer, wishing to bring the matter to a conclusion. "Jack won't be with us. So be it. Dan, you have your work cut out for you. I know you're up to it."

"I'll give it my best," said Dan, elated now that his way was clear.

"You can count on me, too," said Bossman. "I'm still fit most of the time. I'll be sure to stick around and make myself available."

"You must pace yourself, dear," June warned. "Remember what the doctor said."

"Thank you, Chris," said Buyer. "I'm sure we'll need you with Jack gone."

"I never saw this side of you, Jack," said Dan. "Your actions make me very sad. June's got it right, and you've got it wrong. I know we could have worked things out."

"The lawyers are waiting," said Buyer. "Are we ready for the final signing?"

"Let the lawyers come in," said Bossman. "You'd better leave, Jack. Why don't you come back tomorrow to get your things?"

Jack walked slowly out the door before the lawyers entered.

"I thought he was a big man," said Bossman. "Looks like I had him pegged wrong."

"What's wrong with you?" said Helen as Jack sat in the living room watching TV at eleven in the morning. "All you've done for the past week is watch television. Shouldn't you be out looking for a job?"

"Do you think jobs for CEOs grow on trees? I've contacted a few headhunters. Now I wait."

"A man with your proven ability should have no trouble," said Helen, resenting that Jack was unemployed and that his explanation of how it happened was wanting. It was not what she expected at this stage of their marriage, especially with two children nearing college age.

177

"What's proven?" countered Jack. "Six months at the helm of a company doesn't prove very much to an employer."

"So what will you do?"

"Damnit, I won't take a lesser job," Jack said with determination. "Why should I? I've tasted it. It's CEO or nothing."

"Don't be so defensive. I'm not asking you to settle for less."

"For twenty-five years I settled for less. That's enough."

"Okay, I don't blame you," said Helen, "but I hope you'll be realistic. As you say, such jobs aren't easy to find. Why can't we talk? I'd like to know what happened."

"I told you, I didn't like the terms that George Buyer offered."

"Which were?"

"He expected me to step aside and be second to Dan."

"Why would he do that?" said Helen, who thought she was asking a sensible question.

"I don't know," said Jack, evading the truth. "It's over. There's nothing more to talk about."

"Didn't he give a reason?" Helen pursued

"Well, yeah, I suppose."

"I'm waiting."

There was no escaping Helen's persistence. "Damnit, he said it was necessary in order to meld his company's methods with ours. Now let's drop it."

"I think that makes sense."

"It's totally unnecessary—unless they planned to strip me of all authority and call the shots," said Jack in sheer speculation.

"So you'd become a figurehead?"

"That's right. I'd be back where I was before Chris stepped down."

"But why? They'd still need someone in charge. Aren't you the logical one?"

"I don't know. You figure it."

"So that's what your leaving was about?"

"Mostly. There were a few other items I objected to."

"Such as?"

"They were quite incidental—of no real importance, just annoying. Look, Helen, I don't like this third degree."

"I just want to know everything that was said."

"Why? Do you doubt the wisdom of my decision?"

"I'd just like to know. I'm your wife. What happens to you, and why, concerns me."

"Well, they're going to bring Sally back," said Jack, thinking that this would end Helen's relentless questioning.

"You must have been thrilled."

"Don't be sarcastic. I told them I wouldn't agree to that. I'll have no part of her."

"That was very nice of you," said Helen mockingly. "Thank you. By the way, I forgot to tell you. Dan called while you were shaving; he wants to see you."

"I have nothing to say to him."

"Why not? He sounded very friendly. Not like someone who was suing you. I told him you'd be here all morning, as usual. He should be arriving shortly."

"He's not suing me."

"My, that's good news. I like Dan. It saddened me that you two weren't hitting it off anymore. When did he change his mind?"

"It's a long story. You'll find out soon enough," said Jack cryptically.

Helen went to the door when the bell rang. "Come in, Dan," she said. "You're looking well. It's been a long time."

Jack remained seated when they entered the room and refused to take Dan's extended hand.

"Please, sit down," said Helen. "Let me get some coffee."

"Forget it," said Jack. "He won't be here long enough for coffee."

"That's all right, Helen," said Dan. "I already had some. I understand how you feel, Jack, but what's happened isn't my doing. Don't blame me."

The role reversal was lost on Jack. "What do you want?" Jack said, his manner hostile.

"I want you to come back. We...I need you."

"I'd be glad to—"

"You would?" said Dan, looking overjoyed. "That's wonderful, wonderful."

"Hear me out. Not as your subordinate."

"I don't understand what you're talking about," said Helen. "Would someone explain?"

"If I remained on the job, Dan would be my boss. Can you feature that?" said Jack with a laugh

"I didn't choose who would be what," said Dan. "That wasn't up to me."

"Then I have nothing to say," said Jack, turning his face away.

"Look, you'd have all the authority. I won't interfere. I'll give you a free hand because I know you can do the job," said Dan, pulling a chair next to Jack's and sitting down.

"No, I want the title, too. I don't want to work under you."

"Dan sounds entirely reasonable," said Helen. "He's giving you everything you could want. Why are you being so stubborn?"

"Because...because...," Jack stammered.

"Because why? Tell me."

Jack stammered again; his tongue seemed tied.

"Say it, Jack," said Helen, demanding the truth, whatever it was.

"Goddamn him," said Jack, glaring at Dan. "Every black inch of him."

"What did you say?" Dan said, thunderstruck.

"Because...because you're black."

There was a stunned silence. "My god," Dan said finally. "You're no better than all the others."

"I don't believe what I'm hearing," Helen said. "How can you feel that way? You've always professed to be so liberal."

"You can't understand. It's the whole goddamned mess—my having to step down, working for a former subordinate, his color— it's too much. It's plain demeaning."

"I can't win," said Dan, throwing up his hands. "The deck is stacked against me. You're a goddamned hypocrite. Sally told me that Bossman was behind firing me, so I thought we could be friends again, become a team the way we used to be. Now I see that while you were my boss, you only pretended to be my friend. Shit, it wasn't even skin deep. I can't stand the sight of you. Please excuse me, Helen." He started for the door.

"I'll let you out," said Helen. "I want to apologize, Dan. I'm so sorry about this."

"Don't give it a thought. I won't. I'm used to it. It's an old refrain. He's like all the rest of you."

Helen closed the door and returned to face Jack. "I'm disgusted with you," she said. "As Dan says, you're a hypocrite."

"Yes, that's what I am," said Jack, shaking his head.

"Well, I'm not. I like living well. I like the money you make. I'm not about to give it all up without a fight. Swallow your stupid pride. Tell Dan you'll work for him."

"Not on your life."

"That's just it. It's my life, too," Helen said. "You're sacrificing my future because of your ridiculous prejudice."

"You're asking too much. I've made my decision."

"No, Jack. Remember me, your other half, for better or worse? Why didn't you consult me? Why didn't we talk before you did something ridiculous. Now I'm telling you, call Dan. Tell him you'll work for him. If you have to, see someone who can help you. Find out why you feel this way and get rid of it. What you've done isn't rational. Don't take me down with you." Helen turned on her heel and left the room.

Jack sat for a minute contemplating Helen's statements, then he picked up the phone and dialed Sally's number. "Can I see you?" he pleaded when she finally answered. "Please, I've got to see you. Don't hang up." The phone clicked. He slammed the receiver into its cradle and walked out of the house.

No one answered the door when Jack rang the bell to Sally's apartment. He rang the doorbell again, without success. Then he banged on the door until the walls shook. "Please, Sally," he shouted. "Let me in. We have to talk."

Sally finally spoke through the closed door. "I've already told you, I won't see you."

"Look, I'm sorry for what happened. There's an explanation."

"I don't want to hear your phony explanations," she said.

"Sally, I've quit. I'm through."

Shocked, Sally unbolted and opened the door. "You've quit? Why?" she asked as he entered.

He reached for her but she moved away. "It was a lousy deal. A fucking demotion. Christ, how could they expect me to go for it?"

"Did they tell you I would be working for you and Dan?" she asked, suspecting that she may have been partly responsible.

"Yeah. That was a bad idea."

"What's your problem with me?" Sally asked.

"You don't shit where you eat," he said, repeating the phrase that Bossman had used on him.

"Is that what my working for you signifies? You know I'd always stick to business. I would, Jack."

"Well, it's all over now. I won't work for SuperGeneral."

"I still don't understand. Here, sit down," Sally said. "What happened?"

"It's horrible," said Jack, sitting beside her on the sofa. "I'm so damned ashamed."

"Of what? What did you do?"

"I refused to work for Dan."

"Dan's your friend. He's always been loyal," Sally said, confused.

"He's black, Sally."

"So what?"

"Something in me rebels against working for someone inferior to me."

"Inferior to you? Dan?" Sally exclaimed, her voice reaching falsetto. "You don't mean that."

"I do."

"Why? Not because of his color."

"Yes."

"I don't believe I'm hearing this, especially from you. Your people have been victims of prejudice for two thousand years. How can you feel this way?"

Jack got up from the sofa and went to a bookcase, where he studied the book titles and retrieved a book entitled *History of the United States*. "I've never admitted it to myself. It's deep within me. I have this feeling of superiority over Dan. I know it isn't fair, I know it isn't rational. He's capable, he can do my job, but I think I'm better than he is."

"I used to love you...but now I hate you," said Sally, staring at Jack.

"That book in your hand, turn to the Declaration of Independence."

Jack leafed through the pages.

"Let me have the book," said Sally. He handed it to her and she found the page she wanted. "We hold these truths to be self-evident, that all men are created equal...," she read.

"We aren't really created equal," said Sally. "But we must respect one another as if we were."

"Damnit, I know that. You see, I always came to their defense as long as I was on top. I resented Chris because of his prejudice. To think I'm no better."

"You're worse," said Sally. "Your liberalism is only on the surface. You pretended to be on their side. At least Chris didn't."

"Why am I this way? Why do I intellectually believe one thing and feel the opposite?" said Jack, asking himself as well as Sally.

"There's no doubt you have lots of company. Many of us need someone to kick. It makes us feel better about our miserable selves."

"It's my goddamned pride."

"Now you know."

"Yes, now I know. And I'm ashamed. I hate myself."

"What do you want to do about it?"

"What should I do?"

"Call him," Sally instructed.

"Dan?"

Sally handed him the portable phone. "He's at the office." She walked over to a small table, opened a drawer, and withdrew an address book and handed it to Jack. "This is his direct line. I'm supposed to be there in an hour. I'll take you there."

Jack dialed. "Dan, it's me, Jack. Don't hang up. Please don't. I want to apologize. I'm ready to talk. That's right. Will you see me? How about now? I'll be right over."

"Let's go," said Sally as she put on a jacket and withdrew her car keys from her purse.

In the office that was once Bossman's, then Jack's, and now Dan's, Dan was sitting at Jack's old desk.

"Come in and sit down, Jack," said Dan as his former boss knocked on the open door. "But make it quick. I don't have much time."

"Sure, Dan," said Jack obsequiously, taking the visitor's chair that he hadn't sat in since Bossman made him CEO—long ago, it seemed.

"So what's on your mind?"

"I've had second thoughts. I'd like to be part of your team."

"Is that so?" said Dan with irony. "This is quite a reversal. What changed your mind?"

"Discovering my hypocrisy," replied Jack flatly.

"Right," said Dan. "Your kind hide behind your liberalism, don't you?"

"I didn't realize. Well, the truth is, I never admitted it to myself."

"I'm not sure I can trust you, Jack. I try to take a positive attitude toward you people, give you the benefit of the doubt, but I can never be sure that you accept me as your equal. You see, I need that acceptance in order to do this job. I need people who will respect me as a competent human being regardless of my skin color or my kinky hair. Know what I'm saying? Apparently my—what should I call it?—my soul, my essence, if you will, is irrelevant to you."

"That's not true," Jack protested, squirming in his chair. "I've always respected you for your ability. I truly believe you can do the job, as well as and maybe better than I."

"Well, I'm certainly happy to hear you say that. But that isn't the issue here, is it? My competence, that is."

"No," admitted Jack.

"I know what you feel. I've seen it in the actions of your people all my life. Words lie, Jack, but not actions. That's what I go by. You feel you're better than I am in some sick way, don't you?"

"I did, but not anymore."

"Is that so? To what do you owe this sudden transformation?" Dan glanced at the clock on the wall. "Let's see. It must have taken place within the last two hours. A true miracle, I'd say."

"A revelation, Dan."

"A revelation, you say?"

"Look, for the first time I see myself for what I've been," said Jack, feeling that he deserved all that Dan was handing out. "And I despise what I see. It goes against everything I believe. I can't explain where my...my sick, as you called them, feelings about you and your people came from. But now I recognize them, and I'm dealing with them. They're wrong, and I'm trying to make them right. By the way, when you talk about 'my people,' are you talking about whites?"

"That's right. The whites, the dominant ones. You know we black people are cursed living in your society, because there's no way out. We see what you have. You teach us to want it, then you place it beyond our reach."

"So how do you account for your new position? A pretty high perch, I'd say," said Jack, pouncing on the opportunity to retort.

"An aberration," said Dan with a shrug.

"Perhaps. Still, there had to be some whites who appreciated you for what you can do and not for who you are."

"That's true," Dan admitted.

"And I can tell you that there are whites without black prejudice. You may not know who they are, but I know because they condemned me and came to your defense. Sally is one of them. So is Helen. And if you'll give me a chance, I can prove that I will value you as a human being."

"I'm not seeking your intellectual approval," said Dan, pointing out a necessary distinction.

"For the first time I accept you emotionally. I want to be your friend, and I'm prepared to work for you. I want to be on your team. You must believe me," Jack pleaded.

"What about Sally?"

"I can't allow her to work for me," said Jack unequivocally. "We're too involved with each other."

"What's it doing to your marriage?"

"It's really none of your business—"

"I ask as a friend," said Dan, softening.

"Well, thank you. I appreciate that," said Jack, feeling the return of his former warmth toward Dan. "My marriage is no picnic. One of these days, I'll have to find the courage to end it."

"Are you ready to come back right now?"

"Even sooner," said Jack with a smile.

Both men rose from their chairs. "You'll be in my old office. Is that acceptable?"

"That will be fine," said Jack.

Bossman poked his head into the office just as Jack and Dan embraced. "I heard you were here, Jack. Change your mind?"

"Yeah," said Jack, feeling awkward.

"Glad you came around, son," said Bossman as if all were forgotten. "Dan's a good man. You'll be a great team. It's important that the two of you make this company hum. Remember, I now hold stock in SuperGeneral, so I still own a piece of you." He started to leave. "Dan, don't drive him too hard. Nice seeing you back, Jack."

"How are you feeling, Chris?" inquired Jack.

Bossman extended his hand straight ahead of him. "Pretty good. See?" But then his hand began to vibrate. "Well, maybe not perfect," he said, and walked out of the office.

"There goes a damned hypocrite," said Dan. "Were it up to him, I know where I'd be. But my heart goes out to him because he's a suffering human being. Suffering is the supreme leveler, isn't it?"

"No one, not even us 'lucky whites,' is spared," said Jack.

"Take the rest of the day off," said Dan. "See you in the morning."

"See you in the morning," said Jack, "to begin a new future."

The Ultimate Success

R. P. Beckwith here.

The aberrant manifestations of human nature are compelling. Be assured that a person who commits a crime merely acts out wishes that reside in us all. So what holds us back? Fear that we'll be caught? Certainly, that's a major impediment. And why would we be caught? Because as humans we are inherently inefficient. From my experience as a former district attorney, I've found that typically we leave behind a telltale clue. The simple absence of a naked man's socks among clothes left on a beach is the clue that undid our city's benefactor and business leader Ben Ransom.

To keep my hand in the business of intrigue—although I'm retired from public service, I'm not ready to quit yet—I agreed to serve as a part-time investigator for the American General Life Insurance Company. As you no doubt know, an insurance company is a sitting duck for a dishonest policyholder, one who is expert in subterfuge. Let's consider the Ben Ransom case, the fifth that the company has assigned to me and perhaps my most challenging.

It began when Ransom, president of Ransom Pharmaceuticals, held a meeting of his fifty-person sales staff in the cafeteria of his plant in Middle City, a thriving community in central Massachusetts. The men and women sat around tables while Ben stood at a blackboard, which displayed an array of dollar figures.

"Now, I want all of you to impress on our customers that they don't have to pay for the products until they need them," Ben said, emphasizing the words "don't have to."

"You mean, they'll keep the goods in their inventory until they actually sell them?" asked one of the salesmen, looking perplexed at such an offer.

"How will the company know when that is?" said another salesman, seeing a problem, the first of many. "A customer could sell his inventory and simply not pay us."

"That's your job—knowing when that is," said Ben confidently. "Every time you visit a customer, check on the inventory. It's very simple."

"What about billing?" asked one of the saleswomen. "Are we billing the customer right away?"

"The day the goods are shipped," Ben replied.

"When do we get our commissions?" asked a third salesman.

"When the customer pays us," Ben said matter of factly.

The group grumbled, clearly unhappy with the arrangement. Certainly the new policy would boost sales, but the proposal was suspect and loaded with hidden complications.

The first salesman spoke up again. "It sounds to me like we're giving our customers goods on consignment. We're shipping the goods and billing them, but we can't say it's really a sale."

"It is a sale," said Ben, annoyed at the repeated objections. "And it's a good deal for us. Look, the customer is carrying the inventory instead of us. Only the execution of the transaction is delayed. That's all."

"What if a customer refuses to go along?" asked another salesman, despite Ben's visible impatience.

"Tell him that there'll be a price increase next week, but any order he places now is still at the old price. That should convince him. Show him how you're saving him money," Ben stated with a tone of finality. "Now, are there any more questions?"

The silence was broken only by people shifting in their chairs. No one had the courage to tell Ben that his new policy was dangerous and could have dire consequences.

"Good," said Ben. "Now let's get out there and sell. Push to get the customers to cooperate."

As the crowd broke into small conversational groups and the members exchanged their previously unspoken thoughts, the saleswoman who had spoken up earlier approached Ben.

"Mr. Ransom, I think we're making a mistake. I'm a stockholder, too."

"Really? That's terrific," said Ben. "Shows great dedication to our cause. Y'know, I wish all our employees owned a piece of the action like you."

"What concerns me, Mr. Ransom, is that the company will be showing increased sales and profits, but they aren't real. They will only be on paper."

"I hear what you're saying," Ben said, intent on mollifying her. "But you're wrong. You see, we're merely transferring inventory from us to them. It's that simple. And with business slowing these past few months, this program will prevent a massive layoff. You wouldn't want to see that, would you?"

"Of course not."

"So, you see why we must do this. Get out there and load up those customers. Why should they care? They don't have to pay for the products until they're ready. That's your talking point. If customers object, as I said, just tell them about the price increase. You'll be giving them an incentive for taking the stuff now."

"You're very convincing, Mr. Ransom. I'd say you're a pretty good salesman yourself."

"I *am* a salesman at heart. And I'll be on the phone to our contract customers to get them to cooperate, too. Don't worry."

Ben was a super-salesman, to be sure, a man who thought he could sell his way to success and out of any predicament. I have met many like him.

Before I retired ten years ago, I devoted my entire career to public service as a district attorney right here in Middle City. For forty years I put up with the arbitrariness of our judges and the frequent corruption of our police department. Too often I experienced the frustration of seeing the guilty go free or given leniency because society prefers to coddle them. We've lost a sense of outrage. Consequently I have chosen to devote the latter portion of my life to solving crimes, to puzzling out who did the deed, a never dull endeavor, and to digging up facts that lead to a logical inevitability that no judge or jury can dispute.

Six months passed. The salespeople pushed and, despite a recession, the customers cooperated. As sales swelled, the bottom line, at least on paper, broke a record. Ben was thus a hero of the sales force and the workers, and his son, George, who was Ben's production manager, and his daughter, Eve, a stockbroker, who touted the stock of Ransom Pharmaceuticals to all her clients.

But he wasn't Franklin's hero. Promptly at 7:00 a.m., when he knew that Ben began work, Franklin appeared at the door to Ben's opulent office.

"Good lord, Franklin, what's on your mind so early this morning?" Ben said. "Don't stand there; come in and have a seat."

"Speaking as your accountant...," said Franklin timidly, because he expected an argument to what he had to say.

"As opposed to being my friend, I presume," Ben said, in good humor. And why not, because Franklin had only good figures to report.

Franklin laughed nervously. "Your friend, too. Maybe more as your friend."

"I hear some words of advice already on their way," Ben said.

"Not advice. When I give you advice, you do as you damn well please. It's my final warning, Ben. The receivables situation has gotten out of hand. You can't ignore it any longer. And the finished goods inventory is at a dangerous level. You're running out of cash. I'm surprised the bank hasn't contacted you. Or have they?"

"Oh, c'mon, Franklin. Don't be so gloomy. No, the bank hasn't said a word, but I have an appointment with Brad."

"Then they don't know yet what's happened this past quarter?" said Franklin, his thin eyebrows raised.

"That's right. It's only a quarter. I don't see a problem. The bottom line looks great. That's what they look at. So they'll expand our credit line and everything will be fine."

"It's the cash flow, Ben," Franklin said, looking agitated. "Do you hear me? The game is cash flow, not bottom line. They're bound to ask how you got into this mess and demand some changes."

"Relax, my friend. It's nothing that a little more borrowed money won't fix. Take it easy, will you?"

"I'm concerned that you don't have much collateral left," said Franklin, gingerly removing a balance sheet from his briefcase and pointing to some figures.

"The bank will come through; it always has," responded Ben as he glanced at the piece of paper. "Remember, the bank owns a piece of the company. It's on the line as much as I am. They have no choice. I'll get the money; you can depend on it."

Ben saw Franklin as a typical accountant—conservative, certainly not the entrepreneurial type, knows only the numbers, forgets the role of relationships. But Franklin had served Ben well over the years and had acted as a good counter to Ben's more daring approach to business. As Franklin said, Ben always sought his advice and then did as he damn well pleased anyway. Hell, why not, thought Ben, I'm the one on the line.

Shortly after Franklin departed, the phone rang. It was Lily, who knew to call Ben before the office opened for business in the morning. Ben and Lily's affair had been ongoing for about four years.

"Hello. Lily? Yes, I miss you, too. No, not tonight. I've got to prepare for my meeting with the bank tomorrow. No, nothing's wrong. Things couldn't be better. Yes, my sweet, I long for you, too. Tomorrow night, how would that be? By then things will be settled with the bank. Then my mind will be free."

Ah, how tender and exciting is illicit love. There's no law against it, and if there were it would be the most violated law in our jurisprudence. I've observed that as men become middle aged, they often seek a younger woman to reinforce their waning powers. Ben, who was portly and at fifty-eight conscious of his lost youth every morning that he looked into the shaving mirror, found comfort in Lily's adoring fidelity.

At day's end after the office closed, Ben sent out for food to eat at his desk so he could continue working. Finally, weary from poring over the figures to present to Brad at the bank, he went home and settled into his favorite overstuffed chair, burying himself in the local newspaper.

Ben's wife, Chloe, a plain woman in her early fifties, heard him enter the house. As usual, she was in the kitchen busily preparing dinner. Tonight their adult children, George and Eve, would join them in a rare family get-together. Chloe dried her hands, feeling hurt that Ben didn't come into the kitchen to greet her, then went into the living room, pretending to be surprised at Ben's presence.

"Oh, you're finally home," she said as she bent down to kiss him. "How was your day?"

"Fine," Ben said, without responding to Chloe's kiss. He continued reading.

"Do you want to hear about my day?" Chloe inquired.

"Sure, sure," Ben replied without enthusiasm, maintaining his concentration on the newspaper.

"My day…well, nothing happened. Nothing you'd be interested in, I'm sure."

"Good," said Ben, looking up for the first time. "What did you say?"

Chloe sighed. "I'm making your favorite supper tonight."

"I've already eaten," said Ben. "I sent out for food at the office."

"Why? You knew the kids were coming for dinner. That's most inconsiderate of you."

"Damnit, I forgot," Ben said angrily.

"Why does the family always come second, Ben?" Chloe said, exasperated.

Ben lowered the newspaper to his lap. "It doesn't. Not a day goes by that I don't think of you and the kids."

"That's not the same as being with us. You're hardly here most of the time, and when you are, your mind is elsewhere. What's happened to us, Ben? You may be a big shot at the company, but at home you're only a fraction of a husband."

"I said I forgot. Is that a crime? Look, I've got other things on my mind. I don't need your lecturing." Glancing back at the newspaper, he read a headline. "Oh, my god."

"What? What's happened?" Chloe responded, fearing some calamity.

"Crowell Industries is going bankrupt."

"Who is Crowell Ind

"Our biggest customer. They owe us a bundle. Christ, this is terrible. Christ," said Ben, getting up to pour himself a drink.

"What does it mean, Ben? Is it serious?"

"Well, it doesn't help the cash flow, but we'll weather it. Nothing to worry about. It's just not a good time for this to happen. After I see Brad at the bank, everything will be all right," said Ben, returning to his chair and swigging his drink.

"You always know what to do. You're at your best in a crisis," Chloe said, bending down to kiss him again. "The kids should be here any minute. At least have dessert with us."

As Chloe left the room, Ben muttered to himself, "The worst possible time. The goddamn worst possible time." The Crowell account constituted a quarter of his business. If Crowell went under, he would be in real trouble. He knew it wasn't his only trouble. There was—well, he wouldn't think about that. He wouldn't want Chloe to know. She was a worrier. Thank god she thought he could fix anything. And, of course, she was right.

George had a key to the front door and let himself in. He was tall and portly like his father.

"Hi, Dad," he said.

Staring into space, Ben nodded.

George sat on the sofa opposite his father and gazed at him. "Can we talk business for a minute?" George asked.

"Well, do it now," Ben replied, preferring to remain submerged in his own thoughts. "You know how your mother feels about business talk at the dinner table."

"We're getting a pile of returns at the plant—unopened cartons," said George. "I've never seen anything like it. I think you ought to know."

"I'm sure it's nothing to worry about," Ben said. Then he realized that there was something to worry about. "You say the cartons are unopened?"

"That's right, so it's not a quality problem."

"Okay. I'll have sales look into it," said Ben, playing down George's report. He had enough to worry about.

"It's strange. The returns are coming in from all over the country," George persisted.

"Yeah, as I said, sales will—"

"Something's wrong, Dad. Sales should investigate right away."

"I heard you," Ben said sharply. "You take care of production, as you're supposed to. I'll take care of the rest."

"Take it easy. I was only making a constructive suggestion. There's an ugly rumor going around the company—"

"About what?" Ben pounced, increasingly tense.

"That the company's short of cash."

"Who told you that?"

"The workers in my department. They're worried."

"How in hell...It's not true," Ben responded indignantly. "You know we've got a virtually unlimited credit line with the bank. It gets me how crazy rumors start without any foundation."

"Sure, Dad. I told them there was nothing to worry about. You're on top of everything."

Eve, who also had a key to the front door, bounced into the room. "Hiya, guys. What's new? Say, that was nice news about the company, Dad."

Eve was in her early thirties, trim and attractive, an investment broker with the most prestigious house in town.

"Yeah, I meant to mention it," George put in. "The best bottom line ever. I'm proud of you. That's what I told the people: The company's making a nice profit."

"I'd say you're the most popular CEO in town," Eve said proudly as she sat on the arm of Ben's chair and hugged him. "Webster and Company received a flood of orders just since last night. The price of your stock went up three points today alone. I tell everyone they can't go wrong. It's the best investment they'll ever make."

Ben was visibly uncomfortable. "You shouldn't tell them that, Eve," he said. "You know better. Every stock has its risks. The market is irrational—emotional."

"I agree. But I tell my customers that I know your company firsthand, and I know my dad. You're a winner. I can't be that sure about my other recommendations. I even bought more stock for myself."

"You should diversify," counseled Ben. "After I die you'll have plenty of stock in the company. I wish you wouldn't put all your eggs in my basket."

"That's where you have them, Dad. Why not me? Don't they say, like father, like daughter?"

"It's 'like son,' Eve," George said.

"You're nothing like Dad, George. But I am. Anyway, I'm not planning on Dad dying. I don't want company stock that way."

"Life is a fragile thing," said Ben. "You're too young to know that yet. Get to be fifty-eight, you can be gone like a flash."

"Is there something wrong, Dad?" asked Eve.

"Aren't you feeling well?" said George, with some alarm in his voice.

"Don't worry, I'm okay. It's just as you get older you become more aware of how short life is. There's less time for a second chance, and you have a hell of a lot less spark. You can't afford many mistakes."

"But Dad, you don't make mistakes," Eve said with fervor. "You've made a steady climb to the top. I want to be just like you."

Chloe called from the kitchen. "Dinner's ready, everybody."

"Listen, Eve," said Ben, "getting to the top is one thing. Staying there is quite another. It's more frightening, because you have much more to lose."

"Dinner's getting cold," Chloe shouted.

"We're coming. We're coming," George said, rising.

But Ben lingered. "Listen, kids, I'm going to beg off. Tell your mother I still have some work to do to get ready for an important meeting early tomorrow morning." He chuckled. "The wicked have no rest."

Ben left the house without another word and went to see Lily. She would listen to his woes.

The next morning, Ben appeared right on time at the bank. "Well, you're looking fit these days," Ben said, reaching to shake Brad's hand. It was the contrast with himself that Ben couldn't fail to observe. "Oh, to be forty-three again."

"It's the jogging," Brad said, grinning. "I do it every morning."

"Jogging, eh? If I had the time..."

"You make the time, Ben." Brad looked directly at Ben's pot. "It would be good for you. Say, congratulations. The word's out that your sales broke a record and the bottom line...well..."

Ben shrugged, yet he was pleased that Brad had a positive view of things. "Just as I predicted, Brad," he said.

"I'm glad you called. We were about to call you," Brad stated.

"I suppose it's about the credit line, eh? We've reached our limit."

"Well, yes, that, and about some things that are puzzling."

"Brad, you know how it is. You make more sales, you need more cash. Another couple million would suit us just fine—for, say, six more months, until the cash starts coming in from our receivables."

"That's what I want to ask you about. How do you account for the unusual jump in sales this past quarter?"

"It's simple, Brad, very simple. The customers are building inventories and they've asked for time. But they're all solid accounts; they're good for it."

"I see. Well, that's not necessarily the case."

"What do you mean?" Ben demanded, startled.

"When we noticed that you reached the end of your credit line while your receivables were climbing, naturally we got a little nervous."

Ben flushed as if he were having a hot flash. The discussion was going in the wrong direction. It was imperative that he find a way to change it.

"Naturally. I can understand that."

"So we called a few of the accounts to check out their credit worthiness. You know, get some information on how they were doing."

"Sure, sure," Ben said, trying to moderate his rising anger. "But why in hell didn't you call me? I could have told you about any of our accounts."

"Of course we could have done that, Ben, but that's not the bank's procedure," said Brad coldly. "Well, we did it, and we were in for quite a surprise."

"You found they were good for it, right?" Ben said, regaining some self-assurance.

"It turns out that isn't the issue. Sure, they're sound accounts, but they told us they never ordered the goods you sent them."

"There must be a mistake."

"Apparently not. This led us to call several more of your accounts, and they all said the same thing." Brad knew he had Ben, and he wasn't about to let go.

"Well, it's true we told our customers that if they placed their orders before year's end they wouldn't have to pay until next year," Ben said, making the best of a doomed situation.

"The way we hear it, they have no obligation to pay by any particular date. In fact, several of your customers tell us they're returning the goods." Brad sighed. "What are you trying to do, Ben? I think you ought to stop playing games and level with us."

"I'm not playing games," Ben said desperately.

"Okay, okay. But tell us what's actually going on here."

"Well, sales have been dropping off lately. Competition is getting fierce, and it will be a while before the new products we've got in the pipeline are ready for market. So we overshipped a few accounts, strictly a temporary measure, to maintain the bottom line and keep the stock price up. You know how erratic the market is; when it sees sales fall, it goes into a panic. Hell, the bank only benefits from this policy. It secures the value of its twenty-five-percent interest in the company."

How could the bank not see the logic of my argument? thought Ben. Aren't I protecting the bank's interest as well as my own? But Brad refused to go along.

"I'm afraid the bank doesn't see it that way, Ben. What you've done is a deception. The sales aren't real, so neither is the bottom line. Were this information to get out, the stock would plummet."

"How will anyone else know? Tell me."

"What are you going to do with the returned goods? You can't sell them; there's no demand. Do you realize how much money you're tying up in inventory, maybe obsolete inventory that could be rendered worthless once you or the competition comes out with new lines? No, Ben, when the board learns what you've done, there'll be hell to pay. I've been directed to tell you that an emergency board meeting is scheduled for tomorrow morning at nine."

"Tomorrow morning? I have an appointment to meet with the CEO of Crowell Industries tomorrow morning."

"Cancel it, Ben."

"Haven't you heard? Crowell is going chapter eleven."

"Yes, we know. And they're one of the accounts you shipped tons of unordered product to. It's a bad situation. Your meeting with Crowell will be a waste of time. If you get ten cents on the dollar, you'll be lucky."

Brad stood up and extended his hand to Ben, signaling that the conversation was over. Taking Brad's hand, Ben searched his eyes for some sign of empathy. But Brad, impatient to get on with his next task, cast his eyes toward some papers on his desk. It was obvious to Ben that he could expect no mercy from this quarter.

"See you in the morning," said Brad as Ben turned and strode toward the door on rubbery legs.

The board of Ransom Pharmaceuticals consisted of five mature, seasoned men whom Ben had handpicked for their expertise and compatibility with him. Once a quarter they sat around a long table in the conference room and discussed the company's past performance and future strategy. Ben, being the major stockholder, presided and generally had his way on most issues—that is, until the bank purchased a portion of the company's stock and Brad, as the bank's representative, put in his 25 percent's worth.

Promptly at nine that morning, Ben opened the meeting. "I realize, gentlemen, that what we've done looks bad, but it really isn't. It's only temporary. Eventually, we will work off the excess goods." He sounded more than a little defensive.

Clint, a local businessman, responded before Ben's last words had left his mouth. "I'm not so concerned about the logistics of your excess inventory. What I'm concerned about is the dishonesty of your act." Clint scanned the faces around the table searching for their assent and received nods and positive looks. "How did you expect to get away with it?"

"I think you're exaggerating the situation, Clint," said Ben, sensing that he was losing his dominance. "You know from running your own business that you've often got to stretch the limits a little; the bottom line calls the shots, dictates what has to be done. It's sacred and must be maintained. So how can you fault me for what I've done?"

"Because the bottom line you've created is false, Ben," said Franklin, his always loyal accountant. "It's a fiction. I wish you had listened to me more."

Siggy, the company's lawyer, spoke. "Let's get down to the nitty-gritty, gentlemen. Assuming that most of the quarter's billings aren't true sales and that a good chunk of the credit line is tied up in worthless inventory, what do we do? What do you suggest, Franklin?"

Ben interrupted before the accountant could speak. "You're wrong, Siggy. The inventory isn't worthless. Even if we sell it as distressed goods, we can at least recover our cost."

For the first time at any meeting, Siggy ignored Ben's words. "I addressed my question to Franklin," he said, looking to the accountant for a reply.

"Downsize," replied Franklin. "We need a major layoff to cut our losses. There's no alternative. We must do that, Ben."

"Listen to me," Ben implored. "Why don't you understand that this is a temporary situation?"

Siggy again ignored Ben. "In my business, we operate on the assumption of a worst-case scenario. I say eliminate any unnecessary risk."

Brad, who had by now captured the implications of his colleagues' feelings, finally spoke. "Ben, I'd like you to leave the room. We'll call you back in shortly."

Ben was indignant. "What? I should leave? This is my company, and I chair this meeting. You're my friends; you can't do this."

"But we can, Ben," Brad said in his best pontificating manner. "The credit line is overextended. Once that happened, you lost control— read the agreement. Look, I don't feel happy about this; I'm your friend. But there's a limit to what friendship can do. Business has nothing to do with friendship. You must realize that."

"How dare you? This is my business," said Ben, pounding the table with both fists. "I own a majority of the shares. I still control the company. I built it from a garage operation to where it is today with my own bare hands. I *am* the company."

"And where is it today?" Brad asked. "There's no cash; you can't go on. You no longer own a majority. That's what I'm trying to tell you. The bank is picking up its option, as stipulated in the agreement. We're converting the loan into stock, which gives the bank controlling interest. I'm sorry. That's the way it is."

"Damnit, Ben," Franklin interjected. "Why did you persist? I've been warning you for months. Why didn't you listen? You must have known that it would catch up with you."

Ben sat back in his chair, shocked and deflated. "To save the company, Franklin," he said softly. "I persisted because I wanted to save the company. Given enough time, I thought customers would take the goods. I knew it was a dangerous gamble, but what was I to do? Real sales weren't coming. Competition is getting tougher and tougher; prices are falling. I thought it would be a temporary thing. There was nothing else I could do."

"What about pulling in your horns, scaling down?" asked Siggy. "A little hubris, Ben, is that it? You had to be the big deal; you had—"

"Shut up, you bastard," Ben seethed.

There were several moments of awkward silence. "That's enough," Brad said. "If you'll leave, Ben, please."

Ben brusquely grabbed his papers and, trembling, supported himself along the edge of the table as he walked out of the room.

"I think it's time to consider new leadership, gentlemen," Brad continued after the door closed. "Real profits have been declining for two years. The bank has had it with Ben's mistakes. He refuses to acknowledge them, grasp their consequences. He's stubborn, close-minded, and blind to what he's done. And he believes he can do anything he wishes. He's dangerous, gentlemen, a high-stakes gambler. Each of us has a responsibility to our stockholders, of which the bank is certainly a major one. I propose that Siggy take over temporarily while we search for a competent CEO."

"I'm all for that," Clint said.

"What about you, Franklin?" Brad asked.

"I feel like a rat," said Franklin. "Ben and I have been friends since he came to Middle City twenty-five years ago. He's confided in me, sought my advice. He could have used any of the prestigious national accounting firms, but he stayed with my firm, with me."

"We're all in that boat, Franklin," Brad pointed out. "We're all his friends. I've been his banker since day one. But the company's survival is primary. After all, Ben still owns a good chunk of the business. Under current conditions, it may be worth little, but he'll benefit from a turnaround. Can we agree, then?"

All assented as Brad picked up the phone.

"Would you please ask Mr. Ransom to join us?"

Ben entered, then stood without making a move. Brad motioned him to take his usual chair at the head of the table.

"Please sit down, Ben."

"No, I'd rather stand. I take it I'm done as CEO."

"I'm afraid so."

There was a long silence. "I see," said Ben finally. "Well, no hard feelings. You've all done your duty. I wish you luck."

Ben turned and walked out the door without closing it behind him. "I may be down, but I'm not out," he muttered to himself. "I'll beat this. I don't know how, not yet. Just stick around everybody and watch me."

As a criminal investigator, I wish to comment that Ben has done nothing illegal, so his actions to this point are not my concern. Of course, what he has done is unethical, but in business such behavior is routine. The reason? There's so much opportunity. We run into it every day, from labeling on packages to misleading advertising. But desperate men often commit desperate acts, and those are usually illegal.

Ben couldn't face returning to his office. He wasn't ready to go home and deal with Chloe. But Lily, his adoring Lily, was always ready to listen to his woes and offer encouragement.

Lily was at her easel when Ben arrived.

"Well, isn't this a surprise?" she said. "A visit from my honey on a weekday morning." She rushed to embrace him, but it was immediately obvious that he wasn't interested. "Are you all right, Ben? Is something wrong?" His face was still ashen.

Lily was a beauty: auburn hair, trim figure, small, barely five feet, glittering dark eyes, and proud that she had warded off the appearance of middle age so well.

Withdrawing from her embrace, Ben dropped onto the couch that filled a corner of the studio. "Wrong?" he said. "I've just lost my company."

"Lost your company? How? It's yours. I don't understand. No one can take that away from you."

"Oh, yes they can," Ben said bitterly, "and they did. After all I've given to the company. After all the years of business I've given the bank, they've taken it all away from me. Goddamn them."

"What happened, Ben?"

"I'd rather not go into it, not now."

"Of course. It's painful, I know," Lily said softly, sitting beside him and caressing him. "I'm so sorry."

"Thanks, Lily. Thanks for your understanding."

"I'm sure you'll find a way to—"

"Get it back? There's no way," said Ben, shaking his head.

"I mean, to beat this."

"Sure, I'll beat it. I'll start over, that's what I'll do. I may be fifty-eight, but by god I have some life left in me yet."

"So I've noticed," said Lily slyly as she hugged him to her. But Ben, lost in thought, didn't respond. "Do you want to stay with me tonight?" she asked.

"I wouldn't be any good."

"I don't mean that. We could just be together. I'd keep you warm. I'd make you comfortable."

"Lily, my love, nothing can make me comfortable. I won't be comfortable until...until I'm on top again. Do you understand?"

"Of course, dear."

"The problem is my age. Is it too late to start over?"

"We elect presidents older than you, Ben."

"Sure, to run the country, not to run a business. There's no comparison. I can't think of a president who could replace me. I wouldn't hire any of them. Maybe Roosevelt, Lincoln," Ben said and began to laugh. "Imagine Johnson or Nixon keeping a company in the black. And Reagan—inspiring maybe but nothing more than a figurehead. He got us deeper into the red than anyone. Worse yet, there's the second Bush." Ben clasped her hand in his. "You're good for me, Lily. I'm lucky to have you."

"And I'm lucky to have you. If not for you, I'd still be a banker's secretary instead of doing what I love."

"I believe in you, Lily. You're a first-class artist, and someday the whole world will know."

"I don't care about the world. I just want you and my art," said Lily wistfully. "But I don't have you, do I?"

"Of course you do. I'm yours. You know that."

"Certain days, certain hours. That's hardly a full commitment."

"Let's not get into that, okay?" Ben said, standing up.

"Sure, my sweet. You're under stress." She paused before continuing, asking herself, then asking Ben, "What happens next?"

"I don't know. I have to think," he said, pacing. "What do I say to the kids? They've always looked up to me. Especially Eve. Placed their faith in me. Now, they'll see me as a failure. I've let them down. Only yesterday the stock skyrocketed because we showed a terrific bottom line. You hear me, Lily? The company was heading for...for the stars. And in less than twenty-four hours, the board thinks we're heading for bankruptcy and I'm accused of mismanagement. Can you beat that? It's such a shock.

"The suddenness of it. Did it really happen?" he said out loud, although he seemed to be talking to himself. "Overnight I'm worthless. I feel such shame. A failure. I was class president in high school, top man in my college class. Worked hard, strove to be the best, wanted to do only good. And now look at me. Oh, I've had a setback now and then—but small ones, nothing like this. What can I do? Most of my life is over. I can't end up this way."

"Darling, it's not the end. It's a new beginning."

"I hope so. I've never doubted myself before. They've taken away the fruit of my best years. How can it be the same again? Does that mean it will get worse? Can it be better? I'm frightened, Lily."

"Come close to me. Let me hold you," Lily said, pulling him down to sit on the sofa beside her. "I'm with you, Ben. You aren't alone."

Ben was about to take the first step to implement a plan that would make Chloe secure against any eventuality. Although outwardly displaying a positive attitude, he knew that his self-confidence was shattered for the first time in his life, and the consequences could well be disastrous.

As he strode into Franklin's precisely kept office and sat down beside the desk, he felt deflated. But part of him refused to give in to his depression. Part of him kept fighting.

"So it's over," he said to Franklin, slapping his hand on the desk. "All those years you did our books, given us the benefit of your wisdom. It's a goddamn shame, Franklin, a goddamn waste. Don't you agree?"

"I hope you realize I had nothing to do with this," Franklin pointed out.

"Of course. I know it was out of your hands. The bank was calling the shots. But, y'know, Franklin, you didn't have to take their side so blatantly. I mean, you sat there and gave me hell right in front of them."

"I'm sorry. You're right. I shouldn't have done that. But I was so damned pissed that you hadn't listened to me and that, if you had, none of this would be taking place. Christ, Ben, why in hell wouldn't you listen to me?"

"Well, that's spilt milk. I'm here because I believe you're still loyal to me."

"I certainly am, Ben. We grew big together. If it weren't for you, I'd still be running a one-man operation, not the fifty I've got now."

"I was wondering whether you'd be willing to do me a small favor."

"Sure, anything, Ben," said Franklin, welcoming the opportunity to make up for his small infidelity.

"The company has an insurance policy on my life. I'd like you to have it transferred to me."

"If Brad approves, I don't see a problem."

"No, Franklin. Keep Brad out of this. You do it."

"But the company owns the policy. I'll need his approval."

"Why? The company no longer needs insurance on my life. I'm not here. Don't you get it?"

"Well, if you were to die, god forbid, the insurance proceeds would go a long way toward purchasing your shares."

"Tell me, Franklin. Whose side are you on? Since when does the bank need that kind of money? Furthermore, the bank doesn't know about the policy. One of their oversights. I never told them about it."

"Really? I'm surprised that they didn't insist—"

"As I said, it was their oversight. They aren't as sharp as they think they are. So what do you say? Since the bank doesn't know it exists, it won't know a thing about what you're doing."

Ben reached into his jacket and handed Franklin the papers. "Here's the policy," he said.

This was the act that ultimately brought me into the picture some time later. To this day I am not clear about Ben's motivation at the time. Did he have a specific plan in mind that would involve the policy, or did he wish to acquire the policy—as any breadwinner would do—as a matter of course?

"Have the policy transferred to me and make Chloe my beneficiary," Ben told Franklin. "For friendship's sake, okay?"

"It's too late, Ben. I'll need an officer's signature to sign the request. Your signature won't qualify."

"Haven't you ever heard of predating? Draw up a letter, dated last week, and as president I'll sign it."

"Hell, I don't know. It's not the way I do things."

"I know that, Franklin. That's why I trust you."

"I'll do it for you as a friend, Ben, not professionally."

"Okay, but of course you'll still be my accountant."

"Sure, Ben. I'll still be your man, just so long as you don't ask me for anything else that involves the company. You understand?"

"Absolutely. I wouldn't think of it."

Ben began to feel his self-confidence return, as though he had retaken control, albeit in a small way. Winning over Franklin was proof that his persuasive powers were still intact. Yet the facts of his demise were stark. The future appeared bleak, threatening, unconquerable.

After leaving Franklin's office, Ben returned home. Where else was he to go? There was no point in going back to Lily's. He lay on the living room couch, wallowing in defeat, his hand over his face.

Chloe entered the room, startled. "What are you doing here at this hour? What's wrong? Aren't you feeling well?"

"You're damn right I'm not feeling well. I've lost the company. They took it away from me. I'm fired. Can you imagine?"

"Fired? How can you be fired? You're the boss," Chloe said, disbelieving. She sat down.

"I'm not the boss anymore. The bank is."

"I don't understand."

"The bank doesn't like the way I was running things. They've taken over."

"I thought everything was going smoothly," said Chloe. "You never mentioned problems."

"You were never interested."

"I'm interested when you're having problems," she said, her tone like steel.

"Hell you are. When I used to tell you about the problems at work, you said that you had enough of your own running the house, so I stopped telling you."

"Well, surely if the company's problems affect the family, I want to know. You should at least realize that." Feeling that a full-blown battle was about to begin, she tried to contain herself. One disaster was enough.

"So, now there'll be no more problems to tell you about, will there?" Ben said sarcastically.

"What did you do that made them fire you?"

"What did I do? That sounds like an accusation."

"No, dear. I simply want to know what happened."

"I'd rather not go into it. But I can tell you that what I did was for the good of the company. In time, things would have straightened out."

"Can't it be fixed? Have you talked to Brad?"

"For chrissakes," Ben exploded. "The bank is the problem, and Brad is the bank."

"Excuse me, I didn't know. What does this mean? What will you do?"

"I don't know. I don't know," Ben said, blankly staring past her.

"This is the first time I've heard you say that."

"It's the first time I've ever failed."

Chloe walked to the sofa and sat on the edge of the cushion as she reached over to stroke her husband's hair. "You'll find a way. You always have," she said calmly.

"Sure, sure," Ben said as he removed her hand.

The phone rang and Chloe got up and answered it. "Yes, your father is here. I'm not sure it's a good idea to come over right now." Covering the mouthpiece, she turned to Ben. "It's George. He's says he's calling from his car and he's on his way."

"Tell him it's okay," Ben said, grateful for the interruption.

"Your father says come," Chloe said and hung up, pleased that Ben wanted to see their son. It was a good sign. "What are you going to tell the kids?"

"I'll tell them what happened, of course. I've done nothing to be ashamed of."

"I'm worried about you, Ben." Chloe wanted to embrace him and tell him that she believed in him, but she hesitated, knowing that he would repel her affection, as he had for several years. It hadn't always been that way. She blamed the business.

"You needn't be. I'll be all right," Ben said.

"The business has been more important to you than anything else in your life. Now you have us, Ben. You have me and the kids, and we're behind you."

"I'm grateful for that, Chloe. I really am. It's good to know. I've always worked for all of us, not just myself. Sometimes it may not have seemed that way, but you always came first in my mind. It's ingrained in me. I would never desert you."

"Why would you even say that? It wouldn't occur to me. We may have our differences, but I never doubted your loyalty...."

"You know I'll always take care of all of you"

"Yes, I know that. You're a good man, Ben. You mean well."

"Look where it's got me. My god," Ben said covering his face again with his hands.

George, who had let himself in with his key, entered the room panting and excited. "Dad, is it true?"

Ben immediately sat up, wanting his son to see him in his usual commanding position. "Yup, I'm no longer your boss. I've been demoted to being just your father."

"Damnit, Dad," George said impatiently. "You knew why all the material was being returned. Why in hell didn't you level with me?"

"Don't jump to conclusions, son. You don't know the whole story," Ben said defensively.

"Tell us the whole story, Ben," said Chloe. "I want to know."

Ben repeated his litany

"The way I hear it, you also had merchandise shipped to customers without their permission just to make things look good," George said, with challenge in his voice.

"Maybe the salespeople got a little enthusiastic," Ben said sheepishly.

"C'mon, Dad. They wouldn't make a move without you."

"Do you doubt me?"

"Damn right I do. Can you blame me? How do you think I feel? Here I am, in charge of production, and my own father, the CEO, is cheating, deceiving everybody. And, incredibly, you thought you could get away with it. Christ, Dad, I've always admired you."

Ben was contrite. "I'm...I'm sorry, son, I've let you down. I really thought it was the only way I could save the company. I had no choice."

"You could have faced the music and downsized," George responded without mercy.

"Maybe so, maybe so. But that would have been costly, so I chose not to. I made a mistake, but it was an honest one."

George rolled his eyes and looked to his mother. "I called Eve before I left the office. She's on her way over."

"I don't know about business," said Chloe, "but it sounds to me like you made a dishonest mistake, Ben."

"I thought you were behind me," Ben said, glaring at her.

"How am I going to face my people in the plant?" said George.

"How does this change anything for you?" Ben asked.

"It's taken me a long time to win their respect," George explained. "I've had to overcome the fact that I'm the CEO's son. Don't you understand? Your error reflects on me. Your shame is my shame, too."

"There's no shame in what I did," Ben insisted. "Tell them the truth. You didn't know. That's all."

"They'll never believe it; not where blood's concerned. I'm not sure I still have a job."

"Sure you do. They need you," said Ben, standing up and heading for the kitchen.

Eve burst into the room and rushed to her father, embracing him. "I'm sorry, Daddy. George told me what happened."

"Everything will be okay, honeybunch," said Ben welcoming her embrace and sympathy.

"What exactly...how did this happen?"

"The world suddenly learned that the company's bottom line is fake," George offered sourly. "And Dad created it."

"I don't believe it. How—"

"Well, we've been having some problems," Ben said.

"What?" Eve said indignantly. "That's not what you've been telling me. I've been recommending the stock to my biggest customers based on your assurance that the company's future was secure and bright. Don't you realize I stuck my neck out, and now you're saying your story was a lie?"

"I...I...I meant what I said. I felt sure it would turn around," said Ben weakly.

"But you didn't tell me the truth. You lied to me, you lied," Eve cried.

"I'm sorry, honeybunch, I'm sorry." That was all a downcast Ben could say.

"Damnit, Dad," George said, pacing back and forth to let off steam. "How could you have done such a stupid thing?"

Ben buried his face in his hands and sobbed. His family had never seen him cry before. Despite their anger, it shattered them to see him break apart.

Ben raised his head and spoke as much to himself as to them. "Listen to me. You build a business from scratch with your own sweat. You eventually employ hundreds of people who depend on you. You do good work and become an icon in the community. You must not fail; it is not permitted. It would have been so hard to contemplate retreat. Every fiber of me rebelled at the idea. I had to take the alternative. My pride, my soul, my life depended on it. Can you understand?"

Chloe knew her husband, and George and Eve knew their father, and they understood.

A month passed, and Ben had fallen into a deep depression. Chloe and the children were worried as they discussed his condition in the living room.

"All he does is sit in his bathrobe and watch TV," Chloe said in despair. "He doesn't even bother to get dressed, and he's irritable. You can't say anything without his snapping at you. People call, old friends, and he won't talk to them. I've never seen him like this."

"He needs help. A professional," George suggested.

"I've tried to get him to see someone, but he won't hear of it," Chloe said, feeling hopeless.

"Maybe I could persuade him," Eve offered.

"You can try. But get ready for an explosion," said Chloe.

"He's so damn proud," said George. "He may say he's made a mistake, but I don't think he really believes it."

"Of course he doesn't believe it," Chloe said. "He keeps blaming the bank, especially Brad. Did your father ever admit he made a mistake?"

"Let me talk to him," Eve repeated.

Ben, dressed in a bathrobe, strode into the room. "What's this? Some kind of conspiracy going on?"

"Sure, Dad, a conspiracy to see what we can do," said Eve.

"About what?"

"About you," said George.

"About me? I can take care of myself."

"Look at you, still in your robe. Is this taking care of yourself?"

"Shut up, George," Eve said. "Dad, we hate to see you like this."

"Just leave me alone. I'll be all right."

"When, Ben?" asked Chloe. "I'm waiting."

Ben turned to George. "How's it going at the plant?"

"We've cut way back—to less than half the number of people we used to have."

"So business is lousy, eh?" Ben said, feeling redeemed that the new management wasn't performing any better than he had.

"Could be better," said George.

"And how's the investment business?" Ben asked Eve.

"She had sold stock in the company to most of her clients," George said before Eve could answer, "and they haven't forgiven her. See what you've done?"

"Don't you think I know that? I'm well aware of the consequences of what's happened," Ben said angrily.

"George, how could you?" said Eve. "That's a cruel thing to say to our father. Dad, won't you see someone and talk about this? Do it for us, if not for yourself."

Ben had been over this again and again with Chloe. "What would be the use? For chrissake, they'd have to undo all that's happened."

"Only God could do that. Maybe you ought to talk to Him," said Chloe with a touch of sarcasm." Why can't you be realistic? You've always been so sensible."

"Please, for us," said Eve. "It's so painful to see you this way."

"I'll think about it."

"Well, that's something, anyway," Chloe said.

"Actually I've got some ideas about the future," Ben said. "But I'll need you kids to help me."[

Although Ben was depressed and some days stayed in bed, even refusing to eat, gradually he was coming out of it. The thought of a fresh start was beginning to gestate in his mind.

"Of course, Daddy," Eve said, nodding and giving George an encouraging eye.

"Sure thing," George said.

"I'm thinking of starting a new pharmaceuticals business."

"Great, Dad," said George, genuinely pleased.

"I'm glad you approve, because I'd like you to come in with me. We'll need some financing, and that's where you come in, Eve. So both of you will be my partners. It'll be a real family business. Give the old business a little competition, eh? Give the bank a run for its money."

His fresh enthusiasm was a gift to all of them, and they wanted desperately to sustain it. But there was reality to deal with.

"I...I don't think I'd have much luck raising any cash these days," Eve said.

"Why not? Lost your touch? A super saleswoman like you?" Ben said.

"I hate to say this to you, Daddy, but I'm afraid you don't have much credibility anymore."

"Credibility? Hell, I'm still the same guy who built the old business and put this town on the map."

"I know *you* are the same," Eve said, emphasizing "you." "But they've forgotten."

"So, everyone thinks I'm a failure, is that it? Don't they realize that some of the most successful people in the world have failed, some more than once? Walt Disney failed. Did you know that? And look how he came back."

"I can't afford to give up my job," George said. "Furthermore, the bank's counting on me. There's talk about moving me up."

"The bank's the enemy," said Ben sharply. "Why can't you understand that?"

"The bank's my employer. Why can't you understand that?"

"So neither of you will join me, huh? That's the kind of thanks I get for bringing you kids up, sending you to the best schools in the country and—"

"Ben. Stop that," Chloe shouted. "We did it for them, not ourselves."

"Sure, sure. I know. I shouldn't have said that. But I'm disappointed. Somehow I expected you'd have more faith in me."

"We do have faith in you. We do, Daddy," Eve said.

"Please don't blame us. We have our own lives," added George.

"Of course you have. It was just an idea I had. I thought it would bring us together somehow," said Ben.

Avoiding one another's eyes, they lapsed into silence. Then George, feeling guilty over letting his father down, blurted, "I'm sorry, Dad. It's just...I hope you don't take this wrong. It's just that I don't trust your judgment."

"Don't trust my judgment, eh? For most of my life I worked my butt off and made decisions that gave us all of this, a standard of living better than 99 percent of the people in this town. You trusted my judgment when I took a chance and brought you into the business and gave you responsibilities. I did it because I believed in you.

"Sure I made what turned out to be a possible mistake—it's not cut and dried, y'know; there are many players in this. But now you're judging me not on what I've built over the years but on a single unfortunate minor error over which I had no control."

Eve, stinging from the consequences of the company's troubles, had to speak. "Minor error? My stockholder customers sure don't see it that way."

"Is it really that simple, Ben? A minor error?" said Chloe.

"Hell no, Mom," George said. He turned to Ben. "It isn't a minor error, as you call it. You act as if the consequences are unimportant."

"Sure there have been consequences. I shouldn't have said minor, but I know it's not the end of the world. It's only a temporary setback. What I created once, I can do again. Now, are you going to be with me or against me?"

"I'm not against you. It isn't a question of being for or against," said George.

"Sure it is," replied Ben, "because I'm going to bury my old company."

"Damnit, Dad. I admit it bothers me that you'd be competing with us," said George. He hesitated before asking, "When did you plan to start this business?"

"Right away. Look, George, I still have a few bucks. You'd have a salary—"

"There'd be no need," George interrupted. "I have some savings. Why are you so vindictive?"

"You mean after what they've done to me I should forgive those bastards? Anyway, I'd have no choice but to go after my old customers. They all know me. Business is business. We'd be equal partners, George. You'd be your own boss. You'll never have that where you are. Where's that entrepreneurial spirit, eh?" Ben slapped George affectionately on the back.

"It's true, I've always liked the idea of being my own boss."

"With me you'd have it," Ben promised.

"You mean that? Full partner, split down the middle?"

"Absolutely. I'd want it no other way, son."

George pondered for a few minutes. "Okay. I'll give Siggy my two weeks' notice."

Ben suddenly felt like his old self. He hugged George to him, "Atta boy. You won't regret it."

"But no games, Dad. You know what I mean?"

"Games? I don't play games."

"Like what happened at the company."

"That wasn't a game. As I said, it was a necessity. Anyway, with us the books will be open. Maybe I can get Franklin to quit the board and take us on, the way he did the first time around. And I'll get Siggy to do the legal work, draw up a partnership agreement between us. To win in business, you need a good Jewish accountant and a good Irish lawyer. We'll have the benefit of my past experience, George. Round two is bound to be smoother and better."

"I hope so, Daddy," said Eve.

"It looks to me like you lost round one, Ben," Chloe said.

"Maybe, but the fight isn't over. We'll win, guaranteed. Right, George?"

Ben punched George lightly on the chin, prompting George to respond. Father and son swerved back and forth across the room in a feigned boxing match as the women laughed and egged each man on.

Could it be the old days all over again? wondered Chloe. "Well, it's sure good to see your spirit back, Ben. Kids, when your father was younger, when we were first married, he was a living dynamo. There was no holding him back."

"I'm still the same guy, Chloe. A little older, a little wiser, but more determined than ever," said Ben, panting.

"Oh, Daddy, I wish you luck," said Eve. "I'm sorry I can't help. You too, George."

"That's okay. I've caused you enough problems," said Ben as Eve hugged him. "So, onward we go. Tomorrow, round two begins. Break out the wine, Chloe. Let's drink to round two."

Fresh beginnings are marvelous because in them we are innocents. For all Ben's past experience, he still had more to learn. His first lesson began the next day in Franklin's office.

"Sorry to keep you waiting, Ben," Franklin said after motioning him to a chair beside his desk. "Client business, you know."

"No need to apologize, my friend. But this isn't strictly a social call."

"How long has it been now since—"

"The board meeting? Ten years, Franklin, at least ten years."

"All of a month, I'd say," Franklin countered, grinning.

"Yeah, it only seems like ten years. Tell me, are you still serving on the board?"

"Yes, but I'm thinking of resigning. The bank pretty much makes all the decisions. The board has become nothing more than a rubber stamp."

"Not like when we had a board, eh?"

"We were a team then," Franklin said wistfully.

"How would you like to become a member of my new team?" said Ben. "George and I are starting a new business. Same as the old company's, because that's where all my connections are—customers, vendors..

"But not with the bank, obviously," said Franklin.

"Definitely not. Brad is no friend," Ben said firmly.

"What about capital? Most of your net worth is tied up in the company—which, by the way, is still in trouble."

"That's where you come in. With your connections—banks and various moneyed investors around town, your clients—I thought you might set us up, put in a good word."

"You're my friend, Ben," said Franklin sincerely, "and I'd like to help, but I'm afraid too much damage has been done. Your reputation has suffered, Ben. You were number one in this community; everyone believed in you. Now people are so disillusioned that, in effect, you've become a pariah. No one wants to be involved with you. No bank, no investor would be interested."

"The higher you go, the bigger the fall. Is that it?"

"I'm afraid so," said Franklin, looking genuinely sympathetic. Indeed, he felt proud that he had the courage to be honest in dealing with his friend.

"Then we'll find sources outside the community."

"There's a network, Ben. It won't matter where you go."

"Are you're saying I'm finished, that I have no future?"

"Not for a while, at least. Not until this blows over."

"That could take longer than I have."

"I'm sorry to be the bearer of sad tidings, my friend, but you know I've always told you the truth. I'm an expert with figures, with the bottom line, with reality, and you've always depended on me for my expertise. You can still depend on me.

"It can't be over for me. It can't be. Not yet."

"I'm sure you'll find a way."

"To do what? All I know, all I want to know, is business. If I can't start over, I may as well be dead."

"I trust you meant that metaphorically," Franklin said, concerned.

"Sure, sure. I'll find a way. I won't let them beat me down. I'll rise again, my friend, and I want you on my team. You understand?"

"We'll see."

"What do you mean, 'we'll see,'" said Ben, rising from his seat and hovering over Franklin. "What are you trying to say?"

"I can't do it gratis as I did when you started the first time. I need to get paid. I have big expenses now

"You gambled with me once and you made out, didn't you? It'll be like that again."

"What I'm saying is, I can't gamble. I don't gamble anymore," said Franklin, with increasing discomfort.

"You mean you don't believe I can do it again? Is that what you're saying?" Ben demanded.

"Of course not. I'm saying—"

Ben pounded his fist on Franklin's desk, his voice rising. "I'm the same man I was twenty-five years ago. A better man, seasoned, experienced. What in hell is wrong with you? Have you forgotten what I've accomplished? You used to marvel at what I did. Damnit, show a little faith. A little faith."

"I'm sorry, Ben. Damned sorry. I can't be your man this time."

"What kind of friend are you? I appointed you to my board. All those years that you serviced my company meant nothing?" Ben's voice had become a scream as he grabbed Franklin by his shirt and pulled him from his chair.

"You're throwing away the most valuable relationship you ever had. I made you what you are. You were only a pipsqueak until I came into your life. And you're still a pipsqueak. A goddamned, good-for-nothing pipsqueak. Do you hear me?"

"Stop this, Ben," said Franklin firmly as he tore from Ben's hold. "You'd better leave, now."

"You'll regret this," Ben warned in a hoarse whisper. "I'll destroy you, along with the company." He swept the papers off Franklin's desk onto the floor and stormed out of the office.

Ben's second lesson began hardly a week later when he received a call from Brad requesting that he come to the bank to discuss a matter that couldn't be handled over the phone.

"Thanks for coming, Ben," Brad said when they were both settled in chairs in Brad's office. "I didn't want to deal with a certain matter on the phone. Please sit."

"How's the business doing?" asked Ben, nodding his head yes to Brad's offer of coffee.

"Not too bad," Brad said, as he poured two mugs of coffee at a console in the corner of his office.

"That's not what I hear," Ben snorted. "Remember, my son still works for the company."

"Yeah. Well, frankly, things could be better. Sales are off. Though we've downsized, net worth is plummeting into negative territory. It's going to take a while to turn it around. But I have a positive attitude."

"Maybe now you can understand why I had to do what I did."

"I don't see how that would have solved the problem. You only made things worse," Brad said evenly.

"I was buying time," Ben said feeling hot, and not from the coffee. "Why in hell can't you see that?"

"There's no point in going over it again," said Brad, seeing that the past was still raw with Ben. "I've asked you here so we can talk about your assets."

"My assets?"

"Yes, your personal net worth."

"Why do you have to know about that?"

"Well, you signed the company's note with a personal guarantee."

"So? Now you have the company."

"Not all of it. We only have control, and even if we owned all the stock, it wouldn't be enough to discharge the note. As you know, after the bad news got out, the stock declined considerably."

"What are you getting at?" Ben asked nervously.

"Well...I...well, the bank is calling the note. It wants you to make good on it—personally."

"I see. I still have the company stock, of course. There's nothing to worry about, is there?" Ben said as if in a trance.

"Ben, you didn't hear me. That won't come near to covering it. As I said, the company's net worth is now negative."

"So what do you want me to do?" Ben asked angrily, snapping back to reality. "You can't get blood from a stone."

"You have other assets."

"My home..."

"And what's in it. And your car. Remember, you put everything on the line."

"I don't believe what I'm hearing. I don't believe it," Ben said, shaking his head.

"Please, Ben. This isn't easy for me."

"Oh, you poor sonofabitch."

"I'm sorry you're taking it this way."

"How do you expect me to take it? You're trying to clean me out."

"I'm sorry, Ben. Believe me, I'm deeply sorry."

"I'll declare bankruptcy."

"Sure, you could do that. But you'd better leave town afterward. From what I hear, you owe a lot of people besides the bank."

"What am I supposed to do? Go on welfare?"

"Knowing you, you'd find a way to come back."

"After all I've done for the bank, after all the money you've made on me, you'd do this?" Ben said, leaning over the desk.

Wary, Brad moved his chair back. "It's not personal, Ben. I want you to know I'm fond of you. I still want to be your friend."

"Oh, sure. I understand, Brad. I understand. We'll be the best of friends. You know, you're more of a bastard than I figured you were."

Brad watched Ben stand and shuffle toward the door, hanging his head in defeat.

R. P. Beckwith here. Obviously, we have a man in desperate straits. Under such conditions, there's no telling what he will do. He might even commit a crime. Not a capital crime such as murder. He's not the type, poor fellow. He's a victim of the success syndrome. Under our capitalist system, failure is not tolerated. The price is...well, you've seen for yourselves. Yes, I can sympathize with Ben. But I must remain true to my profession: I am first a criminal investigator. The secret of my success is tenacity. I do regret that our city's benefactor and major industrialist has to be my subject

A month later the bank acted on the note and auctioned off Ben's and Chloe's personal belongings on the front lawn of their house, thereby notifying all the neighbors of their plight. Their shame was enormous.

They stayed at Eve's apartment that night, but Ben took off after dinner, saying he wanted to take a walk and think. His walk brought him to Lily's studio.

"Everything's gone. It was so damned humiliating. All our belongings, furniture, even clothing, spread out on the lawn. Swarms of people came; they were like hyenas pawing all over our stuff. Humiliating. Humiliating. My god.

Lily kissed him on the lips. "Oh, Ben. How cruel they are."

"I've rented a small apartment in town. The house was getting too big for Chloe anyway. I'm poor now, Lily, worth nothing. I'm going back to when I was in my twenties, when I had nothing to lose, but then most of my life lay ahead. Now I've lost everything." He shook his head in wonderment. "So again I've got nothing to lose. What a joke my life is. Only now it's not so funny. I keep asking myself, how do you start all over again at fifty-eight?"

"You're still the same man you always were. The same man who succeeded before," said Lily. "And don't you still love me; don't I still love you? Nothing that matters has changed. When you had money, you did wonderful things with it. You made a lot of people happy. You made all this possible—my studio, my art. Without your financial and moral support, I couldn't have become the artist I am now."

"You are an artist because you were born that way. I had very little to do with it."

"That's not true, Ben. Having talent isn't enough. I'd still be a secretary. I wouldn't be painting. Because you believed in me, I'm an artist."

"And a damned good one. Your work is pure, uncompromising. It's not like mine, like business, where you have to make compromises all the time. Sometimes it gets dirty. I admire what you are, what you do. Maybe I should have been an artist, too."

Lily laughed. "Not you, Ben."

"Well, I sure as hell would be starving for a worthwhile cause."

"I wish I felt I was good. Some days I do, but most of the time—"

"My god, Lily, you're stuff's in museums. What more proof do you need?"

"I want to die and come back one hundred years from now and see whether my work is still hanging there."

Ben was feeling lighter. Lily uplifted him so. She was good for him, as always.

"I'd like to help you, Lily my girl," Ben said, embracing her, "but the problem is, I don't want you to die."

"And I don't want *you* to die," she said, gazing into his eyes.

"Death. It would be an easy way out, I suppose. For all I know, my useful life may be over. But y'know, the thought of suicide never occurred to me."

"Let's go away, Ben," said Lily excitedly. "The way we did three years ago. Only this time for good. Let's put all this behind us. I've saved some money.

"Go away? To where? My ruined reputation would follow me wherever we go. I thought about it once but dismissed the idea."

"You're referring to this country," said Lily.

"That's right. This is the only place I know."

"There's a big world out there, Ben."

"You mean Europe or South America or—"

"Wherever you'd like to go. Someplace you've dreamed of but never found the time to visit—or never dared visit because it would be so wonderful that everywhere else would be a disappointment. Do you know what I mean?"

"Well, yes, I do," Ben said, chuckling. "Y'know, I haven't thought of it in years, but since I was a boy I've always dreamed of living on a South Seas island, get to know the natives, learn their culture, become a part of the society. I used to read about Captain Cook's exploration of the South Seas, and I was fascinated with the *Bounty* trilogy, you know, by Nordhoff and Hall." Lily shook her head no. "As a boy I'd gaze across the hills from the west window of our third-floor apartment in the direction of those idyllic islands and daydream about them. My mind would take me clear across the continent, across most of the Pacific, and I'd be there swimming in a lagoon or splashing around in a crystal stream. Absurd, isn't it? A boy's romantic dream."

"Let's do it," said Lily. "Let's go to a South Seas island. Realize your childhood dream. You've been a success, certainly, but this would be the ultimate success."

"This is ridiculous, Lily. I've got responsibilities here," Ben protested.

"What responsibilities? The business is gone."

"For one thing, I must support Chloe. Even if I have to become a bagger at the supermarket."

"Wouldn't your children take care of her?"

"Better yet, say, if I were to die—" Ben stopped to contemplate his sudden recognition of an idea. "With the insurance, she'd be set for the rest of her life."

"Look who's being ridiculous."

"I could disappear, Lily. That would do it."

"Disappear? What are you talking about?"

"Just what I said. I could disappear. Permanently."

"It sounds ominous, Ben. Stop talking nonsense."

"I'm serious. I can't stay in this town. Everyone shuns me. I can't start over here; no one will invest in me, no one will lend me money, no one will even tell me what time it is. My kids are ashamed of me. My wife is grieving over the loss of our old way of life and resents my failure. It's a dead end, don't you see? I have to leave. Would you come with me?" He stopped, waiting for a reply, then went on before she could speak. "I wouldn't blame you if you said no. No one needs a failure."

"Of course I'd come with you. Wasn't it my idea?"

"But my best years are over, Lily. Don't you see that

"No, Ben, your best years are ahead," Lily said, elated. "I must be dreaming. After all these years, I'd actually have you all to myself, on your South Sea island."

"Let's do it. I'll go first, then you follow. We'll meet in L.A. But before I go, I must die."

"Now, Ben, stop joking."

"Not really die, Lily. Make it look like I died."

"How in the world…Wouldn't that be dishonest? I mean, isn't that cheating the insurance company?"

"I've…my company, that is, has paid in plenty over the years. It's time I got something out of it. The policy will more than take care of Chloe for the rest of her life."

"I don't know, Ben. I don't like that part of it."

"Lily, it doesn't involve you. I just can't leave Chloe destitute. Do you understand?"

"Well, I realize that your motive is noble. You're a very kind man."

"It's not for myself. Yeah, I'll miss Chloe and the kids. We've had good lives together. They don't need me anymore. No one will miss me. A failure, a has-been is expendable. Y'know, if I had never been a success I'd be worth more to society today than I am now. A zero, that's what I've become, so that's what I'll be. Gone forever. I'll assume a new identity—a new name, a new past. No one will ever find me. Surely not in the islands."

Lily burst out laughing. "And who will find your body?"

"No body, my love. Nobody finds the body," Ben said with exuberance. "Watch me, just watch me. What island would you like?"

"It's up to you. I'll go wherever you wish, any island, North Pole, Cape Horn, Timbuktu, anywhere. I'm with you."

Ben embraced her again. "Those aren't islands, Lily."

"Well, I know—"

"We'll visit Tahiti, Bora Bora. What about Western Samoa? Would you like to paint pictures on Western Samoa?"

"Yes, my canvases would like that. I'll become a female Gauguin. What will you do there?"

"I'll be your manager, set up a gallery and sell your stuff to the Japanese tourists," Ben said, having figured it all out in only minutes. He was back in his executive mode again and it felt good. "It would be a beginning. I'll take on other artists, eventually establish a string of galleries in major Southeast Asian cities. I've got to dream, y'know. I can't do nothing."

"I know. It sounds wonderful. It *is* wonderful. But how long?" she asked.

"Not long. I'm going for a swim."

"You're so silly, Ben."

R. P. Beckwith again. Ben might have something to say here.

"Any of you out there who thinks it's too late to start over is dead wrong. Look at all the penniless emigrants who came to this country from distant lands. How many of you older folk are doing what you set out to do when you were young? Damn few, I'd venture, even though you've probably had two, three, maybe more careers already.

"Starting over makes sense. This competitive capitalistic society of ours is purely Darwinian. We're in a constant struggle with one another to acquire goods; their accumulation is our symbol of success. It's tough on the nerves, though, and love suffers. Happiness should come from doing what we always wanted to do before we got sidetracked. I've learned this from my failure. Next time around, I'll do it differently."

A week after Ben had concocted his plan to disappear, the four board members of Ransom Pharmaceuticals met. As soon as all were seated, they began discussing the only thing on everyone's mind.

"It's a shame, a dirty, rotten shame," said Clint.

"Somehow I feel we're responsible for his death," Franklin said.

"How can you say that? It was an accident," said Brad.

"A man walks into the ocean naked and drowns. You call that an accident? He was depressed, Brad," said Franklin. "We did it to him."

"I don't think Ben was the type to call it quits," said Siggy. "The police say it was an accident. That's good enough for me."

"We'll never know without the body. I think the company ought to do something for Chloe," said Franklin.

"Did the company have any life insurance on him?" asked Clint.

"As the accountant, you'd know, Franklin," said Brad, saying what was on everyone's mind.

"It had several million on his life. I don't recall the exact amount," Franklin lied.

"Where's the policy now?" Brad asked.

"I...I think he took it over," Franklin replied, pretending uncertainty.

"You think? Don't you know?" Brad demanded.

"Yes, he has it, I'm sure. That is, he had it," Franklin said, cornered.

"Are you saying the company let it go after paying premiums all those years? When did the transfer take place?"

"I think while he was still CEO," said Franklin, beads of sweat forming on his forehead.

"Are you sure?" Clint said. "Because if it happened later, we've got a case of fraud here. The company was sole beneficiary, right?"

"Correct," Franklin replied, wiping the perspiration from his forehead with a handkerchief. "I'll check into it, but I'm sure he made the transfer while he was still running the show. I wouldn't have allowed such a transfer if it happened after his resignation." He turned to Brad. "I'd have checked with you first, of course."

"Well, it's too bad this has happened," said Siggy, who had taken over the management of the business. "A few million bucks would certainly take the company out of the hole it's in."

"Look, gentlemen, let's get down to business. As you know, we're going deeper and deeper into the red. Explain why, Siggy," Brad directed.

"I've cut back to the bone. Sales keep dropping. The new product line won't be ready for six more months. The exchange has halted all trading of our stock. To stay alive, gentlemen, I'm afraid we'll have to start selling assets."

"Maybe Ben had the right idea. At least we had the illusion of being in the black," Franklin said facetiously.

"My friends, I've had enough," said Clint. "I must submit my resignation. My business needs my full attention."

"You don't have to resign, Clint. The bank has reached the end of its rope. We can't pour in any more cash. It's all over."

"What are you saying? Liquidate?" asked Franklin.

"Yes, liquidate, or sell the business, if it's possible, but I think we'd get more from a liquidation. It will incur a substantial loss for the bank either way."

"I'm glad Ben isn't alive to see what's happened to his company," Franklin said, still loyal to his friend despite their rupture. "It was one thing to lose it, but to see his years of struggle and sacrifice go down the drain, that would be too much. His death is a blessing."

"Well, gentlemen, I guess that about does it," Brad said, adjourning the meeting. "See you at the club meeting tonight. I understand it's your turn to be honored, Franklin. It's most generous of you to finance that addition to the library. What are you going to call it?"

"The Ben Ransom Room, Brad. I was his friend."

With Ben gone, George and Eve visited Chloe almost every evening to assuage her loneliness and offer an ear to her expressions of anger over what she was convinced was Ben's suicide.

"Mom, everything will be all right. I can support us," Eve said one such evening.

"How could he do this? Leave us penniless. I knew he felt humiliated. I knew he saw no way to recover. But life must go on. I'm so angry at him."

"No one would trust him anymore, Mom. People overreacted. They wouldn't give him a second chance."

"But why, why destroy himself? I don't understand. He had us.

Didn't we mean anything to him? Weren't we reason enough for him to keep on living?" said Chloe.

"What gets me is the way he did it," said Eve. "It doesn't seem like something he'd do."

"That's right," said George. "After all, he was a strong swimmer. From what I understand, the ocean was calm that day. There was no undertow."

"No, he did it to himself," said Chloe. "I don't doubt it for a minute. The police wondered whether he had a heart attack, but I told them—"

"Dad's heart was strong," said George.

"That's what I told them. He was in perfect health."

"It doesn't make sense," George said.

"None of it makes sense," Chloe agreed. "I can't forgive him. I'll never forgive him. He didn't even leave a body to bury and mourn."

"That's the way it is with airplane crashes at sea. The bodies are lost," Eve said, trying to put her mother at ease.

But those are accidents," Chloe shot back. "This was deliberate."

"How can you be sure? It may have been an accident," Eve conjectured. "He went for a swim and something happened. Maybe a shark. Maybe a floating timber struck him. We don't know whether it was deliberate or not."

"He's never simply driven to the beach and gone for a swim. He's never done it before. No, I think he deliberately let himself drown. He was depressed. He took the coward's way out. It was a selfish act." Chloe could not be dissuaded from her theory.

"Well, at least he isn't alive to see the demise of his company. They gave me notice yesterday," George announced.

"You mean, fired?" asked Eve.

"Not fired, Eve. They're shutting the place down and selling it piece by piece at auction. Every employee received a notice."

"Oh, god, my poor customers. I'd hoped the bank would make a go of it. I kept telling my customers to hang on, not to sell at a loss. Now they've lost it all."

"What about you?" George asked. "You bought a chunk of stock for yourself."

"That's the way the market goes. You win, you lose. I'll manage. But I don't know how to face my customers. Will they ever trust me again?"

"No one trusted your father again," Chloe said. "Why would it be different in your case?"

"What I did was in good faith, Mom. What Daddy did was…well, you know."

"I don't think you can count on anything anymore," Chloe said sadly.

Soon after Ben's disappearance, American General Life Insurance Company assigned me to the case. The company needed the body or some proof, even circumstantial if necessary, that Ben was indeed gone. As part of my investigation, I called Chloe Ransom at her apartment a few weeks after Ben's disappearance. The phone rang many times before she answered it.

"R. P. Beckwith here, Mrs. Ransom. Investigator for the insurance company," I said in my friendliest voice.

"Insurance company? What insurance company?"

"Why, American General Life, ma'am."

"You mean—"

"You are your husband's beneficiary, Mrs. Ransom. Weren't you aware of his policy?"

"I don't know about such matters. Ben never confided in me."

"Well, I have a few questions, if you'd be so kind."

"He's a bastard, Mr. Beckwith, I can tell you that."

Mrs. Ransom seemed like a decent sort, so I asked, "May I drop by? At your convenience, of course. I could be there shortly."

"Yes, come over. I'll be home," she replied.

Immediately upon hanging up, she dialed Franklin. "Franklin, this is Chloe. When you were Ben's accountant, did you know anything about his life insurance?"

"Well," Franklin began awkwardly, "the company used to have some on his life while he was CEO, but, well, of course, after he left…"

"Do you think he owned any himself?" Chloe continued.

"He may have taken some out," said Franklin, loosening his tightening shirt collar. "I wouldn't know, Chloe. While he was CEO he figured that, on his death, the sale of the company would take care of you."

"Yes, well, he never mentioned any insurance to me," said Chloe, convinced that Beckwith must be on a wild-goose chase.

"To be frank, I wouldn't know anything about what he did during those closing days. You see, being on the board, I had to keep our relationship at arm's length. So I'm the wrong person to ask," Franklin said, attempting to end any further discussion that would implicate him. Would that goddamn policy haunt him forever?

"Really? I thought he sought your advice on everything," Chloe said.

"As I say, as a board member I couldn't act on his behalf or give him advice."

"Well, the will didn't mention any insurance, and you don't know of any, so I suppose the insurance inspector who called is confused."

"What insurance inspector?" Franklin said, alarmed.

"He says he's from American General Life Insurance Company and he wants to see me."

"I'm curious, Chloe. After you meet with him, would you let me know what he wants?" Franklin paused, wishing to end the conversation on another subject. "Did you hear that the company is being dismantled?"

"Yes, it's too bad. Maybe it's just as well Ben isn't here to see it. He left me destitute, but I wouldn't wish him to see what's happening. He put his life into the business."

"It cost him his life, Chloe. He couldn't take failure," said Franklin.

"But he had me. He had the kids. He didn't give a damn about us. We were reason enough for him to keep on living."

"How are you managing, Chloe? I mean financially."

"The kids are pitching in. They're wonderful. George will soon be looking for a job, but he's bound to find one. Thanks for asking, Franklin. I'll manage."

She hung up and began vacuuming the apartment, causing me to practically break down the front door to make my knocking heard.

"I'm sorry. I didn't hear you knock right away," she said as she opened the door and stood there in her kitchen apron.

"That's perfectly okay, Mrs. Ransom," I said as she admitted me. I quickly inspected the room. "Lovely apartment. Are you the decorator?"

"It's my passion. I suppose it's all I'm good at," she said, then added, "and so was my husband."

"Your husband?"

"My other passion."

Having heard that their marriage was one sided, I sought verification. "It must be gratifying to know that you were in harmony together."

"I thought so, until...until...goddamn him. How could he do such a thing? How could he?" said Chloe, angry as usual at the thought of her husband's ostensible suicide.

"Excuse me, Mrs. Ransom. Would you be a little more precise? What did he do, in your opinion?" I was hoping to bring her around to seeing another possibility.

"What did he do? Isn't it obvious? Mr. Beckwith, he killed himself, abandoned me, abandoned his family. I still can't believe it. It's so unreal. Yes, he was depressed, but he was coming out of it. He even seemed happy during the last days. I hate him for what he did."

"Hold on, Mrs. Ransom. It could have been an accident. That's the premise on which my visit here is based."

"Never," said Chloe, raising her voice. "Ben planned everything that ever happened to him, except...well, he certainly didn't expect to lose the business. But he wasn't one to give up."

Chloe's description of her husband's typical behavior, that he "planned everything," was most revealing. It buttressed my theory that the allegedly deceased could be alive and having the time of his life.

"A heart attack, perhaps?" I suggested.

"I know that's what the police thought," Chloe said more calmly. "But I don't think so. True, he could have taken better care of himself. But, according to his doctor, he was in excellent health."

"I read about his business misfortune in the paper," I said, trying another approach. "He was obviously under stress—from the business debacle, I mean. As you say, it was a happy marriage?"

"Certainly we had our difficulties," Chloe admitted. "What marriage doesn't? We could have spent more time together as a family. But we made the best of it. We agreed to go our own ways, and that kept the peace."

"Not really a war between you, but more like a perpetual truce?" I offered.

"Yes, you could say that. But I know he loved me. And I loved him. Or did. And as I said, he seemed happy toward the end."

"Curious, isn't it? Would a man who came to some resolution

about his bad fortune, who seemed happy—from what you tell me—would such a man have reason to commit suicide?"

Chloe became thoughtful. "Do you really think...could it have been an accident?"

"Certainly it is in your interest that it be an accident," I said, and went to the nub of my inquiry. "Tell me, Mrs. Ransom, does your husband always wear socks?"

"Socks? I...I'm sorry...what does that have to do—"

"Let me put it differently. Does you husband ever go without socks?" I pursued.

"Ben not wear socks? Of course he wears socks. When he dressed in the morning, they were the first things he put on, even before his underwear and trousers. I don't understand."

"A routine question, Mrs. Ransom. A minor item, really."

She gave me the answer I was seeking.

"You must have a reason for asking. Now I'm curious."

"There were no socks left on the beach among his belongings. They found a wallet, credit cards, handkerchief, underwear, shirt, trousers, belt, shoes, everything that American men carry and wear, but no socks."

"What are you suggesting?" Chloe asked, puzzled.

"Suggesting, Mrs. Ransom? I'm merely stating a fact."

"Then he must have drowned with his socks on," she said quite logically.

"Possibly, possibly. Of course, you realize that the insurance doesn't cover a death by suicide."

"Oh?" she said, genuinely surprised. "I know you said over the phone that he had some insurance. What insurance is it?"

"You needn't worry, Mrs. Ransom. With or without the body, your husband's motives are beyond proving," I assured her, being less than honest.

"Are you telling me that he had a policy on his life after all?"

"Precisely. And a handsome sum at that."

She was incredulous. "Are you saying—"

"Yes, Mrs. Ransom, I expect it will be paid in due time," I said with resignation.

In any investigation, facts lead us from one point to the next. But, as in all important discoveries, the basis for the pursuit of investigative truth derives from our intuition, our human capacity to imagine and process what it doesn't yet know. Although based on a slender theory, I believed that Ransom was alive and well. I had less confidence in my ability to prove it before American General would have to make good on the policy. Ransom could be anywhere, perhaps in the most unimaginable of places on the planet.

"May I ask how much the policy is for?" Chloe asked cautiously.

"You may, and I shall tell you. Ten million dollars. Mrs. Ransom, you are to become a wealthy woman again."

"To tell the truth, I'd rather have my Ben back."

"That is something I'll be working on."

Chloe stared at me puzzled but chose not to seek further elucidation. Had she, I would have changed the subject.

Of course, you follow my drift regarding the marriage. Clearly, it was not a happy one. And the missing socks are a giveaway. Going for a swim in one's socks? Come, come.

Where to begin? As the French say, cherchez la femme. Now, can anyone tell me what fair lady in Middle City disappeared about the same time as my subject? If you can, I'm listening.

Brad put Franklin through the third degree. The subject of their conversation was related to my visit with Chloe. Who knows all the consequences of our actions?

Brad, red faced, stood behind his desk holding a letter-sized piece of paper. "Where did you find this?" he demanded.

"In the files, Brad. Where else?" Franklin said, remaining matter-of-fact, hoping to have a calming effect on his questioner.

"We've gone over the files with a fine-tooth comb. This wasn't there," Brad insisted.

"I suppose your lookers missed it."

"Come on, Franklin. Don't give me that. You had it all along, didn't you?"

"My secretary turned it up," said Franklin, realizing that he couldn't prolong his lie.

"Tell me, why was it in your files?" said Brad, sitting down, knowing the answer already. "This authorization to transfer Ben's policy should have been in the company's files."

Franklin shrugged. "I can't explain it."

"I think you can. You arranged it with Ben, didn't you? The date on this authorization is only two days before he was forced to resign. How could Ben have known we were planning to oust him? He couldn't have. He had no reason to take over the policy personally. Yet despite the pretty steep premiums, he made the change. I believe you colluded with him and predated the authorization."

Franklin seemed confused and found himself gulping for air. "What was the harm?" he said finally. "It cost the company nothing. He asked me to draw up the proper authorization as a favor."

"But you predated it to throw us off the track. It's subterfuge, Franklin. And it cost us a fortune. How much was the policy for?"

"Ten million," Franklin replied meekly.

"Ten million?" Brad shouted. "Good god. And you have the chutzpah to say it cost the company nothing?"

Franklin winced and hung his head. "I never expected him to die so soon," he muttered.

"Here today, gone tomorrow. Ever hear of that old saying?" Brad said, as if he were addressing a child. "Well, we're going to contest the transfer, and you'll have to testify that it was a fraud. The company is the rightful beneficiary. We're prepared to take legal action if the insurance company won't go along."

"If I testify, my reputation is destroyed," pleaded Franklin.

"That's too bad. And if you won't testify, we'll take you to court," Brad announced.

Franklin seemed to recover his composure. "For your information," he said sarcastically, "this whole thing might be moot. I hear that an insurance company inspector is investigating the claim."

What prompted Franklin to come clean with Brad, besides Brad's demand that the policy be found, was learning from Chloe of my investigation. Franklin knew that he had badly bungled the secret of the policy's transfer, and he knew that the existence of the policy would eventually become common knowledge. After all, Middle City is a small town in many ways.

"What?" said Brad, startled. "Investigating the claim on what basis? The policy is valid, isn't it? The transfer to Ben was made."

"Oh, yes," said Franklin, feeling renewed. "I have no idea what the problem is."

"You're laying a smoke screen," accused Brad.

"Look, call the insurance company yourself."

"We'll do that. Now, I want you to sign a statement confirming that the authorization is fake."

Franklin signed, but, as he suggested, it was moot, and not for any reason that either man could imagine.

Chloe, having immediately informed George and Eve of her good fortune, invited them to dinner at her apartment that evening.

"That's what he said. Ten million dollars," Chloe confided, sitting on the couch in the living room.

"And you knew nothing about the policy?" George said in amazement from his father's chair.

"Not a thing. He never said a word."

"I just knew that Dad would take care of you, Mom," Eve said. She patted her mother's hand as she sat on the couch beside her.

"I shouldn't have doubted him," Chloe berated herself. "He was a good man."

"So, if it was a suicide, you say there won't be a payoff?" said George.

That's what Mr. Beckwith, the insurance inspector, told me."

"An insurance inspector. Why an inspector?" George said.

"Who knows? Maybe he was trying to confirm the cause of death. Yes, that's what I think he said, or something like that."

"But the police called it an accident, didn't they?" Eve said.

"And that's what Mr. Beckwith said the insurance company thought it was, too. So he assured me that a payment would be made. But he did say one thing that puzzled me." George and Eve bent toward their mother. "He implied that he would try to get my husband back for me, or something to that effect."

"That's absurd," said George. "If Dad drowned, how could he bring him back? Did he mean he'd try to find the body?"

"I don't know. It's quite mysterious."

"He must have been joking," Eve said.

"I'm sure that's all it was," said Chloe.

I called Brad to ask for an appointment, and he agreed to meet with me three days hence. I arrived on that day promptly at nine. A receptionist ushered me into Brad's elegant office. Brad approached me from behind his desk, his hand extended. "Care for some coffee?" he said.

"Don't mind," I said as he directed me to the chair that Franklin had heated up a few days earlier.

Brad poured two mugs of coffee from the large coffeemaker on the console in his office.

"How do you take it?" he asked.

"Neat, like my whisky," I said, and he smiled. He handed me a full mug, took one for himself, and settled into his desk chair. Then, before I could speak, assuming I had called to see him on a matter concerning the bank's action, he opened with what was on his mind.

"As your office no doubt advised you, we are contesting the transfer of Ben Ransom's life insurance policy. Originally the policy on Mr.Ransom's life was owned by the company. The authorization to—"

"I know the story," I cut in. "No need to review it. I'm not here to discuss the issue of who the correct beneficiary is. That's not my bailiwick."

"So what's the problem? Why did you ask to see me?"

"I'm an investigator, and only that, exploring the validity of the insured's death. It's as simple as that."

"What's to investigate? We know he died," Brad said, ready to dismiss the issue.

"No, we don't, sir, unless by chance you've found the body. Without absolute proof of death, we must investigate. And according to the contract, without that proof, two years must elapse before the company makes good on the policy."

"So your point is that we have approximately another eighteen months to wait?"

"Point one precisely."

"And point two?" Brad said, amused.

"We have reason to believe that Ben Ransom is very much alive."

"What did you say?" Brad said, disbelieving his ears.

"Mr. Ransom is—"

"What in hell makes you think that? If there's no evidence—"

"Ah, but there is evidence. Perhaps only a tiny scrap, but size is not a factor in the investigation business," I said in a professorial manner. Brad was the kind of person I enjoyed talking down to.

"Are you suggesting that Ben has committed fraud?"

"Does that surprise you after the scandal at the company, and the questionable authorization to transfer the policy to him?"

"I suppose not," said Brad, sipping his coffee. "So you're saying he simply faked a drowning and disappeared?"

"A plausible theory to go on, wouldn't you say?" I suggested, seeing that he had little trouble envisioning the entire scenario.

"That sonofabitch. He's even cheating us out of his death," Brad said, most perceptibly.

"Now, I have a question that I believe you can answer," I said. "I understand that you used to have secretary named Lily.

"Sure, Lily Acton," said Brad, his eyes lighting up. "Terrific woman. Efficient, lovely personality. Used to be my right hand. Quit about three, four years ago. Became an artist full time. I don't know how she could afford the luxury, but that's none of my business."

"Did Mr.Ransom know her?"

Brad thought for a few minutes. "Of course. She witnessed the signing of all the papers regarding his company's loans. And she was present at many of our meetings to take notes."

"Are you aware of any relationship between Mr. Ransom and Lily?" I continued.

"None, except here at the bank. Ben was strictly a family man. I doubt if—"

"Family men are the most vulnerable, sir. Aren't you a family man?" I said, smiling.

"Yes, I am."

"And aren't you having an extramarital affair with one of your clerks as I speak?"

Brad appeared stunned. "How did you—"

"It's my business, sir, to know such things. Now tell me more about this Lily. You say she is a full-time artist?"

"Well, yes. The bank has bought some of her paintings. So has the museum. She's very good."

"Perhaps she's self-sufficient and doesn't need a paramour to support her. Would you let me see her account balance?"

"I'm afraid we can't divulge that information," Brad said haughtily.

"Of course I'm free to divulge what I know about you to a certain party who would be most interested," I threatened. In my pursuit as a sleuth, there are no limits to the extent to which I will go to gain information.

"I'll get it for you," Brad responded within the blink of an eye as he picked up the phone and requested Lily's current balance. After listening briefly he hung up. "She's closed her account," he said smugly.

"When was that?" I asked. "Let me guess: August 18 or shortly before."

Brad picked up the phone again and dialed. "When was the account closed?" he asked. He hung up, looking bewildered. "Right on the button: August 16."

I rose from my chair, shook Brad's hand, and turned to leave. "Thank you, sir. I appreciate your excellent cooperation."

"Just a minute. How did you know that Lily—"

"Do you understand French, my good man? *Cherchez la femme.* Look for the woman, and you'll find the man."

I departed with a swinging gait through the bank lobby and onto the street. The sun was bright, and my heart was light. My theory was holding.

If it was impossible to locate Ransom, it was a simple matter to trace Lily. I merely sent a letter to her old address and, because only six months had elapsed, it was returned with a forwarding address on the envelope, a street in Los Angeles.

Armed with photographs of Ransom, I flew to the City of Angels, certainly a misnomer. There at her forwarding address, an upscale apartment building, I looked up the caretaker, who identified the man in my photographs as one who had rented an apartment.

However, I had missed the man and his "wife" by a week. And their names—Lillian and Benjamin something or other. "Williams," said the caretaker.

My theory was now law. I had proof without the slightest doubt that Ransom was alive. The trail was hot. Any forwarding address? No, but on talking with some of the neighbors, pretending to be an old friend, I learned that my prey was enamored of the South Seas. I knew then that their discovery was only a matter of my continuing perseverance.

The South Pacific is a mighty big place, with thousands of islands. Which one would *I* go to for a visit? Tahiti, of course. But I wouldn't stay there. Too many tourists. As soon as I landed I took a cab to Papeete and visited a dozen hotels where my quarry would be inclined to stay—places with all the amenities of an American facility. Bingo, a clerk at one of them said that Lillian and Benjamin Hinsdale had stayed there but had recently left. No idea where to.

Why not visit another island where English is commonly spoken? So began my island-hopping tour across the Pacific.

Finally I found the right island. There they were, the two of them on a beach, wearing sunglasses, sitting in beach chairs, reading and conversing.

"Well, I see that my old company is no more—liquidated. Damn shame," Ben was saying as he tossed his newspaper onto the sand. "If the bank weren't so goddamn impatient—"

"We agreed: No talking about the past," Lily said, annoyed. "Why do you keep harping on it? Why can't you get it out of your system? It's over and done. I'm sick of hearing about it."

"Because it needn't have happened," Ben said adamantly.

"But it did. Damnit, let it go, Ben."

"It doesn't concern you."

"How can you say that? Your bitterness has made you into a miserable person. It concerns me every day. I no longer enjoy being with you," Lily said, returning to her book.

"What are you saying? You don't love me?"

"I love the man you used to be. If you don't become reconciled to the past, I'm leaving for the States."

"Don't talk like that. Don't think it. My life is nothing without you, Lily. You know that," Ben pleaded.

"I'm not so sure. I think your life is nothing without anger and regret. I'm just your sounding board."

"You've got your painting. The trouble is, I'm bored," Ben said with a sigh.

"I'm sorry that selling my art didn't turn out to be a big enough deal for you."

"Paradise isn't what it's cracked up to be," said Ben, staring out at the crystalline blue ocean.

"Then let's leave. I've painted all the scenes I want to here."

"We can't go back to the States. It's too risky."

"Not for me," Lily said, letting her pent-up feelings pour out. "There's nothing to stop me. I miss my life there: the galleries, the museums, the theaters, the concerts. They were my stimuli. Here, every day is like another and my work has developed a sameness. I'm in a rut. I'm not growing. I long for contact with the rest of the world."

"Are you telling me—"

"I want to go home. If you want to come with me—"

"I can't. They'd find me. Chloe would become penniless. I could end up in prison."

Having overheard their conversation from behind a tropical hedge, I decided that it had reached an appropriate point for my entrance. I installed my beach chair in the golden sand nearby and sat down. They stared at me as if I were a sea monster ready to devour them.

"R. P. Beckwith here," I said in my jolliest voice. I stood up, walked over to them, and shook their hands. Their astonishment was palpable. "Beautiful day, isn't it?"

"Just like every day around here. They're all the same," Ben said, refusing to meet my eyes.

"Ah, the South Seas," I said, spreading my arms toward the glittering cobalt ocean. "Americans, aren't you?"

"No. We're from Toronto," Ben said.

"Canadians, eh? I'm an American, and I can't tell the difference between a Canadian and an American." I laughed. "I've often wondered whether a Canadian can tell the difference."

"It goes both ways, Mr. Beckwith. We can't tell either," said Lily, now seeming relaxed.

"I see. Well, of course the real difference is that you Canadians think it's a crime to even jaywalk. You live by the law. Whereas we Americans, well, we take pride in perhaps not flouting the law but in evading it. We have a renegade streak. But you Canadians, you are good boys and girls, aren't you?"

I always prefer an oblique approach when making a kill. It's more civilized.

"True, we don't have much crime in Canada. What do you do, Mr. Beckwith?" Lily inquired.

"Do? I'm a hunter," I said matter-of-factly.

"What a strange occupation. You don't look like a hunter."

"You mean because I'm not wearing a hunter's cap or an orange jacket?"

Lily laughed, obviously at ease. "That's right. Surely there's nothing to hunt in these islands. No wild animals here, except maybe boar."

"Oh, but you're wrong, Ms.…. What did you say your name was?"

"I didn't. Andrews. Benjamin and Lily Andrews."

Ransom had picked up his newspaper from the sand and commenced reading.

"Very pleased to meet you. The islands are abundant with prey. You said Andrews?"

"From Toronto," asserted Lily.

Ben muttered from behind his paper, "What sort of animals do you expect to find here, Mr.… Mr.…."

"Beckwith's the name. The human sort, Mr. Ran…Andrews. Homo sapiens, a most intriguing animal. By the way, I'm from Massachusetts, Middle City. No doubt you've heard of our illustrious town."

Ransom's and Lily's eyes met in panic.

"Never heard of the place. Never been there," said Ben firmly.

"Oh, but I'm afraid you have, Mr. Ransom. And you too, Lily," I said quietly.

Their astonishment rendered them dumb. "Who are you?" Ransom finally asked. "You're not the police. How did you know that I—"

"I'm with American General Life Insurance Company, Mr. Ransom. Remember us? Were you going to ask how I knew you were alive?"

"And in these remote islands," added Lily.

"Should I give away secrets to my adversaries?"

"I'm curious," Lily said calmly. "I thought we covered our tracks pretty well. Really, Mr. Beckwith, it's the least you can do before what you're going to do."

"Well, yes, I suppose so," I conceded. "I suspected that Mr. Ransom was alive when the police found his clothes. There were no socks left on the beach. I doubted that you'd go for a swim with your socks on, Mr. Ransom."

"Son of a bitch," Ben spat.

"Was that all?" Lily asked.

"Certainly not. I questioned the coincidence that both Lily Acton and Mr. Ransom disappeared on the same day, and that Lily closed her account at the bank a couple of days earlier. Although I didn't know that you were having an affair, I did learn through the bank that you knew each other. It's all very logical, don't you think?"

"But we changed our names. How did you trace—"

"Like most people who assume new identities, you retained your first names. All I needed to do was search for a couple whose first names were yours. It was a long shot, of course, but one that works quite well in most cases. After all, it has taken almost two years to find you."

With ten million dollars at stake, American General had good reason not to skimp in funding my pursuit of Ransom. Even if it would take five years, the company would have given me carte blanche.

Ben took a deep breath. "Okay, let's cut to the bottom line. When do we leave?"

"When do *you* leave, sir? Lily can do what she pleases."

"I want to go home," said Lily.

"I'm afraid it will have to be at your own expense," I said. "The company will allow me to cover only Mr. Ransom's fare."

"That's not a problem. I want to be near Ben," she said, reaching for Ransom's hand.

"Forget me, Lily. I'm heading for a stretch in prison," said Ben, nobly.

"That is true. Quite a stretch, I suspect," I said.

"Oh, Ben, I feel relieved," Lily said. "It's over. We can be ourselves again. Wherever you are, I'll be at your side. I'll visit you every day. You can count on me."

"No, Lily. Get on with your life. This wasn't working anyway. You don't find paradise in the world. It's someplace inside you."

I confess having been impressed at Ransom's newly discovered wisdom.

"What about my wife and kids, Mr. Beckwith?"

"Your kids are fine. Eve is still with her brokerage firm and George is working for the bank."

"You mean for Brad? That godamn—"

"Brad's right-hand man, as I understand it, and ready to move into his slot. Brad's been appointed president," I explained.

"Can you beat that? See, Lily, it's not all bad."

"I didn't think it was. You did."

"Except for that son of a bitch," Ben steamed.

"I take it you're referring to Brad," I said.

"You take it right, Mister."

"I don't give him long for the job," I opined.

"Is that right? Why do you say that?"

"Just a hunch. An investigator's intuition, you know."

"How's Chloe?"

"Well, I hope she hasn't spent all that insurance money. She'll have to return it. Obviously, something will have to be worked out."

"I mean, how is she?" Ben insisted.

"Fine, fine. Your showing up will be quite a shock to her. She's convinced that you committed suicide."

"Look, Mr. Beckwith, how about a little mercy? Spare her the shame. Prosecute me in another state. Don't take me back to Middle City."

"You still love her, don't you, Ben?" Lily said.

"She's the mother of my kids. We weren't the happiest couple, but I owe her."

"I'm afraid I have to bring you home. The scene of the crime, you know. Anyway, it's not up to me," I said.

"When do we leave?"

I folded my beach chair and looked at my watch. "Get packed," I said. "We'll depart on the three o'clock flight"

"I could escape right now. Just take off and disappear again," Ben suggested.

"It's over, Ben," said Lily. "Do you want to keep running?"

"If you disappeared," I said, "I'd find you again. Your existence being no longer in doubt foils your scheme to support your wife with the insurance proceeds."

Ben threw up his hands. "We'll get ready, Mr. Beckwith."

"Good. Don't forget to pack your socks."

As the three of us sat abreast aboard the plane heading for the States, I got to thinking about all the unforeseen consequences that resulted from a series of lies. A business ruined, a family dismembered, a romance broken, an insurance company richer, an investigator triumphant, all because a man tried to solve his life's problems by twisted means. Case closed.

Now, I understand the company is ready to assign me to another case right there in Middle City. It involves a bank president who is suspected of stealing the bank's funds. Whom do you think it might be?

A Son's Father, a Father's Son

A Tale of Two Wars

All the local celebrities were there: the mayor, the governor, even the chief justice of the state supreme court. Bradley Blodgett, sixtyish, looking patrician—he was president of the largest bank in town—stepped to the microphone from his place at the head table to make the introduction. The room, normally reserved for wedding receptions and bar mitzvahs, was enormous. Spread before Bradley were scores of round tables around which men in tuxedos and women in gowns were seated.

"We have among us a man of outstanding generosity," Bradley began, "a man who has contributed more to the quality of life of our citizens than anyone in recent memory. The Sidney Randall Wing of City Hospital, the addition to the art museum, the new swimming pool at the high school—I could go on and on—would not have been possible had not our good friend and community benefactor, Sid Randall, provided the funds. How does one thank this man? He has said he wishes no thanks. Nevertheless, for our sake if not his, we proffer our thanks. Would Sid kindly come to the lectern?"

Rising from his place at the head table, Sid walked slowly, almost reluctantly, to stand beside Bradley. His ruddy, bony face betrayed unease, as if he were only doing what was expected. He stood almost a head shorter than Bradley, who held a silver plaque toward the audience. Handing it to Sid, he said simply, "It's a mere plaque, hardly enough to represent what's in our hearts, but, anyway, here it is, my friend."

Sid, putting on his best face, accepted the plaque with a grin and read the laudatory inscription silently.

"I...I'm quite bowled over," he said. "But no thanks are necessary." He paused for several moments, as if that was all he would say, then he began again. "Let me tell you a story. One day, J. P. Morgan was extolling his good works to a visitor in his office. He had established this foundation, made that grant, helped orphans, supported the downtrodden, et cetera. Suddenly there was a knock on the door. "Come in," he said, and in walked a bedraggled man, obviously a bum. "Alms for a destitute man," the bum said. "Would you kindly spare a starving man a dollar?" "Get out of here, you bum," J. P. said, and he threw him out bodily. The visitor was astonished by this act of selfishness. It didn't make sense. "Why didn't you give him a dollar? After all, it's only a pittance and you're worth millions." "You don't understand," said J. P. "That was my ex-partner."

Some in the audience guffawed and some snickered, but not Jay Edson, Sid's brother-in-law and partner. Jay didn't think Sid's story was funny.

Sid continued: "When I came here after the war twenty years ago with hardly a penny in my pocket, this city gave me the opportunity I needed to start my business. It gave me a reprieve on taxes, it provided the guarantees I needed to raise finances, and it's here that I found the loyal staff and dedicated workers who have made my company a success. In effect, you made me your partner; unlike Morgan, you gave me that dollar. So, you see, I am the one to be grateful. My contribution to our community's welfare would not have been possible were it not for you. I appreciate the honor, this glorious plaque, which I'll hang in my office to read every day. But it is truly undeserved. Thank you."

As Sid withdrew to his place at the head table, the audience stood in unison beside their tables and applauded; some shouted their approval. It was an evening that made Sid's family proud: his son, Ken; his wife, Edith, who stood beside him adoring, applauding; his nephew, Bobby, who was Jay's son; and Jay, who quickly forgave him for his offending story. Edith embraced her husband, and they kissed as the audience kept up their applause. Sid was quite the man of the hour, of the year, of the decade, of the World War II generation. Were it not for Sid, this small, unworldly central Massachusetts city, which had seen the demise of its major industries from foreign competition, may well have become a miniature urban slum.

The year was 1970. The war in Vietnam was in progress and our country's casualties were unacceptably rising. Due to the war, the economy was strong. Sid's company was operating around the clock, hardly able to keep up with demand for its electrical components, especially from that of its largest customer, the U.S. government.

Ken and Bobby, cousins only months apart in age, would be graduating from high school in a few months and be eligible for the draft. It was cause for consternation to Sid and Jay, each of whom was ambitious for his son and expected that they would both come into the business and eventually become their successors.

The boys accepted this, although Ken reluctantly. Loving and admiring his father and wishing to please him, he went along for now and reserved the right to change his mind when the time came. There was the service and college ahead, plenty of time for some future event to intervene that would derail his father's expectations for him.

Bobby, meanwhile, couldn't wait to get college over with and join the company. He knew of Ken's feelings; the two had discussed their future often. So Bobby aimed for the top, hoping—no, expecting— to replace his uncle when Sid was ready to step down.

At every opportunity, Jay was laying the groundwork in subtle ways to make it happen, even though it was years away. For example, he would review the company's financial statements with Bobby and explain each figure in detail. He kept Bobby informed about every new product being developed and had him visit the facility again and again so that he became familiar with the staff and they with him.

Edith often had Jay and Bobby over for dinner. Jay's wife had died in middle age some years before. "Jay needs a home-cooked meal to remind him of what it's like to be loved," Edith would say to Sid. To Jay she would say, "You should find a good woman and marry her."

But Jay showed no interest in anyone, although there were plenty of opportunities. He still pined for his dead wife. After Mildred passed away, he would say, "I still have my career with the company. And I have her memory. No one can match that. It's enough for me."

It was on such a dinner evening that the subject came up of the boys' immediate future after high school graduation. Ken's girlfriend, Sheree, was also present. She had arrived early to help Edith, and to help Ken set the table; to her amusement, he never got the place settings right. "For someone as smart as you, I don't understand why you don't remember," she said, laughing. Ken only shrugged.

Sid was sitting in the living room reading the newspaper. Suddenly he got up, paper in hand, walked into the dining room, and said, pointing to a page, "Do you see what they did? It's terrible. How in hell could they?"

"What on earth are you talking about?" Edith said. "Please get ready. Jay and Bobby will be here any minute."

"They shot those kids in cold blood. Innocent kids."

"Who shot who?" Ken said, walking over to his father to see the paper. Tall and gangly, he towered over Sid.

"The National Guard shot them in cold blood—defenseless college kids."

"Oh, that's awful. Where did it happen?" Edith asked from the kitchen. Roundish and small, she moved smoothly and quickly around the kitchen like a ballroom dancer.

"A college called Kent State in Ohio. Never heard of the school. Do you know it, Ken?"

"Sure do," Ken replied. "It's a big school."

"The kids were demonstrating against the war. I don't agree with them, but they do have the right," Sid said.

"Well, I do agree with them," said Ken firmly.

"We're over there fighting communism, son. We're fighting for our way of life."

Ken had heard this before. It was Sid's mantra about the war. "Baloney," Ken said calmly.

"Let's not start this argument all over again," said Edith, poking her smooth, moonlike face into the dining room. "Go and wash up, Sid."

After Sid left the room, she said to Ken, "By now you should know better than to argue with your father about the war. You can't win."

"Yeah, I know," Ken said.

The doorbell rang, and Ken welcomed his uncle and cousin.

"Hi there, Kenny, my boy. How ya doin?" said Jay, placing his arm around his nephew's shoulder. He was as tall as Ken but considerably more portly. They had similar personalities: cautious, good-natured, and straightforward when dealing with others. No doubt the two had some genes in common. Jay liked Ken despite the threat—rather the perceived threat—to Bobby's future.

"Hi, Uncle Jay. Hi, Bobby."

"What's new, Ken?" Bobby said, expecting nothing new.

Bobby's personality was unlike his father's. He was somewhat of an iconoclast, prone to irreverent outbursts, the consequences be damned. His build, portly and of only medium height, also differed from his father's, so much so that there was no obvious clue that the two were related.

"Graduation. That's what's new," Ken replied, as they wandered into the dining room, where Sheree was finishing setting the table.

"Yeah, that shit. You going?"

"Of course I'm going. I'm graduating. Aren't you?"

"Going?" Bobby said playfully.

"Yeah...and graduating."

"Well, I'm graduating, but I'm not going."

"You sure as hell are going, you hear me?" Jay declared as he entered the dining room. "If your mother were alive, she'd insist."

"If Ma were alive, I'd go of my own free will," Bobby said with a tinge of resentment. "Hi, Sheree. What's new?"

"Only you, Bobby. You're new." Sheree was petite, brown haired, brown eyed, slender, and in love with Ken. She was a year behind him in school.

"Oh, you've got a witty girl here, Ken."

"She's much more than that, Bobby."

"Uh-oh. Something's up."

"We'll tell you about it later."

Bobby nodded, his eyes glistening with anticipation, as Sid entered. "Hello there, Bobby. Glad you made it, Jay."

"Same here. Got things back to normal at the plant."

Preceded by the aroma of seasoned pot roast, Edith entered with a platter of food as Jay kissed her on the cheek. "Oh, Jay! How are you, Bobby? Let's all sit. Help me get the rest of the food, Sheree."

"Damned good cook, my sister."

"Listen, Jay," said Sid as they took their usual places, "despite the problem you had, did that order go out that I asked you about?"

"Sure did, Sid. Right on the button."

"Good."

"This is no time or place to talk business," said Edith, returning from the kitchen with Sheree. "I prohibit it." She turned to the boys. "So both you boys are graduating at the same time. Isn't that nice? What are your plans, Bobby? College?"

"I'm leaving the country, Aunt Edith. Goin' up north."

"What? Not to Canada," said Sid contemptuously.

"You heard him, Sid," Jay interjected. "He doesn't want to be cannon fodder the way you and I were in World War II."

The decision for Bobby to leave the country was Jay's. Planning his son's career from the day he was born, Jay made sure that no eventuality—neither war nor revolution nor natural disaster—would interfere with Bobby's advancement to top man in the company. And Bobby, who rebelled in small, tentative ways against his father's control, nevertheless went along, because he believed he was the best choice for the job.

"You never told me, Bobby," Ken said, surprised.

"It's something you don't advertise. You don't want the fuckin' draft board to get wind of it," Bobby said.

"You don't talk like that at the dinner table," Jay reprimanded. "Talk civil like or don't talk at all, ya hear me?" Then Jay turned to Ken. "So what are you going to do? Let them take you?"

"Take him?" said Sid. "He's volunteering, aren't you, son?"

"I don't agree with the war, but I suppose it's my duty."

"No, it isn't," said Edith firmly. "There are plenty of others who can go. Why does it have to be you? When your father was fighting in the Pacific, I waited, living in fear that I'd get a letter from the war department. I don't want to have to live through it again with my son."

"I think it's wonderful that you were here waiting for him, Edith," Sheree said. "I want to do the same for Ken."

"Of course you do. Ken is lucky to have a girl like you," Edith said, reaching over to pat Sheree's hand.

"Not as his girlfriend, Edith. I want to be his wife," Sheree said, having planned with Ken to break the news that evening. No one was surprised. Ken and Sheree seemed destined for each other, although no one expected them to be married right away.

"You're...you're only a child," said Edith. "Still in school. What are you saying?"

"So that's what's new," said Bobby, nodding his head toward Ken.

"I graduate next year," said Sheree, "and I'll go to college while Ken is away. I'll be here when he returns. Didn't you marry Sid because he was leaving? That's what Ken told me."

"Yes, yes," spouted Edith, trying to control her emotions. "But you're both so young."

"Weren't you and Dad young too, Ma?" Ken said. He sidled over to Sheree and kissed her.

Sid answered for his wife. "We were young, still..." He paused, flashing back in his mind to those early years. "Still, we made out okay."

"I say take all the love you can get, because you can suddenly lose it," Jay stated, referring to his own happy but cruelly truncated marriage.

"Well, why does Ken have to volunteer?" Edith said. "If he doesn't go, he and Sheree can wait. Let's you and me talk later, Sheree, after dinner."

Ken's and Sheree's eyes met in a knowing glance. They anticipated that Edith would have more to say in private. "Sure," Sheree replied with a sigh.

"They'll draft him, Edith, if he doesn't volunteer," Sid said. "This way he has a choice. Y'know, a kid fresh out of high school doesn't stand much of a chance to get a rank. Anyway, it's his duty. I fought for this country, and now we're under attack again."

"We're not under attack, Dad," Ken said. "It's a civil war that's none of our business."

"Then why in hell are you going?" Bobby asked.

"Because maybe by being there I can help end it. We're bound to win. Then it will be over."

Bobby thought that Ken was naïve. How could he make a difference? The entire country was in an upheaval over the war. The government was obsessed less with winning than proving that it was on the right course. Practical Bobby wouldn't fall into that trap of fighting for a false cause. Yet, there was a certain beauty in Ken's innocence. Bobby admired his cousin's idealism, his wish for a better world. Unlike Ken, Bobby felt that because he couldn't change the world, he'd do the smart thing: adapt to it.

"That's good thinking, son," Sid said. Turning to Jay, he continued, "Did you hear what they did to those kids at Kent State? Shot them in cold blood."

"Yeah, I heard it on the radio as we were driving over. What in hell are they demonstrating for? Now, Bobby here—"

"They want the war to stop," Ken said. He knew that if he were enrolled at Kent State, he too would have been demonstrating with the others.

"That's a lot of crap. We're going to win this war; that's how it will stop," Jay said.

"They still have a right to demonstrate," said Sid.

"Yeah, I suppose," said Jay, still doubting that they had any reason to.

"And they didn't have to shoot at some defenseless kids with real bullets," said Sid. "Hell, something like that could never have happened in our war. We respected everyone's rights."

"Sure, like the rights of the Japanese Americans," Ken said sarcastically.

"Who was demonstrating then, Sid?" Edith inquired. "I don't recall any demonstrations on our campuses."

"Yeah, Sid, don't you remember?" said Jay. "No one wanted us to get into the war. It was none of our business. If it hadn't been for Pearl Harbor...hell, the government was doing the demonstrating, putting the Jap Americans in concentration camps like Ken says, and anyone with a German name had to watch out."

"Nowadays we demonstrate all the time, Ma," said Ken. "The blacks are demonstrating for equal rights, and some are getting killed for it—blacks and whites."

"I think it's a stupid war," Bobby said, slamming the palm of his hand on the table. "They're never going to get me."

"He's all I got, folks," Jay said, looking lovingly at Bobby. "I don't want to lose him, too. So I'm shipping him off."

"I know exactly how you feel, Jay," Edith said, nodding emphatically. She couldn't fathom her husband's wish that their son participate in the fighting. Didn't he know that Ken might be incapacitated, might never come back? She attributed Sid's return from war to sheer luck. Could she be lucky a second time?

"Sid, do you want Ken and Bobby to go through what we went through when we were their age?" asked Jay. "I sure as hell don't."

"Most of us survived, didn't we?" Sid replied. "We came out better for it and went on to become the most successful generation our country has ever known. It taught us to be tough and to keep fighting against the odds. And that's what I did in business. Where do you think my doggedness comes from?"

"Yeah, you built a great business, Sid, and I'm grateful you brought me into it, but it wasn't the war that taught you how to do it. It was the depression, when you watched your parents fighting for survival. You and I learned as kids that hard work and perseverance gave us the things we needed, and after the war it gave us even more. Look at what you are, head of a big business, one of the most respected and admired men in the community. I hear some of the bigwigs in town would like you to run for mayor."

"Idle rumor, Jay," said Sid, dismissing the idea with a sweep of his hand. "I'm a businessman, not a politician. They're different breeds."

"I think Jay is right," Edith said. "I don't think fighting a war teaches anything except killing and doing terrible things to others. And I don't want my son to participate in it."

"Don't worry, Ma. I'm not capable of doing anything terrible."

Sheree placed her arm across Ken's shoulders. "He's the kindest person I know," she said, gazing at him.

"In war, son, it's kill or be killed," said Sid.

"I could kill if I had to," Bobby said.

"Sure you could," said Sid, ending the momentary silence elicited by Bobby's blunt remark. "And so could Ken. Only he won't know it until he has to deal with it."

"What about the other horrors?" said Edith, obviously repulsed by such talk of killing. "The awful bombings, and what the invading armies do to enemy civilians. I heard—"

"To the victors go the spoils, Edith," Sid said pontifically. "It's as old as the ages."

"Wouldn't a little generosity work better? When the Russians went into Germany, I heard they did terrible things to the Germans."

"Hell, we Americans weren't exactly angels, Edith," Jay said.

"You mean—"

"Sure, we raped and pillaged."

"You did? I never heard that," said Edith, astonished.

"Oh, not all of us. Only our bad ones. You must have seen the same thing when you went into the Philippines, Sid."

"Oh, sure. We had some bad ones too."

"Well, I know that Ken isn't capable of treating others cruelly,"

Edith declared. "As Sheree says, he's a naturally kind boy." She patted Ken on the head as she would a favorite pet.

"Ma, I couldn't hurt a fly," Ken said, then laughed as he recalled having swatted flies with a vengeance.

"Couldn't hurt a fly, eh?" said Sid, dismissing what he interpreted as Ken's naïveté.

"Boy, are we different," Bobby said. "Anybody stands in my way—whoosh, I cut him down. That's what you've got to do in this world to get ahead."

"Who in hell told you that?" said Jay indignantly.

"I don't know. It's the way I think, that's all."

"What about you, Ken? How do you think?" Sid asked.

"I know you want me to come into the business, Dad."

"Answer my question. Would you let someone keep you from reaching a goal?"

"Not if the goal was important to me. But I don't see why I'd have to destroy my opponent."

"Or your competitor," Sid said impatiently. "In business you can have no mercy for those who seek to destroy you. You must understand that, son."

"I do, Dad. I certainly do."

"Okay. Sure, I want you to come into the business. It's an opportunity few boys have. But I want you to go to college first, get a good education, learn how to think."

"I'm all for college, but not to study business."

"What do you mean?" asked Sid, looking suddenly ill at ease.

"That's what Bobby's going to do in Canada, study business," Jay said approvingly. "Then after the war's over, he'll come back and join us in the business, won't you, Bobby?"

Sid ignored Jay's reference to Bobby and turned to Ken. "Of course you're going to study business," Sid said with finality.

"No, Dad. I have something else in mind."

Sid was becoming increasingly upset. Why couldn't Ken understand the golden opportunity he was offering him?

"Such as?"

"Astronomy."

Sid looked as though he had been struck by a blow.

"Surely, Sid, it makes sense," Edith entreated. "He's been fascinated with the stars ever since he was five. Remember that telescope we bought him, how he'd go outside at night to look at the stars? I could never get him to come in for bed."

"Kid stuff, that's all," Sid said, discounting the idea with a slash of his hand through the air. "Out of this world, that's what it is. Out of this world. Ridiculous. I thought he'd be over it by now."

"I'm really going to war to please you, Dad. I think just like those demonstrators at Kent State. They know we have no reason to be over there. I don't believe in it, but I'm going because it's my duty—to you as much as my country."

"I went to war because I loved my country and we were threatened; that's why you must go," said Sid. "We must protect our American way of life. I don't expect you to go because of me."

"But I am. I'm doing this for you, and when I return it's your turn to do something for me."

A silence fell over the room. Sid broke it with a nervous laugh. "Well, I see you know how to negotiate," he said.

"Oh, he sure does. Learned it from you, eh, Sid?" commented Jay, trying to ease the tension. Jay was always the peacemaker, even in business. It was he who bargained with the union, because Sid always blew up during negotiations.

"I don't want any part of your business," Ken said, his eyes piercing his father's. "I'm going to learn about the universe and spend the rest of my life at it."

"That's a wonderful thing to do. Isn't it, Sid?" implored Edith.

"We'll wait until he gets back, then we'll decide," Sid said, refusing to give credence to his son's preference.

"Not *we*, Dad. *I* will decide."

"We'll see." Things had gone too far; it was time to change the subject. "How would you like an after-dinner drink, Jay?"

"Don't mind if I do."

"Let's sit in the living room." The men retired to the living room and Sid poured drinks.

"All right, boys. Help clear the table," said Edith. "Come with me in the kitchen, Sheree."

Sid was not happy with his son. Although he worried that he might not have his way, he thought that—given time—he could bring Ken around. As for Jay, Ken's decision to take up another profession offered an opening for his Bobby that he had not

251

anticipated. Edith had only two wishes: that her son not go to war and that he and Sheree not marry right now.

If such conflicting agendas are the stuff of family politics, these concerns were minor compared with the unpredictable future event that would sully their family harmony.

"I really think you'd be wise to wait until you at least finish high school before getting married," Edith cautioned Sheree as they cleaned up the dinner dishes. "What do your parents say?"

"I haven't told them yet."

"At your age, won't you need their permission?"

"I suppose so."

"What if they don't approve?"

"We'll elope. I'll fake my age," Sheree said defiantly.

Edith grew wistful, recalling her early days with Sid. "It won't be easy when Ken's gone. You'll worry every moment of the day and night, especially when you're alone in bed trying to sleep. Is he safe? Will he come back?"

"I'll worry even if we aren't married. I love him, Edith."

"There's a difference when you're married. I don't want to sound hard-hearted, but what if he doesn't come back? It's my worst nightmare, but it's always a possibility. I have to be realistic, and so must you. Finish school first, go to college, don't foreclose on future opportunities. Your life as an adult hasn't begun yet. Everything's ahead. Be free until you know that your decision can be permanent."

"What have you got against me, Edith?"

"Against you?" said Edith. "Dear Sheree, I've nothing, absolutely nothing against you." She embraced the girl. "I always wanted a daughter, and I'd be proud to have you as part of our family. But I'm trying to spare you the pain you'll have to endure if you marry Ken."

"I'm sorry," Sheree said contritely. "I didn't mean—"

"I know, dear. I know how you feel. Look, if Ken doesn't go, if by some miracle he changes his mind about enlisting and isn't drafted, I'd have no objection to the two of you marrying, but only after you graduate high school. Then you'd have only my blessing. Would you agree to that? But if he does go, will you wait until he returns for good?"

"I'd like to think about it."

"Of course. Please do that."

While Edith and Sheree were talking, Jay and Sid were in the living room discussing their respective sons.

Having Bobby's future in mind, Jay came right to the point. "I'm surprised to hear that Ken doesn't want to join the business. I figured you planned on grooming him to succeed you someday."

"First time I've heard of any other plan. He doesn't know what he wants. Astronomy! Who in hell takes up astronomy? Crazy scientists, that's all. Where did he get such an idea? He's too smart to be buried in some observatory. When his stint in the service is over, he'll change his mind."

"Yeah, I'm sure he will. But what if he doesn't?"

"If he doesn't—"

"Sid, look, you and me, we've got ten years give or take a couple before we retire. It'll be here before you know it. Maybe your boy will be tied up in the war for another three, four years. Then he has four years of college after that."

"What are you getting at?"

"What I'm getting at is, Ken will have only three years at most to get ready to take over. You and I know that's not enough time. He'll need at least five years to learn the ropes. Even more time than that, I'd say."

"Well, who says I have to retire in ten years?"

"Nobody. But with your ticker, I think it would be smart, don't you? One heart attack is enough."

It was frequently on Jay's mind that Sid's heart could have an unscheduled attack much sooner, but he thought he'd better not say it. Dedicated to getting along as a means of getting ahead, Jay was in the habit of censoring his true thoughts, a not uncommon habit with most people in business.

"Well, it's true, I don't have the energy I used to have. But I suppose when you get into your late fifties, that's normal."

"And it doesn't get any better, Sid."

"How in hell do you know? We're the same age."

"Yeah, well, I know how vulnerable we are. Life is just a slender thread, and sometimes it snaps without warning. Mildred...you know how it was. We went to bed just fine, then I woke up in the morning and there she was, lying dead beside me. Not asleep, but

253

dead. Gone from me forever. Christ!" Jay buried his face in his hands, as distraught as if it had happened the night before.

"It's tough, Jay. It's damned tough, I know. Being mortal is a curse. It's a trick God plays on us." Sid's face reddened, betraying a welling rage that he didn't fully understand. "We're given damn little choice. The things that happen, they're too irreversible."

"Right," Jay responded, startled at Sid's outburst. "What I'm getting at, Sid, is life is goddamned short, and you and I can't keep up this pace the way we have been. You know what I mean? The kids have to take over, and they, or one of them, must be taught everything about the company, and soon."

"I couldn't agree with you more."

"Yeah, but what if Ken sticks to his guns? Know what I mean?"

"No, I don't."

"I'm talking about Bobby, Sid. My son and your nephew, Bobby. He's enrolling in college in Canada this fall, then business school. If Ken doesn't want to join us when he gets out, Bobby's there to do the job, all college trained. In fact, he can start even before Ken comes aboard. It will give us some depth in the organization

"Look, this is all much too premature," said Sid, wishing that this line of conversation would end.

"Well, I'm giving you something to think about, that's all."

"Thanks, Jay. I'll think about it." But Sid intended to do no such thing.

"That's all I ask," Jay said, relieved that the subject was finally on the table for future discussion. "This is one helluva war over there, isn't it? I pray that Ken makes it in one piece."

"I'll pray every day. Ken is smart. He'll make it just fine," Sid said, as if what he willed would become fact.

"It's all luck, Sid. Smarts don't always work. If a bullet has your name on it, that's it. How was it with you? You never talk about it. When I tell you how it was with me in North Africa, and the slaughter at Anzio, you just listen and say nothing about yourself."

"Nothing like that happened to me."

"You mean it was all roses for you?"

"Certainly not."

"Yeah, I heard the Japs were worse than the Germans—more determined, loved to die for the emperor, that kind of stuff. But what about the natives, the Filipinos? You liberated them. They must have loved you. It wasn't that way for us in Germany."

"Look, Jay, I'd rather not get into it. Okay?"

"Okay, Sid. If it's too painful, I understand," Jay said, perplexed by Sid's mounting annoyance.

Edith entered the room with Sheree, followed by the boys. "Well, everything's cleaned up," she said. "Let's all watch some TV. Turn on *I Love Lucy*, Sid."

The rest of the evening was lovely. Such togetherness as they sat laughing at the antics on TV was salve to Edith's heart.

After Sid's talk when he received the plaque, Bradley Blodgett had taken Sid aside and asked to meet him at his office at nine Monday morning. Bradley wouldn't reveal the purpose of the meeting but said that it had nothing to do with business.

Sid had forgotten the appointment when at nine sharp his visitor appeared. They shook hands, and Blodgett, at Sid's direction, settled into a comfortable chair opposite Sid's desk.

"The city is in bad financial shape," Blodgett began, tenting his hands, "and it's time we acted, did something radical, to straighten things out."

"Are you asking for a donation? If you are, you know I'm quite willing to contribute," said Sid.

Blodgett waved his hand, dismissing the offer. "Of course, money always helps, but we need something of a more permanent nature— a changing of the guard. You and I know that the administration is downright incompetent. As a banker in town, I'm concerned. The city will never attract more businesses with its spendthrift record. And business is the lifeblood of the community and, of course, my bank."

Sid was impassive, curious about what Blodgett was leading up to. "How can I help?" asked Sid, as he always did when approached.

"I knew you'd offer," Blodgett said.

"Of course, Brad. I meant it when I said I owed my company's success to this community."

"You owe yourself first, Sid. As your banker, I know better than most how you built the business from practically nothing. But what I'm about to ask is much more than has been asked of you before."

Blodgett leaned forward, to make sure Sid would not miss the next words. "I...we'd like you to be our next mayor."

"Mayor?" Sid said with a snort. "I'm a businessman, Brad, not a politician. The two don't mix."

"Precisely. That's why we're in such a mess. We need someone at the helm with business savvy. That's why all the businessmen and women in town have asked that I approach you."

"Why not hire a city manager?"

"He wouldn't make a difference. The goddamned city council would ride roughshod over him. We need someone strong who knows what's right and demands that it be done. You get my point?"

"Running my business is a full-time job, Brad," Sid said, repositioning himself in his chair.

"You needn't give up all your responsibilities here. Jay is practically your alter ego. Couldn't he take over some of your work?"

"True, true," Sid said, to his surprise beginning to entertain the idea. "Doesn't the mayor have three more years before his term is up? The election is a long way off."

"That's correct. But you've got to start early in this business, Sid. That'll give us three years to lay the groundwork. At any rate, I'll bet you swamp any opponent they pick to run."

"They, meaning the council?"

"They're in bed together, Sid. The lot of them, nothing but self-interested conspirators. You must know that."

Sid shrugged. "As long as they left us alone, I had no gripe."

"Of course they leave you alone. After what you've given this town, they wouldn't dare touch you." Blodgett realized that Sid was perhaps a bit naïve about politics, after all. He would need some educating.

"Frankly, I don't think much of politicians," Sid said. "They're shortsighted and concerned only with their own survival."

"Ah, but that's where you could make a difference, Sid. You don't fit the mold. You would bring decency and honesty to the scene. You would perform in the tradition of our forefathers," Blodgett said with enthusiasm, breaking from his usually measured manner.

"I think you're laying it on, Brad. Don't you?"

"I mean on a small scale, Sid. But I'm sincere."

Why even consider politics? Sid asked himself again. He had always rejected requests that he join one town committee or another.

Doing things by committee, making compromises to arrive at decisions was not his way. Either you take a leap and suffer or reap the consequences, or you make no decision at all. Furthermore, he knew that politicians say things that they think the electorate wants to hear, not things that they truly believe. That was not Sid's way. Furthermore, he hadn't met a politician yet whom he respected, and he knew many of them.

But Sid had already had one heart attack, making him conscious of his mortality as never before. He wished to leave a legacy beyond that of his business, which he suspected would be merged eventually into a multinational and lose its identity after he was gone. In fact, if it turned out that Ken wouldn't take over the business, he might consider a merger while he was alive. Being mayor, especially one who would make a difference, would place his name in the history of the community along with the good causes he funded that carried his name. It would be another step, albeit perhaps a small one, to ensure his immortality.

Sid took a deep breath, then grinned. "Okay, Brad. I'll be your man."

Blodgett stood and reached for Sid's hand. "Good, my friend. For the time being, leave things up to us. You'll be our next mayor, guaranteed."

THREE YEARS LATER

What a difference three years can make. They can pass like moments or take an eternity. Ken and Sheree didn't marry, but for reasons other than Edith's reservations. No, Sheree's parents, whose permission she needed because she was still a minor, refused. Not that they objected to Ken. He would have certainly been a prize, the son of the wealthiest, most prestigious man in town. They felt she should finish her education—graduate high school and complete college—before marrying. And it did occur to them that Ken might never come back from the war or, if he did, return severely handicapped from wounds. They didn't want their daughter "tied down with a cripple," as they put it. Reports of a high American casualty rate were rife.

So Ken joined the army and went to Vietnam. Bobby went to Canada. And Sid and Jay's business prospered as the war created a thriving economy—and a disunited nation.

As Blodgett predicted, Sid was an effective candidate for mayor. He worked at it full time, knocking on doors and making rousing speeches that had practically everyone in town cheering. He appealed to all strata, from business owners to struggling widows and unskilled workers, all of whom were fed up with the past administrations. All counted on Sid to bring honesty, impartiality, and responsible management to city hall. The sidewalks would be repaired, and taxes would fall. He was a shoo-in, bound to win by a landslide.

That evening, after a nonpolitical speech in which Sid was given the Man of the Year award, Jay accepted Sid and Edith's invitation to come home with them for a nightcap. Edith took the men's coats and hung them in a closet as Sid and Jay sauntered into the living room.

"What a terrific evening," said Jay with genuine admiration as Sid poured three after-dinner drinks. "Your speech wasn't obviously political, but its implications oozed politics. How did you do it?"

"I'm so proud of you, Sid," Edith said as she walked up to him and kissed him squarely on the lips. "Our new Man of the Year. You're my man of the year, and all the years of my life."

Sid beamed at her, then turned to answer Jay's question. "I have no idea how I did it. It's one thing to be running for mayor, but the honor of being chosen Man of the Year..." Sid shook his head in incredulity. "Frankly, I was bowled over."

"Why, with what you've done for this town—the library wing, the hospital, and the thousands of people you've put to work here—this town owes you. You've made it the flourishing place it is."

"I suppose I've helped."

"And now you'll be mayor, so you can do more than help," said Jay. "You can make this town the best in the state...hell, the nation."

"I don't understand why you won't give yourself credit," Edith said as she sipped her Kahlua.

"I'm just an ordinary man, no better than anyone else," Sid said, studying the opposite wall.

"Nor worse," said Edith. She moved to him and sat on his lap. "I'm so proud of you, Sid."

"Maybe worse," Sid said, casting his eyes to the floor.

"C'mon, Sid," said Jay.

"You're being ridiculous," Edith said, getting off Sid's lap, looking slightly distressed.

Jay stood and spoke in a partly admonishing, partly admiring tone. "Jesus, Sid. As long as I've known you, you've been straightforward, and generous and acted honorably. Your employees love you. You have friends galore. I'd bet my life that you'll win by a landslide. Take it from me, most of humanity is worse than you."

"Well, I'm certainly grateful to everyone. I took advantage of an opportunity, of which there were plenty right after the war, to make it big. That's all I did."

"But the way you did it, Sid. The way you did it. It's beautiful," said Jay.

True, Jay owed his success to Sid and would, of course, praise him. But he also recognized Sid's entrepreneurial genius, his decisiveness and ability to forecast the consequences of his actions, so that time after time they turned out to be right. As for Jay, if he lacked such abilities, he was loyal, straight, and a leveling influence, valuable to the business and Sid in his own right.

"I owed it," Sid said cryptically.

"Owed it?" Edith looked distressed. "What did you owe? To whom?" she demanded.

"To myself."

"I don't get you," said Jay, puzzled.

"I'd rather not go into it. Okay?"

"Sure, sure," said Jay, suspecting that he was treading on ground that he too would rather avoid.

"I've never heard you talk this way," Edith said, concerned.

For a few moments they fell silent, and Sid considered how to change the subject. He was saved by the ringing doorbell. Edith went to the front door, where she found Ken standing resplendent in his uniform.

"Ken! It's Ken. You're home. You're home," she cried as she flung her arms around his neck. "Oh, my son."

"Hello, Ma," Ken said kissing his mother on her cheek. His voice was subdued, and Edith released him, sensing his strange soberness.

Having come to join Edith at the door, Sid hugged Ken to him and held him there.

"Good to see you, son."

"Hi, Dad."

"It's good to see you, son. Good to see you," Sid repeated, at a loss for more profound words to express his elation.

"Let me get into this welcome party, too. Whaddaya say, Kenny?" said Jay as he took Ken's hand and shook it vigorously.

"Hi, Uncle Jay."

"What a surprise. Why didn't you let us know?" said Edith.

"It was kind of sudden," said Ken apologetically.

"Is the war over?" Sid asked with a laugh.

"Maybe. Who knows in this war? But that's not why I'm here."

"We're not winning, are we?" said Jay.

"We've lost it, Uncle Jay. It was lost before we began. And the Vietnamese are the biggest losers of all."

"It sure as hell isn't like our war, is it, Sid?" asked Jay.

"How long will you be staying, son?" Sid asked.

"Only a few days. I have to report to Washington."

"Washington? You on some important mission?" Sid asked, rolling his eyes.

Ken smiled. "I'm only a grunt, Dad. People like me don't go on important missions."

Sid patted Ken on the back. "Just curious. Well, then you must be on an unimportant mission. Come in, sit down. Want a drink?"

"No, thanks."

"We're celebrating your father's being voted Man of the Year earlier this evening," Edith explained. "I wish you'd been there to hear his wonderful speech. You have a father to be proud of."

"That's great, Dad. Great. I'm sorry I missed it."

"Thanks, Ken," Sid said, his eyes glittering with happiness over his son's approval and his own pride at seeing him in uniform.

"I'll have that drink, Ma," Ken said, looking more relaxed. Edith filled a small glass and handed it to Ken as the four of them sat basking in the warmth of their togetherness.

Ken finally blurted, "I have only a few days' leave, because there's a problem that has to be cleared up."

"A problem?" Sid asked, looking mildly alarmed. "What kind of problem?"

"A problem, that's all."

"Can't you tell us what it's about?"

"I'd rather not, at least not yet."

"Anything *that* secret sounds like important stuff, eh, Sid?" said Jay.

Ken changed the subject. "How's Bobby," he asked Jay

"Doin' just fine. He'll be finishing up next year, then on to business school…. Well, I gotta go," Jay said suddenly. "See ya again, Ken.

"Aren't you going to stay for some coffee?" asked Edith.

"Thanks, but I've got to be at the office early in the morning. Anyway, you'll want to get the scoop from your son. Good night, everyone."

Jay walked out the door and down the steps. There were other reasons for his abrupt departure. Ken's presence magnified Bobby's absence, and Jay suddenly felt lonely and incomplete without his son. Soon after his wife died, Jay showered all his attention on Bobby, who became Jay's purpose in life. He was determined that his son would surpass him and become the giant success that he had failed to be.

In addition, Jay needed time to think about the business and wanted to go for a walk in the cold, bracing air before driving home across town. Sid's being mayor was bound to change his role in the company, and maybe Bobby's.

"Oh, it's so good to have you home," Edith said to Ken. "How was it over there? Was it terrible?"

"Everyone is the enemy, and nobody is. It wasn't that way with you in the Philippines, was it, Dad?"

"Not at all. We were welcome. There was no question who the enemy was."

"Still, Sid," Edith commented, "I remember your letters saying that the Filipinos didn't have much use for Americans."

"After a while, after the Japs were driven out or captured, we treated the people like second-class citizens in their own country. Our boys were interested only in their women," Sid said evenly.

"We do the same to the Vietnamese now," said Ken. "We call them Gooks."

"Is that so? We coined the word back in my time." Sid shook his head, intrigued that the American deprecation of people of another color and a less powerful nation was passed on from one generation to another. "But I hear reports that we're killing innocent civilians and torching villages."

"They're suspected Viet Cong villages, that's why," Ken said.

"But do you have proof before you do such a terrible thing?" Edith inquired, hoping that Ken had had no part in it.

"No, there's no proof. The village is suspected of harboring Viet Cong sympathizers. The people won't help us."

"Maybe they don't know anything. Maybe they just want to be left alone. Maybe they fear retribution from the other side," Edith pursued.

"Yes, maybe. Anyway, I don't think what we did is right even if they're sympathetic to the Cong."

"Have you ever been on...that kind of mission?" Edith asked fearfully, immediately regretting the question.

"Once or twice," Ken said hesitantly.

"And you killed civilians, burned their homes?" Edith said, horrified by the image and of her own headlong persistence. Why couldn't she drop this line of questioning? Though part of her didn't want an answer, she felt compelled to know. She looked to Sid for encouragement but he remained impassive.

"No, I didn't, Ma."

"But you were there?"

"Yes, I was there. I had no choice. I didn't participate. I pretended."

"Thank God," Edith said, relieved. She knew that Ken was too moral a person to commit, on his own, acts of violence against the innocent. But she also knew that, like dogs in a pack, the pressure of group bonding could override an individual's conscience. Sid had told her that such things happened in his war.

"Didn't your commanding officer see you holding back?" Sid demanded, now intensely curious.

"Yes."

"That's all? Yes?"

"He was pretty pissed off at me."

"I can imagine. You made the rest of them feel like criminals. They were doing their job, and you judged them."

"Now, Sid, how can you say that? You know that Ken did the right thing," Edith said, satisfied with Ken's story.

"No, he didn't," said Sid. "He was part of a unit, a team, and it's imperative that they stick together. In the army you follow orders; there's no alternative. Anyhow, no civilian could understand," said Sid, somewhat heatedly.

"Are you telling me I should have joined in? Is that what you're saying?" asked Ken, incredulous.

"No, of course not. I mean…" Sid sounded uncharacteristically confused.

"Then what in hell do you mean?" Ken demanded. But Sid was silent. "Look Dad, I'll be paying the price anyway."

"What price? You say you're clean. Is that right?"

"Right."

Sid shifted uncomfortably in his chair. "Then what are you saying?"

"They're holding me accountable along with the others," said Ken, looking straight into his father's eyes.

"Accountable?" Sid and Edith chimed in unison.

"Well, we…they raped some of the women. The village turned out not to be Viet Cong."

"Not you, Ken. Not you, son," Edith pleaded.

"I told you I wouldn't have anything to do with it."

"But can you prove it?" Sid demanded.

"I don't see how."

"Won't the others back you up? Your commanding officer?" said Sid, pushing for more.

"Of course not. Why should they? They don't know what I did or not do in the confusion."

"Then it's your word against theirs." Sid was already sizing up the legal implications, searching his mind for what action to take, for the right lawyer to defend his son. "What was the size of the unit?"

"A platoon."

"Christ."

"I don't know what will happen. A court-martial for sure, then maybe prison. I don't know," Ken said, hanging his head.

"Not prison. Dishonorable discharge, maybe. I can pull some strings in Washington. We've got contacts."

"There were some killings, too," Ken added reluctantly.

"Oh, oh, how awful. What a thing for you to see. You poor boy." Edith got up from her chair and sat beside Ken and stroked him.

"The raped women were killed, weren't they," Sid said, as if it were a given.

"Yeah, they were killed, Dad, and some of the kids," Ken replied, his voice hardly audible. He continued in a bitter tone, "When we saw that they weren't Cong, we didn't want to leave any witnesses to what we did."

"You sure you weren't involved? How could you not be?"

"Don't you believe me, Dad?" Ken said plaintively, hurt that his father was for the first time doubting him.

"How can you, Sid?" Edith said, indignant that there could be any doubt as to Ken's innocence. "How can you not believe your own son? You've known him all his life. You know he isn't capable of doing such a dastardly thing."

"Under certain conditions, even the best of us can do dastardly things. It's part of being human, our dark side. Take my word for it," Sid said, his voice rising.

"You've got to believe me, Dad."

His father's faith in him was as crucial as life itself. Constantly struggling to balance his own needs with his father's wishes, Ken wasn't ready to risk Sid's disapproval. He knew that some day there would be a confrontation, but not yet, and not over this. He needed his father's support now more than ever.

"Are your buddies confessing what they did?"

"No."

"Then they're innocent, too," Sid said, the word "innocent" reeking with sarcasm. "What happened was committed by some phantoms? Is that right?"

"I saw them do it. I know which ones did the raping and the killing."

"So you'll have to testify against them." Suddenly, Sid saw the scenario played out. Ken would be the innocent witness. There would be no consequences, after all.

"How can I testify? If I do, they'll point a finger at me, too," Ken said.

"Why are you grilling him like this, Sid?" Edith shouted. "Stop it. You act like he's one of them." Having not an iota of doubt concerning Ken's innocence, Edith felt that things had gone far enough. "Let's change the subject," she said calmly. "Did you know that in addition to being made our city's Man of the Year your father is running for mayor?"

Ken was relieved that his mother had come to his rescue. "That's great, Dad. And I wish I had been at the Man of the Year ceremony."

"I wish you'd been there, too. I spoke of you, how I hoped you'd take my place some day, that our family would continue in the

tradition I established. I told them you were a better man than I."
Then, staring off into space, imagining a future of trouble and plans
gone awry, Sid added, "But now...now that's all questionable. Our
family name will be shamed. Our reputation ruined. My candidacy
at risk before it has even begun."

"I'm sorry, Dad." Ken buried his head in his hands, tears filling his
eyes.

"I so looked forward to you coming into the business," Sid said
longingly.

Ken looked up as tears coursed down his cheeks. "I had no control
over the way things worked out. War is crazy. Nothing goes the way
you expect."

"You had no control over your impulses, goddamn you," Sid
exploded.

"No, Sid," Edith shouted, "goddamn you for thinking this of our
son. What's wrong with you?"

"Maybe I shouldn't have come home," Ken said desolately.

"Don't say that," Edith consoled him. "We've been waiting years
for this day. Your father isn't himself. He'll come to his senses."

"Okay, okay," Sid blurted. "I'll give him the benefit of the doubt."

"What doubt?" said Edith. "Can there be any doubt? What's
wrong with you, Sid?" Edith felt outrage wash over her.

"Gee, thanks, Dad," Ken said bitterly. "Look, I've been traveling
all day. I'm tired. If you'll excuse me, I'm going to bed."

"You do that. Have a good sleep. God knows you need it," Edith said.

"Sleep? I haven't slept in weeks," said Ken as he left the room.

"You've got to stop accusing him," Edith declared. "Why won't
you take his word for it?"

"Because I know how it is in war," Sid replied with conviction. "I
know. All civilized constraints are out the window. Our dark side
bursts through the veneer. We do things we'd never do at home."

"Are you speaking from experience? Is that what you're doing?"

"Of course not," said Sid, averting his eyes from Edith's. "I've seen
things, that's all."

"Well, he is our son. Our only child. We've got to believe him, and
believe in him."

"I want to. Believe me, I want to, Edith. But after this, my dreams
for him are dashed. Can you understand that?"

"You mean your dreams for yourself."

"Don't be ridiculous. I have no more dreams. I've achieved far more than I ever dreamed I could. My dreams are behind me."

"Why can't he still come into the business?"

"How could he? Everyone will know what he's done."

"He hasn't done anything. Don't you understand?" said Edith, her outrage mounting again.

"What I mean is, he's bound to be found guilty and punished. Just being accused is enough to give him a black mark in the public's eye. And you can be certain that the whole episode will be well publicized. Something like this can't be kept under wraps. He'll never command the respect of our employees or our community. Can't you see that?"

"Oh, Sid, what a terrible mess this is."

"That leaves only Bobby to take over. I don't want him running the show. He'll kill it. You know how he is—shoots from the hip, cares only about himself. He's no leader."

Edith had never heard Sid talk this openly about their nephew. She liked Bobby even though he was Ken's opposite—outgoing, a kind of renegade, unpredictable, but frank and open. "Does Jay know how you feel?" she inquired cautiously.

"I haven't told him yet. Don't worry, Edith, we'll find a place for Bobby, but it's not at the top."

"Then train Ken to take over," Edith said. "I think his idea to become an astronomer comes from childhood dreams. We all have them. Of course, I know they aren't practical. I'll work on him. He's grown up a lot in three years. I can see it. If he knows how much you need him, if you show him that you trust him..."

"If only I could believe him, I could handle it better. If only I could believe him, I'd go to the mat for him."

"But you are going, Sid. Aren't you?"

"I'm not sure. I'm just not sure."

The next morning Ken called Sheree, and they met, at Ken's suggestion, in the city park. He wanted to avoid dealing with her parents and, for the time being, his own. His father's reaction baffled and depressed him. Sid was always his biggest booster, always at his side in every contest, every argument. Ken had come to realize that his wish to be an astronomer was only a childhood fantasy, after all.

The service demonstrated for him the power of organization, the rewards of teamwork, the value of responsible leadership, and the tragic consequences of blind leadership. It gave him a new appreciation for his father's enterprise.

At this point he would at least consider joining his father's company, but he needed his father's trust. Ironically, now that he had come around to his father's point of view, that trust was in question. The door that had always been open was now closed. Perhaps there'd never be a confrontation, only silent rejection.

After Ken and Sheree kissed and held each other for a long time, they sat holding hands. Ken told her that he had only a couple of days' leave. When she asked when he would return, he withdrew his hand from hers and said it would be a long time, maybe never.

"Why are you saying that?" Sheree asked startled. "What's wrong, Ken? What's happened?"

Ken described the Vietnamese village incident, his own refusal to take part in it, the court-martial of members of his platoon for what they did, and the likelihood that he would be found guilty by association. There was no way he could prove his innocence. The court-martial would probably result in a prison term for all the participants.

Sheree was shaken. "But you did nothing, Ken. How can they punish you for what you didn't do?"

"I can't prove it, Sheree. Don't you understand? We're a platoon, a unit; all of us are in this thing together. We stand by one another. That's the way it is."

"It's stupid. You're individuals, and you're responsible only for your own actions, aren't you?"

"No. That's the point, we're not. We're bound together, trained to think as if each man is the extension of the other. I am guilty in the army's eyes for what anyone in the outfit does."

Sheree couldn't see the logic of Ken's predicament. Would women be the same way? she wondered. Would women so bond together that each would share the blame for another's irresponsible act? Not a chance, she thought. If women were running the world, there'd be no war.

"But what about heroes, their acts of bravery?" Sheree persisted. "They receive the medals as individuals. Explain that."

QUINTET

"Heroes do things that are above and beyond what is expected of them. They perform outside the team, taking the initiative in a crisis."

"But isn't that what you did by not taking part in the atrocity? I mean, Ken, you deserve a medal for *not* acting."

Ken laughed. "You're grasping at straws, Sheree." He hugged her to him. "They don't reward a soldier for doing nothing."

"You mean for being a decent human being. Did you try to stop the others?"

Ken hesitated, finding the answer hard to express. "No," he said finally. "I should have. That's my biggest regret. I did nothing." His words sounded stilted, as if not heartfelt, as if they were lies, as if, perhaps, they were a simplification of how he felt, of what actually happened.

"But why? You knew what they were doing."

"I was afraid they would shoot me. I'm a coward, Sheree, a goddamned coward. You don't know. They went wild; there was no stopping them." He began to sob, and she reached for him and held him close to her.

"I believe in you, my darling. We'll get married right away and see it through, just the two of us."

"No, Sheree. I won't put you through this." How he loved this girl of his, so much so that he refused to bind her life to his until he knew he was free and their happiness was assured.

Sheree, however, having already delayed their marriage once, gave no consideration to what might happen next. She was confident of Ken's innocence and felt that now more than ever he needed her by his side. If he went to prison, so be it. He was still the same man she loved, and that's all that mattered. Of course, she knew there'd be hell to pay with her parents, but now she was in college, no longer a minor, and free do to whatever she wished.

"I love you, Ken. I've waited three years. Don't make me wait any longer. No matter what they do to you, I want to be with you."

"We'll see. I can't think of marriage right now. My whole future is up in the air. Try to understand, Sheree. I need more time to see how all this shakes out. Okay?"

She realized that pressing the point was futile; the timing was wrong. She would delay awhile longer and try again when she knew he was ready. "Certainly, my darling. I'll be here waiting."

268

As soon as Ken arrived in Washington, he sought out his closest friend in the platoon, Roger Baxter, who, like Ken, volunteered right out of high school. Raised in a Chicago slum by a single mother, Roger was a brash fellow, a heavy drinker who used hard drugs, chased women, and expected to make a career in the army. He needed "structure" he said, echoing the advice of his priest.

Although it would seem incongruous that Ken would have such a friend, the fact was that, like a marriage of two unlike people, they complemented each other. Whereas Ken was cerebral, Roger was practical. Ken was patrician; Roger was earthy. Ken lived by principles; Roger lived by his wits. Ken admired Roger for his ability to adapt, to fix anything with what was at hand, and for his uncanny perception of reality. Roger admired and respected Ken for his impeccable honor and acceptance of someone like him.

Ken and Roger talked outside the barracks to avoid anyone who might be listening.

"Did you ask your dad's lawyer about our situation, the way you said you would?" Roger asked, hoping that Ken's rich father would have a legal advisor who could come to their rescue with a helpful angle.

"Forget it. My father thinks we deserve whatever we get."

"That figures. Parents don't give a damn about their kids anymore. Maybe it's good I never had a father."

"I don't understand him. He refuses to take my side. He was never like this."

"Well, we ain't angels, Ken. What do you expect?"

"He won't take my word for anything anymore." Ken kicked up a plume of dirt angrily.

"Your word? Look, friend, don't expect sympathy from anyone. We did what we did, that's all there is to it. We just have to face the music. You'd better get that into your head."

"But I didn't do anything."

"Jesus, Ken, don't give me that shit. We're all in this, every goddamned one of us."

"Did you see me doing anything?"

"I'll say this, I didn't see you not doing anything. I was too busy. What about you? Did you see me?"

"Frankly, no. It was all so terrible, a blur."

"Well, I did plenty. Okay? But you can't prove what I did, and I can't prove what you say you didn't do."

Roger was Ken's last hope as a witness to his innocence. It was a given that none of the others would support him. Because they were consumed with banding together in common defense, he may as well join them.

The incident soon made national headlines, and news of Ken's participation exploded across his hometown. The powers behind Sid's candidacy were extremely disturbed. "Like son, like father," some of them sneered dismissively. But to most, the serious concern was that the publicity about the son was bound to reflect on the father. How tenuous is a good man's reputation? Here was proof that a lifetime of service and philanthropy can be sullied by a single stroke, even in the eyes of one's beneficiaries. Sid was not surprised by what followed. On schedule, Bradley Blodgett asked to meet Sid in his office at nine on Monday.

"This thing with Ken. What's your take on it, Sid? Level with me now," Blodgett said somewhat sheepishly.

"He says he wasn't part of it. Yes, he was there, but nothing more. That's what he says," Sid replied coldly.

"And, of course, as his father you believe him."

"As his father, I have to believe him. Wouldn't you do the same for your son?" Brad began to interrupt, but Sid cut him off. "I know, *if* you had a son. Well, you've got a daughter. You'd believe her."

"I would, Sid. That's the way fathers are. We raise our kids to be decent, to have morals and principles, but the damned world out there keeps corrupting them," said Brad, unsure how to move the subject from the general to the particular.

"We can't blame the world, Brad. We can only blame ourselves."

"True, and that's the problem. What Ken did—"

"Just a minute, Brad. No one has proved anything yet," Sid said, controlling a mounting indignation.

"Of course, I mean what he's accused of having done." Seeing Sid's defensiveness, Brad paused to realign his approach. "I'll be frank."

"By all means be frank," said Sid dryly.

"It seems to be rubbing off on you. People are skeptical. I mean, they don't want a mayor whose family is tainted with scandal."

"You know this for a fact?" Sid shot back.

"Well, we didn't take a poll, if that's what you mean."

"So, what you're saying is that my sponsors think the people wouldn't want a 'tainted'—isn't that the word you used?—guy like me as their candidate after all."

"To put it bluntly, yes," said Brad, avoiding Sid's gaze.

"Well, okay, Brad, I'll withdraw my candidacy, and you can all go to hell." Sid rose from his desk chair as a signal to Brad that he had better leave.

"I wish you'd understand, Sid. We don't have a choice. You're no longer a winner."

"Brad, I've never been a true winner. I've only been lucky."

"I'm still your banker, Sid. I'm on your side, but I'm only one man. If it were up to me alone, I'd not be doing this. You'd still be my man."

Sid placed his arm over Brad's shoulder and led him to the door. "Y'know, Brad, throughout history it has always taken only one person, just a sole individual, to make a difference in the world, either for better or for worse, and obviously you're not one of them."

A YEAR LATER

Another year of life's twisted course. Ken and his platoon received a mild punishment, a dishonorable discharge; and after amnesty was in the air, Bobby returned from Canada. The war was over and America was defeated, bewildered over the ineffectiveness of its might and feeling shame over its discovered inhumanity.

The Randall family was reunited, everyone assuming that they would take up where they had left off before the war. But, of course, it was an impossible hope. The war had changed everything.

It was late in the evening in the Randall's living room the day after Bobby had come home from Canada. Edith, having served one of her famous multiple course dinners, was reclined on the couch sipping a glass of wine. Sid sat in his favorite armchair.

"Isn't it great having both boys back home?" said Jay, standing at the fireplace, his arm resting on the mantel, which held his glass of wine. "Thanks for inviting me and Bobby over, Edith."

"I thought it would be nice if we celebrated as a family. It's the first time we've been together in years," Edith said, glowing. Surrounded by those dearest to her, she basked in a new sense of wholeness.

"Yeah, and now that the war is behind us, everything can get back to normal. Thank God, eh, Sid?"

"It was a dirty war, and it will take years for our country to feel clean, if ever," Sid said, a tinge of bitterness in his voice.

"Really, do you think so?"

"I wish you'd stop dwelling on it," Edith said impatiently. "The past is past, Sid."

"Well, it's too bad that Ken got swept up in it the way he did," Jay said.

"You too, Jay," said Edith. "Stop it. Let's talk about something else."

"Seems like there's going to be an amnesty, so Bobby's free and clear. He's transferred to State College here to finish his business degree."

"I'm glad for him, and it must be nice for you now that you have him home for good," said Edith.

"Oh, I've missed him. While he was in Canada he grew up, y'know, and he's come back a man. I'm sure you found it the same with Ken." Jay looked from Sid to Edith and back again.

"Ken grew old, Jay. He grew old almost overnight," said Sid. "And so did I."

"Yeah, it was a terrible thing that happened. But now he's home."

"His reputation as a human being has been stained," said Sid.

"The stain will fade," Edith counseled. "Time makes all things fade."

"Some things can never fade. They last until you die."

"Damnit, Sid, lighten up. Our sons are back," Jay said, disturbed by the direction of the conversation.

"He hasn't forgiven him, Jay," Edith said, sitting up. "My son is innocent, because he did nothing bad, but no matter, Sid still thinks his son is guilty."

"Christ, Sid, all he got was a dishonorable discharge," Jay said. "You want him to sprout wings?"

"The military court found the commanding officer responsible, so he took the hit," said Sid. "But the rest of them—well, they did what they did. I don't call that exoneration. As individuals, we are responsible for what we do. You don't pass off that responsibility on someone else."

"They were under orders, weren't they?" Jay said.

"There's something higher than taking orders. It's called acting according to one's conscience. Would you call the German guards that ran the concentration camps innocent? After all, they were only under orders."

"You make me so angry. You just won't believe him. You're so...so impossible," Edith said, knocking over her empty glass onto the floor where it broke into shards.

As she hastened to pick up the pieces, an awkward stillness filled the room, until Jay could tolerate it no longer. "So I suppose he's going to college and take up astronomy, or something like it?"

"No, he's changed his mind," Sid said.

"He wants to take some time off, travel around the world for a year or two, then he'll decide what to do," Edith explained.

"Obviously, he can't take over for me," said Sid.

"Because?" Jay asked.

"Well, his past is too fresh."

"In time, Sid, it will be forgotten," said Edith.

"Y'know, Bobby will be ready in another year. You and I have to seriously think of the succession, Sid."

"I'm well aware of the need," Sid said. "Between you and me, I don't have the motivation anymore. I'm ready to step aside."

"What can I do to lift your spirits, dear? Tell me what to do," Edith said, going to his chair and patting his shoulder.

"Perform a miracle and undo the past, that's all," said Sid, squeezing Edith's hand.

"Oh, Sid, dear. Why can't you find a way to believe in your son?"

Jay wished the subject of Ken's guilt would go away. It was consuming his sister's marriage. And he was alarmed at what it was doing to Sid's morale. He was losing his passion for the business, perhaps even for living. Jay had never seen Sid so troubled. It was a dangerous situation, because the succession was now of critical importance. "So, Sid, what about Bobby? If not Ken, then it has to be Bobby."

"I'm afraid not, Jay. I'm sorry, but I don't think Bobby is up to the job."

"Of course he is," said Jay vehemently. "He's got the education, he knows the fundamentals—"

"I don't doubt that. But it takes more than an education to be a leader. I don't think he has the right stuff, not for the top job. He's not the type to dedicate himself to a cause. We can use him as a division manager. I think that would be more his speed."

"Where is this coming from? When did you come to this conclusion?" Jay said, outraged.

"I've watched him. I know him."

"No, you don't. As I said, he's come back a different person than when he left. You don't know what he is."

"We don't change, Jay. Our personalities are set long before we go to college. He's a good kid, I don't doubt it for a minute. And I'm all for bringing him into the business, but not as my replacement." Clearly Sid was implacable.

"Did you know about this, Edith?" said Jay, turning to face his sister.

"I don't interfere in business matters. You know that."

"So you have known what Sid thinks and never said anything."

"Had I told you, would it have made any difference? What would you have done?"

"Well, I would have...well...Look, Sid, I'm going to fight you on this. I'm going to appeal to the board."

"As a major stockholder and board member, you have that right. Bear in mind, I'll fight back."

Jay knew that he'd lose, because Sid ruled the board; the members always listened to his advice and followed it.

"Then who do you have in mind?" asked Jay. "Hell, Ken can't be your man."

"Maybe when he gets the past out of his system."

"You just said that's not possible, that it will haunt him—and you, I take it—forever."

"He'll have to learn to live with it. I think he's a survivor. He'll heal and get on with his life. Isn't that the way most of us handle tragedy? You've talked about the atrocities you witnessed in Europe. Do you still wake up at night screaming? Not anymore, right, Jay? I did for years, but now I sleep the night through, that is until this goddamned thing with Ken."

"I keep telling you to take a pill," Edith said. "He won't take pills, Jay. He'd rather stare at the ceiling and make us both suffer. When he's awake, I'm awake. I went through it for years after his war, and now we're doing it again after Ken's."

"I'll be frank, Sid," said Jay, deciding to step into the fray, "even if Ken gets his feet back on the ground, even if he's qualified for the job with regard to education and personality, he's the wrong man. Edith says he's innocent, and that's good enough for me, but the newspapers called him a rapist, maybe a killer, and there's no way to erase that publicity. You'd never hire a stranger with that reputation, justified or not, for any kind of management job let alone the top one. Ken is out of the question, Sid. Face the facts."

"Maybe you're right," said Sid with unexpected equanimity. "Maybe not Ken, but certainly not Bobby."

"I hear them coming in," said Edith just as the boys entered the room and flung themselves on the sofa.

"Hi, Aunt Edith," said Bobby as Edith hugged and kissed him on the cheek.

"It's good to have you back, Bobby."

"Hi, Uncle Sid," Bobby said, reaching to shake his uncle's hand. Sid nodded but said nothing.

"I could use some of that wine," Ken said, rising and pouring a glass. "Want some, Bobby?"

"Got anything harder?"

"In the liquor cabinet, over there," Edith said, pointing.

"That's okay. I'll take some wine."

Ken poured Bobby a glass and handed it to him.

"Since when have you been drinking, Ken? Service make a man of you?" Jay said.

"Yeah, a man," Ken said, stung by his uncle's remark. "It's frightening, isn't it?"

"I didn't mean—"

"Oh, it's okay, Uncle Jay. Men do terrible things, like drinking wine."

"Shit, you should try pot, Kenny," Bobby said. "That'll send ya where you want to go."

"I catch you smokin' that stuff, I'll—" Jay threatened.

"You'll what?" challenged Bobby.

"If I see any of it around, I'll throw it down the toilet. That's what I'll do."

"You'll have to find it first."

Such talk had gone far enough for Edith. "I hear you have only one year left at business school and you're transferring back here," she said to Bobby, as if the altercation between father and son had never occurred.

"Yup. I spent the war fighting the girls off up in Canada, and now the government says it's okay to become an American again. So here I am."

"He's getting the kind of education I never got," Jay said. "Who thought of going to B school during the depression? These kids have it made. Our parents couldn't afford to send us to college, could they, Sid?"

"No, but we had the GI Bill, the best thing this country ever did. That's why we're making out, and our country is leading the world."

"Do you hear that, boys?" Jay said. "Education, it's the road to success. Right, Sid?"

"That's right, and that's why we're the most successful generation in history. They were smart in Washington back in those days. Instead of dumping all us ex-GIs into the labor pool, they sent us to college. Not like today, when the good of the nation comes second."

"The GI Bill was damned brilliant, I'd say," Jay interrupted.

"I got a good general education at State," Sid went on, ignoring Jay's remarks. "And because I didn't know much about business, I went to school nights and learned a balance sheet from a P & L statement. The GI Bill paid for all of it."

"Oh, I forgot," Jay said. "You went nights, didn't you? Boy, that seems like a long time ago, Sid."

"Why didn't you go to college, Jay?"

"I had to go to work to support my parents. Our dad was worn out from welding in the shipyard during the war and couldn't work anymore. Remember, Edith? Maybe not. You were only a kid. People who work with their hands wear out sooner than the rest of us, y'know. Bear that in mind, boys. You'll never get rich working with your hands."

"It was almost thirty years ago, Jay," said Sid, becoming nostalgic. "Remember how you were on the road drumming up orders while I was in the cellar of our rented house with one injection molding machine making electric switch plates.

Edith always loved to hear this story, because it took place during the years of optimism and hope and their youth. It was the best years of their lives, in spirit if not in material terms.

276

"I used to help with the books," said Edith. "We worked hard, but we never complained. And I was very much in love."

"The good bad old days, eh? Because we had a purpose, Edith. It was called success," said Sid.

"You hear that, boys?" said Jay. "A purpose, something to work for, that's the key."

"I think Ken has the right idea," said Bobby. "Do some traveling. Actually, I'd like to take a year off, too. Maybe you and I could carouse together, Ken. Whaddaya say?"

"Hell you will. You're goin' to finish B school and come into the business," Jay decreed. "Build a career and become a success. Haven't you been listening to what we've been saying?"

"I guess I'm all for that, too," said Bobby, shrugging.

"Said with enthusiasm, eh, Bobby?" Sid remarked sarcastically.

"Well, I think Ken's idea—travel—is educational, too."

"I'm not doing it to get an education, Bobby," Ken said.

"I realize that. You expect to find something, right?"

"Just myself, nothing more."

"Hell, I know who I am. That's as easy as looking in the mirror."

"I used to think I knew myself, but no longer," Ken said sadly.

"We can never know ourselves completely until we're tested," said Sid, locking eyes with his son.

"So, I was tested, and apparently I failed. According to some, anyway," Ken said, meeting his father's gaze squarely.

"You haven't failed," said Edith. "You were unjustly accused. How can you doubt yourself?"

"It's a legal thing," said Sid. "Suppose he did nothing, which he claims?"

"It's the truth, Dad," Ken shouted in frustration.

"According to our law," Sid persisted, "if a man kills another man, his associate is just as guilty as he is."

"Maybe I was justly accused, maybe I deserved everything that was meted out, maybe I deserve even more punishment than I got. I don't know what's true anymore."

"No, Ken, you know the truth," said Edith, "and you must believe in it, and yourself."

"The truth is how you see it, Edith. What happened is one thing, but that's not enough. The truth is a matter of opinion," said Sid.

"What in hell are you talking about?" Bobby interjected.

"How dare you talk that way to your uncle," said Jay. "He's talking about facts. That's all."

"Facts? Who can argue about facts?" said Bobby. "What's opinion got to do with it? Vietnamese women get raped and killed; those are facts. Either it happened or it didn't happen. Either you did these things or you didn't. If I was ordered to do them in the line of duty, I'd do it. But Ken didn't. I believe him. He isn't capable. So why don't you all lay off him?"

"Shut up, Bobby," Jay screamed. "Just shut up."

Bobby's outburst shook Jay, for he could see that by contradicting Sid, Bobby failed to see his own interest. Or, worse, perhaps he didn't much care whether or not he was in line for taking over from his uncle. Otherwise, why would he come to Ken's rescue and jeopardize his standing with Sid?

But that was not the case. Sid was impressed, and surprised. He recognized the rationality of Bobby's approach and his unselfish support of his cousin as something new, something he hadn't seen in his nephew before.

"Do you really think those boys were ordered to do what they did?" Sid asked Bobby.

"Well, their commanding officer was held responsible, wasn't he?"

"You mean you don't think they acted on their own, or at the very least interpreted their orders with a free hand? Is that what you're saying?"

"This is ridiculous," Ken said. "It's not black and white; it's not that simple."

"I know it's not simple. It never is, but someone is responsible. You can't duck it," Sid said.

"To the victor go the spoils. Isn't that what you said, Uncle Sid?" asked Bobby.

"Apparently you have the luxury of admitting your dark side, Bobby," said Sid.

"That's not a luxury, Uncle Sid."

"But for some of us it would be. Take it from me."

There was a long silence as everyone avoided the other's eyes and looked down at the Oriental carpet. Finally, Jay broke the silence.

"Time to leave. Let's go home, Bobby."

"I want to stay awhile and talk to Ken."

"See you all later then," said Jay. "We've got more talking to do, Sid."

"No, Jay. I've said all I have to say. You do what you want," Sid replied.

"Good night, Edith, Ken."

"Good night, Jay. Listen to Sid. He knows what's best," Edith said, her eyes pleading for peace between them.

Jay walked to the door but before closing it behind him said, "Edith, as your brother, your happiness means everything to me. Don't worry about a thing. Sid will see the light."

"Go on, you sonofabitch," said Sid, laughing.

"Why don't you and I leave and let the boys talk?" Edith said, reaching for Sid's hand and pulling him from his chair and into the next room. "It's such a pleasure to have you boys back. Good night."

"Good night," said the cousins in unison.

There were no competitive feelings between Bobby and Ken. For one thing, as Jay had come to suspect, Bobby was willing to accept that Ken had to be favored for the top position in the company. After all, wasn't he the president's son? For another, Bobby didn't think that Ken wanted the job and if he took it he'd be miserable and eventually fail and quit. As Bobby saw it, Ken was hardly the entrepreneurial type. Moreover, Bobby believed almost as a religion that fate was always on his side; sooner or later only the best would happen. And it was this belief that gave him a feeling of self-assuredness and an ability to take things in stride, which was rare. You could say that he was genuinely a free spirit.

Clearly, Ken had none of these qualities. Although Ken admired Bobby for his irreverence and daring, he took life seriously and felt the need for reasons and causes, perhaps even absolute truth. Before he could accept anything, he had to understand it, and he understood Bobby. He understood that Sid failed to see that Bobby was the better choice for taking over the business. Though the cousins came from different backgrounds and were headed in different directions, their appreciation for each other and their mutual wishes coincided. They were more than cousins; they were friends

As soon as Sid and Edith closed the door behind them, Ken reclined on the couch where his mother had been and Bobby sat in his uncle's chair.

"Damn, you're a lucky sonofabitch," said Bobby. "I wish I could just take off and be a vagabond like you. They plan every minute of our lives, don't they?"

"They try to," Ken said.

"You'd think they'd discovered some kind of nirvana, and nobody in his right mind wouldn't want it."

"I suppose they see us as their ticket to immortality," said Ken, thinking of his father's pressure on him to train for the stewardship of the company.

"Hey, Kenny, that's going a little overboard, don't you think?"

"I don't know. I think my dad wants to keep his name and his achievements alive after he's gone. You know, when you visit an old burial ground, all the gravestones are covered with mold and dirt, and many are so eroded you can hardly read the inscriptions. Why? Because the people buried beneath the stones are forgotten. If they made a difference, how would we know it? They may as well not have existed."

"Why should I want people two hundred years from now to know about me?" said Bobby. "My life is now; I want people to know who I am while I'm alive, that's all. After I'm dead, who cares?"

"I haven't figured out why we're here in the first place," said Ken with a laugh.

"I know why I'm here, Kenny."

"You do?"

"Sure. To become a wheel in the business in another year. Look, I'll level with you. Your dad isn't far from retirement. My dad wants me to go for the top job. And I expect that Uncle Sid would want it for you. I think there's going to be a fight. But I want you to know I wouldn't stand in your way."

"Do you want the job, Bobby?"

"Yeah, to tell the truth I can taste it."

"Then go for it. I'm not in your way."

"You mean that?"

Ken thought it judicious not to mention that for a time he had entertained the idea that maybe he ought to follow his father's wishes concerning the business. But he had more recently come to the conclusion that his damaged reputation made it impossible. If his father hadn't awakened to that fact, he was bound to soon enough.

"Absolutely. I don't want it. Anyway, even if I did, after what's happened, I wouldn't be eligible."

"Trouble is, I don't think your dad cottons to me," said Bobby.

"I'm in the same boat, only worse. He doesn't believe or trust me. But you're all that he has, unless he brings in a stranger. And I don't think he'll do that. He has always appointed family to management positions. Isn't every one of his VPs a relative?"

"So, you're going to take up astronomy stuff? Is that it?"

"I don't know what I'm going to do. I hope in time I'll find out. Maybe I'll join the Peace Corps, do some good for somebody," said Ken, getting up and pacing.

"Christ, I admire you, Kenny."

"Thanks, Bobby, but I don't see what's to admire."

"I know what I want, and I know where I'm going, but everything I do is for myself."

"No one can blame you for that. I'm the same way."

"You don't see it, do you? How in hell can Uncle Sid not see you for how you are?"

"About this thing that happened, he refuses to believe me. I don't know why. You can't imagine how much it weighs on me. I want his respect so damned badly. What do I have to do to win it? The only thing left is for me to leave and get on with my life. So that's what I'm going to do."

Sheree and Ken met again at the same park bench as before, not for the reason of privacy this time but to keep their meeting a secret. Sheree's parents strongly objected to their daughter being involved with "a rapist and murderer." But as with Edith, Sheree believed Ken's story without a scintilla of doubt. The more strongly her parents objected, the more determined she was to see Ken. She was ready to marry him at a moment's notice. But it was Ken who delayed again, this time because of his need to be free of any entanglement, although to escape what, to find what, to bury himself in what, he could not say.

"You don't want to be tied to someone like me," Ken said.

"Someone like you?" Sheree protested. "What do you mean someone like you? What's wrong with you?"

"Do you want a list?"

"Ken, you are the same man who went away, and—"

"No, Sheree, you've got it wrong. I'm not the same man," Ken said, caressing her cheek. "The only thing that's the same is my love for you, but nothing else."

"Isn't that all that matters, that we love each other?" Sheree begged.

"Why should you have to suffer for my sins?"

"What sins? What are you talking about? You haven't done anything wrong."

"What I've done or haven't done isn't the issue," Ken said impatiently. "It's what the world thinks I've done that counts. Don't you see?"

"I don't care what the rest of the world thinks."

"But I do, Sheree. I do, damnit."

"Why? Why? We'll fight the rest of the world together."

"We can't win," Ken said, looking skyward at the rustling, innocent leaves falling from the tree beside them. How he wished to be as free as one of those windblown leaves.

"I've never heard you talk like this," Sheree said, startled.

"So you see, I have changed."

"Yes, you have, and I don't like it."

"Neither do I. But I can't help it. It's the way I feel." He took her in his arms and held her. "I have to leave, Sheree."

"Take me with you," she said as tears welled up in her eyes.

"I've got to do this alone. I've got to sort things out first."

"Well, when you do, will you send for me wherever you are?"

"I will, Sheree, I will," Ken said, and they kissed as if it were their last time.

Sheree no longer had illusions about Ken, about their chance of ever marrying. Empathizing with his suffering, not wishing to cause more pain, she was unable to vent her frustration over his refusal to include her in his life. True, she didn't want to wander the world with him. She didn't wish to spend her life living in the shadow of his mysterious guilt and the stigma of his past. An old-fashioned woman, she wanted to settle down, have a home and children. But she had no control over her love for him. It was as much a part of her psyche as consciousness itself. So she became resigned to the possibility of unfulfilled love. Who knew how many more years would pass before Ken would be ready, if ever?

The next day, late in the afternoon, Edith and Ken sat in the living room across from each other. Edith had decided it was time the two had a heart-to-heart talk.

"Come here, Ken, sit next to me on the sofa. Before your father comes home, let's talk."

She knew her son's pain and sought to assuage it. She also knew that his future wasn't turning out as she had envisioned it. She had long ago become reconciled to Sid's obsession with the business and neglect of her, but she loved her husband and was proud of him. All in all, he was a good man and, in his way, a loving one.

Ken was like his father in some ways, particularly with respect to his integrity and his serious approach to life. But he was the opposite in other ways—in his sensitivity, his scholarliness, and his ability to express affection. Between her two men, her life had been fulfilled. But now life had turned gray, and it was time to intervene.

"There's nothing to talk about, Ma. I'm all talked out. Anyway, it doesn't do any good. Everyone has his mind made up about me," Ken replied, despondent.

"I've made up my mind, I definitely have," said Edith. "You are the same as you were before you went to war, no worse. Only better— older, more mature, more thoughtful."

"No, Ma. You're wrong. I don't feel good about myself anymore."

"Oh, Ken. You have no cause to feel that way," Edith said as she patted his hand.

"I'm an outcast in my own town, in my country."

"Don't listen to them, Ken. Don't listen."

"It's not a matter of my listening. It's their actions. They shun me. When I go to the supermarket, I can feel the coldness at the checkout counter. When I go to the bank, the tellers slam their windows shut on me. All my old high school chums avoid me. I have no more friends, except for Bobby. Then there's Dad. I can't stay here any longer, Ma. I can't live where I'm ostracized."

"Come, let me hug you," Edith said, reaching for him and holding him to her. "My poor boy. I feel so helpless. I'm overwhelmed with sadness for you. But I'm sure in time it will all be forgotten and your life will return to normal."

"Maybe so, maybe not. But I have to deal with what's happening now, Ma. I have to leave."

"I know, son. You want to travel. That will be good for you. I've always found travel mind-expanding. In this country we think our way is the best in the world, that we are the center of the universe. But we aren't. There are other ways that are as good and maybe better. We are so judgmental, so stuck on our rightness, so busy that we don't take time to be alive. Your father...he's like the rest of us, but not you. I don't know what we did, but you're...well..."

"Different. I've never fit in, Ma. I've always been on the perimeter at school, not excluded but never part of the in-group. Not like Bobby, who was always popular."

"Bobby runs as deep as a trickle of water. I never understood how you two could be such fast friends."

"You've got him wrong, Ma. Dad does, too. Bobby knows himself; he knows where he wants to go. He's lucky," said Ken, genuinely admiring and envious.

"He's lucky his uncle is willing to take him into the business. Your dad says he'd make a good car salesman. That's how I feel, too."

"Why do all of you underestimate him? He'd be a perfect CEO to succeed Dad," Ken said, truly baffled.

"I don't know about that. That's your dad's business. I don't want to talk about Bobby. I want to talk about you, about us. You're my business, and I want you to come back from your travels in a year renewed and ready to join your father."

"I can't do that, Ma."

"Of course you can. He'll be ready to accept you, I know he will. I'll make sure of it. I'll bring him around the way I usually do," Edith said, already formulating a strategy.

"Ma, I don't want to return."

"What did you say? Not return, Ken? This is your home. If there's anyplace in the world where you're welcome, it's here."

"I want to live in a foreign country, begin fresh, make new friends. Do some good where it's needed." Ken's face lit up with the prospect.

"In exile? Self-imposed exile?" Edith said, shaking her head vigorously from side to side. "Ken. Son. That's not necessary. The past will all be forgotten. It's just a matter of time."

"I don't think people will forget. I don't want to live in a place where I can't prove my innocence. And it's more than that. Our system is corrupt. I don't believe I can find justice here."

"I know, I know. But do you think it's less corrupt someplace else? Where in this unfair world do you think you can find justice?"

Besides her son's unjust punishment, she thought of her husband's forced withdrawal from the mayoral race, then her mind leapt to the Holocaust, the worst injustice of all.

"I don't know. I'll just keep looking," Ken said, determined.

Knowing that Ken was still young enough to be optimistic, and hesitating to voice her true belief that her son's quest was bound to fail, Edith said instead, "Oh, my wonderful boy. A mother has dreams. You'd be in the business and marry Sheree and we'd have grandchildren, and they'd stay with us while you and Sheree went on vacation. It would be like starting life all over again for you, and for us. But right now, such a dream is just that, isn't it? And I'm afraid it will always be."

She sighed in resignation. "I think I hear your father at the door. We'll talk again."

Sid entered, threw his briefcase on the desk in his study, then sauntered into the living room. Ignoring Ken, he kissed Edith on the cheek, picked up the newspaper on the footstool before him, and fell into his favorite chair.

"Hi, Dad," Ken said. Sid didn't respond. "Well...," Ken murmured, then got up and left the room.

"You must stop this," Edith remonstrated. "He's your own flesh and blood. What has he done to you?"

"Damnit, Edith, I don't want to discuss it," Sid replied, annoyed and tense.

"You're certainly in a foul mood."

"Who wouldn't be after dealing with your brother?"

"Why, what has Jay done?"

"He's gotten to every goddamned board member. They've had me on the phone all day."

"About Bobby, I suppose."

"Yeah, about Bobby."

"What have you got against him? Hasn't he done what was expected of him? He's in business school and he's willing to do anything you ask. What more do you want?"

"I don't like him. It's a personality thing. He doesn't have a conscience. He's the kind of guy who'll stop at nothing to win."

"You've always said that in business you'd deal with the devil if it was good for the company. I'm sure you don't think the devil is very nice."

"There's a limit. I wouldn't have the devil run my business."

"So, according to you, Bobby is the devil?"

"Of course not. He's an opportunist."

"You're bitter because you can no longer dream of having Ken take over someday. So you're taking it out on Bobby," Edith said as Sid got up and poured himself some wine. "Ken thinks Bobby would make a perfect CEO."

"All he's doing is appointing a surrogate to make up for his own failure. Can't you see that?"

Edith knew that arguing with Sid would get her nowhere. She knew from years of fighting for her point of view that once Sid made up his mind he stuck to it as if his life depended on it. And perhaps, in his need to be right, it did. But occasionally she won when she thought the issue was important enough.

"Sid, I want you to talk to Ken."

"We've talked. There's nothing more to say."

"He says the same thing," Edith said with a laugh. "I mean really talk—no recrimination, no anger—listen and talk. He sets such store by what you think of him. And unless you accept him, he'll have a hard time accepting himself."

"Many of us have a hard time doing that. And some of us never succeed at it. I can't help him, Edith. Nobody can."

"Do you know what his plans are?"

"Sure, he's going away."

"Yes, and he's not coming back."

"Did he say that?" Sid said, suppressing his alarm.

"He's turning his back on us, on his country. And do you know why? Because he feels he's been done an injustice. He'll never be able to prove his innocence here. So he's going into exile, Sid. Do you realize what he's doing? It's self-imposed exile." Edith's voice broke, and she began to sob.

Sid put aside his drink and held her. "Now, now, Edith. Calm yourself…. Ken said that?" Sid couldn't stand to see his wife weeping. Whenever she wept, he felt like doing so himself. Only then could he join her in suffering. All his love for her became concentrated the instant she began crying.

"He's so disillusioned," said Edith, blowing her nose amid her tears. "If you would show some faith, some concern, that would mean so much to him. He's our son, Sid, our only child. Even if he were responsible for those bad things, I'd still love him. Don't you love him?"

"Yes, Edith. I've never stopped loving him. I'm just angry and disappointed. We're his models, and he failed to—"

"Then show him some compassion. Please, Sid, I'm pleading with you. Talk to him once more."

"Damnit Edith," Sid responded heatedly. "Don't you hear me? I'm done talking to him."

"Just once more. Please, Sid. For my sake, if not his. Don't let him leave without telling him you love him.

Sid stiffened, struggling with himself to give in. "Okay, okay, once more. But this will have to be it."

"That's all I ask. He's in his room. I'll get him. You two can talk while I get supper ready."

Edith had won a major concession. She had banked on Sid's love and sympathy for his son to override his condemnation. She had always known that Sid's outer hardness hid a soft interior that expressions of love could, at the right place and the right time, pierce. In her estimation, this time and this place were right.

Waiting for Ken to appear, Sid picked up the local newspaper again and perused it, noting that the city was running in the red and that taxes would have to be raised. He felt a surge of regret that he had withdrawn from the race for mayor. Maybe he should have become a candidate independent of the cabal. Why had he given in to Blodgett so easily? He'd have had the city on a fiscally responsible budget, that's for sure. Why should he have to pay for his son's sins? No, such thoughts were hypocritical. Who is without sin? Didn't he have his own to pay for?

"Ma says you want to see me," said Ken upon entering the living room.

"Sit down. There, on the couch. Care for some wine?" Sid asked, starting to rise.

"Don't mind. Stay where you are. I'll get it."

"No, you sit. I'll do it," said Sid as he poured a glass which he handed to Ken, then returned to his chair. "Your mother tells me you're planning to go away for good."

"That's right," said Ken. So that's why he was here, he realized. His mother had appealed to his father to talk him out of it.

"Turning your back on your country. Isn't that what you're doing?"

"What did my country do except turn its back on me? I defended it to the best of my ability, and in return I'm ostracized."

"I see."

"Do you really? Do you, Dad?"

"Well, I wouldn't call your punishment severe, certainly not cause for the extreme rejection you're about to make," Sid responded with strained contempt in his tone.

"My feelings and actions have nothing to do with the punishment I received. I have no trouble accepting punishment, even though it was undeserved. It's being unjustly marked that makes me so angry."

"Why was it undeserved, as you say? You were there."

"I know you say that's enough; it's the law. I don't give a goddamn for the law. You've got to understand the circumstances. I had no choice. What was I to do, run out on my platoon, become a deserter?"

"I had such high hopes for you. I want to believe you," Sid said.

"Why can't you? I don't understand. What's stopping you? Why can't you take my word? I don't know what to say to you. My denials mean nothing," Ken said, his temper mounting.

"I know what we are capable of."

"We? Which 'we' are we talking about? You or me?"

"All mankind. We, all of us, are capable of reverting to our animal nature."

"Sure, that may be. I witnessed it, but not everybody is like that. Some of us have empathy that overrides everything else. Some of us are capable of being noble."

"When we can afford it."

"No, Dad. It's not a matter of affording it. It's as much a part of our nature as our animal instinct. Don't you believe we also have a bright side?"

Sid was impressed. Clearly Ken had thought through his predicament, its moral and legal implications. Despite the calumny heaped upon him, the rejection he was enduring, and what he had witnessed or partaken in, his belief in mankind remained intact.

Remarkable, Sid thought. Holding no such opinion himself, Sid concluded that Ken was simply naïve and idealistic, which was typical of someone his age. Just wait until he accumulates a few more years of living, thought Sid.

"Listen, son. Would you call me a good man, an empathetic man?" Sid asked, confident of Ken's answer.

"Yes, I believe you have a good heart. You're kind. And our entire community worships you for the man you are."

Sid laughed. "Hah, what do they know? Ken, I'm a fraud," he shouted, emphasizing the last word. "A fucking fraud."

Taken aback, trying to contain himself, Ken said, "No, Dad. I know you."

"Know me? Ken, we never know each other, least of all do we know ourselves."

"Remember, I live here with you," said Ken, unsure whether his father was leading him on. "I see how much you love Ma. Despite your refusal to accept me, I still believe you love me."

"I do, son," Sid said, walking over to Ken and touching his arm.

"How can you call yourself a fraud? Where does that come from, Dad? Why do you say such a thing?"

"Because I do know myself. Few of us have the opportunity to make that discovery. I have seen what I am. I'm not as innocent as everyone thinks."

"Is anyone innocent? I've done things I'm ashamed of. I'm not pure. I..." Ken faltered, afraid to confess his own misdeeds or discover any that his father may have committed.

"Sure, we don't carry our shame with us. Most of it fades so we can live with ourselves. But if the shameful deed is too great—"

"I know. Just to bear witness is hard to live down. Take it from me," Ken said.

"So you've learned that none of us is innocent."

"Sometimes even doing the right thing has a price." Ken immediately regretted his statement. Its implication that he withheld information, that there was more to his story, must not be divulged. Hoping his father wouldn't pick up on it, he added, "I know only about myself, Dad. I can't know about others."

"But you know what others are capable of doing, isn't that right?"

"Yes," Ken said, pinned down.

"I've tried to lead an exemplary life, Ken. I wanted your mother and you to be proud of me." Sid refilled his glass, and while his back was turned he continued in a hoarse whisper. "I've tried to make up for what I've done. And I think I succeeded. As I look back on my life, yes, I've compensated for my bad deed."

Ken felt an oncoming panic. "What are you talking about, Dad?"

"It's so hard for me to talk about this. I buried it; I thought it was over and done long ago. It was under control. Then this terrible thing your outfit did in Vietnam brought it all back."

"When you were in the war? Is that it?"

"Yes. I've never told anyone what I'm about to tell you." Ken watched his father's hand tremble as the wine spilled from the glass.

"You don't have to tell me anything," Ken said, mortified at seeing his father beginning to come apart. "I mean it, Dad. It isn't necessary."

"But it is, you hear. It is. It's time I came clean. I owe it to you." Sid turned to Ken and remained standing as he fought to regain his composure.

"I don't want to hear it, Dad."

"You're going to, goddamnit," Sid screamed. "It's the only way I can forgive you. Do you understand? So listen."

Ken sat back in astonishment, letting his father continue.

"We were on a patrol in the bush in the Philippines, just a squad of us," he began then stopped as his voice cracked. Clearing his throat he continued.. "We were looking for Jap snipers when we ran into this nipa shack. Inside were three young Filipino women, prisoners that the Japanese soldiers were using for their pleasure." Sid paused and stared off into the next room as if the scene were transpiring there. "I've asked myself a thousand times, why did they have to be there? It's like an accident, a twist of fate. You can't explain it."

"Dad, don't go on. I've heard enough," Ken said as he got up from the couch to leave.

"Sit down!" Sid commanded. "This is for both of us. Get it?" Ken nodded and sat down. He understood. If only he could be as candid, but how could anyone understand all of his story? His father went on. "So I don't have to tell you what happened. You already know, eh? I don't have to go on, do I, for your sake? But I do, for my sake. You're going to listen—for me. Do you understand?"

"All right, Dad. I'll listen—for you."

"Good lad." Sid looked into the adjoining room again, envisioning the scene he was describing. "We entered the shack. The girls were cowering, afraid, you see. We told them we were Americans, that they didn't have to be afraid, but it didn't seem to make any difference. They were still frightened. Americans, Japs, what did it matter? We were men and we hadn't had a woman in years. One of our boys called them whores and began slapping them around. If the Japs can use them, so can we, someone said. God, the poor girls; it was terrible. We went crazy, absolutely crazy. We raped them."

"You mean..."

"Me, too. Yes, I joined in. I was no better than my buddies."

"But they were whores."

"No, Ken. The Japs used them that way, but they weren't whores voluntarily. They had been decent Filipino girls, fifteen or sixteen years old. They had no choice."

"I understand. You had to do it, didn't you? The others forced you. I mean, if you didn't join in, they might have turned on you."

"If only that were true. If only...No, no question, I wanted to. At first I watched, then something in me broke loose from all civilized constraints and I went wild. I liked it, that's the awful thing about it. I actually enjoyed it. I felt all-powerful. I saw a part of myself that I hadn't known before. I did something I didn't know I was capable of.

"But it didn't end there." His shoulders heaved, and Sid began sobbing. "God, God, I must go on. I've got to say it."

"Take it easy, Dad." Ken rose and embraced his father. "I'm listening."

"Thanks, son," Sid said, gently withdrawing from the embrace and calming himself enough to go on. "After we were done, we began arguing over what to do with the girls. Someone said that if they talked, we'd be in trouble. I knew what was coming. So I stepped out of the shack and knelt on the ground, despising myself. Then came the shots." Sid slumped into his chair. "Instead of doing the responsible thing and defending the girls, instead of at least protesting, I let it happen because I was afraid of being discovered. I can hear the shots now. I can still hear them."

"My God, Dad." Still standing, Ken watched his wretched father wallowing in shame.

"I should have stopped them. I could have done something, but I didn't. We reported that the Japs killed them, and no one questioned it. I've spent the rest of my life trying to atone for this. All of us have secrets, Ken, but few have secrets as dark as mine. I came back from the war a hero just for having fought for my country. Until this moment, no one knew except the two other boys in the squad. Not your mother—least of all her—not your uncle, no one else. I thought I had buried it for good, except…Well, I've said enough."

"So you appreciate my feelings," said Ken, relieved.

"Yes, I understand. You forced me to deal with myself once again. You reopened a wound that I thought was healed. I didn't want to face up to my crime again. I know what you've gone through. Forgive me, Ken. Please forgive me."

"Of course I forgive you, Dad."

Ken reached for his father's hands, tugged him from his chair, and held him in a long embrace. "Thanks for what you just did. I know how hard it must have been."

"Good lad. But if you can forgive me, you can forgive yourself," Sid said.

"I'll try. But I confess it's easier to forgive someone else."

Still holding each other, Sid said, "I'm ready to believe you. My deed was far worse than yours. I want us to be friends again."

"I love you, Dad."

Edith entered to find her men at peace, embracing. "What's this? My two boys making up. I'm so pleased. At last we're a family again."

"Now, about your coming back home," Sid said. "You must return. Go to school in Europe. Study there. I'll take care of the finances. You could come into the business, take over eventually, but if you want to do something else, I won't object. Whatever you want to do is okay with me."

"I think Bobby should step into your shoes, Dad. I'm not right for the job. He's got the stuff."

"That's what I keep telling your father," Edith said, nodding vigorously.

"He's got you all fooled," Sid said adamantly.

"No, Dad. He gives it to us straight. We see him just as he is. There's no pretense. He's tough. Isn't that what it takes? Isn't that what you always said? 'You must be tough in business. There's no room for feelings.'"

"I'll think about it."

"Well, that's something," Edith said, directing the men into the kitchen. "Come, supper's ready. Bring your wineglasses with you."

Within a few days, Ken departed the United States. Although his father agreed to finance anything he wished to do, he accepted only with the provision that the money would be a loan. Before leaving, he and Sheree discussed their future together. He told her that he had to travel alone, and she told him that she would go with him.

"I'll be back in a year," he said. "You'll be out of college then, and we'll get married. But I have to do this by myself, Sheree. Please understand."

"Why?" she begged. "What are you looking for?"

"Looking for? I suppose to find out how I fit into this world. I don't know yet. Look, I want to be totally anonymous; I want to bury myself in other cultures, be with totally new people, and forget this country."

"Why can't we do it together?"

"Because I must be completely free. I may be living and traveling under difficult conditions. I'm used to it, but you aren't. I love you, Sheree, and I'm yours if you'll wait. Just one more year."

Sheree agreed amid tears. It was their second parting. At least there was hope.

ANOTHER YEAR LATER

During that year Ken traveled around Europe, educating himself not in a formal sense but in how the rest of the world lived. From Europe he went to Egypt; then Israel, where he lived for some months in a kibbutz; then India; then Tibet, where he found a culture being methodically destroyed; then Indonesia; then the Philippines. There he met and was a guest of some of his father's grateful Filipino friends from the war. From them he learned that his father had built a school, which carried his name, for their small farming village. He had also contributed to the restoration of their bombed-out church, even though he didn't subscribe to their faith.

After a few months of exploring the archipelago and living with a primitive tribe in the mountain forests of Mindanao, he moved on to Japan, where he visited Hiroshima and Nagasaki, and from there to Africa, where he offered his services to a French agency dedicated to alleviating the suffering of the people in war-torn southern Sudan.

Sid eventually agreed to bring Bobby into the business and groom him to be his successor in five years. Sid's plan was to remain for a time as chairman to see that his nephew performed effectively. If he didn't, Sid would replace him. Jay agreed to this condition, convinced that Bobby would surprise him with his inborn acumen and would cause the company to grow as never before. Jay knew that he would have to play the role of honest broker should any disagreement, especially in style, develop between his son and his brother-in-law.

Peace had returned to the family and the nation. But a phone call that Sid received from one Perry Axminster threatened to shatter the calm. Mr. Axminster said he was passing through and asked to drop by the office to say hello. Sid consented, reluctantly. He hadn't seen or heard from Perry since their discharge from the army and over the years dreaded that he would someday appear.

When Axminster entered the office, Sid saw that, even though they were the same age, his visitor looked a good ten years older than he. Indeed, Sid would not have recognized him on the street. A heavy drinker and smoker, no doubt, Sid thought. Perry wore a soiled open-necked shirt that revealed loose, aging skin. His bloated face had several days' growth of beard.

"Goddamned long time, eh, Sid?" Perry said, extending his hand to meet Sid's across the desk.

"Have a seat," Sid said, motioning Perry to a chair squarely in front of him.

"I heard you'd done pretty good, Sid, but I never expected all this," said Perry as he surveyed Sid's elegant office.

"Just luck, Perry," Sid said, shrugging. "Being in the right place at the right time. You couldn't fail after the war."

"Well, I sure as hell wasn't in the right place at the right time."

"Is that right? I'm sorry to hear that. What have you done with your life?"

"Well, I'm what some would call a drifter. I do odd jobs. My wife left me years ago, took my two kids. To tell the truth, Sid, my main occupation is alcoholism. I'm an alki, or was. Been off the wagon for a couple of years now."

"So what brings you up this way?" Sid inquired, at least appreciating Perry's honesty about himself.

"My daughter lives up north. Haven't seen her in years. I thought I'd sponge off her for a while. Hey, enough about me. You got kids?"

"One, a son."

"Yeah. S'pose he's with you in the business?"

"No, he's abroad right now."

"Oh. Was he in the war?"

"Yes, he was."

"A shitty war. Nothing like our war, eh, Sid?"

"I suppose you could say that. In some ways it was the same," Sid said, shifting uncomfortably in his executive chair.

"Have you heard about George?"

"George?"

"Yeah. Jesus, Sid. George from the squad. You know, George."

"No, I haven't heard. What about George?" Sid asked, not sure that he wanted to know.

"Dead."

"I'm sorry to hear it."

"You know how he died, Sid? Fucking a whore in New Orleans. Ain't that like him? Had a heart attack. Lucky he didn't have one at the shack. Remember the shack, Sid?"

"What's on your mind?" Sid said, containing his impatience.

"Nothing much. Just a social call. Now that there's only the two of us, I thought it was a good idea to renew our acquaintance."

"Well, Perry, it's good to see you again," Sid said, motioning to rise.

"Same here, Sid. But before I leave, I got to ask you a favor. For friendship's sake, would you be willing to lend an old buddy a few bucks? Not much, maybe five hundred or a thousand. I mean, I'll bet you'd hardly notice it."

Sid stood motionless, speculating whether this was a one-time touch or had long-range implications, and whether there was a tinge of blackmail in the request.

"Sure," said Sid, withdrawing a checkbook from his desk drawer and making out a check for five hundred dollars while Perry scanned the opulent office again.

"Thanks, Buddy," Perry said, checking the amount. "Let's get together again. Swap some stories. Eh, Sid."

Sid escorted Perry politely to the door, restraining his wish to throw him out. Immediately he began contriving a strategy to ensure that "getting together" would never occur. But he knew it wouldn't be easy.

When Sid arrived home that evening, still stinging from Perry's visit, he was further disturbed to learn that Edith had consented to receive one of Ken's war buddies at their home in a few hours. After supper, Sid retired to his favorite chair to read the local newspaper while Edith sat in her rocking chair knitting.

"Didn't you tell him that Ken isn't here, that he's in Africa?" Sid asked, annoyed.

"Of course I did."

"Then why does he insist on seeing us?"

"Well, he said that he was one of Ken's buddies in the service and he wanted to meet you."

"I don't get it. Why would he want to see me?"

"Don't ask me. He said he was passing through town and had heard that your company was a great place to work. Because he's a friend of Ken's, I saw no harm in it."

"Of course there's no harm in it, but there's nothing to be gained from it either. I've had enough of people passing through town," Sid said, dropping the newspaper onto his lap in resignation. "He's looking for a job. He as much as said so."

"Why are you so touchy about this? We'll get a chance to meet one of Ken's service friends."

"Ken never mentioned him to me. What did he say his name was?"

"Roger."

"Roger what?" said Sid impatiently.

"I didn't ask. Stop giving me the third degree. He should be here any minute now."

"I'm glad you didn't invite him for dinner."

"After the way you're behaving, I'm glad I didn't, too." The doorbell rang. "That must be him now."

"You get it."

"Why don't you leave the room if you don't want to meet him? I'll tell him you're not here."

"I want to know why he wants to see me."

That was hardly the truth. Sid wanted to find out what the man had to say about what happened in Vietnam. Not that he hadn't finally believed Ken. Wouldn't it be useful to get another point of view? he rationalized. But hadn't he and Ken brought the issue to closure? So why couldn't he drop it? Does most of a lifetime of feeling shame linger right up to the end?

"I take it you're Roger," Edith said as she opened the door. "How do you do."

"Howdy, ma'am."

Sid stood up to greet his visitor. He'd make the best of it. Edith led the guest into the living room.

"This is Ken's father," Edith said.

"Pleased to meetcha, sir," Roger said, extending his hand.

Sid took Roger's hand unenthusiastically. "Have a seat," he said.

"Would you like some coffee?" Edith offered as Roger sat stiffly on the couch.

"Don't mind if I do," said Roger, and Edith disappeared into the kitchen.

"So, you were in the same outfit as my son in Vietnam," Sid said, hoping, without appearing too obvious, to steer the subject in the desired direction.

"Yes, sir, the very same platoon, same squad."

"And what brings you here?"

"I hoped to see Ken, and meet you too. Ken and I used to talk about home, and he told me about your company and how it's such a terrific place to work."

Most people who visited Sid were looking for something. Usually when friends or relatives or even strangers called on him, he would ask right off, "What can I do for you?" Rarely did they reply "nothing." But this time Sid wanted something from Roger, so he did the asking. "Where are you from?" he continued.

"You never heard of the place. A small town in Ohio."

"So what do you do?"

"I s'pose mostly I'm a maintenance mechanic. I can fix anything."

"A pretty handy guy to have around, eh?"

"Yup, I s'pose, except nobody wants me, Mr..."

"Sid's okay. Why not? You look very employable to me."

"Well, you know. Ken was lucky. He had a built-in job waiting for him. With my record, I'm what they call persona non grata."

"You're referring to your service record I take it?"

"Keerect, sir."

"For your information, Ken doesn't work for me. He's in Africa," Sid said matter-of-factly.

"That's what the Mrs. told me. What in hell's he doing there?" Roger said, looking incredulous.

"I guess you'd call it 'finding himself.'"

"Yeah, that's Ken all right. But not me, I don't have that kind of problem. I was wondering, sir, whether there's an opening for a guy like me—you know, an all-around fix-it type—at your company."

"Well, you'd have to go through personnel. Why don't you apply there? If we can use you, I'm sure they'll put you on."

"Well, sir, I'm not so sure. My service record, it's not the best."

"I see."

"There's no erasing the fucking past. Excuse me, sir. I mean, just the past. I s'pose it stays with you as long as you live."

"That's quite true," Sid said, crediting Roger for his insight. "You've learned a profound lesson: Everything that happens in your life influences everything that's going to happen."

Edith entered with a tray holding three cups of coffee, sugar, cream, and cake. She set the tray on the coffee table and distributed a full cup to each of the men, then offered them sugar and cream. "Did I hear you say you were in the same outfit as Ken?"

"That's right, ma'am, over in Nam. Same platoon, same squad."

"And when you came home..."

"Yup, court-martialed, too. Just like Ken was. We were together in the same lockup for a while."

"You received the same punishment, I presume?" Sid said.

"Yeah, everybody got a dishonorable discharge except the officer in charge."

"Did you think that was fair?" Sid pursued, marveling at Roger's openness.

"No, sir. We did what we did. It got out of hand. Actually, our commanding officer tried to stop us. We wouldn't listen."

"What? You say he tried to stop you?"

"Yes, sir, he sure did, but it was too late. Everything was out of control."

"Did that come out in the trial?"

"No, sir. He felt responsible and said the blame should fall on him.

Nobody spoke up. Anyway, it wouldn't have done any good. In the army it's—what do they call it?— protocol to hold the man in charge responsible."

"And that's the way it should be. In business, too," Sid said.

Edith was puzzled. "Didn't Ken say his officer didn't interfere?"

"Ken said that? I'm sorry, ma'am. I don't mean to contradict him, but our officer almost went off his rocker with guilt after we were choppered out. He wouldn't have anything to do with us anymore."

"But you were a participant?" Sid said, not needing the answer, of course.

"Yes, sir. We were all participants, except our lieutenant."

"Not, Ken. Not our Ken. He's not capable...He stood apart from what happened," exclaimed Edith.

"Is that what he said? Hmm. Well, if that's what he said..."

"Don't you know?" Sid asked accusingly.

"Look, I'm sorry. If that's what he said, then that's what he said," replied Roger. "I shouldn't be talking about it. It's done and over and it's no use digging it up again."

"I'm asking. A simple answer, yes or no. Did you participate?"

"Yes, sir. I told you I did," Roger said. Then after a long silence, he added, "But I'm not proud of it. Something snapped in me. I guess in all of us."

"Then you know whether Ken took part, too," Sid pursued.

"Sid, I don't want him to answer. Don't answer him, young man. I don't want to know."

"Well, I do," said Sid. "I have to know."

"You do know, Sid," said Edith. "You've heard Ken's side. You've had it out with him and made peace. Let it be. I beg you."

"I think I'd better leave," said Roger, placing his half-empty cup on the tray and standing.

"No, sit down," demanded Sid. "I want your answer."

"Sir, I'm leaving. Tell Ken I was asking for him," Roger said, striding toward the hall door.

Sid caught up with him and swung him around.

"Listen to me," Sid screamed, holding onto Roger's arm. "Just answer yes or no. Was Ken a participant? Did he do what everyone else was doing? Goddammit, answer me."

"Stop it, Sid," Edith shouted. "Stop it. Let him go."

"Listen to your wife," Roger said, pushing Sid away with a powerful thrust, almost knocking him off balance.

"You won't answer, will you?" Sid said, starting to lose his temper. "Your kind stick together. You're protecting him, you sonofabitch. You're murderers. You hear me? Goddamned murderers. Get the hell out of my house."

"Good-bye, sir, 'bye, ma'am," Roger said calmly as he opened the door and walked quickly into the dark.

Sid stood motionless looking after him, then slammed the door so hard that it shook the house. His heart was pounding furiously.

"Listen to me, Sid," said Edith, worried that his anger would bring on a heart attack. "Calm down. Come into the living room and sit with me." She led him by the hand to the couch. "Will you listen?" Sid nodded. "Remember, Ken said there was a lot of confusion. How could this man know? All he knows is what he did himself. I believe our son. And Sid, does it really make any difference? Does it really?"

"They protect each other," Sid muttered as his heartbeat moderated. "I suppose I can't blame them. That's how it is in a platoon. We protect each other."

"What's done is done. So let the past be. Let yourself relax." She rubbed her hand up and down his back.

"If Ken lied to me..."

"Before he left, you no longer doubted him. Why now? You became his loving father once again. What did he tell you? He must have convinced you of his innocence."

"Yes, I believed him."

"Then don't go back. Don't let a stranger do this."

"You're right, Edith. I can't let him do this to me. You're right." Sid stared at his wife admiringly for her wisdom and steadfastness.

"Anyway, it doesn't really matter whether he's innocent or not, does it? Not if you love him."

"You don't want to know the truth, do you?" Sid said, as if making a momentous discovery.

"Does the truth matter? Isn't to love also to forgive?"

"To forgive ourselves as well, Edith. Forgive ourselves. What can you expect? We're only human, after all."

"Being human isn't so bad. What's there to forgive about that?"

"Our dark side, my love."

"I must live a sheltered life. I don't see it in people, not in our friends, not in Jay or Bobby, certainly not in you and gentle Ken, my two loves."

"It's there, Edith. The devil is in all of us."

"Not in you, Sid. You are the finest, most honest, most respected man anyone could know."

"I'm a fraud. I've got everybody fooled. The whole damned world, including you, Edith. Even including you."

"Oh, Sid, you are so ridiculous," Edith said, laughing. "What an outrageous thing to say. I know you better than anyone in the world. You can't fool me. I know you."

"Edith, I have something to tell you."

Sid repeated the account he had related to Ken, not as graphically but with all the essential elements, including the guilt over his failure to step in and prevent the killing of the girls. As he told the story to Edith, it came home to him that if Ken were innocent, he must also be condemning himself for his own failure to act on behalf of the Vietnamese. Why hadn't he questioned his son more, learned the details of what went on? Why? Because he didn't want to know. The details were bound to be too familiar, replicating his own experience, reviving his self-disgust.

"Until now I haven't forgiven myself for what I did that day, and for what I didn't do," Sid said.

Edith's reaction surprised him. Instead of disbelief or revulsion, she offered a calm, thoughtful response. "You were only a kid then, thrown in with older men, susceptible to their influence. You're not that boy today, Sid. You weren't that boy when I married you before you left."

"Then you forgive me for what I did?" Sid said, incredulous at her reaction. Did this mean that for all those years he needn't have kept his secret from her, after all?

"Sid, I love you for the man you are. I don't care what you did back then. You aren't that person anymore." Studying Sid's face, Edith paused, then added, "Are you? What would you do today?"

Sid considered her question, a question he had never asked himself. She was correct. He couldn't possibly do such a thing today. The price was too high.

"Today, I'd willingly sacrifice my life to save those girls," he said. He had borne his guilt under the assumption that through the years he would always remain the same. Given similar circumstances, he figured he'd do it again. "People don't change," he had always said. But some do, including him. Was it chemical or hormonal or simply a maturing that now enabled him to take charge of his impulses and do noble things?

Isn't that the nature of living, of growing older and acquiring a perspective so that one can forecast the consequences of one's actions and do the right thing? Yes, he was truly no longer that kid who had surrendered to his animal drive, and he could take heart that at least his conscience had intervened, refusing to let him take part in the final act.

"Thank you, Edith, for your understanding," Sid said in genuine gratitude.

"Our love for each other is all that matters, Sid." They embraced, and Sid glowed with relief.

Ken was completely caught up in his work to alleviate the suffering in his poor African village. It was all the more tragic because it was futile; neither side in the struggle cared for human life. He labored day and night, helping the villagers plant crops and build homes. He taught the children some English and taught the adults about the rest of the world.

He worked himself to exhaustion and fell ill. Because there were no facilities nearby to diagnose his illness, it remained a mystery. He grew progressively worse, losing more pounds than his normally lean body could afford, which prompted the agency he worked for to contact his parents.

Edith and Sid were beside themselves with worry. Sid recalled his own illnesses during the war while overseas: malaria, dengue fever, jaundice, and diarrhea, all of which he contracted, and elephantiasis, which struck down some of his buddies. Now there were rumors of new diseases, more virulent than any known previously, coming out of Africa.

Sid assumed his take-charge mode. "I'll go there and bring him back," he told Edith. "Don't worry, I'll make it."

Edith wanted to accompany him, but Sid wouldn't hear of it. "It's a difficult place to get to. It'll be easier if only one of us goes. You stay here and get things ready for him."

Of course Edith did worry, not only about Ken but Sid, whose heart could well give out under the strain of such a journey. And what's to get ready? She knew that it was only a ploy to prevent her from taking an active role in Ken's rescue.

Both her men could die in the effort. Perhaps Sid should have assigned someone else. Yet the fact that he was going all-out to personally bring back their son was proof to her that his love for Ken overrode his doubts and was unequivocal.

Sid flew to the city nearest to Ken's village that had a jet airport; from there he took a small plane to an airstrip that was a three-day trek away from the village. He found a guide with two assistants and rented two all-terrain vehicles, which they drove until the roads ran out. From there they went on foot for a day and a half, the packs on their backs filled with cans of food and simple medications that the agency had requested.

The trek was difficult for Sid. The years had severely diminished his stamina such that he had to stop often to rest. The chief guide, concerned about whether Sid could go on, offered to have one of his men accompany Sid back to the vehicles while he retrieved Ken, but Sid would have none of it.

"I can do it," he insisted. "Just take it a little slower." Sid paced himself, and took an occasional nitroglycerine tablet. It was important to him that he rescue Ken himself, even at the cost of his own welfare. No one else, no matter how capable, would do. To Sid, the mission was indeed a rescue—from a primeval world in which the dark side of man ran rampant in senseless killing and destruction.

Sid found his son gaunt, wasted, a physical remnant of the boy who had left almost a year earlier. Ken was conscious when his father entered the tent and knelt beside his cot. He wound his arms around Ken's bony body.

Seeing his father's mortified, tear-stained face, all Ken could say was "It's good to see you, Dad" before he closed his eyes and fell into a somnolent silence.

"I'm bringing you home, Ken." Sid saw his son's eyelids flutter in response.

After providing the agency workers with the food and medicine from their packs, the guide and his assistants moved Ken to the stretcher they had brought with them. Although the workers invited

Sid's party to spend the night, Sid refused. As long as there was light, they would move out.

The workers expressed their gratitude for the provisions and medicine, explaining that local hostilities had made it impossible for them to replenish their supplies. They warned Sid and his companions of the danger and told them to be watchful.

Each of the four of them, packs loaded with plenty of water, took a handle of the stretcher and set out. For one and a half days, they followed the roughly marked trail to the terminus of the dirt road where they had left the vehicles. During the few occasions in which he was conscious, Ken found his father solicitous. He encouraged Ken to fight for his life, not to give up. Sid tried to impress a single image on him: They were going home: to civilization, to Edith and Sheree, and to all the other people who loved him.

Finally they arrived at the point where they had left the vehicles. But they were gone, apparently stolen. The guide and his assistants cursed the government in dialect; they were sure that the soldiers were the thieves. Discouraged, they sat on the road commiserating with one another.

As was his custom in business, Sid demanded that they take immediate action: They would continue on foot. But it was more than two hundred miles, the guides argued. Sid countered that they would be on a rough dirt road, certainly better than the trail. Furthermore, didn't they stand a chance that some vehicle would come along and pick them up? After discussing Sid's argument among themselves, they agreed to go along, as if they had any other choice.

By dint of his resolve, Sid became the lead man. He had won the guides' admiration. They saw that Sid was willing to die before he would give up bringing his son home—the same thing they would do for their own sons.

Despite his waning endurance, his torso soaked with perspiration, his joints stinging, Sid pushed on mile after mile, summoning up strength by sheer will. He allowed the guides to choose when to stop and rest. In his younger years, this is how he had dealt with disappointment and failure: by refusing to give in. To fight and persevere was his way.

After another day of carrying the stretcher down the road, a decrepit pickup truck came along. The driver, a farmer, stopped, listened to their story, and, after Sid promised to pay him whatever he asked, agreed to take them to the town with the airstrip. Directing the guide to sit in the cab beside the driver, Sid and the assistants placed Ken in the back of the truck and clambered aboard. During the four-hour trip, Sid cushioned his son in his arms against the jolts caused by the rutted road.

Finally they arrived at the airstrip at the edge of town. Sid paid the farmer and took down his name and how to reach him so that he could reward him further later. He said good-bye to his guides, to whom he gave a substantial bonus for their loyalty and dedication. Each one shook his hand.

While waiting for the small plane to arrive, Sid found the local doctor, who came to the airstrip to examine Ken. The doctor was at a loss to diagnose Ken's ailment. He said he could arrange for blood tests, but the blood samples would have to be flown to a lab in the city and the results would take time. Meanwhile, all he could do was give Ken pills to make him sleep. Using the doctor's phone, Sid arranged for a private jet to meet him at the city airport to take them across the Atlantic. He called Edith.

"The doctor here gave him something to make him comfortable. He's stabilized," Sid reassured her.

"What's wrong with him, Sid? Don't spare me. I want the truth."

"The truth is, Edith, they don't know. It could be malaria or something else. Once he's back in the States, we'll get him to a hospital and bring in a tropical medicine specialist."

The remainder of the journey went like clockwork. Edith and Sheree were waiting with an ambulance at Boston's Logan Airport terminal when Sid's private jet landed. Ken was unconscious and with fever during the reunion and remained so throughout the night in a Boston hospital.

Days went by. Tests revealed a rare virus for which there was no known medication. The disease had to run its course. So Ken was removed to the hospital in their small central Massachusetts city, where in a private room of the Sidney Randall Wing he would be near his family and made as comfortable as possible.

Ken could survive or he could die; only time would tell. But he had periods of awareness during which he would communicate briefly. Edith and Sheree and Sid visited him around the clock. Sometimes

Jay and Bobby would join them, making it a family reunion around the bed. That was against hospital visiting rules, of course, but this *was* the Sid Randall Wing. Edith often brought an entire home-cooked meal to the room for all of them so they could share that time together. Even when Ken was too weary to participate in the conversation, it was like listening to beautiful music to hear them talk among themselves.

During one of his more alert periods, he asked to talk to his father alone. How grateful Edith was that Ken and Sid would confide in each other. She took Sheree by the hand and left the room, telling her, "They're more than just father and son, Sheree. They're friends."

Ken thanked Sid for rescuing him. He said he realized he might not survive, but Sid's valiant effort to bring him home meant everything to him.

"You can make it, Ken. Just keep fighting to live. You can make it," Sid repeated, giving the only counsel he knew.

"Dad, if I don't make it—"

"Ken, don't even think it. Do you hear me? That's an order."

Ken managed a wan smile. "I want you to know that I told you most of the truth about what happened in Vietnam."

"I believe you, son. But it doesn't matter. I don't care what you did or didn't do."

"But I didn't tell you everything, Dad. I want you to know everything."

Sid wasn't sure whether to cut Ken off or to listen. His only wish was to please him, put his mind at ease as much as possible. "Okay, kiddo, I'm listening."

"I tried to stop some of my buddies, Dad. You must believe me. I said I didn't to protect myself, but the truth is I did."

Sid was confused by Ken's statement. Why would he need protection for revealing all that happened? "I believe you. Now, take this before you say anything else," said Sid, holding a glass of water near Ken's parched lips so he could sip from a straw.

"They threatened to kill me if I interfered."

"You mean your buddies? Is that what you mean?"

"There was no stopping them. Do you understand?"

"I understand," said Sid. He knew how determined Ken was to tell everything, just as he had been when telling his own horror story. "You did a courageous thing trying to stop them. I'm proud of you."

"No, Dad. You have no reason to be proud of me. You should be ashamed. They were killing those women and their children. I had to stop them."

"Don't condemn yourself for that, Ken. Your attempt to stop them was an act of nobility. I wish I had been as brave and decent as you." Sid saw that Ken was becoming agitated. "Look, take it easy, son. I'm glad you told me how it was. Now lie back and get some sleep."

How ironic this was. His son had committed the one act that he regretted most of his life not doing, and for which his conscience had given him no peace.

"You don't understand, Dad."

"Sure I do," Sid said. "Remember, I've been there."

"I killed my buddies, Dad. I shot two of them when they wouldn't stop."

"You...you say you shot them?"

"I'm a murderer, Dad." Ken sobbed silently. "You have a murderer for a son. You'll be well rid of me."

Sid was shocked, but he quickly spoke. "No, no, Ken. You've got it all wrong. You stopped two murderers. Yes, you took justice into your own hands, but you were trying to prevent a worse injustice — the killing of innocents. And you saw at the court-martials that no one who perpetrated those acts was given a just punishment. No, Ken. You did the only thing your conscience demanded that you do."

"I don't know, Dad."

"I do. I know." Sid stood and paced back and forth at the foot of the bed. "Who else knows about this?"

"No one. Only you. No one saw it happen. They thought it was the Cong who killed them."

"Then we'll keep this between us."

"You mean, you forgive me?"

"Forgive? Why son, I've never been prouder. Now, it's time you tried to sleep. Get well, get well for Ma and Sheree and me, because whether you feel you deserve it or not, we love you."

Gripping Ken's hand in his, tears filling his eyes, Sid was overwhelmed as he watched Ken close his eyes and slowly lose consciousness, mumbling, "Thanks, Dad. I love all of you, too."

Sid sat silent for a while listening to Ken's breathing, thinking about what he had just heard. How Sid hated war and what it does to the finest among us, what it did to Ken, to him. Long after it's over, its effects remain indelible within us, and within the generations that follow. Look at what it has done to this loving boy, Sid thought, good to the core, sensitive to the needs of others, a model youth. Our dark side, buried deep within us, makes us killers and the killers of killers. Where will it end?

Sheree and Edith returned, but Sheree remained outside the door of the room so she wouldn't interrupt Ken and his father. Edith entered cautiously and saw that Ken was now asleep.

"It's time to leave, Sid," she said.

"Where will it end?" Sid muttered, mostly to himself.

Edith took Sid's hand as they stood gazing down at Ken's wasted, motionless figure.

"He's come home, Sid. It will end here."